UNDER the CAJUN MOON

MINDY STARNS CLARK

HARVEST HOUSE PUBLISHERS

EUGENE, OREGON

The author is represented by MacGregor Literary.

Cover by Dugan Design Group, Bloomington, Minnesota

Cover photos © Florea Marius Catalin / iStockphoto; VisionsofAmerica / Joe Sohm / Getty Images

UNDER THE CAJUN MOON
Copyright © 2009 by Mindy Starns Clark
Published by Harvest House Publishers
Eugene, Oregon 97402
www.harvesthousepublishers.com

Library of Congress Cataloging-in-Publication Data
    Clark, Mindy Starns.
    Under the Cajun moon / Mindy Starns Clark.
        p. cm.
    ISBN 978-0-7369-2624-9 (pbk.)
    1. Cooks—Fiction. 2. Fathers and daughters—Fiction. 3. Cookery, Cajun—Fiction. 4.
Cajuns—Fiction. 5. Louisiana—Fiction. I. Title.
    PS3603.L366U63 2009
    813'.6—dc22

                                                        2009019246

Printed in the United States of America

        09 10 11 12 13 14 15 16 17 / DP-SK / 10 9 8 7 6 5 4 3 2 1

In loving memory of my father,

Robert M. Starns, M.D.

1929–2008

Louisiana born and bred, he passed along to me his joy in this land and its waterways. An avid reader, he taught me the value of a tale well told. To combine both for this story has been incredibly fulfilling.

And with love to my father-in-law,

John C. Clark Sr.

Though a Yankee through and through, your enthusiasm for New Orleans makes you an honorary Southerner. Thank you for your love and support through the years!

ACKNOWLEDGMENTS

Many, many thanks to:
John Clark, my loving husband, story shaper, and best friend
Emily and Lauren Clark, my incredibly sweet and helpful daughters
Kim Moore, paragon of patience and editor extraordinaire
Members of my online advisory group CONSENSUS
Everyone at Harvest House Publishers
Ned & Marie Scannell
Chip MacGregor
ChiLibris

Thanks also to:
My Cajun cousins, the Bourgs: Brett, Rhonda, Jesse,
Tabitha, Virginia, Katrina, Jared, and Joel, and Brett's
parents, Druis and Catherine Bourg. Y'all rock!

Don Beard, Kirk Bachmann, Cajun Jack and Dawn of Cajun Swamp
Tours, Erin Compton Daniels, Jeff Gerke, John Heald, LUMCON, Marc
Preuss, Sisters in Crime, John Sonnier, Amy Starns, Andrew Starns, David
Starns, Jackie Starns, Sarah Starns, Mr. and Mrs. Elward Stephens, Erin
Sullivan, Chef George Thomas, Kimberly Walden, and Shari Weber

And last but not least:
Thanks to all who repeatedly lift me up in prayer,
especially my FVCN Small Group:
Brad, Brian, Chuck, Fanus, Mariette, Robin, Tracey, and Tracie

ONE

Ringing.

Something somewhere was ringing and just wouldn't stop. Slowly, I opened my eyes. As I came more fully awake, I realized that the ringing was a telephone, and that the telephone was on a bedside table next to my head. Blinking, I looked around, trying to remember where I was.

Where was I?

The ringing persisted. I fumbled for the phone with one hand but the noise stopped before I could even lift the receiver. Licking dry, cracked lips, I let go of the phone and moved a hand to my forehead, feeling for a fever. My skin seemed cool, though I did have a splitting headache.

What was wrong with me?

More important, where was I and what was I doing here?

Carefully, I raised myself onto my elbows, my head throbbing with the effort. Looking around the dark room, it didn't seem familiar. To my right, judging by a thin rectangle of light, was a window covered by heavy drapes. Was I in a hospital? There were no machines running nearby, no tubes coming from my body. Looking down, I could see that I was fully dressed. At least I recognized my own Theory suit, though the cream linen looked wrinkled in the dimness. Somehow, I had a feeling that I wasn't in a hospital but rather a hotel.

Light. I needed light to figure this out. Ignoring the thousand pounds of mush inside my head, I sat all the way up. Making sure of my balance, I stood and stepped to the shades, pulling them open.

"Agh!" I cried, covering my eyes with a hand. The glare was blinding.

Fumbling frantically, I felt my way back to the bed and sat on the edge, my heart pounding. In all of my thirty-two years, I had never had anything like this happen to me, had never once woken up in a strange place without knowing how I had gotten there. After a few seconds I lowered the hand from my eyes and gingerly opened them again, thinking that if this was a hangover, I must have had one doozy of a night. Except that I didn't get hangovers. I rarely even drank.

Looking around, I felt sure I was in a hotel room, though it wasn't one I recognized. The decor was bland, if a little worn, and though there were no suitcases on the floor, my purse was sitting on the dresser. Standing again, I moved to it and looked inside, but nothing seemed amiss. My wallet was there, and a quick count of the cash it held assured me that no money was missing. Glancing around for some clue as to where I was, I spotted a small vinyl notebook imprinted with a fancy logo and the words "Maison Chartres."

My own image in the mirror above the dresser caught my eye, and I paused to study it. I looked like me—or at least a disheveled, exhausted version of me. My long ash-blond hair was a tangled mess, my blue eyes bloodshot and tired.

Where was I and how had I gotten here?

Moving again toward the window, I placed my hands on the glass and looked out. I was on the first floor, and judging by the unique architecture outside, I was in New Orleans, the city of my youth. I wasn't familiar with this particular hotel, but given the name it was probably on Chartres Street, in the French Quarter.

The French Quarter.

Vague memories of yesterday began edging their way into my brain. My mother's phone call. My father's injury. My frantic flight from Chicago to New Orleans.

From the airport, at my mother's insistence, I had driven to our family restaurant in the French Quarter to meet with my parents' lawyer and handle some paperwork before going to the hospital to see my father. I remembered that much.

Suddenly, the phone on the bedside table began to ring again. This time, I leaped toward it and snatched it up quickly.

"Hello?"

"Yes, hello. This is the front desk," a woman's voice said. "I'm sorry to bother you, but I thought I should tell you that the police are on their way to your room. They've been very persistent. Apparently, someone else in the hotel called in a complaint about noise."

"Noise? What noise?" The only noise I had heard was the ringing of the phone. I wanted to ask if the woman knew how I had gotten here, but before I could even form a coherent question in my mind, there was a pounding at the door. I quickly concluded the call and made my way toward the sound.

Rounding the corner of what I assumed was a bathroom, I realized that this wasn't just a single hotel room but, in fact, a suite. The front room was as dark as the bedroom had been, and I stumbled through it to get to the door. Once there, I swung it open, revealing two policemen standing in a sunny courtyard. Just the sight of their crisp uniforms and no nonsense expressions flooded my soul with relief. Maybe they could help me figure out where I was and what was going on.

"Sorry to disturb you, ma'am. Is everything all right?"

I blinked, wondering where to start.

"Ma'am? Have you been a victim of domestic violence? 'Cause we can take you out of here right now and bring you somewhere safe."

"Domestic violence?" I asked, reaching a hand to my cheek, wondering if they saw something I hadn't noticed in the mirror, a cut or a bruise.

"We had a complaint of noise. They said it sounded like two people having a big fight."

I took my hand from my face, swallowed hard, and tried to think of how to reply. Before I could say another word, one of the cops stepped forward into the room, causing me to take a step back.

"You're obviously confused, ma'am. Let's take this one thing at a time."

He was speaking in the measured tones usually reserved for small children and senile adults. "Are you physically injured in any way?"

Again looking down at my wrinkled suit, nothing seemed amiss. I ran my hands over my arms and down my sides, but I didn't feel anything painful or unusual.

"No. Physically, I think I'm fine."

"All right. How about him? Is he okay?"

As I looked to where the policeman pointed across the room, I gasped. There, in the light that spilled from the open doorway, I could see someone sprawled out on the couch. It was a man, dressed in a dark brown suit, eyes closed and mouth open.

The second cop came inside and went over to him, shaking his shoulder and saying, "Sir? Sir?"

Watching them, I realized that the sleeping man looked familiar. Then it came to me. He was the lawyer I had met with last night at the restaurant, at the request of my mother.

"Are you under the influence of something?" the cop asked me now. "Are you on drugs?"

Drugs. That must have been it. I must have been drugged.

"It's hard to explain. I—"

"Excuse me, ma'am," the cop interrupted, not waiting for my answer but instead responding to a grunt from his partner, the one who was now kneeling beside the couch.

Suddenly I couldn't wait for this guy to wake up and tell us what was going on. But then the cops both stood and turned to look at me even more strangely than before. That's when I realized that the man on the couch wasn't going to wake up at all.

The man on the couch was dead.

TWO

Life should have an "undo" function. If one simple click could move time backward by a step—just one single step—then maybe that would make all the difference between success and failure. Between right and wrong.

Between life and death.

If I could, I thought now as I stood in the hotel doorway and looked across the room at the body of a man I could hardly recall, I would go back and undo that precise moment, yesterday, when everything had first begun to go wrong.

I had been in downtown Chicago, filming my second guest appearance on a local public television show, *Business Time Live*. During a commercial break, my assistant, Jenny, had come over and whispered that my mother was repeatedly texting and calling, and that she urgently wanted to talk to me. As the show only had seven minutes left, I told Jenny that my mother would have to wait and that I could call her back as soon as we were off the air. I didn't bother to add that surely the woman who had barely given me the time of day my entire life could survive another seven minutes. Looking unsure, Jenny had ducked away just as the break came to an end.

"Welcome back to *Business Time Live*," the host said as the cameras began rolling again. "I'm your host, Tony Gray, and today's guest is

Chicago resident and international business etiquette expert Chloe Ledet." Turning to me with a polished smile, he continued. "Chloe, you've given us some fascinating information here today, but let's get specific. Say I'm a business executive used to the American way of doing things. What's going to get me in trouble when I'm out of my element?"

Putting thoughts of my mother out of my mind, I had jumped back into the interview with my full attention, explaining the various faux pas that Americans frequently committed in international business situations—from accidentally making offensive gestures with their hands to wearing the wrong clothes to saying the wrong things.

"In fact, Tony, if we were in parts of Africa right now, just the way you're sitting would be incredibly insulting to me."

"How so?" he asked, animatedly looking down at his own posture.

"With your leg crossed over the other one like that, you are exposing to me the sole of your foot, something that's unacceptable in certain cultures."

"You've got to be kidding," he said, placing both feet on the floor. "It's like a minefield out there!"

"Absolutely, Tony, and those mines pop up around clothing, gifts, business cards, introductions, protocol, and so on. That's why I always advise my clients, no matter which country or culture they're going to be dealing with, to take time to learn about it first. Respecting other cultures is good business. Proper etiquette is the grease that oils civilized society."

"Well, Chloe, thank you so much for all of your excellent advice today. Before we close, I wanted to take a minute to ask a more personal question, one that my viewers are eager to hear the answer to."

Like a deer caught in headlights, I was afraid I knew exactly where he was going, but I had been helpless to stop him. Looking back now, I found it ironic that even as Tony was bringing up the topic of my famous father, neither one of us had known that man's very life had been hanging in the balance.

"Tell all of us what it was like growing up as the daughter of the great Chef Julian Ledet. The man's a legend. As beloved as Paul Prudhomme. As accomplished as Mario Batali. As recognizeable as Emeril Lagasse.

Did your fascination with good manners originate in Ledet's restaurant, maybe even as a small child?"

Tony continued to smile as he waited for my response, but I was furious. He had known the question would upset me, but he had gone there anyway.

"Well, Tony," I replied evenly, "the great Chef Julian Ledet may have been famous, but to me he was always, simply, 'Daddy.'"

Tony knew that wasn't exactly true, but it was the only answer I was giving him on live TV. I couldn't believe he had blindsided me with the very topic I had told him was off limits, one that had hounded me my entire adult life.

"When you were growing up, did he cook fancy meals at home or just at the restaurant?" Tony persisted.

"Mostly at the restaurant."

I knew what Tony was getting at, and I wasn't going to go there. He wanted me to share my poor-little-rich-girl story of lonely meals in boarding school dining halls or at home in front of the television, eating reheated leftovers by myself. I had told that to him in confidence when he took me out to dinner just last week. Now he was trying to get me to repeat myself on national television—even though I had made it clear that I was sharing those things in confidence.

"How about you? Do you cook too, Chloe?"

"Only if microwaving counts," I joked, glancing at the clock to see how much longer he was going to drag this out. Ninety seconds left, which meant he had no choice but to move on.

"Well, to bring this back around to the topic of business, just one more question," he said, leaning toward me in his chair. "What's the secret behind Chef Julian's Secret Salt? Its unique color and flavor have made it a best seller in gourmet shops and professional food outlets for many years, despite the fact that quantities are often limited. Where does it really come from?"

"Come on, Tony. You know better than that. That's like asking Colonel Sander's daughter to reveal her father's eleven herbs and spices."

Laughing, Tony agreed. He shook my hand and thanked me for

coming, and then he turned directly back to the camera and gave a plug for the next week's show.

As soon as we were off the air and the tech had removed the microphone pack from my suit, I thanked Tony for the interview and asked that he please never call me again—not for another appearance on his show or a second date.

Marching from the room, I could hear him calling after me.

"Come on, babe, what's the big deal? That's just good TV!"

I wasn't going to dignify his comment with a reply. As I passed through the studio door and into the hall, I could hear Jenny's tiny footsteps tapping along behind me.

"I'm so sorry, I can't believe he pulled a stunt like that," she said as she fell into step beside me, her brown curls bouncing as we walked.

"Don't apologize, Jenny. It wasn't your fault. It was mine, for going out with that sleaze in the first place."

"Hey, you! Ice Queen!" the sleaze called from behind us. "You left your complimentary fruit basket in the green room."

Jenny told me that she would handle things and then meet me at the car.

"You know, you really crossed the line in there, mister," Jenny said, turning on her heel as I reached the heavy door and pushed it open. As I stepped out into the Chicago sunshine, I couldn't help but smile at the tiny tornado who served as my right arm and chief defender. Tony Gray might be six foot three inches of glorified muscle, but against Jenny he didn't stand a chance.

Tony couldn't have known this, but calling me "Ice Queen" had been a particularly cruel blow. That was the nickname I had earned as a teenager, when my ugly-duckling adolescence had given way to a more swanlike appearance, leaving me tall and striking but also confused and frightened. After years of being ignored, suddenly I found myself getting attention from every direction. The problem was that what people saw on the outside didn't match up at all with who I still was on the inside. Over time, my best defense had become a sort of cool, reserved demeanor. That my eyes were an icy blue didn't help, and eventually I earned the nickname

"Ice Queen." What no one had ever understood was that underneath all of that ice was a teenager's aching heart, pumping with a desperate need to belong and to be loved.

I slipped into the car and dialed my mother's number. As I waited for it to start ringing, I noticed movement in my side mirror and turned to see what looked like a fruit basket walking toward the car on two tiny legs. Jumping out to help, I cradled the phone against my shoulder as Jenny and I wrestled to get the huge mountain of fresh fruit onto the backseat of my new sports car.

"I knew I should've gone with the convertible," I quipped.

"The pineapple's stuck," Jenny grunted, pressing down the top until the whole thing finally popped through. At that moment, my mother finally answered.

"Chloe? It's about time!"

"Hello, Mother," I said, glancing toward Jenny. "What is it? What's wrong?"

"You have to come to Louisiana. Now."

"Why? What's going on?"

"We need you, Chloe. It's your father. He's been shot."

He's been shot.

And that was it, the "undo" moment that I wanted to take back. Now that I was standing in a room with two policemen and one very dead body, here was another. I had a feeling that my life was about to be filled with all sorts of undo moments.

Somehow, the cops had come there in response to a report of possible domestic violence, and they seemed intent on sticking with that first impression. I tried to explain, but they both seemed so sure, in fact, that it took a while for them to actually listen to what I was saying. I told them I had almost no memories of last night, absolutely no idea how I had gotten there in that hotel room, and that I had obviously been drugged and brought there without my knowledge or consent. Finally, they grew so frustrated with my adamant insistence about the bizarre nature of the situation that they told me to wait and save my complicated story for the detective.

In the meantime, one of the cops led me to an empty suite next door and told me to have a seat on the couch and wait for the arrival of the detective. Silently, he stood guard in the open doorway, keeping me safe. I assumed the other one was securing the scene.

Still confused and incredibly frustrated, I was actually glad to have some peace and quiet to think things through. My brain still felt foggy and my headache was getting worse.

As I willed the fog to clear, the realization that a man was dead began to sink in. The poor guy was dead! However it had happened, I mourned for his passing and for his loved ones, who would be finding out the sad news any time now.

A cluster of curious hotel guests began gathering in the courtyard outside, trying to get a peek at what all the hoopla was about. Wishing they would all go away, I called the front desk and asked them to send over something for a headache. Soon a hotel employee appeared with a bottle of water and a packet of generic ibuprofen. I swallowed the pills immediately, leaned my head back against the couch, and closed my eyes.

From the sound of things, the room next door was buzzing with all sorts of activity. As I continued to wait for the detective, I tried to grasp more memories from my befuddled brain.

I remembered dropping Jenny at the office and then running home to pack after my mother's call. I remembered racing to the airport, catching the flight that Jenny had arranged for me, hoping I would arrive while my father was still alive.

I remembered descending toward the New Orleans airport several hours later, nervously holding my cell phone in my hand and waiting for permission to turn it back on so I could call to see where things stood. Outside, as the lights of the city had loomed into view, I had felt that odd disconnect of coming home once it wasn't home anymore. Astounded by the unreality of the situation, I'd had to admit that I always expected one day my dad would die from a heart attack or a stroke brought on by a fit of rage at some poor dishwasher who had missed a spot on a plate, or a waitress who had given a patron the wrong kind of spoon. Never had I expected to hear that he'd been a victim of gunfire.

But that was exactly what had happened. According to my mother, around noon today my father had been the victim of a hunting accident down at his favorite stomping grounds in the swamps of south central Louisiana, an accident that had left him with a gunshot wound to the leg. The bullet had struck an artery, causing him to lose several pints of blood before help had finally arrived. Paramedics had taken him to the nearest hospital, which was in Morgan City, gotten him stabilized, and then air-lifted him to Oschner Hospital in New Orleans. Even as I had been en route to New Orleans myself, my father had been having major surgery.

Reaching New Orleans at last, I dialed my mother's number the moment I could after the plane landed, hoping she would report that my father's surgery was successful and that he had regained consciousness.

The call had gone to voice mail, so I simply told her I had arrived in New Orleans and would be at the hospital as soon as I could get there. Once I hung up, I tucked my phone away, gathered my things, and waited what felt like an eternity for the plane to be secured at the gate and the doors to be opened.

Thanks to Jenny who had booked me in seat 1C, I was the first one off the plane. The airport was quiet, and I was able to move quickly up the hall and into the main area, which was lined with empty restaurants and darkened gift shops. Taking the escalator, I reached the first floor and strode briskly past baggage claim to the rental car desk at the far end of the hall. As I got closer, I was relieved to see that there was only one person in line. When it was my turn, the young man at the desk processed my rental quickly, and by the time I got back to baggage claim, the buzzer was sounding and the conveyor belt was just kicking into action.

Watching for my bags, I thought about my relationship with my parents. Things were complicated, but I did love them. Just knowing what they were both going through had knotted up my insides like a fist. I kept hearing my mother's voice saying *We need you, Chloe*. I wasn't sure if I had ever heard those words from either of my parents before.

We need you.

The physical trauma of a gunshot wound would be hard enough on anyone, but it didn't help that my dad was getting on in years. I was a late-in-life baby for him, so it was easy to forget that by now he was almost in his eighties. He had always seemed so healthy and vibrant, especially when he was with my mom, who was still stunningly beautiful and younger than him by fourteen years. But I had to remember that he wasn't as young as he seemed, not at all. Even if he survived this, it was definitely going to take a toll on him.

My bag had been one of the last to come out, but after a quick shuttle ride I had claimed my rental car and climbed inside. There, I had forced myself to sit quietly for a moment, take a few deep breaths, and try to gather my wits about me.

I hadn't been back home in a long time, longer than I wanted to admit. Had it been two years? Three? All I knew was that if my father died before I had a chance to see him and say goodbye, I would never forgive myself.

What kind of daughter was I, anyway?

My cell phone rang just as I was about to start the car, so I waited, answering instead. It was my mother returning my call, saying that she had been in the recovery room with my father when I had phoned from the plane.

"How's he doing?"

"He's hanging in there. But he needs you to do him a very big favor, Chloe. I know you want to come straight to the hospital, but he desperately needs you to handle an important business matter for him first. You've got power of attorney, you know, so you're the only one who can do it."

I pinched the bridge of my nose and closed my eyes. My father and I had signed power of attorney papers a good ten years ago, when I was in my early twenties, just out of college and embarking on my career. At the time I hadn't understood why he had chosen me for such an important role, so afterward I had gathered up the nerve to ask him why he had designated his daughter rather than his wife. What my mother didn't know and would never know was what he said to me in reply. *You're a smart girl, Chloe, not like your mom. She may be the most beautiful gal in New Orleans, but she's also one of the dumbest. You know how much I love her, but if anything ever happens to me, I need to know you'll be handling my affairs, not her.*

At the time, I was offended on my mother's behalf but deeply flattered on my own. Mostly, I was shocked by the rare vote of confidence coming from a man who constantly found fault in those around him, especially me. He was right about my mother in the sense that certain things confounded her, particularly things that involved paperwork or finances. I, on the other hand, had taken after my father, who was born knowing how to do business. His trust in me was well placed, but even then I had hoped I would never be in a position to actually prove it.

Yet there I was ten years later, and the first thing my mother was asking of me was the last thing on earth I wanted to do.

"What if Dad doesn't make it? Can't this wait?"

"No, it can't. Please, Chloe, just do this one thing and then you can come."

She rattled out my instructions. I was to go straight to Ledet's, our family restaurant in the French Quarter, where I was to meet up with their lawyer and sign some business contracts he and my father had been working on.

"Dad's not selling the restaurant, is he?"

"Goodness, no. He's buying something. Some property. The lawyer knows what it's all about. You just have to sign the paperwork."

Incredible, I thought as the knot in my gut slowly began to shift upward toward my heart. My father was practically at death's door, yet even in his last, desperate moments it was more important for him to know that a business matter was handled than to see his daughter's face one last time and tell her all of the things he had never been able to say before.

Things like *I love you, Chloe*, and *I'm sorry, Chloe*.

Now, sitting on the couch in the hotel room and thinking of my father, I tried to remember if I had ever made it to the hospital last night. Somehow, I just knew that I had not. Frantic, I looked up at the policeman who was standing watch and asked him if he knew anything about Julian Ledet.

"Julian Ledet, the chef? Yeah, I heard he got shot yesterday."

"Do you know if he's still alive?"

"Why do you want to know?"

"Because I'm his daughter. I came to town so I could be with him at the hospital. They weren't sure if he would make it through the night."

"Far as I know, he's still alive," the cop replied, eyeing me strangely. "At least I haven't heard otherwise."

We were interrupted by the appearance of a man wearing a brown suit the same shade as his bowl-cut hair. Speaking with a downtown "N'Awlins" accent, he introduced himself as Detective Walters, though it came out sounding more like "Wahtus."

He sat down on the chair to my left, looking as though he was ready for a nice long chat. It wasn't until that moment that I began to grasp the gravity of my situation. My father's life was hanging in the balance at the hospital, but instead of being there with him I had woken up this morning in a strange hotel room, one with a dead man on the couch.

Now I could only hope that the detective had come to give me an explanation, because I sure didn't have one for him.

THREE

FRANCE, 1719
JACQUES

It was time for the final beating.

Jacques reached for the flat sheet of gold and placed it on the work surface in front of him, thrilled that after an entire month of casting, rolling, and beating, casting, rolling, and beating, over and over and over, this incredibly long and boring and tedious job was finally almost finished. That simple thought filled Jacques' mind with a joy and relief so great he felt like shouting. Given that his presence was supposed to be a secret, though, Jacques knew he could do no such thing—nor even speak very loudly, for that matter, lest the farmer who labored in the surrounding fields hear. He kept silent but was unable to conceal a grin as he worked.

"You're looking mighty pleased with yourself," Papa said softly from accross the room, pausing to sit up straight, wiggle his shoulders, and move his head from side to side in a stretching motion. Goldsmithing was hard on the back and neck.

Jacques gestured toward the rack against the wall, its shelves bending from the weight of one hundred and ninety-five brass fleur-de-lis statuettes covered in gold leaf. Just five more and they would be finished!

"I'm smiling because this tedious commission is finally drawing to a close. Oh, how I long to get out of this stuffy workshop and breathe some fresh air! Then it's out of isolation for us both and back to the city and a normal life."

"Back to Angelique, you mean," Papa teased with a wink.

"Back to the angelic Angelique," Jacques agreed, grinning.

Papa chuckled, which sent him into a bout of coughing. His agonized wheezing and choking had become a familiar sound in the past few weeks, a desperate refrain that echoed repeatedly off of the walls of this stifling place. The old man had quicksilver poisoning, incurred several weeks ago when he was preparing the amalgam for water gilding and had accidentally inhaled mercury vapors. Irreversible and incurable, quicksilver poisoning was also eventually fatal. Immediately he had changed processes, switching to mechanical gilding instead, which was more tedious but safer. By then, however, it was already too late.

As his health had grown worse, and knowing he would not be able to finish the job alone, Papa had written to Jacques, instructing him to close up their Paris shop, tell everyone that he was off to visit an ailing aunt in Provence, and head to the eastern banks of the Seine. There, he was to purchase a rowboat, load it with as much nonperishable food as it would carry, and set off upriver, watching for a leather apron that would be hanging from a tree along the northern shore.

Jacques had done exactly as instructed, reaching the location just two hours outside of the city. He had hidden the boat on the wooded bank, retrieved the apron, and then slipped into the building sight unseen.

Once they were together, Papa had more fully explained what was going on, saying that he was working on orders from the palace itself, doing the highest-paying job of his entire career. His orders stipulated that the work had to be done alone and that if he told anyone else what he was doing he would forfeit the entire payment. As he had already put in so many hours of hard labor on this job before he took ill, he had made the only choice available to him that would allow him to earn the money he was due: He sent in secret for his son, who was young and healthy and would be able to help him finish the task.

Jacques had been heartbroken to learn of his father's illness but had tried to remain optimistic. At least their working conditions were not too terrible. The building the palace had conscribed for this top secret project was well supplied, a roomy old blacksmith shop converted for goldsmithing. As there was only one cot, Jacques had been forced to sleep each night on a pallet on the floor, but otherwise he was comfortable. Meals were delivered to Papa twice a day by a neighboring farmer's wife, and by supplementing those meals with the food Jacques had brought, both men were well fed. Jacques hid whenever the meals arrived, but otherwise they had been left alone to do their work. As long as they kept the doors closed, conversed softly, and only stepped outside for air in the nighttime, no one had seemed to notice or suspect a thing.

Except for Papa's lingering ill health and the tediousness of the project, Jacques had to admit that the past few weeks had been enjoyable, a respite from the busyness and noise of their life in the city. Jacques' mother had died when he was only a boy, so he and his father were used to being alone together.

But then yesterday Papa had taken a bite of bread and managed to lose a tooth in the process. At that moment, his eyes met his son's and Jacques could no longer ignore the obvious. The old man was dying, and Jacques could not begin to conceive of what life would be like without his Papa, the man who had been there for all of his nineteen years.

Trying not to think about that for now, Jacques returned his attentions to the fine sheet of leaf in front of him. Running his dagger in a crisscross pattern through the gold, he managed to cut the sheet into numerous, perfect squares, two centimeters each. When that was done, he put the dagger away and carefully began piling each square one upon another, intermixed with delicate pages of calfskin vellum.

After he had stacked all of the squares and pages, he gathered the entire pile and gently forced it into a parchment case. That, in turn, was slid sideways into a second case. The double packaging would allow Jacques to hammer the outside with vigor without disbursing the layers of gold inside.

Jacques stood and carried his valuable parcel toward the beating bench. As he went, he sensed his father's gaze and once again looked at the man, whose pale skin and sunken cheeks made him seem so much older than his years.

"Son."

"Yes, Papa, what is it? Am I doing something wrong?" Jacques paused in the middle of the room, ready for the expected reprimand. Ill or not, Papa was always correcting and teaching him. This time, however, the older man simply shook his head and spoke, his open mouth revealing the dark place where his newly missing tooth used to be.

"No, son. Now that we're almost done, I was just thinking how thankful I am that you came out to help. I know you don't love smithing as I do, but you have worked without error or complaint, and I appreciate it more than you know. You've done a good job."

"Why, thank you, Papa."

As the old man gruffly cleared his throat and looked away, Jacques felt his own face flush with heat. Papa did not dole out compliments often, but when he did he was sincere. With renewed vigor, Jacques continued toward the beating bench and set the package down on top of its marble square.

"Someday," his father continued in a more lighthearted tone, "you will earn the title of master goldsmith for yourself and can carry on my mark. Who knows, perhaps you'll even be named royal goldsmith. You would be invited to live at the Louvre, and all thoughts of station would no longer be an issue for Angelique's parents."

Jacques smiled at the dream, but that's all it was. A man didn't get to be a royal goldsmith without an enormous amount of talent, dedication, knowledge, experience, and hard work. Jacques was no stranger to hard work, and he had experience and knowledge, but in his heart there was no dedication, and in his soul, not nearly enough talent. His father spoke in grandiose ways, but they both knew the truth, that Jacques lacked any true artistic ability, certainly nothing approaching the skills of his father. He was good enough to serve as a technician and aid to a master but would never be a master himself. He could hardly sketch a pair of candlesticks, much less render them to the client's expectations in three dimensions. The fact that he hadn't yet created a masterpiece sufficient to earn him consideration as a guild member was proof enough of his lack of talent.

Still, warmed by the glow of his father's compliment, Jacques did what he could do very well, taking care to center the parchment on the marble square of the beating table. He checked the leather apron that hung from the front, positioning it so that it would catch any gold that might accidentally escape the carefully-wrapped sheets, and then he reached for the large hammer. Jacques hefted the fifteen-pound tool in the air and then banged it down against the center of the package.

Hefting again, the beating began to take on a necessary rhythm as Jacques hammered the pile with his right hand and turned and moved it with his left. As a young man, beating had been a skill that Jacques had had trouble mastering—and he had had the blue thumbs to show for it. Now, however, his moves were done with such smoothness and dexterity that he was able to turn the pile after every second stroke without breaking his rhythm or missing a blow.

He had been beating gold leaf all month and now did it mindlessly, almost as if he were in a trance. Usually, he passed the time by thinking about Angelique, about her perfect hands and tiny waist and lilting voice. Were she not titled, they would have gotten married by now. As it was, though goldsmithing was generally considered the most genteel of the mechanical occupations, his station was still below hers, which meant that her parents would not even grant him audience for a proposal. The way he saw it, he needed to become so rich through his father's shop that her parents would accept him as a viable match despite his lack of title.

But would Angelique wait long enough for that to happen? She said she would. She said she would do whatever it took to become his bride. That, of course, had led to an argument between them, for if she was really willing to do whatever it took, then she would simply defy her parents' wishes and join hands in marriage now.

Ah, well, Jacques thought as he hammered and turned, hammered and turned. *Perhaps the past month apart has convinced her to take such a bold step.* He would know soon, as the moment this job was finished he was going to return to Paris, seek her out, and once again ask her to marry him. Perhaps this time her answer would be an immediate and enthusiastic "Yes!"

On the other hand, a beautiful, eligible, titled young woman in Paris had many opportunities to find a more suitable husband than a mere gold-smith. For all he knew, her love had already begun to fade, her dedication to wane, and her affections to seek out another. He wouldn't know for sure until he looked into her eyes. Until then, he would have to content himself with the knowledge that, from the moment they had met in the Tuileries Gardens two years ago, it had been love at first sight for both of them. His love had never wavered since. He only hoped hers hadn't, either.

Jacques worked on the package for what felt like hours. When he was finished with the beating, he carried the package over to Papa's table and waited patiently as the man pulled out the contents and used his loupe to examine the leaf.

"Perfect," Papa finally pronounced, and Jacques heaved a deep sigh of relief. He would be happy if he didn't have to pick up another beating hammer ever again.

"So, Papa," he asked, wiping the sweat from his brow with his forearm, "any guess yet as to what these statuettes are for?"

"I already told you, son, what they are or how they'll be used isn't our concern. We're being paid to make them and to keep quiet about it."

Jacques didn't reply but instead retrieved his agate. Despite Papa's comments, as Jacques held the stone firmly in his hand and began the final polishing, he kept wondering about the palace's need for two hundred gilded fleur-de-lis statuettes. If the royal orders had been for statuettes of solid gold, at least then Jacques might better understand the importance of discretion. But these were merely gilded—gold leaf on brass—and worth infinitely less. Given that, why such secrecy over mere trinkets?

What was the palace planning to do with them?

Furiously polishing the shiny surface, Jacques could only hope that someday they would learn the answers to those questions. Given that the quicksilver poisoning was going to cost Papa his life, Jacques felt he was owed that much.

FOUR

The detective pulled out a pen and a notebook and asked me to tell him everything from the very beginning. I tried, starting with my mother's phone call at the TV studio yesterday and ending with the drive from the airport to the French Quarter. Beyond that, I said, everything was rather foggy, though it was coming back to me bit by bit.

"Why don't you take a few more minutes to think about it," the detective said, patting me on the arm. Then he excused himself to go next door, saying he would be back soon.

"But maybe you can help me," I objected as he stood to go. "Do you know anything about what's going on here?"

"Sorry. I'm still trying to get up to speed myself. Let me take a look next door. I'll be back and we can talk some more."

Alone again except for the uniformed cop at the door, I closed my eyes and tried to recall more of last night, to remember what had happened after my mother told me I had to go to the restaurant to sign papers before I could come to the hospital to see my father. I remembered driving down the interstate toward the French Quarter, my hands clenched around the steering wheel like a vise.

As I had passed the exit for the hospital, a slow-building anger had begun pulsing through my veins, anger and hurt at thirty-two years of rejection from the two people on earth who were supposed to love me unconditionally. What a joke! Nothing had changed here, nothing at all. Even in their darkest hour, my parents cared more about some stupid signed papers than they did about me.

Why was I even surprised? My whole life I had been nothing to them but an afterthought, a mistake, an inconvenience to be handled. No wonder I craved rules. I had grown up watching two parents ignore the most basic rule of all: that the one thing they most owed me was *themselves*.

Furious, I felt like pounding the steering wheel and railing into the dark, empty quiet of the car. I wanted to yell at a nonexistent passenger as if my father were sitting right there and ready to hear the cries of my heart. I held it in, though, lest passing drivers see and think I was crazy. It wasn't easy, as this whole situation had managed to push every single one of my buttons. I may have been an adult with a well-rounded life and a successful consulting business, but things like this reduced me to that same little girl who spent her life quietly watching from the sidelines as the world revolved around her parents and their needs. Rounding the broad curve at the Superdome, I couldn't help but think what a perfect metaphor the massive, looming structure was for my parents and the way they dominated their surroundings at every turn.

Taking the next exit, I left the Superdome behind and made my way south toward the river. As I went, I did the breathing routine I'd learned in exercise class, trying to get my heart rate down. By the time I turned on to the narrow, even streets of the French Quarter, I was finally calm enough to think straight. I could do this. I could meet with Mr. Peralta, sign his papers, and maybe even take a minute to talk with Sam, the restaurant's former manager and probably the closest thing I'd ever had to a loving father figure. Though Sam had retired from Ledet's several years ago, he still lived behind the restaurant in a second-floor apartment that overlooked the courtyard. Spending time with Sam was always the highlight of my trips home.

World-famous Ledet's restaurant was on Royal Street near Toulouse, squeezed between an antique shop and an art gallery. My parents used to call it their "first child" as a joke, but to me it was their only child—and I was just a visiting distant relative. I pulled right up front but saw no valet to take my car, so I continued on toward a hotel parking lot half a block away. Soon, I was strolling through the warm April night, still wearing the linen Theory suit I had put on earlier for the TV show.

When I reached the door of Ledet's, a surge of emotion filled my throat. How many times had I walked through this very portal, feeling like an outsider in my own family's restaurant? Pushing that thought away, I tried to open the door but it was locked.

Surprised, I stepped back to look at the sign over my head, just to make sure I was in the right place. I was. I tried the heavy glass door again and then peered inside. The front hallway was darker than usual, but I thought I could detect light and movement out in the courtyard. I knocked but no one responded, so I decided to go around and try the service entrance off of the side alley. As I turned to go, I saw a man coming toward me on the sidewalk, briefcase in hand.

"Chloe?"

"Yes?"

"Kevin Peralta. Your parents' attorney? I don't think we've ever met."

Jolted from the memory of last night, I gasped, my eyes popping open.

Kevin Peralta.

My parents' attorney.

The man who now lay dead on the couch in the suite next door.

Leaning forward, I rested my elbows on my knees, closed my eyes again, and tried to recall what had happened next.

In front of Ledet's restaurant last night, I had been startled by Kevin's appearance because he wasn't the Mr. Peralta I had been expecting. Seeing the confusion on my face, Kevin explained that I was probably thinking of his father Ruben, who had died of cancer the year before.

"I've taken over his practice," he added.

I expressed my condolences, and in turn he tried to offer words of comfort about my own father's precarious state.

"I know it's scary right now, but it's going to take more than a gunshot wound to stop the great Julian Ledet," Kevin said. "He's too stubborn to take this lying down. I guarantee you the feisty old guy is going to be back on his feet in a couple of days, shouting at the nurses about the hospital food."

"Maybe."

"No, really. Can't you just picture it?" Suddenly, he put one hand on his hip, puffed out his chest, and began bellowing in a perfect imitation of my father. "Nurse, you call this *Jell-O*? My *dog* could make better Jell-O than this! The *fleas* on my dog could make better Jell-O than this! Get it out of my sight! Bring me some flan!"

By the time he was finished, I was nearly crying with laughter. You had to know my dad to get that imitation just right. Obviously, Kevin knew my dad very well.

"Chloe? Is that you?"

Kevin and I both turned in surprise to see a man standing in the open doorway of Ledet's. It was the fill-in bartender, the guy Ledet's always called in to sub when the regular bartender couldn't make it.

"Hey, Graze. How are you? Long time no see."

"Hi, Chloe. I'm sorry," he replied, holding the door wide so we could step inside. "Your mom told me to leave the door unlocked for you, so I opened up the back. I thought you'd be coming in that way."

"We would have tried that next. Don't worry about it." We stepped inside and waited as he again locked the door. "So what's going on? Is the restaurant closed tonight because of my dad's situation?"

Looking surprised, Graze said no, that Ledet's was always closed on Mondays.

"Oh, right," I relied, feeling stupid.

Graze led us away from the elegant entranceway and through the main dining room, which was dark.

"If you're closed, what's going on out there?" Kevin asked, gesturing toward the courtyard.

Just as I had thought, there were about ten or fifteen people milling around among the greenery and fountains and café tables.

"Private party. A wedding shower for two Ledet's employees who are getting married. That's why we've got some staff here tonight, a cook and a waiter and a dishwasher. And I'm running drinks."

He named the happy couple, saying that one was a captain and the other was a sous chef, so it was a joining of front and back house. As I didn't recognize either name, I figured that both of them must be newer employees. Turnover in the restaurant industry was notoriously high, especially in the high-pressure environment of five-star restaurants like this one, and except for a few old-timers like Sam who had managed to stay in the same position for years, it wasn't unusual to see new faces every time I came home.

Graze led us toward one of the smaller dining rooms. The lights were on inside, and as he opened the double French doors and swung them wide, I saw that the center table had been set for two.

"Your mama said to give you a room to yourselves and to fix y'all some dinner. But first, can I bring you something to drink?"

"Just water for me, thanks," I said. "I won't be here long enough to eat dinner."

Kevin ordered a drink for himself, and I told him to feel free to order food as well. Just because I had to leave soon didn't mean he couldn't stay and enjoy.

Once Graze left to get the drinks, Kevin lowered his voice and asked about the man's odd name.

"Graze? It's his nickname." I went on to explain that in restaurant lingo, those who pilfered cherries and olives from the bar were known as "grazers," and they were many bartenders' biggest pet peeve. Legend had it that somewhere in this guy's career, he had said "Don't graze! Don't graze!" so much that it earned him a permanent moniker.

"Got it. *Graze*. I thought maybe he used to be a cemetery worker or something, and you were calling him *Graves*."

We laughed, which was a good feeling, and I couldn't help thinking how much easier Kevin was making this whole experience for me. Like the valve on a pressure cooker, the laughter was helping me let off steam.

Graze returned with our beverages and some menus, urging me to have at least a little something to eat so that my mother wouldn't become angry with them for not following orders to feed me. I was indeed hungry, but I didn't want to take up even one minute more than necessary before heading to the hospital.

"This paperwork is going to take a while," Kevin said, as if he could read my mind. "You might as well. We'll work as we eat."

"But—"

"Look at it this way, Chloe. I know you want to see your dad, but right now he wants you here, doing this. If you don't take the time we need to get this done, you know what'll happen. He'll be upset with you for going there instead."

Kevin was right, of course, so finally I had surrendered to the moment and accepted a menu. As I did, my heart surged again with hurt and anger. With my father stuck in the hospital and me taking his place there with Kevin, I had no doubt which of my father's two children—the restaurant or me—he loved more.

Now, looking up from my place on the couch in the hotel room, I asked the cop at the door if he thought the detective would be gone much longer. He didn't know, so I stood and stretched a little. Feeling antsy, I put my hands on my hips and twisted from side to side, glad to realize that at least the headache was finally fading a bit. The memories continued to surface as well.

Alone in the private dining room with Kevin, I had called my mother to check on how things were going at the hospital, but again her phone went to voice mail. Leaving a message and then putting mine away, I had turned my attention to Kevin, who was still looking at the menu and wanted my opinion of the various dishes. I was embarrassed to say that it had been so long since I'd eaten there that many of them were unfamiliar to me. Of course, the menu's centerpiece was still my father's signature dish, Croûte de Sel Rose, which translated to "crust of pink salt." Julian Ledet was known for it around the world, the same way Paul Prudhomme was famous for his blackened redfish.

Many restaurants offered salt-encrusted fish, of course. Prepared by placing a fish and some herbs in a pan and then literally covering them with a mound of salt, the dish was baked in an oven; when it came out, the salt would have formed a solid crust on the outside, allowing the fish to steam in its own juices on the inside. Though it wasn't uncommon fare, my father's version was unique indeed, as he made it with his own special salt, the same salt that was packaged and shipped from an undisclosed facility in south Louisiana and sold as "Chef Julian's Secret Salt" in fine stores around the world.

On the TV show, Tony had tried to get me to talk about my father's salt and where it came from, but the truth was that the source was known only to the great Julian Ledet himself. Given that it was pink in color and slightly bitter in taste, I had always had a feeling it was imported either from Hawaii or the Himalayas, both of which were known for pink salt. Wherever it came from, my father always called it the perfect cooking salt because its bitterness gave way to a uniquely delicious flavor during the heating process.

I decided to go with Aunt Alma's crawfish bisque, a delectable dish that had always been one of my favorites. I didn't recognize the waiter who came to take our order, but he was obviously a pro, as was every one who worked at Ledet's. My father would stand for nothing less than excellence.

When the waiter left and we were alone, Kevin reached for his briefcase and balanced it on his lap. As he opened it up and flipped through the contents, I thought again how handsome he was. Watching him, it had suddenly struck me that part of my mother's motive for the meeting might have been to matchmake. It drove her crazy that I was thirty-two and not married, for she simply couldn't understand the point of going through life without a mate. With her, I had always defended my singleness, saying that I poured so much of myself into my career that it wouldn't be fair to a spouse. What I would never admit to her was that sometimes the loneliness pierced so deep that I would have traded every professional and financial gain I'd ever made for the love of a good husband. It wasn't very modern of me, but that was how I felt. I didn't want children, but marriage was something I longed for deeply whenever I allowed myself to really think about it.

Given that most of the guys I knew were looking for easy hook ups with little emotional involvement and zero commitment, I didn't date much. Now the first guy I'd met in a long time who seemed decent and kind was dead in the next room. Glancing at the cop who stood watch in the doorway, I resumed my place on the couch, rubbed my temples, and tried to remember more about last night and what had gone so horribly wrong.

FIVE

FRANCE, 1719
JACQUES

After going undetected for so long, Jacques couldn't believe that on the final morning he was nearly spotted. He and Papa had worked late into the night to finish polishing the last two statuettes, so they hadn't roused when the cock crowed. Both men, in fact, were still sleeping the morning away when a loud rapping was heard at the door, jolting them from slumber.

Thinking it was the farmer's wife with lunch, they were scrambling around trying to hide Jacques' pallet when the bolt on the door twisted as if by key and then began to swing open. Immediately, Jacques dove onto the floor and rolled up under the cot. His father smartly slid his blanket so that it draped down the front of the messy bed, and then he rose and crossed to the other side of the room, probably so that whoever was entering would not have their eyes trained in Jacques' direction.

"So you *are* here!" a man's voice said, sounding startled. "Why didn't you answer my knock?"

Papa replied in truth—or at least partial truth—that he had been up late finishing the job the night before and had chosen to sleep in.

"Well, put your trousers on, sir. It's time to load up these trinkets so I can deliver them to the palace. In the box you will find cloths to protect the statuettes. Wrap all but the top layer. Leave those unwrapped, please."

Jacques was trying to calculate how long it would take them to load all two hundred statuettes when the man spoke again.

"First, help me with this cart, would you?"

"Uh, sure. Can you give me just a moment to pull myself together?" Papa asked, which Jacques knew really meant *Can you give me just a moment to sneak my son to a better hiding place?*

"Just hurry," the man barked, but it didn't sound as though he was going to step outside to leave Papa to his privacy.

By the sudden brightening of the light, in fact, Jacques realized that the man had swung open the larger door. Carefully, he tried to look down toward his feet, to make sure they were hidden even in the glare of the morning light, but he just couldn't be sure. Saying a prayer that he wouldn't be spotted, Jacques focused on lying as still as humanly possible.

Listening closely, he could hear what sounded like the squeaking wheels of the empty cart that had thus far sat unused in a corner of the workshop. Next came the sound of clanking and grunting as the man and Papa wrestled with something obviously heavy. Jacques winced as soon as the coughing started, knowing that Papa wasn't up to doing whatever he was having to do, not at all. Finally, the man seemed to realize that as well, for Jacques heard him tell Papa to move out of the way so he could do it himself.

After a good bit of shuffling and scraping and clanking, there was a single, low squeak, like the opening of a door or cabinet, and then all went silent for a moment.

"I don't understand," Papa said, clearing his throat.

"You don't need to understand," the man replied. "Here's the next part of this job. We need you to melt these down to bars, every last one of them. I'll be back to get the bars day after tomorrow, and then you can go home."

"Bars," Papa said, "so these are...real?"

"Fourteen carat, solid gold. And you had better account for every ounce."

"Of course. But the sumptuary laws—"

"Exempt. I was told you might want to see the certificate."

Jacques heard the rustling of paper, and though he wasn't exactly clear as to what was happening, if it had to do with sumptuary laws, then that meant Papa was making sure he wasn't being asked to do anything illegal.

"Yes, I see," Papa said finally. "This is acceptable. Thank you."

More movement and then the man spoke again.

"Listen, I need to water my horse. You fill the trunk with your little treasures and then I'll be on my way."

"Yes. Certainly."

After the man had unhitched his horse, Jacques heard footsteps walking away and the gentle neigh of the horse in the distance. Still, he remained frozen until he heard a whispered "all clear" from his father.

"What's going on, Papa?" Jacques replied softly, sliding out from under the cot. "What is he asking you to do?"

Jacques crouched beside the cot and looked toward the front of the workroom. There, framed in the light of the door, were two carts, each one weighted down with a large, identical wooden trunk.

"Don't let M. Freneau see you," Papa hissed. "Go. Get out of sight."

Jacques glanced outside to make sure the well-dressed man in the powdered wig was still tending to his horse and facing away from the building, and then he made a quick, quiet dash to his usual hiding place, a narrow wardrobe near the back door into which he could just fit his muscular frame. As he pulled the door closed, he saw his father shuffling laboriously toward the trunks at the front of the room.

The coughing resumed almost immediately, and it was all Jacques could do not to pop out of the wardrobe and take over. Fortunately, after a few minutes he heard M. Freneau outside calling toward Papa.

"Listen, take your time, old man. I will pay off the farmer for your meals. Maybe they'll give me a hot breakfast as part of the deal."

Papa managed to stop coughing long enough to reply that that was fine. Jacques listened as the stranger mounted the horse and trotted away. As soon as he could no longer make out the rhythmic clattering of the horse's hooves, Jacques stepped out of the wardrobe and moved toward his father.

"Let me do it, Papa," he whispered. "You keep watch."

The old man didn't even put up a fight. He just nodded wearily, coughing some more, and dragged a stool to the threshold, positioning himself where he could see up the road but not be seen.

Jacques propped opened the trunk, pulled out the stack of fabric squares inside, and began running back and forth between the shelves and the cart. One by one, he wrapped the finished statuettes in the fabric squares and placed them down into the trunk, wondering why Freneau had brought two trunks when one was obviously going to be enough to hold them all.

After stacking the first fifty or so Jacques was breathing hard, though whether from exertion or the fear of being caught, he wasn't sure. He paused to step around the corner and check on his father. The man was perched heavily on the stool, his head resting against the rough doorframe, his eyes glued to the road. For the first time ever, Jacques realized that his strong, capable father looked utterly weak and small. How quickly this final turn for the worse had happened!

"No sign of him yet, Papa?" Jacques whispered.

"No. I will tell you when I spot him."

Quickly, Jacques returned to his work, though before he loaded any more statuettes he took a moment to roll the cart closer to the shelves. That, indeed, made the loading a lot easier. Standing in place now rather than running back and forth, Jacques was able to load twice as fast. In the end, as he'd estimated, all two hundred statuettes had fit inside the one trunk, but just barely. He brought over the other cart, thinking that as long as Freneau hadn't returned yet, he might as well divide the load after all and shift things around a bit. Swinging open the lid of the second trunk, however, presented quite a surprise.

It was already full. Inside was what looked like two hundred more of the same statuettes. Jacques did a double-take, as he was now looking at two identical trunks sporting two identical loads, the only difference being how he had stacked his, vertically rather than horizontally, as the other ones were.

What had Freneau said to Papa? Something about "the next part of the job" and "melting down to bars"? Why did he want these melted down?

Obviously, they had been made by someone else. Had their workmanship been inferior?

Jacques picked up one of the statuettes from the second trunk and took a moment to study it closely. It looked fine to him. In fact, it looked as though it had come from the exact same mold as the ones they had been making. How could that be?

What was going on?

Jacques carried that statuette to the first trunk, lifted one from there, and compared them. They were identical.

"Jacques!"

Jacques' head jerked up at the rasp of his father's voice. Quickly, he returned each statuette to its trunk, closed their lids, and dashed toward the front door.

"What is it, Papa?" he hissed. "Do you see M. Freneau?"

"I see a cloud of dirt up the road. It's likely him."

As fast as he could, Jacques ran back, grabbed one of the heavy carts, and dragged it to the doorway. He was about to drag the other as well when his father came inside, holding his stool, and urged Jacques to get in the wardrobe. Without a word, Jacques did as he was told.

There in the narrow, dark space of his hiding place, Jacques couldn't see but he could hear a little. First came the cloppity-clop of the horse outside, then Freneau's voice saying something. Once he came into the building, his tones sounded angry. Straining to listen to the conversation between him and Papa, Jacques realized that Freneau wasn't mad at him, he was griping about the farmer's wife, who had only been willing to give him a single cold biscuit for his trouble.

As the two men talked, it sounded as though they were working together to attach the horse to the cart. Freneau said something again about returning day after tomorrow at noon to pick up the bars, and then with the sound of hooves moving more slowly this time, he clattered away.

Jacques waited in the wardrobe, listening for Papa's "all clear," but it never came. Finally, unsure what to do, he took a risk and pushed the wardrobe door slightly ajar. He didn't see anyone, so he pushed it a little further and then gasped.

There, lying on the ground in the open doorway, was Papa.

"No!" Jacques cried, running to his father.

"Once he was gone, I simply lost all strength," Papa rasped, trying to struggle to his knees.

"Of course you did," Jacques said, lifting up his father from the ground and helping him toward the bed. He would have carried the man entirely, but he didn't want to humiliate him. "You had to work too hard. You weren't up to that."

"At least he is gone now. Close and lock the door, son, and bring me some water."

Jacques did as he was told, his heart pounding in his throat the whole while. His father simply couldn't die! He was too young! It was too soon! Trying bravely not to cry, Jacques held the cup to his father's trembling lips as he took a few sips. Jacques didn't even visibly react when he pulled the cup away only to see that yet another tooth had come out and was lying there in the water at the bottom.

"Papa, please hold on," Jacques whispered, tossing out the contents of the cup and setting it aside. "I can't lose you yet."

Papa closed his eyes and tilted back his chin, his breathing labored and long. They had known too many men in their business who had died this way, first the breathing, then the teeth, and then finally the internal humours. It wouldn't be long now.

"Jacques, you must finish this job for me. There is one thing left to do."

"What does it matter now, Papa?"

His father opened his eyes and looked straight at him.

"I am a master goldsmith," he replied sternly. "It matters."

Jacques nodded, wiping at his damp cheeks, promising he would make sure the work was done and done well. Kneeling there on the floor, Jacques listened miserably, trying to concentrate as his father explained that he was to melt down the statuettes that were in the remaining trunk and cast them as gold bars.

"I'll have to separate out all of the metals first," Jacques corrected.

"No, son. These aren't gilded. They're solid gold."

"What?"

There in the quiet workroom in the dim light of morning, Jacques' father explained that the statuettes only looked similar on the outside to the ones they had made. On the inside, these were solid fourteen-carat gold, as opposed to theirs, which had been brass statuettes covered in gold leaf.

"I don't understand. We didn't make these. How is it that they look exactly the same? How could someone else have matched your design so precisely?"

Papa thought for a moment and then swallowed before speaking.

"It was the other way around. When I first came here to do this job, I was given the finished molds and told to use them. We matched *their* design, Jacques."

"But why, Papa? What's going on?"

"It's not our business to ask. We have been well paid to do a job and keep quiet about it, and that's what we're going to do. *You're* going to do. Do you understand?"

"Yes, sir. I understand."

Jacques stayed where he was for the moment, and soon his father's breathing changed from shallow, agonized gasps to the deeper, even wheezes of sleep. Jacques laid the blanket over his father's resting form. Then slowly, sadly, he got up, brushed himself off, and forced himself to do exactly as his father had told him.

First he got dressed, splashed some water in his face, and ate a hunk of leftover bread to calm his churning stomach. Then he crossed the room to where the remaining cart waited by the door and slowly rolled it toward the worktable. He stoked the furnace with fuel, and as it heated up he gathered the tools he would need: the crucible, the muffle, the tongs. Finally, his heart heavy, Jacques opened the trunk and reached inside for the first of two hundred fleur-de-lis statuettes that he would be melting down to a liquid and then casting as gold bars.

It wasn't until that moment that he realized the man had mistakenly carted away the wrong trunk.

SIX

Still thinking back to last night, I remembered Kevin pulling out a file folder for us to discuss before closing up his briefcase and setting it on the floor. I wasn't sure where that file folder or the briefcase were now, but I didn't recall seeing either in the hotel room next door.

Was that it? Had someone drugged both of us just to get their hands on that paperwork? Maybe that was what had happened, only somehow Kevin's body had reacted differently to the drug than mine, and he had ended up dead.

But when had we been drugged? Where, and how? Surely not at Ledet's, my own family's restaurant. Closing my eyes yet again, I strained to remember what had happened next. We were there in the restaurant, our orders placed, Kevin holding the file folder in his hands.

"Ready to get started?" he had asked.

"Yes, I am," I replied, eager to sign the papers, eat a fast meal, and then get myself to the hospital as soon as I possibly could.

Kevin began by explaining the basic situation, saying my father had called him first thing that morning and told him to make an offer on a property down in south central Louisiana. The place he wanted to buy was an eighty-acre tract of high ground, much of it wooded, that sat in the Atchafalaya Basin between the river and a clear, deep bayou. For many years it had been my father's favorite hunting and fishing grounds, the place he went whenever he wanted to relax and regroup.

"You're talking about Paradise, where he was today when he was shot," I replied. The land he wanted was owned by Alphonse Naquin, an old friend of my father's, one with whom he'd had a falling out a few years ago. "My dad's been trying to get Naquin to sell that place to him for a long time. The answer was always no."

"Well, this time your dad had a new approach. He was so excited about his offer that he felt sure Naquin would accept it this time."

"What was the offer? It must have been a big one."

Kevin hesitated, glancing at the paperwork.

"Yes, it was, but your father also came up with a deal clincher, one that would surely convince Naquin to sell. Julian told me to make the offer and draw up the contracts, and he would sign them in a few days, once he got back to town. That's what I need you to sign on his behalf."

"Sounds simple enough, but why can't this wait? Why am I here tonight when I need to be at the hospital with my dad?"

"Because of what happened next. Your father was shot a short while after he and I talked. Before he even called for an ambulance, he left a message for your mother, telling her to let me know that this land deal was extremely important and I was to push it through as fast as humanly possible."

"Well, that figures," I mumbled. "Leave it to Julian Ledet to be wheeling and dealing even as he's lying there, shot and bleeding. Good grief."

"I don't know, Chloe. His message was a little weirder than that. It didn't sound like his typical 'wheeling and dealing,' as you put it. Not at all."

"What do you mean?"

"From what your mother told me of his message, it sounded as though the shooting incident and this land deal were somehow connected. I believe his exact words were 'Now that I've been shot, the deal is even more important than before.'"

"What do you think he meant?"

"I don't know. But then it gets even weirder. After that, his message urged your mother to get this contract signed as soon as possible, before they come after her too."

"What?"

"Those were his exact words, that she needed to act quickly, 'before they come after you too.'"

I sat back in my chair, thinking about that for a minute, trying to get down to the bottom-line implication. I thought he had been shot in a hunting accident, but now it sounded as though it might not have been an accident at all.

"Are you saying someone shot my father on purpose? That they came after him and shot him and now they are going to come after my mother unless this deal goes through?"

"Quite possibly."

Blinking, I had tried to reframe the whole situation with that incredible, horrific thought in mind.

"Why would someone do that?"

"I have no idea."

Now, of course, as I sat in this sunny hotel room and Kevin's body lay next door, I knew that my father's concerns had been justified. Whatever was going on, not only had he and my mother been endangered, but apparently his lawyer and even his daughter had been pulled into it too.

"Excuse me, I need to see the detective," I said to the cop.

"He'll be back in a minute. Just hold your horses."

I appreciated the man's protective presence, but his etiquette left a little to be desired. Standing beside the couch, I began to pace as even more memories of last night came flooding back to me.

"Who shot my father, Kevin?" I had demanded.

"I don't know, Chloe, but obviously something's going on."

"Surely it wasn't one of the Naquins," I had said, my mind racing. "That wouldn't make any sense. Why would you shoot someone who wanted to buy something from you, even if you didn't want to sell?"

"No, that makes no sense. Besides, I know Alphonse Naquin and his whole family. There's no way any of them would have done something like this."

"Who, then? Who else would benefit from the sale of Paradise, so much so that my father got shot over it and my mother's safety hinges upon it?"

"I don't know who, but I have an idea about why. Remember I said that when your dad and I talked this morning, he wanted to raise the amount of money he was offering for Paradise, plus he was throwing in a deal clincher? One that would guarantee that Naquin would finally be willing to sell?"

"Yes."

"I think whatever's going on has to do with that deal clincher. It's kind of...um...unique. I knew about it, but I have a feeling you're going to be very surprised."

I stared at Kevin, waiting for him to spell it out. Whatever incentive my father had thought to include in a real estate transaction, surely it couldn't have ended up getting him shot.

"Unique how?" I asked tiredly. "Just tell me, Kevin. What did he throw in to sweeten the deal?"

"Believe it or not, it has to do with treasure, Chloe. Buried treasure."

I hadn't replied but merely sat there, staring at him blankly.

"You know, like pirates and gold and all of that?" Kevin had continued. "You're probably not aware of this, but your father is half owner of a treasure. He found it himself years ago when he was just a young man. With only a few exceptions, he has kept that treasure a secret ever since."

"A treasure," I said evenly, resisting the urge to roll my eyes. "Kevin, you're going to need to start from the beginning on this one. You're right about one thing. This is the first I've ever heard about my father and a treasure."

"Okay. A long time ago, back in the early fifties, your father was down at Paradise and tracking a deer when he discovered buried treasure. I don't know the details of how he found it, but I do know that the first thing he did was run get his friend Alphonse to come and see."

"What was it in? An old wooden pirate's chest?"

"No, more like a disintegrated canvas bag."

"And what was inside? Coins? Jewelry?"

"Statues."

"Statues?"

"Yes, tiny statues that looked very old and very valuable. Right away, your father and Naquin agreed that no matter what the treasure ended up being worth, they would split it down the middle, fifty-fifty. That was their own personal decision, but it's interesting that Louisiana civil code dictates exactly that."

"Exactly what?"

"That when one person finds treasure on another person's land, it is to be divided equally between the treasure finder and the landowner."

"Tell me more about what the treasure was. Statues?"

"Little statuettes, really, about the size of figurines. There were sixty of them, all identical, each about four-inches high, shaped like a fleur-de-lis, and made from solid gold."

I sat up straight, realizing I had seen the very item he was describing. I had grown up in the same house with it, for that matter. As far as I knew, it was still sitting where it had always been, in a glass case in my father's study, next to his most prized possession, the ribbon he had earned upon graduation from the Cordon Bleu cooking school in Paris. As a child, I had been fascinated by that ribbon—probably because I couldn't understand why my father thought it was so precious—but I had never given the gold statuette next to it much thought.

"You said there were *sixty* of them? Where had they come from?"

"Your father and Naquin had no idea. Their best guess was that it had been buried there by pirates."

"Out in the middle of a swamp?" I asked skeptically.

"Oh, yeah. That area was a prime hiding ground for pirates back in the day. Here, take a look at this."

Kevin pulled a page from his file and handed it to me. I looked at it to see the heading: "Found Treasures in the State of Louisiana." Below that were listings of numerous treasures, the dates they were discovered, and the places where they had been discovered. "Jefferson Island, found in 1923, 3 boxes gold coins dating fm. 18 & 19 century," read one. Scanning the locations listed, I was surprised to see that Kevin was right. The swampy parts of the state seemed to be where almost all of these treasures had been buried.

"Of course, there are enough treasures yet to be found that they fill entire books. Treasure hunters study various legends and rumors and then go out searching for the treasures based on that information—and sometimes they find what they're looking for. Usually, though, treasures are simply stumbled upon purely by luck. Like with your dad, or like that group of shrimpers out of Mobile, who pulled up their nets only to find them full of Spanish gold coins."

Kevin's story was interrupted by the appearance of the waiter with our salads. He flitted around us for a moment, offering ground pepper and refilling our water glasses. After he was gone, I handed Kevin back his sheet of paper and he continued.

"Anyway, your dad and Naquin were excited about the treasure, especially because both of them could really use the money. Naquin made a fair wage working for an oil company, but by that point he had four kids and another on the way, and he wanted to build a bigger house. Your dad was just twenty-one, working in a New Orleans restaurant and trying to figure out how he could afford to go to a good culinary school. They knew that both of their lives could change for the better with this treasure, but that they would have to be careful."

"Why careful?"

"Because if it really was pirate treasure and they made their find public, there was a good chance it could be taken away from them. Foreign governments will sue over treasure, you know, especially if they can prove it was seized by pirates from one of their own country's ships. Considering that these statuettes were fleur-de-lis, the symbol of French royalty, your dad and Naquin had a feeling that if they tried to sell them on the open market, the French government might show up and claim the statuettes, leaving them with nothing."

"So what did they do?"

"They tossed options around a while and finally decided to get some professional advice. They shared the news of what they had found with one other person: my father, Ruben Peralta. He was in law school at the time, and they were hoping he might be able to advise them from a legal standpoint about how to proceed."

Kevin went on to describe what his father's legal research revealed.

From what he could tell, there weren't any hard-and-fast rules about how to prevent a treasure from being legally seized by another government. Ruben suggested that they continue to keep the treasure secret while doing some historical research to trace back its origins. If they could prove the treasure's location was legitimate and not due to theft or piracy, then they could go public. If they found that the treasure did tie in with pirates or some other sort of shady dealings, they could choose to go public anyway and take their chances with lawsuits, or as a last resort they could always keep it private, melt down the statuettes into ingots, and sell them for the value of the gold.

"How could buried treasure ever be legitimate, though?" I asked. "I mean, come on. It had to be pirates. An honest person would keep their valuables in a bank vault or a safe, not buried in the backyard."

"You're thinking like a modern person, Chloe. How about before there were any banks in Louisiana? Or how about the people who didn't think banks were safe? And don't forget the Civil War, when a lot of money and valuable items were hidden away in some very unusual locations to keep them from being confiscated."

"All right, I see your point."

"Of course," Kevin added, "for your dad and Naquin, melting down the gold was a risky thing to do, financially speaking, because if these statuettes were something important, historically and/or artistically speaking, that extra value would melt away."

We were again interrupted by the waiter, who came to take away our salad plates, refill our water glasses, and let us know our entrées would be out in just a few more minutes. I sat quietly, trying to process everything, until he was gone.

"So what choice did they make, Kevin? What happened to the treasure?"

"Long story. I'll just give you the highlights. Because both men needed some fast money, they agreed to melt down just enough of the gold to carry them over but save the rest until they were able to do their research. They kept out five statuettes and hid the rest of the treasure in a location known only to the two of them. They held on to one as a souvenir of sorts. Your dad showed it to me at the house. The other four they melted down. Gold was selling at forty dollars an ounce back then, so they netted more than fifteen thousand dollars from melting down just four of the statuettes."

"You're kidding!"

"No. Of course, they had to pay a commission to my dad for handling the details. I mean, you can't exactly melt gold on the stove and then bring it to your local bank. He made things happen in that regard, and he also saw that the treasure was kept secret even while the IRS was correctly compensated so that there would be no problems with the tax laws. But even with his fee and the taxes, there was still enough to send your father to Cordon Bleu in Paris and get Naquin into a new house. In fact, your father had enough money to stay over in Europe for a few years after he graduated, just to study the cooking techniques of the various regions. By the time he came home, he was one very well-educated chef."

I had heard numerous stories over the years about my father's insatiable quest for cooking knowledge and his love for Cordon Bleu and his vaga-bond days in Europe, but now that I knew more of the story, slowly the pictures I kept in my mind were having to realign themselves. He wasn't just a poor kid from the Quarter who made good; he was a poor kid from the Quarter who got lucky and then made good. When I was growing up, he was always driving home the point that hard work and dedication can get you anywhere. Somehow, much of that rhetoric felt like a lie once I knew he had had a secret treasure footing the bills.

The waiter came back with our entrées at that point, and I was glad for the opportunity to collect my thoughts.

The man set my delicious-smelling bowl of crawfish bisque in front of me, but Kevin's Croûte de Sel Rose was a little more complicated than that. Part of the dish's appeal was the elaborate presentation it required. Much like Caesar salad or bananas Foster, the final steps of serving salt-crusted fish lent itself to a bit of tableside drama. Kevin and I both watched the waiter act out that drama now on our behalf, not an easy task considering that this performance usually involved the assistance of several attendants, silent workers who would hover at the waiter's elbow and provide each tool as he needed it, much like a scrub nurse in an operating room.

As our waiter was working alone, he simply laid out an array of tools, a cutting board, and a plate on the empty side of our table. Turning his attention to the hot pan in which the fish had been baked, he tapped along the solid crust with the back of a heavy spoon, breaking the seal and releasing the aromatic fragrance of the herbs. Next, he used a special pair of tongs to separate the crust along its fault line, pushing each side back to reveal the tender, juicy fish inside. Once the salty package was wide open, in a quick, careful movement with yet another tool, he scooped out the whole fish and set it down on the waiting cutting board. There, he filleted it perfectly, right along the bone, and placed the resulting meat on the empty plate. Trading tools again, he used a slotted spoon to scoop out some tiny red potatoes and pearl onions from the pan and add them to the plate. He used a pastry brush to whisk away any errant chunks of the salt, and then he topped the whole thing with a meuniere sauce.

"This isn't going to be too salty?" Kevin asked as the waiter finally set the plate in front of him and gathered up his tools.

"No, sir, not at all. Enjoy!"

Kevin took a bite of the fish as the waiter again left us alone. I could tell by his closed eyes and rapturous expression that he found it even more delicious than he had expected. I enjoyed my bisque with equal enthusiasm, feeling as I did a twinge of pride at the fact that Julian Ledet was my father. The man had his flaws, but truly he was an artist and a genius when it came to food—regardless of how he had paid for his education way back when. In the restaurant that bore his name, though he no longer prepared the food himself, he had created the recipes for most of the items that were served there.

"Ms. Ledet, may we see your hands, please?"

Startled, I opened my eyes to find myself back in the hotel room. Detective Walters and another woman were standing in front of me expectantly. Kevin was dead, I reminded myself, and though I knew there was still more of last night for me to remember, the two people standing here and staring at me were obviously waiting for something.

"Excuse me?" I asked, blinking

"Your hands. May we see your hands?"

I held my hands out in front of me. As I did, I noticed for the first time since waking up in this strange place that my perfectly manicured fingernails were dirty.

SEVEN

As the woman and Detective Walters studied my hands, I tried to remember how my fingernails could possibly have gotten so dirty.

"Uh-huh," the woman said to Detective Walters as she studied my nails. Then, before I could stop her, she pulled out a pair of nail scissors and a plastic bag and clipped off my right thumbnail at its base.

"What are you doing?" I cried, pulling back and staring at her.

"I need the tissues and dried blood under your fingernails as evidence," the woman replied, reaching out again and grasping my hand in a firm grip.

Blood? Dried blood?

"How would I get blood under my fingernails?" I asked, watching in disbelief as she finished one hand and started in on the other, destroying with a few quick snips a sixty-dollar manicure.

"More than likely from the scratches on your friend's cheeks," she replied.

Stunned, I looked up helplessly at Detective Walters. He didn't say a word but merely pantomimed the scraping of his fingernails across his cheek.

Were they serious? Did they really think I had killed Kevin? That was ridiculous!

Once the woman finished with my fingernails, she sealed up her plastic bag, thanked the detective, and walked away. He looked down at me and told me not to go anywhere, that he would be back in a minute. Then he followed her out of the room, and I was left alone again except for the cop at the door. Looking at him now, I finally realized that he wasn't here to protect me. He was here to keep me from leaving.

I knew if I had indeed killed Kevin myself, my only hope lay in remembering how and why. Could I have done it in self-defense? Near panic, I forced my mind back again to the memories of last night.

Kevin had explained the rest of the story as we ate, saying that neither my dad nor Mr. Naquin had been able to turn up any information at all about the origin of the statuettes. Of course, they hadn't exactly been experts at historical research, and there was no Internet back then to make it easier. Finally, Ruben had offered to do the research on their behalf, but at a price. If he was able to find proof that the treasure was free and clear, he wanted a share of the profits. His offer seemed fair, so the three men signed a contract to that effect. Because Ruben was just starting out in a law firm and didn't have much spare time, progress was slow. Eventually, the whole thing turned into a hobby for him, one that he did on the side whenever he could.

Ruben kept at it, telling the others to be patient, but eventually my father reached the point where he wanted to melt down the rest of the treasure—or at least his half. There were fifty-five statuettes left, and gold was still hovering around forty dollars an ounce, so his share, melted down, would have given him a little more than a hundred thousand dollars. He was an accomplished chef by that point and eager to create a first-class restaurant, one that could compete with the likes of Antoine's and Broussard's and Galatoire's and the rest. In the late sixties, that much money would have allowed him to buy the building he had in mind, renovate it, and cover all operating costs in those first crucial months until the restaurant began turning a profit. Most men in that position would have taken on partners, but my father wasn't interested in giving anyone else a say in how he did things. This was to be Julian Ledet's baby from start to finish. He needed the treasure to make that happen.

Ruben, on the other hand, was convinced that the treasure was worth at least three times that much intact, so he came up with a clever alternative. They could handpick several wealthy investors, ones who knew how to keep their mouths shut. Julian would tell them about the treasure, describe the conundrum they were still in about trying to find its true origins, and offer his share as collateral. If the restaurant was a success, they would get back their initial investment plus a healthy rate of interest. If the restaurant failed, they would get the value of their initial investment paid back in gold statuettes. At that point, it would be up to each investor whether he wanted to melt down his share and sell it for the going rate or hang onto it until the research was complete and the statuettes' true value could be determined.

Except for the statuettes, that part of the story fit in with what I knew about how Ledet's got started. My impression had always been that my father owned the restaurant free and clear but that a few well-heeled friends had helped him to get it going—and that he had done so well so fast that he had been able to pay them all back in full within three years. One of the investors, Conrad Zahn, was involved in local politics, and he had also been pivotal in helping my father navigate through the complicated red tape of renovating the historical structure that would house the restaurant.

"Okay, I think I have a pretty good understanding of what went on back then. What happened with the treasure?"

Kevin dabbed at his mouth with his napkin and then spoke.

"Ledet's was a huge success, so the investors got their money back plus interest, and your dad's share of the treasure remained intact. Unfortunately, in the meantime my father's research turned up at least one tie between the statuettes and the French crown. It wasn't enough to prove that the treasure belonged back in France, but it definitely gave them reason to keep it quiet a bit longer. Time passed, and your father's restaurant did so well that he was no longer hurting for money. Naquin, on the other hand, was getting up in years and was tired of waiting for the treasure's big payoff. He tried to convince your father that it was time to make a decision once and for all."

"What was the problem?"

"They couldn't agree on how to get that payoff. All along, your father maintained that the smartest move was to melt down the gold and sell it as ingots, saying a bird in the hand was worth two in the bush. Naquin, however, couldn't stand the thought of destroying what might be an important historical find, especially given that it would be worth far more money intact. He wanted to take the treasure public and try to sell it, even with the risk that a foreign government might swoop in and take it all away and leave them with nothing. Given how much time had already passed since they first found the treasure, it seemed to Naquin it was a chance worth taking."

"I have to agree with him."

"Yes, well, your father didn't. The two men argued about it for years but never reached a solution. They finally had a parting of ways last year. Gold was selling at almost eight hundred and seventy dollars an ounce at that point, so the gold alone was now worth more than four and a half million dollars. I can't even imagine the value of the treasure intact. Twice that much? Three times? Ten times? Regardless, your father wouldn't budge. Naquin had had enough and cut all ties."

"How sad, that such good friends would allow money to destroy a relationship."

"I know. Adding fuel to the fire was the fact that your father was just about to buy Paradise from Naquin when they had their big blowup over the treasure. In retaliation Naquin canceled the sale on the land. Even though his family doesn't even want Paradise anymore, Naquin stubbornly hangs onto it. To be honest, I think the only reason he still lets your father go down there is just to torment him by hanging it over his head like that. That land is Naquin's biggest weapon in their fight over the treasure."

"Sounds like two stubborn old men, both digging in their heels," I said. I was still trying to wrap my head around all that I had learned. "So now that I understand the situation with the treasure, go back to what you were saying earlier. What was the deal clincher my father told you this morning, the one that would finally make Naquin willing to sell him the land?"

"Believe it or not, your dad decided to let Naquin win the battle over the treasure. He wants Paradise so badly that he's giving in. If Naquin will sell him the land, in return your father will allow Naquin to have his way with the treasure and take it public."

"After all these years of fighting, my dad's the one who surrendered? That's not the Julian Ledet I know. He once gave Sam the silent treatment for an entire month just because he didn't like the way Sam had the staff folding the napkins."

"I was as shocked as you, but when we spoke this morning, your father sounded very happy about it, almost jubilant. He was ready to wave the white flag with glee."

"Did he give you a reason for this uncharacteristic hundred-and-eighty-degree flip?"

"No. He just said that he loves Paradise so much he wants to own it for himself, even if it means risking the treasure. After we hung up, I thought about it some more and finally decided that maybe he's ready to retire and wants to build a house down there or something. That was the only explanation I could think of."

"Are you kidding? My mother would die before she'd let that happen. She'll never live anywhere except New Orleans."

"Well, whatever your father's reason for the about-face, he was excited about it. He wasn't resentful at all."

"Knowing him, he probably found more buried treasure there or something and wants to buy the land so he won't have to split this one fifty-fifty or fight over how to deal with it."

"I doubt it, for two reasons. First, that land has been gone over with a fine-tooth comb many times since the treasure was found in the hopes of discovering more, all to no avail. Nothing else is out there. More important, the laws are designed to protect the seller in situations like this. Even if your dad bought the land and then found more treasure, for a certain number of years half would still revert back to Naquin even though he didn't own the land anymore."

"Okay, tell me about Naquin. What was his reaction when you told him my father's offer?"

"Unfortunately, Alphonse Naquin is out of town on a fishing trip and can't be reached. He doesn't know yet."

"I bet he'll be shocked when he finds out."

"Are you kidding? To my knowledge, no one has ever won a battle of wills against Julian Ledet. I'd say Naquin is going to be dumbfounded."

It occurred to me that if Naquin was currently out of town, my father's urgency in completing this transaction was moot. I said as much to Kevin.

"I know. But once I do find Naquin, having the signed contracts with me will definitely speed things along. Your dad wants me to hurry, and the best way I know how to do that is to handle this end of things first."

I asked to see the contract I had come to sign. Reading it through, it seemed fairly standard to me. I was no lawyer, but I had been involved with enough business transactions to be familiar with the paperwork.

"Is there any reason I shouldn't sign this?" I asked, looking up at Kevin.

"Not really," he replied. "Although, now that your father's been shot, and he left your mother that strange message, I would understand if you feel you need more information first."

"Maybe I can help with that," a deep voice suddenly said from the doorway.

Kevin and I both looked up, startled. It was Sam, my father's closest friend and one of the brightest spots in my whole life.

"Sam!"

As I rose from the table, I realized he looked older than when I'd seen him last. The hair at his temples was grayer, the line of his posture more stooped.

"Hi, baby," Sam replied, the smooth brown skin of his face crinkling into a smile as he opened his arms. I moved around the table to rush into them, thinking that on this difficult day it was about time that someone somewhere gave me a big hug.

Sam was there, and he always made everything all right.

"Sam," I whispered now, still sitting on the couch in the empty hotel room, my long fingernails shorn, my heart suddenly aching with fear.

If Sam had been there last night, where was he now? Was he okay? If so, could he explain what was going on? My cell phone was in my purse in the room next door, so I grabbed the telephone on the table next to me and, without asking for permission from my guard, dialed nine and then the number of Sam's apartment. There was no answer, so when it went to the machine I simply left a message saying it was Chloe and that I was at the Maison Chartres hotel and needed him to come right away if he could. I wasn't sure where on Chartres Street we were, but given that Sam's apartment was between Royal and Bourbon, it shouldn't take him long to get here once he got the message. *If* he got the message.

Hanging up, I knew Sam also had a cell phone, but I had never committed that number to memory. I had programmed it into my cell a few years ago, but it wouldn't have mattered now anyway, I realized, as the cop was glaring at me sternly and telling me to stay off of the phone.

"I need to call my mother," I protested. "I need to find out about my father."

"Not right now. Maybe later."

What was I going to do? Where was Sam? Had I really killed Kevin?

Before I had a chance to go back again to the events of last night, Detective Walters suddenly entered the room, sat across from me again, and apologized for taking so long.

"Have you been able to remember anything else about last night, Ms. Ledet?" he asked, pulling out his pen and holding it poised above his notepad. The expression on his face was one of benign interest. Though he obviously thought I was a murderer, he was doing a good job of making it look as though he was giving me the benefit of the doubt for now.

"Yes, I have remembered some," I said slowly, wondering how much to tell him. If I started spouting off about buried treasure, he would surely think I was crazy. On the other hand, my only defense was the truth. Crazy or not, I had no choice but to tell him all that I had been able to recall thus far. My father and Mr. Naquin might not appreciate my giving away the information about their secret treasure, but the more fully I could explain, the better chance I had that Detective Walters might actually believe me—no matter how incredible my story sounded.

Slowly, I explained everything I had managed to remember thus far.

As I did, it almost looked as if the detective was starting to believe the incredible tale of how I had come to town to see my father, stopped first at the restaurant to meet with his lawyer and sign some papers, and ended up learning about a secret family treasure.

He listened intently, making notes and interrupting me frequently for clarification. I ended what there was of my story by saying I felt sure at some point last night I had been given a drug that had rendered me unconscious—and I had remained that way until the police banged on my door this morning. I said I had no idea how Kevin had ended up here as well, dead no less, or why I might have scratched his face. But I suggested that they draw some of my blood so that we could find out what drug I had been given. For that matter, they should test Kevin's too, I said. Perhaps both of us had been under the influence of some substance—one that had rendered me unconscious and killed Kevin. That wouldn't explain why I had scratched his face, but it might help us start piecing this puzzle together.

The detective called in a technician, who donned a pair of rubber gloves, pulled out the necessary supplies, and promptly took a vial of blood from my veins. As he finished and walked away, I wondered if it might be time for me to get myself a lawyer.

"Let me get this straight," the detective said, using the phrase he had already uttered about fifteen times since I started my story. "You don't remember when or where it happened, but you believe that last night you were administered a twilight drug?"

"Yes...a twilight drug. Isn't that what they call the stuff that knocks you out and erases your memory?"

He nodded.

"That's it. I feel sure of it. I was given a twilight drug."

There was still more of the memory to recover, of course, and I couldn't know what lurked in the fog at the back of my brain, but at least I had been able to recall some of what had happened. Now I just needed to think more about Sam, about what had happened after he arrived. I said as much to the detective.

"Okay, well, why don't you think on that while I go check a few more things," he replied. Without another word, he got up and left the room, tucking pen and paper back into his pocket.

Closing my eyes, I again leaned back against the couch and rested my head. Sam. What had happened last night with Sam?

At the restaurant, I remembered embracing him and thinking how thin he felt. He had always been a wiry sort, but now he felt positively skeletal. We pulled apart, and for some reason, just the sight of my old friend caused my eyes to fill with tears. Blinking them away, I invited him to sit down with us and asked him how he was holding up. He and Kevin shook hands and exchanged greetings as I returned to my seat.

"I'm hanging in there," Sam had said as he pulled out a chair, "but I feel like I've aged ten years in the last couple of hours. I've been running around like crazy ever since your mother called me and told me your father had been shot."

"Do you have the details of what happened?" Kevin asked.

"Yes, please tell us what you know," I said.

Sam nodded, placing the tips of his fingers together and bouncing them against his chin in a familiar gesture of contemplation. He began to explain, but most of what he told us we already knew, that my father had been down at Paradise when he had been shot earlier today, probably around noon. As soon as it happened, my injured father had called my mother, but she was at the spa and had her cell phone turned off. Unable to reach her, he had hung up and tried the house, finally leaving a message for her there, telling her what happened and for her to rush this whole contract through as quickly as possible. Apparently, once he left that message, he hung up and dialed 911 for help. He was still alive but unconscious by the time the paramedics found him.

"Excuse me, would you folks like something else to drink?" Graze had suddenly interrupted from the doorway. "Hey, Sam. I'm sorry, but I didn't see you come in. Would you like a brandy or something?"

Sam turned around toward the bartender, who was holding a tray of small glasses filled with a bright red liquid.

"What have you got there, Sazeracs?"

"Yeah, these are for the party outside. You want one?"

"Gimme three and then give us some privacy, would you?"

"Yes, sir."

Graze placed three of the red drinks in front of Sam, who grunted in frustration and said, "Not three for me, Graze. One for me and one for each of them."

At times like that, Sam always reminded me of my father. Between the two of them, they managed to keep the staff on their toes. The big difference between them was that my father corrected with the intent to humiliate, while Sam corrected so the person would get it right the next time.

Not wanting a Sazerac, I ordered a cup of decaf coffee instead. After Graze was gone, I reached out and placed my pale hand on top of Sam's dark one.

"Why don't you take a deep breath? You're scaring me. I'm afraid you'll have a heart attack or something."

Sam did as I suggested, closing his eyes and inhaling deeply. Next to me, Kevin finished his meal and then started on his Sazerac, sipping it contentedly. To me, though the drink may have been the signature cocktail of New Orleans, I always thought it most closely resembled cough syrup.

"Okay," Sam said reaching for his glass and taking a long sip. "I'm okay."

Considering his current state, I didn't want to rush him. On the other hand, I really needed him to keep going with what he was saying.

"Your poor mama," he finally continued. "She didn't even know anything had happened to Julian until she got home from the spa about 1:00 p.m. and checked her messages. By then, your daddy had already been airlifted to Oschner's."

The timing made sense, given that my television show appearance had been from 1:00 to 2:00 p.m. While I was being grilled on live TV by Tony, my mother had arrived at home, heard my father's message, and started trying to reach me soon after.

"Who shot him? How did the accident happen?" I asked, hoping Sam would confirm that it was indeed an accident and not intentional, as Kevin and I suspected.

Sam set his drink down and met my eyes.

"It was no accident, baby. Whoever shot your daddy, it sounds like they shot him on purpose."

"We were afraid of that. But *why*, Sam? Why?"

"I wish I knew," Sam said, looking from Kevin to me and back again. "He was calling from his cell phone when he left the message, so there's a lot of static and skipped words and it's hard to hear. You can sure make out that he's been shot, though."

"Wait a minute, I'm confused about something," I said. "My father always told us that Paradise didn't get cell phone reception at all. One of the things he always liked about it was that no one could ever bother him while he was down there. Now you're telling me that he made not one but two calls from there this morning? What happened? Did a new cell tower go in or something?"

Kevin shook his head.

"No, he called from the marina a few miles away. That's how I first knew he was so excited, because he had gotten in his boat and driven it all the way there just to contact me."

I looked at Sam, who shrugged.

"When Julian left the message for your mama, he was somewhere out on the water, from what I understand. Anyway, your mama made a bunch of calls and finally learned that he had been found alive but unconscious. She wanted to go down to the hospital at Morgan City, but they told her they would only be stabilizing him there and then airlifting him up to New Orleans, so she drove to Oschner's and waited for him there instead. She called me from the car to tell me about the message and asked me to go by the house and listen to it myself and see what I thought."

"And?"

"And it was pretty garbled. I listened to it about ten times and finally gave up. I ended up bringing the tape to a friend who has professional sound equipment, and I'm hoping he can clear up the noise and let us hear what your daddy actually said. My friend didn't know how long fixing the sound might take or how much he would be able to recover, but he said he'd do the best he could. After I dropped the tape off with him, I drove on to the hospital so I could see your daddy and be with your mama. When I knew you were coming here, I thought I should come and tell you all this in person. Once we find out what else is on that tape, we'll know a lot more about what happened."

"I wish I could hear it."

"Well, here. For right now you can look at this. I wrote down what I could make out from it."

Sam dug in his pockets, finally retrieving a folded piece of paper and holding it out to me.

"Thanks, but I don't understand," I said, taking it from him. "What difference does the tape make now? Can't my father just tell you who shot him?"

"Oh, Chloe, I thought you knew. Your daddy's still unconscious, baby. He has been since the paramedics got to him."

"But my mom said he survived the surgery and was in recovery."

"I'm sorry, Chloe. She should have told you. He's alive, but he's back in intensive care. He's still in a coma, honey."

EIGHT

The detective suddenly breezed back into the room, and I was about to tell him about Sam and my father's phone message when he sat, looked me deeply in the eye, and spoke.

"Okay, why don't you tell me how this all really happened, Ms. Ledet? I'm thinking this Peralta guy drugged you and brought you here to his hotel room. He tried to take advantage of you but you woke up, and in defending yourself you accidentally killed him. That's how it really happened, isn't it? You fought him off, knocked him out, and then smothered him with a pillow?"

I gasped, putting a hand to my mouth.

"Is that how Kevin died? He was smothered with a pillow?"

"Come on, let's not play games. He was drunk, you were hysterical, it happens. You were only trying to defend yourself, right?"

Looking into the detective's eyes, I was silent for a long moment, wondering how so much could go so horribly off track so fast. This man was so sure I was guilty, but in my gut I knew I wasn't. I couldn't even kill a spider or a fly. How on earth could I possibly have taken the life of another human being?

The phone message. My mind kept spinning around that phone message, the one my father had left for my mother, that Sam had then written down and shown to me last night.

"I have to think," I whispered, closing my eyes and pressing my hands against my temples.

Last night. The restaurant. Sam had given me the piece of paper on which he had scribbled down what he had been able to hear of the message. Graze had shown up with my coffee at that moment, placing it and a small pitcher of cream on the table in front of me. After he left, I unfolded the page in front of me and read the words Sam had jotted there.

> *Lola, it's Julian. I've been shot! I need help! Pick up if you're there. Oh, Lola, it hurts. Look, I was out at the camp work... remember...trying to steal...shot me...straight to bins, but... from there too...bins totter...I know exactly what's...how many people are...but...why...you're in danger too. Don't trust anyone except Sam and Alphonse, not even the police... radio...finish the job. So much blood...coordinates...talked to Kevin a little while ago about a business deal...drawing up contracts. Now that I've been shot that deal is even more important than it was before. You have to act fast, Lola. Get that contract signed before they come after you too...think you know things you don't...Chloe can handle the details... told you we had an insurance policy...recipe. I just didn't know...get me killed...911. I love you, Lola.*

I had read it through several times, just trying to make sense of his words, to fill in some of the blanks with guesses.

Don't trust anyone except Sam and Alphonse, not even the police, he had said.

Not even the police.

Opening my eyes, I looked at Detective Walters, a strange calm coming over me. I wasn't sure how or why, but at that moment I knew without a doubt that I had been framed.

"I'm sorry, but I have nothing further to say without a lawyer present."

The detective's shoulders slumped visibly, intentionally, as if to say what a disappointment I was to them all.

"Very well. I'll be back. Don't use the phone and don't go anywhere."

The detective left the room, and once again I was alone with the cop standing guard. Terrified, I leaned my head back and closed my eyes and thought about praying for help. I believed in God, but I had never seen Him as the sort of entity who got involved in day-to-day things, more like an all-powerful Creator who sat up on some heavenly throne and directed the after-death traffic. *You donated money to good causes, so you're in. You helped a little old lady across the street, so you're in. Oops, you coveted and lusted, so you're out.*

To me, people who turned to prayer only when they had no other hope seemed like the kind of friends who showed up at your door only when they needed something. I wasn't that kind of person, not even with God.

In fact, I realized, the last time I had prayed was probably around Christmas, when I went to a big church in Evanston to hear my neighbor sing in a cantata. The pastor had closed the service with a lovely prayer, and I had found myself caught up in the moment, joining in with his words in my mind. But that had been more of a responsive thing and not of my own volition. Here in this hotel room, though I would have liked to ask God for some help, it didn't seem...well, very polite of me. I hadn't spoken to Him in a long time, so I had no right to call on Him now.

Instead, on my own, I tried to think through the ramifications of all that was going on. I desperately needed to get to my father. I also needed to find out more about the missing words from that tape. My heart lurching, I knew that most of all I needed to find Sam and see what had happened to him and make sure he was okay.

How had I ended up on a bed in a strange hotel, the handsome young lawyer I had just met last night dead on the couch in the next room? Poor Kevin, smothered by a pillow! Surely it was obvious that whoever had done that would have had to have been much stronger than I. Kevin was tall and very muscular, judging by the cut of his suit last night. I was also tall but quite petite, and there was no way I would have been any match for him, even if I was hysterical, as the detective proposed.

Then again, if we *both* had been drugged, that would have made things simpler. In theory, I might have been strong enough in that situation to hold a pillow over his face until he stopped breathing. Nauseous at the thought, I opened my eyes and sat up straight, knowing in my very core that I hadn't done it.

I hadn't killed anyone, hadn't done anything wrong at all.

Sitting there on the couch, my mind went back and forth over all I had been able to remember thus far, again and again, until finally more began to come back to me. I remembered reading the scribbled phone message several times, finally looking up at Sam in astonishment and then thrusting the paper back toward him.

"I'm sorry, but I have to get to my mother," I had said frantically, pushing my chair back and standing up. "I can't believe you left her at the hospital alone! Can't you see from this that she's in danger?"

I had run from the room and through the dark main dining room toward the front door. As I went, I tried to calculate how long it would take me to get my car from the parking garage and drive back toward to the airport as far as Jefferson, which was where the hospital was located.

Both men were calling after me, but they didn't catch up until I was at the front door.

"Chloe, please!" Sam said, reaching out a hand to stop me before I could unlock it.

"Sam, I'm sorry, but I have to go. My mother shouldn't be alone right now."

"Your mother hired herself a bodyguard, baby. I stayed with her until he got there."

"I still have to go, Sam. I need to be with her and with my father."

"I know, but if I let you walk out of here and something happens to you, I'll never be able to live with that. If she's in danger, you could be too."

Defeated, I looked down at the floor—at the gorgeous rose aurora marble that simply screamed wealth and elegance the moment patrons walked in the door. If my father ever came back to us, I would ask him if it had been worth it. When a single bullet could take it all away in a flash, was any of this worth it in the long run?

Sam placed a hand on my shoulder, and that one simple touch was all it took to make me lose it completely. I burst into tears as the anxiety and desperation of the last few hours finally began caving in on me. Once again I turned into Sam's embrace and buried my head against his shoulder. Through half-closed eyes, I was grateful to see him waving Kevin away so that we could have some privacy. My sobbing went on for a while, and all I could think of as I cried was how furious my father would be if he were here right now to see me make such a scene in his restaurant. Never mind that it was empty. The hard-and-fast rule at Ledet's was simply that there was never to be any drama in the front of house. All histrionics were to be reserved for back of house only, behind the closed doors leading to the kitchen.

When I finally pulled myself together, Sam handed me a cloth handkerchief and waited as I cleaned myself up. Though Sam had always been a loving presence in my life, his wife had usually been the one to dry my tears. After Eugenie passed away, Sam was all I had left. At her funeral, he and I had cried on each other's shoulders.

"I'm sorry," I said. "I don't know what came over me."

"Hush now, baby. You just needed to let out a little steam."

"Sam, why is all of this happening?"

He took a deep breath, shaking his head from side to side.

"I don't know. Why don't we go back and sit down and try to figure out a plan for keeping you and your mother safe until we hear back from the fellow who's transcribing the tape? After he does that, we might have a better idea about what happened to your daddy."

I nodded and began walking back through the dark main dining room, asking Sam why he hadn't just given the tape to the police.

"Because of what he said, that your mother was not to trust anybody except me or Alphonse Naquin, not even the police."

Taking my seat, I apologized to Kevin for my behavior out in the lobby, but he just waved my words away.

"Tha's all right. You had a tough day," he said, his speech slightly slurred.

Judging by the empty glasses in front of him, I could see that he was on his third Sazerac. Considering that just one could put a grown man under the table, I had a feeling he was well on his way to being plastered. With a deep sigh, I had to admit that once again a fellow who seemed promising upon first impression was not going to work out. Getting drunk in an elegant restaurant was bad enough, but doing it in the midst of a business dinner was something else entirely.

Trying to ignore Kevin's inebriated state, I asked Sam if he thought I should hire myself a bodyguard too.

"I'll guard your body," Kevin slurred, "with pleasure. Oh, I'm feeling dizzy. Excuse me while I put my head down."

With that, he pushed aside his empty plate and rested his head in his arms on the table, his actions sounding the death knell on any possibility of a relationship with me. Looking equally aggravated, Sam turned around and glared toward the main dining room until Graze passed by. Sam called to him and asked if he would please bus the table.

Graze did as Sam asked, quickly gathering our empty plates and glasses.

"And don't bring the man any more alcohol," Sam added. "Can't you see he's had more than enough?"

"I only brought the one round, sir," Graze replied defensively.

"Somebody else brought in more from the party," Kevin said from his position on the table. "He said they were left over."

Before any of us could even respond, Kevin began to snore.

Good grief. I could sure pick 'em.

Once Graze had left, and with Kevin asleep, Sam and I were able to talk in private. I asked him how we needed to proceed, both to ensure my safety and that of my mother while allowing me to go down to the hospital to be with my father. Graze had taken away our water glasses, so as we talked and Sam drank his Sazerac, I found myself sipping my coffee, even though it was barely warm at that point.

Soon, however, I began to feel woozy. I blinked, studying Sam's face, which was suddenly going in and out of focus. I put down the cup, wondering if Graze had misunderstood and spiked it with a little alcohol or something. It had tasted kind of odd, but I just figured that's because it probably had chicory in it, which I never really liked.

I was about to ask Sam if he was feeling strange too, but I couldn't get the words to form correctly in my mouth. Instead, what I wanted to say came out sounding like gibberish. Sam looked at me, startled, his brow wrinkled in confusion and concern. I wanted him to know that someone had tampered with my drink, but unable to speak, all I could do was point at my cup and then at myself. Before he could even catch on to what I was trying to show him, everything faded to black.

The drug had been in my coffee.

One of Kevin's drinks had obviously been drugged too.

I had no doubt that we had both been unconscious ever since. If so, then there were no more memories left to tell me what had happened next. All I had to go on from here on out was a dead body. That, and some dried blood and tissue under my fingernails.

Feeling suddenly cold, I shuddered to think of what had been done to us once the drugs had kicked in last night. Obviously I had been framed, but why? Had someone literally dragged my nails across Kevin's face as both of us snoozed away, unconscious? Aching in the pit of my stomach, I thought of Sam. Had he been drugged too? More than anything, I hoped he was all right, but I had a sick feeling that he wasn't, not at all.

Before I could do anything about this final bit of recovered memory, Detective Walters came bursting into the room with a gleam in his eye. He produced a pair of handcuffs.

"Chloe Ledet, you are under arrest for the murder of Kevin Peralta."

"I was framed."

"Yeah, and I've got evidence. Get up."

"What evidence?"

The detective didn't answer but again told me to stand. As I did, he instructed me to turn around so he could handcuff my wrists behind my back.

"I want a lawyer," I said, bile rising in my throat.

"You'll get your lawyer," he replied, locking the cuffs firmly in place.

Putting a hand on my elbow, he led me out of the hotel room and into the busy courtyard, reciting my Miranda rights as we went. Standing tall, shoulders back, I ignored the curious and scornful gazes of all of those around me. I simply looked straight ahead and told myself this would all be straightened out soon enough.

I allowed myself to be escorted to the police car that was waiting out in front of the hotel. The detective opened the back door of the vehicle and gestured for me to get inside, and then he placed a hand on the top of my head and pushed me down. At first I thought he was trying to force me for some reason, but then I realized he was merely protecting me from banging my head against the low curving side of the door frame.

Worse than the walk of shame through the hotel courtyard and lobby was the time spent sitting in the car while waiting to leave. I was looking around and trying to get a better idea of where on Chartres we were exactly, but as I did, I realized that every single person who walked by made a point of looking in at me. The whole scene was so surreal, in fact, that I did the only thing I could do: I closed my eyes and pretended I was somewhere else, somewhere safe and quiet and peaceful, where the biggest problem I had was figuring out what rules of etiquette might apply.

NINE

FRANCE, 1719
JACQUES

At first, Jacques was merely frustrated at the fact that M. Freneau had taken the wrong load. How could this have happened? Was it Jacques' fault, for moving the carts? Was it his father's fault, for not double-checking to make sure he was sending off the wrong one? Or was it Freneau's fault, for talking and griping when he should have been paying attention to what he was doing? Now the man had left with the same load he had brought, and Jacques was holding on to one of the statuettes he and his father had made. The two trunks may have looked the same, but there was no doubt this was the wrong one because they had been stacked differently on the inside. The carts had been slightly different as well. Freneau's was shinier and newer, and theirs had rust on the frame and was made of darker wood. Even if the two men hadn't bothered to look inside the trunks, shouldn't they have noticed that the fellow was hitching the horse to the same cart that he had unhitched only a short while before?

This was ridiculous! Just to make absolutely sure that *he* wasn't the one in error, Jacques carried the statuette over to his father's work area and grabbed a scriber and a loupe. There, he looked through the loupe as he made a tiny mark in an inconspicuous place on the statuette. As he expected, the gold leaf scratched easily away, revealing the brass underneath—at least to his experienced eye. The man was supposed to have taken away the gilded statuettes and left the solid gold ones behind. Instead, he had done the exact opposite. Sick at heart, Jacques smoothed over the scratch with his thumb, put away the tools, and returned the statuette to the trunk. unsure of what to do. This would be a simple problem to solve if he had a horse and the freedom to be seen. As it was, his hands were tied.

Reluctantly, Jacques went to his father and shook him gently until he opened his eyes. Jacques told him what had happened. After Papa had expressed his aggravation at the ridiculous turn of events, he began blaming himself, asking how he could have been so careless, so stupid. Jacques protested vigorously, saying that considering he could hardly breathe at the time, it was probably all he could do not to collapse before the man was out of sight.

Once Papa accepted Jacques' logic and had calmed down a bit, he propped himself up and the two of them puzzled over a solution. Even if he had a horse, Papa wasn't healthy enough to gallop up the road and get to the man himself. Jacques could certainly do that, but Freneau might recognize him as Papa's son, and how would he explain his presence way out here in the middle of nowhere? Surely Freneau would put two and two together and figure out that Papa had been violating the confidentiality of their agreement. Not only would all of their hard work go unpaid, but Papa's reputation for discretion would be sullied forever.

Lunch arrived in the middle of their conversation, so while Jacques hid again in the wardrobe, Papa gathered his strength to answer the door, take the food from the farmer's wife, and ask if they had a horse he could borrow. She said no, so he asked if there was any way she or her husband could deliver a message to Paris immediately on his behalf, something he was willing to pay handsomely for. Despite the large sum of money he was offering, she declined, saying they might be able to do it near the end of the week but not today. He thanked her anyway and bid her good day.

Once she was gone, Jacques and his father shared the meal she had brought and continued to discuss their options. They considered simply waiting until Freneau returned in two days for the gold bars and telling him then. But there was a good chance that by that point it would be too late. Whatever the palace was up to with the gilded statuettes, they might be needing them without room for delay.

After much conversation, Jacques came up with a plan. He paced back and forth as he laid it out, a complicated game of hide-and-seek involving a letter, a courier, and an elaborately constructed deception. At the conclusion of his description, Jacques smiled with pride. As far as he could tell, it was a plausible plan, as long as Papa, a man known for his honesty and integrity, would be able to pull off a few lies.

"No," Papa said softly.

"I know it's not a perfect plan, but if you—"

"No, Jacques, no more lies. One lie always begets another. The first lie was when I brought you out here in secret a month ago rather than send for M. Freneau and honestly tell him about my ill health. All of our sneaking and hiding, that has been a constant lie, and all because I didn't want to surrender this valuable commission. At what cost, though, have I done this? At the cost of teaching my son to construct such a fanciful and complicated story? Bah! It is not worth it. Not at any price."

With an energy he hadn't demonstrated in days, Papa strode to the work table, pulled out pen and paper and ink, and furiously scribbled out a missive. Finally, he put the pen down, blowing on the page so the ink would dry, and then he folded it into thirds. He reached for a lit candle and tilted it over the seam, allowing a few drops of wax to drip into a warm glob. Then he put the candle down and, into that warm glob of wax, he carefully pressed his goldsmith's mark.

"Here is your letter for M. Freneau," Papa said, a calmness finally taking back over as he crossed the room and handed it to Jacques. "Bring it to a courier in Charenton or all the way to Paris yourself, whichever is faster. But no more lies, yes?"

Jacques took the letter, nodding his head but also letting his frustration show.

"And if they find out you broke confidentiality and withhold payment, what then?" Jacques demanded, studying his father's stern face. "You gave your *life* for those little statuettes, and now you're ready to sacrifice your payment as well? Think of all our hard work, Papa! What was it for, if not for the money?"

Papa didn't reply at first, but instead he sat on the edge of the cot, Jacques' questions echoing in the dusty silence around them.

"What was it for?" Papa rasped. "Maybe it was just for *time*, Jacques."

"Time?"

"To be together. To carry out a job well done, side by side. To have one last month with...you."

Papa looked up as he finished speaking. After a moment, despite the shame that burned his cheeks, Jacques forced himself to meet his father's gaze. How did Papa always know words that were so right and true, words that could cut through sinfulness and pride like a dagger through gold leaf?

"You are right, Papa," he whispered. "Of course. You are always right. No more lies."

Nodding, Papa laid down and stretched out.

"You are a good son and a good Christian, Jacques. If I die, 'twill only be a temporary parting, you know."

"Will you wait for me in heaven, Papa?" Jacques whispered, pulling the blanket up over the old man's shoulders.

"Right there at the pearly gates, my son. Now, go and do what you must do, but hurry back."

Trying not to cry, Jacques moved quickly. He doused the fire in the furnace and gathered his things. Before he left, he paused in the rear door-way, taking one last look into the dim, hot room and the man lying on the cot, the great man whom Jacques loved and admired and had always seen as his hero. Giving that weary hero a final wave, Jacques moved out into the sunlight. He didn't fear Freneau's impending anger over the mix-up or the possibility that the palace would learn their confidentiality had been violated and, in consequence, would decide to withhold payment.

His only fear was that Papa would be dead by the time he got back.

TEN

Mentally speaking, I managed to separate myself from what was happening to me the whole time I waited in the police car and throughout the drive to wherever we were going, which ended up being a massive tan structure a few miles north of the interstate.

As they led me into the building, I saw two things that shocked me back to my current reality: across the street, a row of bail bondsman shops, and directly in front of me, a high fence topped with tangled rounds of barbed wire. This was the real deal. Central Lockup.

Numbly, I remained mute as I was processed into the system. I was glad when they finally took off the handcuffs, gladder still that they used no ink in taking my fingerprints. Instead, a woman held and rolled each finger in turn across a pad that was linked to a computer, and the prints were taken digitally. I may have lost my long nails, but at least I didn't have purple fingertips once we were done.

I didn't really start shaking until they took my mug shot. Somehow, standing there and holding a sign below my chin and looking at the camera, I finally began to feel the gravity of my situation. I had been framed for murder! As the camera flashed in my eyes, I knew this was all part of an elaborate setup, and that it had to do with my father and Alphonse Naquin and their long-hidden treasure. For some reason, someone wanted me out of the way and in jail, even if it meant killing someone else to put me there.

They let me make a phone call once I was processed, but as I stood there with the telephone in my hand, I didn't have a clue as to what number to dial. I thought about phoning my mother, but in a situation this extreme, I knew she would be pretty much useless. I could call my father's lawyer, but apparently he was dead and I was the one who had killed him. Finally, I tried calling Sam again but got no answer, which didn't surprise me. For all I knew, he was somewhere else going through his own fog of confusion and disaster—if he was still even alive. In the end, I called the one person in my life who was utterly dependable and completely competent: my assistant, Jenny. When she answered, I explained my situation, saying that I was still in New Orleans and there had been a horrible mix-up, and that I had been arrested and put in jail.

"I'll take the next plane to New Orleans and come get you out of there," she cried.

"No, please don't come. I just need you to make some phone calls."

Giving her the numbers, I told her to call my mother and tell her what had happened, and then to keep trying Sam's number until she got through. Most important, I said I needed her to find me a lawyer, the very best criminal defense lawyer in New Orleans. I told her the police were so sure of my guilt that I had refused to answer another question until I had a lawyer present.

"Good move," Jenny replied.

The officer who had given me the telephone gestured to me to wrap it up, so I told Jenny that I needed to go.

"Find me a lawyer as fast as humanly possible," I repeated.

As I hung up, I watched another prisoner coming in, one who was struggling violently against her handcuffs as they attempted to process her.

As she wildly cursed and writhed, my mind filled with the image of being forced into a cell with a dozen more like that.

A policewoman led me out of the room, down the hall, and into what looked like yet another processing area, a series of cubicles manned by police personnel. A scarred wooden bench was against a wall, and I was instructed to sit there.

"You behave, and I won't have to lock you in," she said, gesturing toward a row of metal hooks that protruded from the wall above the bench. I wasn't sure exactly what she meant, but I had a feeling that the hooks were there to connect to handcuffs or other types of restraints.

I didn't know what I was waiting for, or how long I would have to sit there, but an old wooden bench in the hallway beat a dirty barred cell with other prisoners hands down, so I kept my mouth shut and remained perfectly still. I tried to listen to the various conversations going on around me, but mostly the cops in the next room were just chitchatting about a recent ballgame, about what they did Saturday night, about what they planned to do next Saturday night. Finally, someone came out and spoke to the cop who was standing guard over me, and the next thing I knew, she was bringing me to what looked like an interrogation room. It was small with pink walls and a two-way mirror at the end. At the center of the room was a table with several chairs around it. I was told which chair to take and so I sat and again I waited.

After what felt like an eternity, there was a small knock at the door and a man stepped inside. He spoke with the policewoman, who left the room, and then he approached me and shook my hand, introducing himself as Mike Donner, my new lawyer. I was so relieved that I nearly blurted out the first thing that popped into my mind: *Are you sure you want the job? Apparently I've been known to kill lawyers!*

He joined me at the table, pulled out his briefcase, and began telling me just a little bit about himself and his firm. He ended by saying that he was the best criminal defense lawyer in town but that the best didn't come cheap.

"I've spoken with your mother, and she has assured me that if you can't pay my bill, she will."

This was not an auspicious beginning, but at this point, I didn't have much choice. I replied that I was quite capable of paying for his services and that my mother's assistance in that regard would not be needed. Once those formalities were out of the way, he seemed to relax a bit and urged me to relax as well.

"I just want to hear, in your own words, the sequence of events that brought you here today. Take your time, and tell me the whole story."

"I'd be happy to. But first can you tell me if my father still alive?"

"Yes, but from what I understand he's in a coma."

I exhaled deeply, relieved to know that despite all that was going on and all that was going wrong at least my father hadn't died during the night. Folding my hands and placing them on the table in front of me, I started at the beginning, at that moment when Jenny interrupted me during my television appearance to give me the message that my mother had been urgently trying to reach me. Unlike Detective Walters, who had constantly interrupted me to clarify things and ask questions in an apparent attempt to confuse me, Mr. Donner just listened quietly, took notes on a yellow legal pad, and responded with the occasional nod or grunt. When I was finished with the whole tale, I wasn't sure if he believed me or not. I supposed it didn't really matter. It was his job to defend me regardless.

When it was his turn to speak, he began by commending me for not talking to the police any more than I had.

"I wish you hadn't said anything at all to them, but this is better than nothing."

He went on to tell me of the strongest evidence the police had against me thus far, a preliminary match between Kevin's scratched face and the blood and tissues under my nails. Mr. Donner said that they wouldn't have DNA results back for a while but that the blood type was a match, as was the tissue structure. Worse, by evaluating blood and saliva stains, police had determined that the pillow I slept with under my head last night was the same one that had been used to smother Kevin to death at some point prior to midnight.

Even the lawyer seemed to turn up his lip a bit at that one, as if to say what a cold fish I must be to kill a man and then take a long rest on top of the murder weapon.

Donner then launched into a description of what would happen next, which seemed to have nothing to do with my guilt or innocence at this point. Apparently, the state was required to give me a bail hearing within twenty-four hours. Strikes against me were the nature of the charges—that is, murder in the first degree—and the fact that I was from out of town and did not live here. Very much in my favor, however, were the facts that

I was a responsible business person with no criminal history, I had strong ties to this area, including a father whose very name was synonymous with New Orleans, and the fact that my father was currently in a hospital and needed me there.

"I feel confident you will be released on bail, hopefully by this time tomorrow."

He acted as though I would be pleased to hear him say the word "released," when in fact I was still dumbfounded at the word "tomorrow."

"Do you mean I have to spend the night here? In jail? With criminals?"

"I know the prospect of that sounds quite horrifying to you, but this is just Central Lockup. You might be okay here. Prison, on the other hand, is a different matter altogether. Believe me when I say I'm going to do everything in my power to keep you out of there."

"And what happens if we go to this bail hearing and the judge denies bail?"

"Let's cross that bridge when we come to it, shall we?"

I closed my eyes, telling myself I would most likely be out of jail by this time tomorrow. After that, I would be in a position to put things together and ask questions and track down whoever had really killed Kevin and framed me—not to mention shot my father.

In the meantime, I just needed to find some way to survive.

ELEVEN

Detective Walters questioned me at the station with my lawyer sitting in. He asked me all of the same questions, but Donner wouldn't let me answer most of them. I wasn't eager to be shown to my cell, but the whole process was so incredibly aggravating that by the time we were done, going almost anywhere other than there was a relief.

I spent the next few hours locked in a small cell with a sleeping woman who was probably in for prostitution, given the outfit she was wearing. Other prisoners were led past, but fortunately no one else was ever put inside with us, and my roommate never woke up. Most of the time, I tried to ignore the stench of the open toilet that sat just a few feet from my bed. Worse than the smell, though, was the noise. It never stopped, not the yelling and catcalls from one cell to another, nor the clinking and clanging of bars and chains and doors. My senses were assaulted from every side, and even my skin felt scratchy and chafed under the orange jumpsuit I had been given to wear.

My stomach was growling by mid afternoon, which really surprised me. How could I want to eat at a time like this? I reminded myself that hunger was a normal bodily function, and that so far I had had nothing to eat all day. Of course I was hungry. Between the processing and the interrogating, somehow I had slipped through the cracks and not been given any breakfast or lunch.

I had no watch or cell phone to keep time, and there was no clock in sight, but the hours ticked by at an excruciatingly slow rate. At one point, I was so insanely bored that I found myself wishing my roommate would wake up, just so I would have someone to talk to. Finally, I was given a change of scenery when a uniformed officer came and got me from my cell and brought me to a room similar to the one I had been in earlier.

"Why are the walls in these rooms pink?" I asked, trying to make conversation. The policewoman gestured toward a chair and shrugged, answering that pink was supposed to be calming according to some psychological studies.

I didn't reply what I was thinking, that I felt sure the psychologists weren't talking about this particular shade of pink, which was hideous and had quite the opposite effect.

Once I was seated, another person came into the room and the woman left. This guy was older, in his early sixties, with closely shaven hair and the bearing of a cop. He wore slacks and a shirt, rolled up at the sleeves.

"Hi, Chloe. How you doing?" the man said in a familiar tone, seating himself across from me at the table and sliding a paper bag toward me. "I had a feeling you might be wanting something good to eat about now, so I brought you a muffuletta from the Napoleon House. It ain't Ledet's, but it's better than the mystery meat you'll get in this place. Sorry it's a little messy. The guy at the charge desk had to go through it."

Even without opening the bag, I could smell the heavenly scent of baked bread and sliced meats coming from inside.

"Oh, I'm sorry. Looks like you don't remember me. I'm Wade Henkins. I'm a good friend of your father's." Squinting, I studied his face for a moment and thought he did look vaguely familiar. "Last time I saw you, you were about nine years old and had a snapping turtle clamped to your finger."

I gasped, the memory suddenly flooding my mind.

"Of course! You saved me! I thought that turtle was going to take my finger off."

"He could have, if he'd been full growed. But he was just a young 'un. From what I recall, you were pretty brave about the whole thing."

I pictured the entire scene, which had taken place out in the courtyard at Ledet's. There had been a pond and fountain there, stocked with turtles and fish, and I had always loved them. I remembered that I had come home from boarding school on vacation, and I had been so happy to see my long-lost turtle friends that I had actually reached into the pond to pet one of them, a new one I hadn't noticed before. I was quite shocked when that cute little turtle whipped open his mouth and clamped it down on my finger. Still, even at the age of about nine, I knew my father's rule regarding drama in the front of house. Thus, with merely a whimper, I immediately ran to the kitchen for help, the turtle holding on for dear life. Mr. Henkins was working security at the restaurant and had intercepted me in the back hallway and saved the day, somehow disengaging the turtle and telling me that it wasn't my fault, that my daddy had no business keeping a snapping turtle in a public place that should have only box turtles, and what a brave little girl I was. Looking back at it now, I knew it wasn't bravery that had kept me from screaming; it was the fact that screaming was against the rules. I was nothing if not a good little rule follower.

"I'm not feeling very brave right now," I said, looking at the man across the table. "You're a policeman, aren't you? Can you tell me what's going on?"

"Yeah, I'm a cop, but I'm here in an unofficial capacity. I was with your daddy yesterday, Chloe, not long before he was shot. I can't be involved with the case from the police side of things because I'm actually a material witness to some of what went on down there. But when I heard what happened to you, I had to come check on you, see if you were okay, and see if I could intervene any way on your behalf."

Relief flooded my veins. I was finally with someone who could help me get out of here, not to mention tell me what had happened to my father down in Paradise. Suddenly, my hunger got the best of me, and with apologies and thanks I took out the big sandwich he had brought and began eating it right in front of him, relishing every bite.

"I don't quite understand your situation," he continued, "but being that I know you and your family, I'm willing to give you the benefit of the doubt."

"The benefit of the doubt, that's all I ask. I've been set up, Mr. Henkins, probably by someone who wants me out of the way. I don't know who or why, but I'm sure it ties back to whatever is going on with my father. I was drugged last night at Ledet's, and I woke up this morning in the middle of a murder scene. I know it looks bad, but not only did I not kill Kevin, I don't even know where we were or how we got there."

Mr. Henkins looked at me for a long time, as if he were sizing me up. His steely gaze was a bit unnerving, but I had a feeling it was an interrogation technique he used to make criminals crack. As I had done nothing wrong, I simply returned his gaze without blinking. Then he broke our stare and asked me to tell him everything, from the beginning.

Thus, for what seemed like the umpteenth time that day, I went through every part of my story. He listened intently, asking a few questions for clarification, but otherwise keeping silent. When I was finished with the whole thing, he shook his head, an angry expression on his face.

"More than likely, both of you were drugged and carried out of there in some way that didn't attract attention. I've been telling your father for years that he needs to beef up Ledet's security systems. He has mounted cameras in there, but half the time they're not even on."

"Cameras?" I asked, hope suddenly surging through my veins. "Mr. Henkins, do you think there's a chance that what happened last night at the restaurant got caught on film?"

"Call me Wade, please. Sorry, Chloe, I already checked. Detective Walters said no such luck. Turns out the cameras weren't on because the restaurant was closed."

With his words, my flash of hope went up in smoke.

"But at least the detective went there and checked out my story?" I asked, grasping for more hope. "I've been thinking about who was there last night, like Graze or our waiter, or the people outside at the party. At least one of them had to be in on this. Do you know if the detective even bothered to interview them?"

"Yeah, he did. He said he's talked to everybody and come up with nothing."

My mind racing, I asked Wade about the security system at Ledet's, if there was anything else there that might help my case.

"No, and your father's a stubborn fool. The wine cellar is fully wired, of course, but the main restaurant doesn't even have a basic alarm system. Makes me nuts, especially when he hires me to come in and work some big event and I see how easy it would be to upgrade security around there."

I asked Wade to tell me what he knew about what had happened to my father yesterday morning. As he talked, I took another bite of the muffuletta, relishing the tang of the olives and how they blended with the oily tenderness of the meat.

"He was down at Paradise, calling around to see if anybody wanted to come over and do a little work for him. A couple of the guys went and helped out, same as they always do. I was there visiting my brother, so I tagged along. We worked hard, but it was fun."

"What were you doing?"

"Clearing brush. There's a bunch of old blackberry bushes up in there, but the area was so overgrown he couldn't get to 'em. We came in and cleared the way. Took us all morning, just so he could make a pie."

"By any chance, did the topic of Alphonse Naquin come up?" I wondered if maybe the guys who went there working had been the ones to convince my father to change his stubborn position over the treasure.

"Not that I recall. Why?"

"Doesn't matter. Keep going."

"Okay, well, while we was working we noticed a couple of fellows we didn't know out on the bayou, making a lot of noise. They were rowdy and drunk and kept passing by in their fishing boat, calling things out and laughing and stuff. Ten o'clock in the morning and they were already wasted. At the time, we didn't think too much of it. Lot of guys like to drink when they're fishing."

"Hmm."

"We finished around noon, and your dad said if we wanted go into town for groceries, he'd whip us up a nice lunch. The other fellows had to get to work, but I was free. Goodness knows, I never turn down a meal from Julian Ledet! I borrowed his truck and went to the store." Wade's expression grew more somber. "You sure you want to hear the rest of this?" he asked, and I simply nodded. "Okay, well, I guess I was gone a while, maybe forty-five minutes. When I got back out to Paradise, I couldn't find your daddy. What I did notice were a bunch of empty beer cans out by the dock, and what looked like blood in the water and on the grass. Oh, and my boat was gone."

Taking the last bite of my sandwich, I listened to his tale in rapt attention as he continued.

"I didn't know what had happened, but something just didn't feel right, you know? Especially after seeing those rednecks out on the water earlier. I was hoping your dad had gone out fishing and the blood was just from something he'd caught and skinned there by the dock. I gave him an hour, but when he didn't turn up I called the police. Turns out, he had just been found 'bout six miles north of there, up in a little tributary. He was on my boat, unconscious, blood everywhere, just floating along in the water."

"Who found him? How?"

"He had called 911 before he passed out. They used the GPS signal from his phone to track him down. He's lucky they got there as soon as they did. Any longer and he'd have been a goner for sure."

"What about the men you had seen earlier? Were they caught?"

Wade shook his head.

"Not only were they not caught, nobody else along that waterway claims to have heard or seen them. I don't know what that's about, but they were so noisy I can't imagine we were the only ones who heard them out there. Then again, maybe they weren't drunk at all. Maybe it was just a show they were putting on for our benefit, maybe as a way to come in close enough to do whatever it is they did to your father."

"Was anything stolen? Could it have just been a random crime?"

Wade shook his head, saying no and no, that there weren't even any strange footprints in the area, despite the fact that the ground was muddy. His guess was that they never even stepped off the dock onto the grass.

"What about the other men, the ones who had been there working with you earlier? Could one of them have done something?"

"No way. They're good people, Chloe. Your daddy and them have known each other for years. Besides, they all left when I did. Looking back, I wish they hadn't. 'Cause then Julian wouldn't have been there defenseless and all alone."

Trying not to picture my poor father out in the swamps by himself being ambushed by a group of assassins posing as drunken fishermen, I asked Wade if he had any theories about all of this. He hesitated, glancing toward the two-way mirror. Then, giving me a meaningful look, he simply suggested that we talk again soon.

From the expression on his face, I knew there was something important he wanted to tell me that he couldn't say in this setting, where he might be overheard. He wrote down his phone number on a scrap of paper and gave it to me, saying to call him as soon as I was out on bail.

"Anyway," he continued in a more casual voice, reaching out to pat my hand, "I don't know what good it has done for me to come here except to let you know that there's a friendly face on the force looking out for you."

"I appreciate that more than you can imagine. And I look forward to talking with you again soon."

As he stood to leave and called for the policewoman to return me to my cell, I asked if by any chance he might have some pull to get my bail hearing moved to today instead of tomorrow. He looked at his watch and let out a low whistle, saying that it was already after three but he'd see what he could do.

"Depends," he said. "I'll try. But whether it's today or tomorrow, let me give you some advice. When you go up before the judge, emphasize your current hardship. You ain't even seen your father yet and he could be dying. Given that he's a local celebrity and all, that should help get you out of here."

I thanked him profusely for the advice, the sandwich, and the most important thing he'd given me of all: a glimmer of hope.

Back in my cell, I was still going over our conversation in my mind an hour later when the guard showed up at the cell door bearing the outfit I had been wearing when I was arrested earlier today.

"Get dressed," she said, pushing the crumpled wad of fabric through the bars. "Bail hearing's in fifteen minutes."

TWELVE

After a day filled with shocking events, terror, and misery, the bail hearing was surprisingly anticlimactic. My lawyer breezed in at the last minute, looking somewhat irritated that the hearing had been so abruptly rescheduled from tomorrow to today. When it was our turn to go before the judge, things happened very quickly. Terms I didn't even understand were tossed back and forth between the judge, my lawyer, and a woman I assumed was with the district attorney's office. At one point the judge asked me if I had anything to add, so I simply did as Wade suggested and focused on my dying father and how desperately I wanted to be by his side while he was still alive. In the end, with a single tap of a gavel, I was released on bail, which had been set at five hundred thousand dollars.

It took nearly another hour of paperwork and legal jargon and the securing of the bail money before I was released, but I didn't care. I was free, I was out of there, I was not going to have to spend the night in a cold cell next to an open toilet and a drugged-out hooker.

Before my lawyer and I parted ways, he gave me one small bit of interesting news. He said that there were already two chinks in the state's case against me, which he was hoping to exploit. Apparently, the hotel room I had woken up in this morning had been rented last night by someone other than Kevin Peralta. The desk clerk on duty at the time couldn't remember much about the man who came in last night and asked for a room on the first floor, but he was shorter and older than Kevin, with dark hair, a mustache, and a full beard—at least some of which may have been fake. Unfortunately, there were no security cameras there, the man had paid cash, and he had registered under the name "John Doe."

"John Doe? The clerk didn't think that was weird?"

"As long as his money's green, I don't think they care."

The lawyer went on to say that there was also something suspicious about the phone call that had brought the police to the hotel this morning on a complaint of noise. Not only had no one else at the hotel heard any noise, but the call itself had come from a cell phone, not from a nearby hotel room. Incredibly, the cell phone in question belonged to Kevin Peralta himself.

"Not that Kevin called the police himself, of course. He was already dead at that point. But the call was made from his cell phone. We can use that to support our claim that someone set you up. I'm going to contend that whoever drugged you both and killed Peralta then stole his cell phone and used it to call the police, making sure they would discover the scene before you could have had time to wake up and spot the dead man on the couch and run away."

"I would never have run away," I said, appalled that he would even suggest such a thing. Had I woken up on my own, looked around in an attempt to figure out where I was, and discovered Kevin's body, the very first thing I would have done was call the police. Offended, I moved on to my next question. "Any ideas yet on how the murderer got us into that hotel suite in the first place?"

"Witnesses at Ledet's say that none of them saw the two of you leaving but that they did see Sam Underwood once you were gone. He told them that he had cleaned and closed up the private dining room you folks had been using so they didn't need to worry about it. Then he left. They took—"

"Wait, what?"

As that fact sunk in—that Sam hadn't been drugged as well—the lawyer repeated his words, finishing his sentence this time.

"They took him at his word, and no one else went into that room until the police got there today. Despite what Sam had said, it had not been cleaned."

"Did they get our glasses, as evidence?"

"There were no glasses on the table, only plates and silverware and some dirty napkins."

What had Sam done? How could he have gone off and left me there? What was going on?

Feeling utterly lost and bereft, I tried to imagine Sam as a killer. No matter how I tried to frame it in my mind, it just didn't compute. Sam was no killer.

Then again, neither was I.

"I know you don't care, but I really am innocent," I said.

"Of course. All my clients are innocent," he replied, and then he turned and walked away, calling back to me that I should contact his secretary in the morning to set up an appointment for one day next week.

Taking a deep breath and trying hard to control my irritation, I decided to focus on the fact that I was free, for the time being at least. I hoped that would be one appointment I wouldn't have to keep, as I was going to do whatever it took to prove my innocence and clear my name in the meantime.

Right now I just needed to find a way back to the hotel parking garage in the Quarter where I had left my rental car last night. Once I had my car back, the first stop would be the hospital. At some point, I also needed a hot shower and a change of clothes. After that I would regroup and try to figure out my next steps.

When I had been given back my purse and cell phone, I asked the woman at the pay window if she could give me the number of a local cab service. She told me I probably didn't need to call anyone as a few cabs were usually lined up at the bottom of the courthouse steps.

I walked in the direction she indicated, my high heels clicking against the marble floor as I went. Stepping outside, I saw that there were, indeed, some cabs at the curb.

There were also several news vans and a cluster of reporters milling around in front of them. I tried to duck back inside, but it was too late. They had seen me and were already making a mad rush up the wide stone steps.

Bursting into the building, the media people cornered me as a group, flinging questions at me and pointing microphones and cameras in my face. I was mortified, not just that my story had become news but also because I hadn't even seen a mirror since waking up this morning. I could only imagine what my hair and face must look like, not to mention my wrinkled and dirty clothes.

Without answering any of their questions, I managed to push my way free, made it outside, and descended the steps as fast as I could as they clattered along behind me. As I neared the bottom, one guy jumped around in front of me, again blocking my way. Trying not to look like a deer caught in headlights, I mentally cursed my lawyer for abandoning me when he surely must have known this would happen.

"No comment, no comment. *Á ca oui!* Can't you see the lady has no comment?"

Someone had swooped into the group from the side, and, with his back to me, began herding the reporters away. I couldn't see who it was, only that it wasn't my lawyer, nor was it Wade or Sam. It was someone much younger than any of them, much more physically fit. When he finally turned around toward me, I thought his face looked familiar, but I couldn't place his name. About my same height and age, he was wearing Levis, a dark T-shirt, and a backwards-facing baseball cap.

Suddenly, he startled me by putting his hands on my upper arms and pulling me close so that he could whisper in my ear.

"See dat building 'cross the street?" he whispered in what sounded like a Cajun accent. "Go in through the front and out the back and get into the black truck that's sitting in the parking lot. Keys are under the mat. Drive two blocks up Broad and pull into the Piggly Wiggly. I'll meet you there *bien vite.*"

Feeling like an idiot, once he pulled away I just stood there, staring at him. I wasn't about to get in the car of someone I didn't know, especially not now, given all that had been happening. Still, he was willing to handle the reporters for me, and I surely needed help there. He turned back around and again held out his arms to block them. Glancing at me over his shoulder, he seemed irritated that I was still frozen to the spot.

"Chloe! *Va-ten!*" he snapped, which I assumed meant "Get going."

"Who are you?" I managed to reply. "As much as I appreciate your help, I don't go places with strangers."

"I'm not a stranger. I'm Travis Naquin, Alphonse's grandson. Now go. *Depêche toi!*" Hurry up.

Travis Naquin? I remembered him now.

From the corner of my eye, I watched for a break in the rush hour traffic and then dashed across the street at the exact moment when I could make it safely across without anyone else being able to follow me. As I did, I could hear Travis calling after me.

"*Hé*, Chloe, bring me a bag of Zapp's and some sweet tea when you come back out, would you?"

Given that I was walking into a minimart, I had to guess that he had said that for the reporters' benefit. They would wait where they were, expecting me to return, only I wasn't going to. Very clever. I had a feeling that in a few minutes Travis would say something like, "Let me go see what's keeping that girl," and pull the same stunt, slipping out the back and jogging up the road to our rendezvous point out of view from the courthouse.

I stepped inside the store, which was empty except for an Asian man behind the counter. He didn't say a word but merely smiled and pointed toward a doorway. I went through it, down a hall, and out the back. Sure enough, a big black truck with mud-covered fenders was waiting just outside. It was unlocked and the keys were under the floor mat.

There was no question that this was the vehicle of a backwoods boy, a true Louisiana Cajun. Between the Popeye's wrappers on the floor, the shotgun mounted in the rear window, and the fishing weights that littered the front seat, about all this vehicle lacked to make the image complete were alligator-skin floor mats.

As I gingerly climbed inside, I tried to remember what I knew of Travis Naquin. He and I were the same age and had actually gone out on a date once when we were teenagers. I didn't remember much about him, though I did recall that the date hadn't worked out too well. I had no idea what he was doing here now, but if he had important information that could help me figure out what was going on, I was eager to speak with him.

Better yet, he could give me a ride back to my car in the French Quarter. Then I could retrieve it from the parking garage where it had spent the night and most of the day and drive as fast as possible to the hospital, where I hoped my father was still alive.

As I started up the truck and made my way onto Broad, I thought about the reporters and their frenzied attack. My sincere hope was that this story was going to remain local. Even though my father was an international celebrity, there was a chance that a scandal involving his daughter just might slip under the radar as long as the local affiliates didn't make too big of a deal out of it. If the story went national, I couldn't bear to consider what this whole thing might do to my business. Chloe Ledet was supposed to be the very epitome of refinement and good taste. Somehow, I didn't think a first-degree-murder charge lent itself to that image. Even if I were proven innocent, my reputation would have been sullied forever.

I was still thinking about that when I almost overshot the store I was looking for. Turning quickly, I pulled into an end spot, turned off the car, and moved around to the passenger seat. As I did, I saw Travis coming toward me on the sidewalk, not a single reporter in sight.

"That wasn't so hard," he said as he climbed into the car. "I wonder how long they'll wait around till they realize we've given them the slip."

He settled into his seat, but instead of reaching for the ignition, he turned to face me, pulling off his baseball cap as he did and smoothing back his hair.

"Thank you so much for helping me out back there, Travis. Could you possibly give me a ride to my car in the French Quarter?"

"Sure, but I think we'll have a better chance of a clean break if we sit here for a few minutes to let them realize we're gone and take off as well."

"All right."

Except for the brown hair that was a little too shaggy, Travis Naquin was far better looking than I remembered.

"I can't believe you didn't know who I was," he said, shaking his head, a dimpled smile revealing straight, white teeth. "I recognized you immediately."

"It was just so out of context that it took me a minute. What are you doing here? Please tell me you've come on behalf of your grandfather, who sent you to explain everything to me, including who shot my father and who killed Kevin Peralta."

"*Mais jamais,* I'm sorry to tell you but that's not it. I haven't seen my *grandpere* for a couple days. I came to town to try and find Sam Underwood. I've been looking for him all afternoon, but it's like he's disappeared off the face of the earth. I was about to give up and head home when I turned on the radio and heard them saying that you were being released. I was already on Canal and about to get on the interstate, so I just kept going straight and came here instead. I hope you don't mind."

"How did you know about the reporters?"

"I was out front a little while, waiting for you. I figured they were too. When I saw them racing up the stairs to get to you, I worked out a plan of escape. Sorry it took so long, but I had to move my car and make friends with the guy in the minimart first."

"Well, thanks. I felt like a lamb at the slaughter."

"Really? You looked cool as a cucumber. As always."

I glanced at Travis, wondering if that was an "Ice Queen"-type dig or an attempt at a compliment, but from his expression I simply couldn't tell.

"Anyway," he added, "I know you had a heck of a day, but I'm hoping you might know where Sam is or help me find him."

"How would I know where Sam is? I've been in police custody."

"When I talked to him last night, he was heading to the Quarter to meet with you. It's really important that I find him. I've got something he needs."

"Did you try his apartment?"

"Calling on the phone and banging on the door, yes I did."

"How about Ledet's?" I asked. "He's retired now, but from what I understand he still comes over for family meal every day."

"Family meal?"

"That's when the staff of a restaurant eats together before shift starts—not menu items, of course, but still good stuff, baked chicken, lasagna, things like that. Sam has an open invitation and he's there almost every day. They didn't say if he had come today?"

"Well, see, that's the thing. Considering that your daddy's in the hospital and you're in jail for murder, the folks at Ledet's aren't saying anything to anybody about anything. They treated me like a *gui-gui ga ga*, in fact."

"*Gui-gui ga ga?*"

"A nosy country bumpkin."

"I'm sorry about that. They can be kind of snobby in there. It probably had less to do with the questions you were asking than the fact you came into the restaurant wearing jeans and a T-shirt."

"Yeah, and a baseball cap to boot. Oh, well. I figured if anybody knows where Sam is, you would, either because he told you where he was going today or because you killed him last night and stashed the body."

I glanced sharply at Travis, irritated to see that he was grinning.

"You think this is funny? I've been charged with first-degree murder."

"Did you do it?"

"No!"

"I didn't think so. See, that's why it's funny, because even though I haven't seen you in probably fifteen years, I already know you're the last person on earth who'd commit a crime, especially not a murder, especially not if that murder was a crime of passion."

I thought about that for a moment.

"Are you saying I'm not capable of passion?" I asked cooly, trying to remember our long-ago date. Had he put the moves on me and I turned him down? I simply couldn't recall how that particular evening had played out.

"*Mais non, cher,* just that you were always so prim and proper and worried about rules. Murder is the ultimate rule breaker, a massive disruption of the natural order of things. It's one of the ten commandments, for goodness' sake. I just couldn't imagine such a major rule being broken by the same girl who once scolded me for speeding up to get through a yellow traffic light and shamed me into giving back the extra fifty cents in change the guy at the movie theater had handed me by mistake. If you're anything like you used to be, Chloe, you aren't capable of murder. *Maigre tout,* you probably wouldn't be capable of taking a video back to the store unless you'd rewound it first. Murder? No way. I'd stake my favorite hat on that."

Well. I was speechless for a moment, trying to decide if I was offended by his exaggerations or flattered at how fully he had me pegged.

"Glad to know that as my life hangs in the balance you're willing to risk a hat," I said finally, causing him to throw his head back and laugh.

"Touché, *cher.*"

"Look, I haven't seen or spoken to Sam since last night, right about when I realized that someone had put a drug in my coffee." I didn't add the latest bit of news I had received from my lawyer, that for some reason Sam told the other employees that Kevin and I left and he had cleaned up the room. Those were both lies, but I knew Sam and Sam didn't lie.

I didn't know what to think.

"Where's your grandfather, Travis? Somehow, I have a feeling he could explain a number of things."

Travis shrugged.

"I don't know. He does this a lot, goes off on a fishing or hunting trip and disappears for days on end. My *grandmere* said he left home two days ago, saying, '*Je vous vois quand je vous vois.*' That's their code for 'I'm going off to fish and think, so don't rush me, don't bother me, and don't expect me. I'll see you when I see you.'"

"'Don't rush me, don't bother me'? That must be some marriage."

"Sixty-three years this month, so I guess they're doing all right, then."

I looked out of the side window and ran a hand through my hair, my filthy hair that hadn't been shampooed since yesterday morning. I was tired and snarky and ready to be done with this whole mess. Most of all I wanted to see my father. I also desperately needed to talk with Sam myself.

"My car's parked near Ledet's," I said. "If you'll get me back there, I'll go with you to Sam's apartment first before I leave for the hospital, and we can go inside and take a look around to see if we can figure out where he might've gone or what's happened to him."

"Breaking and entering? You sure that doesn't violate your parole?" Travis teased, reaching for the ignition.

"It's not parole, it's bail, and for your information I have a key."

"*C'est convenue.* I mean, that's convenient. At this point, I'm ready to do whatever it takes, even if that means consorting with a felon."

"You're one to talk. Just because you're helping me now doesn't mean I should trust you. I barely remember you at all."

"Yeah, well, I remember you a little too well. Come on, *cher*. Let's go."

THIRTEEN

FRANCE, 1719
JACQUES

The noise and bustle in the town of Charenton assaulted Jacques' senses from every side, a likely consequence of living in near isolation for an entire month. It didn't help that he was in a place he did not know well, dealing with people he had never met. And everywhere he went, it seemed he was jostled or bumped or shouted around. He had passed the famous Home of Charenton on the outskirts of town, where all of France sent their insane, but in Jacques' opinion things in the center of the village seemed insane as well.

Jacques finally located a courier service, one that listed on its delivery roster "Isle de la Cite, Paris." Papa's letter was addressed to the Palais-Royal, so that would work. Stepping inside, Jacques thought a whole crowd was waiting in line, but as his eyes adjusted to the light, he realized it was simply a husband and wife and their five rowdy children. Jacques stood near the door for a moment, listening to the children fight with each other as their parents conducted their business with the man at the counter. Unable to handle the din, Jacques finally decided he would prefer to wait outside.

At least there was a sidewalk there where he could stand and lean against the wall as he waited, sidewalks being a luxury that Paris proper didn't have room for. From this spot Jacques was able to ignore the loud arguing of the children inside while he observed the busyness of the street, the noisy mix of people and buggies and commerce. Was normal life always like this and he had just never noticed before? How immune one must become to busyness when living directly with it.

"In just an hour!" a man shouted to someone else as he ran past Jacques and nearly crashed into him. "Is it to be outside their offices?"

"No, it's at Les Halles, not Rue Quinquempoix!"

Jacques couldn't help but roll his eyes. He didn't know what they were talking about specifically, but Rue Quinquempoix, or what Papa called "the street lately gone mad," was the center of financial speculation in Paris, the likes of which France had not seen in quite a while. The excitement had begun several years ago, when a Scottish financial wizard named John Law had aligned with the regent and created La Banque General. Since then Paris, and indeed all of France, had been going mad for speculation. The way Jacque understood it, John Law's bank was based on credit and paper money, two things Papa was very wary of.

Of course, there was no denying that many people were becoming quite rich these days, trading stock and buying shares in Law's Compagnie des Indes, whose offices were located at the heart of the speculation district on Rue Quinquempoix. Despite the frenzy, Papa continued to be cautious of speculation on principal, saying that paper lacked the integrity of gold, that sooner or later values would be unrealistically inflated, and that what was going up surely had to come crashing down. Jacques trusted his father's judgment, but sometimes he wondered if Papa was wrong and there really was something to it after all. From what he understood, shares first bought at five hundred were already trading for fifteen hundred!

Either way, at least the upward shift in income was good for the goldsmithing business. The nouveau riche almost always began their elevated lifestyles by procuring the latest fashions for themselves and their homes, and often that meant the shinier the better. The gold and silver boutique in the Place Dauphin that Jacques ran for his father had made more money in the past year than it had in the previous five combined. Sales were up all over town, and energy pulsed from Rue Quinquempoix as if speculating involved the very creation of life itself.

Jacques' thoughts were interrupted by more loud arguing from inside the courier's office.

"I think he's going to give one to every good little girl in the city," one of the children's voices cried.

"Don't be stupid. There's only two hundred in all," a boy replied. "I think they're for future soldiers, like me."

It sounded as though the noisy family was about finished with their business, so Jacques moved closer to the door, waiting as they tumbled out.

"Mommy, if you get a gold statuette from M. Law, can I have it?" one of the girls asked, tugging on her mother's skirt.

The mother's face looked weary as she glanced at Jacques, scolded all of the children, and kept ushering them out of the door.

"You're all being silly," she said to her children. "If we got one, it would belong to our entire family, not any single one of you, so that's enough of that. What could children possibly want with a fleur-de-lis statuette anyway, even if it is pure gold?"

"I'd use it as my dowry someday!" one of the daughters said.

"I'd put it on the mantle and declare myself king!" one of the sons cried.

"Well, stop this endless quarreling because it doesn't matter. We're not going to Les Halles and that's that. We don't even know what the statuettes are for or if our family would get one, and we cannot afford to travel all that way just to find out. Now move along!"

En masse, the family headed down the street and away from Jacques. Trying to process in his mind the conversation he had just heard, he stood frozen in place, heart pounding in his throat.

"May I help you, sir?"

Jacques glanced numbly at the store clerk, who stood waiting at the counter inside.

"Sir? May I help you?"

"Uh...excuse me. I'll be back," Jacques said. Then he wove his way through the crowded street as quickly as possible, catching up with the noisy family at the corner.

"Pardon!" he said, repeating the word until the family realized he was talking to them and stopped.

"Yes, what it is?" the man asked. Standing there beside him, concern came over the woman's face as she seemed to recognize Jacques from the courier's office moments before. She glanced back up the street and then down around her, as if she feared she had forgotten one of her children.

"I'm sorry to bother you, and this is terribly rude, but I couldn't help but overhear your children's conversation. May I ask what you are all talking about regarding solid gold fleur-de-lis statuettes?"

At this point, the children had stopped fighting to cluster around their parents and look up at Jacques curiously.

"Where have you been, monsier? On the moon?" the oldest boy asked, earning a quick reprimand from his father for his rudeness.

Jacques explained that he had, indeed, been out of town for nearly a month and had just returned.

"Everyone's talking about it," the man answered. "It's a special give-away, a tremendous sort of contest. No one knows yet what it's all about, but rumors have been flying for two weeks that the palace goldsmiths in Paris have been casting little statuettes from pure gold, each one of them to be given away for *free*. It was just rumors, understand you, but then yesterday posters went up all over town." He gestured toward a sign that had been affixed to a stake and set in place across the street. "The signs confirm it, that two hundred solid gold fleur-de-lis statues will be given away today at two bells at Les Halles to any and all citizens of France who meet one very specific qualification. I daresay the whole city will be there just to see what that qualification is and if they happen to be one of the ones who meets it."

"Two o'clock?" Jacques asked, his heart racing even faster.

"Yes," the man replied, squinting up at the clock on the church bell tower. "Half an hour from now."

Jacques thanked them for their help, and as they turned to go he darted across the street to read the sign for himself, crossing directly in front of a fast-moving team of horses.

"Be careful, monsieur!" the driver scolded from his perch atop the sedan as he brushed past without incident.

Giving the man an apologetic wave, Jacques focused his attention on the sign. It said:

LADIES AND GENTLEMEN,

M. JOHN LAW AND THE NEWLY FORMED

COMPAGNIE DES INDES

ARE PROUD TO ANNOUNCE THE GIFTING OF

TWO HUNDRED SOLID GOLD FLEUR-DE-LIS STATUETTES

TO ANY AND ALL GOOD CITIZENS OF EUROPE

WHO MEET ONE VERY SPECIFIC QUALIFICATION.

COULD THIS MEAN YOU?

PRESENTATION TO TAKE PLACE

TWO P.M., AUGUST 18, 1719,

AT LES HALLES IN PARIS.

ALL ARE WELCOME TO ATTEND AND ELIGIBLE TO WIN.

Sick to his very core, Jacques didn't understand much of what was going on, but he knew one thing for sure: He had to get to M. Freneau and tell him about the mix-up before the event started. As he could not trust so urgent and necessary a task to a paid courier, Jacques would have to deliver the news straight to Les Halles himself, regardless of the personal consequences. A private violation of confidence was nothing compared to the public disaster this would surely become if M. Freneau delivered the wrong statuettes to M. Law, regardless of what their intentions were to do with them after that.

FOURTEEN

As Travis drove toward Canal Street, I pulled out my cell phone to call Wade Henkins. He didn't answer, so I left a brief message asking him to call me back.

Traffic was heavy on Canal, and after sitting through two revolutions of a light and barely advancing, I suggested that Travis take some side roads. He wasn't familiar with the city, so I directed him in a series of turns that zigzagged us to St. Philip, which would lead us down to Royal.

As we neared Louis Armstrong Park, I noticed a rowdy group of teenagers who seemed to be harassing a homeless man. They had surrounded him and his shopping cart in a circle, and they were taking things out of the cart and tossing them to each other over his head as he desperately tried to grab them back. We were waiting for a light to change, and for a moment I thought about jumping out of the car and racing to the poor old man's aid. The way my luck was going, though, someone would whip out a weapon, someone else would call the police, and before I knew it I would be back behind bars.

"Would you look at that." Travis said under his breath, suddenly veering onto the sidewalk with his truck and slamming on his brakes right where the incident was taking place. In one smooth motion, he put the car in park and reached behind me to pull the shotgun from its rack.

Before I could say a word, he was out of the car and facing the gang, the powerful-looking shotgun held casually at his side. I held my breath. Though I understood the motivation for Travis' gesture, I questioned the wisdom of going one against seven, even if that one was armed.

"*Comment ca vas?* Having a little fun at somebody else's expense?"

"Why don't you mind your own business?" one of the boys replied, looking warily at the gun.

"Well, see, I was minding my own business, but my Boss twelve-gauge here, he just couldn't stay out of it. Me and him, together we kill our first alligator when I was just nine. A nine-year-old boy who can shoot a gator right between the eyes at point-blank range, you think he'd hesitate to fire on a group of punks trying to bully a defenseless old man?"

The boys stared at him for a long moment as they seemed to consider the weight of what he said. Then they slowly raised their hands and backed away. Travis remained right where he was, the gun still held loosely at his side.

As I watched and waited, all I could pray was that a police car wouldn't come driving by right about now, see a lunatic with a shotgun, and slap us both in jail. Considering that I was already wanted for murder, a second offense would likely lock me up for good.

Still, I had to admire Travis' bravery. He never wavered, holding his position until every one of the boys had gone down the street and out of sight.

"Here, let me help you with that," Travis said to the old man, who was gathering his things from the ground where the boys had dropped them. I was about to jump out and help as well when the old man snarled at him.

"Like the kid said, mind your own business," he snapped, clutching a broken umbrella to his chest.

I was offended for Travis' sake, but he merely laughed and wished the man a good day. He got back in the truck, returned the gun to its rack, and pulled back onto the road. We were both quiet for a long moment.

"Did you really kill an alligator when you were nine?" I asked.

"Actually, I was seven, but I didn't think they'd believe that, not to mention I didn't want to sound like I was bragging."

With that, we crossed into the French Quarter.

As the sun set somewhere off in the distance, lights were starting to turn on and the narrow streets were coming alive. Traffic was snarled here too, but suddenly I didn't mind. I simply rolled down my window and inhaled the familiar scent of my hometown. There was something about the French Quarter at this hour, something so mysterious and magical, that for a brief while it pushed away the misery of my day and all that had been going on.

As we inched past old pastel-colored buildings, their simple lines embellished with wrought iron railings, tall windows, and heavy, elegant doors, I simply let my senses take it all in—the smells of gumbo and hot pralines, the sounds of laughter and music, the sight of lazy balconies overhanging the sidewalks, their flower boxes bursting with vivid blossoms and trailing vines. It was warm for April, and the air was so sticky it clung to my arms and face like a veil. Tourists and locals alike made their way down sidewalks lined with hawkers, street performers, and an occasional Lucky Dog vendor.

At one corner, an old man sat on a crate, eyes closed, playing "Amazing Grace" on a saxophone. The sound was haunting and lovely, its melody bouncing from the stucco walls lining the street on both sides.

New Orleans.

Part of me loved it so very much, loved all that was beautiful and unique about it. I loved the Spanish architecture, the laissez-faire attitude, the way days stretched into evenings that stretched into nights, and nobody seemed to worry about getting anywhere or doing anything more important than enjoying the here and the now.

But another part of me, a significant part, didn't love this city at all, couldn't forget what it had come to symbolize to me as a child. When I was very small, we lived in the Garden District in an elegant old house on Prytaria. A nanny lived with us because my parents were never home. My father was busy being the chef and owner of one of the best restaurants in town, and my mother served as the hostess there. Once a week, though, the nanny would drop me off at the restaurant so she could take her day off. To make sure my parents would let me stick around, I learned to be invisible, neither seen nor heard. I didn't mind. I had the fish and the turtles to talk to, and there was always Sam's wife, Eugenie, in their apartment out back. When I would get bored with folding napkins in the kitchen or hanging out in the courtyard, I would make my way up the back stairs, and Eugenie and I would bake cookies or clean house or, if I was lucky, curl up on the couch and just read picture books together.

When I turned six and was ready to start first grade, my parents put an end to my life as I knew it, sending me off to an exclusive girls' school near Vicksburg, Mississippi. There, though the place itself wasn't bad and I had a few kind teachers, I mostly learned to bottle up my feelings of loss and fear and loneliness and simply exist. For a long time, I survived only for trips home. Of course, my parents never altered their schedules for my sake, but at least when I was home I could count on spending more time at Ledet's since we no longer had a nanny. Hovering out of the way in a corner of the kitchen, I would watch my father for hours, barking out orders that were obeyed without question, working his magic over rows of sizzling pots and pans. Sitting in a chair behind a potted plant in the lobby, reading, I would look up at every new click-clack of heels against the rose marble floor to see the beautiful dresses of the women coming in to dine.

Most beautiful of all was my mother, who looked like an angel as she floated about the restaurant, greeting people at the door, leading them to their tables, pausing to say hello or correct a waiter or adjust a tablecloth. She was tall and elegant, her posture perfect, her impeccably tailored clothes not quite able to hide the curvy figure underneath. She wore her ash-blond hair swept into a chic French twist which accentuated her long, delicate neck and the signature diamond teardrop earrings that always graced her pretty earlobes. And then there were her hands, those graceful, dainty hands that were always moving, always busy, always attending to the most minute of details. Sometimes, over the top of my book, I would study those hands and wonder how it would feel to have them stroke my cheek or braid my hair—or even simply write me a letter when I was away at school.

Sometimes, I felt like a stranger in my own family.

Things took a turn for the worse when I was twelve. When I came home from school that Christmas, it was to find that my parents had sold our house on Prytaria and moved us into an even bigger, more elegant place all the way across town on Lakeside Drive. Though it was beautiful there—and my fancy new bedroom even looked out over the sweeping, green lawn and Lake Pontchartrain beyond—I couldn't have felt more abandoned. Because they were farther away, my parents now had to leave for work earlier and got back later. Worse, even when I was home on break, I was rarely given the option of going into the city with them anymore. Instead of quietly hanging out at Ledet's with everyone else, taking in the sights and smells all around me, I was left home with nothing to do in a four-thousand-square-foot house all by myself. My parents said a kid didn't belong sneaking around a stuffy French Quarter restaurant when she could be free to enjoy the fresh air and sunshine of the lake area. In truth, I think my mother was just embarrassed of me at that point, as I was all gangly arms and legs, frizzy blond hair, and sporting a double row of braces on my teeth. At least if I stayed at home, people wouldn't have to give me those sympathetic little glances, as if to say how sad it was that I hadn't taken after my beautiful mother after all.

The few times I did get to tag along to the restaurant, there would be new faces on staff, new changes to the decor, things that made me feel that I didn't even know the place anymore. As I got older, I grew into my long arms and legs, finished with the braces, and discovered the value of makeup and hair straighteners. Once the duckling was a swan, I found that I was welcomed back, but by then I had almost lost interest.

I still went in with them, but instead of skulking around Ledet's all day, I began to venture outside the restaurant and into the Quarter. I would stroll the busy blocks, watching the people and listening to the laughter and feeling above all else that the whole place was one giant club, a club to which I had been denied membership. At seventeen I studiously avoided Bourbon Street and its rows of smelly bars and creepy strip clubs, but otherwise the whole Quarter was mine to explore. I would often end up at Café Du Monde, where I would sit at a table by myself, eat beignets and drink coffee and watch the crowds weave in and among the artists and psychics and performers who lined Jackson Square. At those times, my heart would yearn to be a part of something, something inclusive, something bigger and better and more important than my own little world of one.

Then I would finish my last sip of café au lait, brush the confectioners' sugar from my lap, and head back to Ledet's, back to the restaurant that bore my family's name and had nothing to do with me at all. If not for the welcoming arms of Sam and Eugenie Underwood, year after lonely year, I might have one day simply curled up and floated away, never to be seen again. Instead, though my own parents barely acknowledged my existence, I was grounded by the fact that there were two people who did love me, who cared what happened to me, and who actually listened when I spoke and laughed when I made jokes and held me when I cried.

Over the years Eugenie battled the triple burdens of her race, diabetes, and high blood pressure, growing heavier and more sedentary with each passing day. The last time I had seen her, she must have weighed three hundred pounds, but Sam proudly gazed at her as though she were still the saucy young waitress he had met at Mother's restaurant years before when he'd gone to apply for a job and come away with the job and the waitress' phone number.

Eugenie died during my senior year at college, and I had skipped class and caught a flight to New Orleans as soon as I heard. Sam had given his beloved wife a full-out jazz funeral, complete with a horse-drawn hearse, a six-piece band, and plenty of spare umbrellas for the parade of mourners. To lead us en masse from the church to the cemetery, the band started out with a mournful, heart-wrenching version of "Just a Closer Walk with Thee." During the service, I had sat with my parents. But as we walked toward the cemetery and the music played, I discreetly separated myself from them and inched closer to the front of the procession, just to be near Sam. He must have sensed me there, because at one point he turned and looked around until he spotted me and then waved me up, insisting that I walk beside him. Between quiet sobs into his handkerchief, Sam told me I was the closest thing to a daughter he and Eugenie had ever had.

Together, Sam and I walked in time with the music, in turns holding each other up and audibly sobbing as we went. For me, it had been a very uncommon and public display of emotion, one that would later earn a reprimand from my mother despite the fact that I was twenty-one at the time and far too old to be scolded by her. It didn't occur to me until later that perhaps what my mother had called embarrassment had actually been jealousy. Maybe she thought I wouldn't cry that hard when it came her turn to be laid to rest.

It was true that I was nearly inconsolable with grief that day, mourning the woman who had touched my life with such love. By the time we reached the cemetery, the band had worked through the sad songs and was picking up the tempo. I had never understood why people were always dancing and laughing at jazz funerals. But then Sam explained that we had mourned the goodbye for ourselves, but now it was time to rejoice the passing into heaven for Eugenie. As the band burst into a rousing version of "Panama," Eugenie's favorite song, I finally got it. We sang and danced the second line toward her grave for what felt like hours, brown skin and white all glistening with sweat in the hot afternoon sun. After the dancing, I had prayed, prayed that when she got to heaven God would welcome her as lovingly as she had always welcomed me.

Truly, had it not been for Sam and Eugenie, I might have broken my ties with this city altogether, years ago.

"Are you okay, Chloe?"

Startled from my thoughts, I turned to see Travis staring at me curiously. I realized that we were on Royal, crossing Orleans, and that a single tear had somehow made its way down my cheek. I wiped it away impatiently.

"I'm sorry. I was just thinking about Eugenie's funeral."

"Sam's wife?"

"Yeah. She was a very special lady."

"*Mais oui.* I remember."

"Speaking of ladies, I need to call my mother." I dug my cell phone from my purse, dialed my mother's number, and was relieved to hear her answer. This would be the first time I had spoken to her since I'd been arrested.

"Mom? It's Chloe."

At the sound of my voice, she burst into tears. I was surprised but touched, especially when the crying went on for a block and a half. Once she had calmed down enough to speak, though, I quickly realized that much of her outburst had come not from love or concern about my ordeal but from the mistaken assumption that I had killed a man. She went on and on, demanding to know what could have possibly gone wrong to make me do something like that.

My own mother thought I was a murderer? Even Travis, a guy I hadn't seen in fourteen years, knew I was innocent. Yet here was Lola Ledet, sniffling into the phone about how could this have happened and what were we going to do and surely she had raised me better than this. I just let her keep going, telling myself that she hadn't raised me at all. The faculty and staff at boarding school did. Sam and Eugenie did. The nanny did. My mother, on the other hand, had been merely a bystander.

Now she was a bystander *and* a traitor.

FIFTEEN

The conversation with my mother was made even worse by the fact that I was having to have it in front of a virtual stranger. To his credit, Travis rolled down his window and pretended not to listen, but even so it would have been hard not to hear, considering our proximity.

"Look, Mom," I finally interrupted, "we can talk about all this later. Right now I'm trying to find Sam. Do you have any idea where he is or how I could reach him?"

She did not, as apparently she also had been calling around trying to find him all day. Ledet's manager had told her that no one there had seen him and that Sam hadn't even shown up for family meal, which was unusual for him. As we neared St. Peter, I noticed a car pulling out of a metered space off to the side and gestured to Travis that he should park there. He made the turn and attempted to parallel park his big truck in the tight space.

"All right, Mom, one more question. Last night Sam took the tape from your answering machine and brought it to someone who could enhance the sound. Do you know where he brought it?"

Travis grunted as he eased carefully into place. Ignoring him, I listened to my mother, who was trying to remember what Sam had said. There was no question in my mind that my father's shooting and my framing were directly related. I had done a lot of thinking today, and I had the feeling that the best chance of finding the shooter and proving my innocence began with that tape.

"I'm sorry, but I don't remember."

"Did he say a person's name?" I prodded. "Maybe the name of a business? Whoever it was, they have some high-tech equipment. Where did Sam take it? *Think*, Mother."

"I'm trying, Chloe. You have no idea how difficult this has all been for me!"

"Oh, yeah, and a day in jail has been a real walk in the park for me!"

"Don't be rude, darling. You know better than that."

Speaking of rude, Travis had finished parking the car and was now tapping me on the arm. I waved him off but he persisted. Finally, I asked my mother to hold on and cupped my hand over the phone.

"What?"

"*C'est moi.* It's me."

"It's you what?"

"I'm the guy you're looking for. The recording. Sam brought it to me."

Travis popped a CD from the player and held it up to show me. Handwritten in marker on the top were the date and words *J. Ledet Phone Msg.* He opened the glove compartment and pointed to a small digital tape sitting atop a typed sheet of paper. "Last night, before he came and met you at the restaurant, Sam brought this tape to me at my studio. That's why I've been trying to find him, to tell him what I was able to figure out."

Without responding, I took my hand away from the phone and asked my mother if by any chance the name she was trying to recall was Travis Naquin.

"That's it, Travis! Alphonse's grandson. Of course, how could I have forgotten? He's some bigwig music producer, has a whole studio and everything. Sam thought he might be able to help."

"All right, Mom, that's what I needed to know for now. I've got to go."

"Wait. When are you coming down to the hospital?"

"Soon."

"I hope so. So many people came to see about your dad that my bodyguard finally made me move into a private waiting room for safety purposes. I'm going stir-crazy in here all by myself. I need someone to talk to."

Her words were not lost on me. She wanted me there not to comfort me or to help me figure out what was going on, but because she was bored and tired of being by herself.

"I only get to see your father once an hour," she added pitifully, "but of course he doesn't say a word. It's awful for me."

"Goodbye, Mother," I said, disconnecting the call. Closing my eyes, I took a deep breath and let it out slowly, counting to ten.

To his credit, Travis didn't offer any platitudes to make me feel better. Instead, he quietly waited in silence as I pulled myself together.

"My phone's battery is getting low," I said finally, unzipping a side pocket of my purse and pulling out my car charger. "May I plug it in?"

"Of course, *cher*," he replied, gesturing toward the power outlet.

"Thanks." I plugged in the charger and propped the phone in a cup holder. Then I turned to Travis and asked him to tell me about the message. "Were you able to recover the missing parts? Do we know who shot my father?"

"No, we don't know that. I was able to clarify a few things and pick up some external sounds, but overall I was disappointed. Between swamp gasses and mineral deposits, south Louisiana is brutal on cell phone transmissions. For the first part of the call, the sound was broken up by external interference, so the missing words can't be recovered. The only parts I could recover were near the end, when it wasn't a transmission problem but simply of matter of your father's voice growing weaker and being drowned out by other noises."

"Can I hear it?" I asked, wondering if I was going to be sorry for asking.

"Sure. Take a look at this first."

He handed me the page from the glove compartment, and I looked at it to see that it was a typed transcript of the tape similar to the one Sam had handwritten and shown me last night. This version included some words in parentheses, and everywhere a gap appeared, indicating missing words,

Travis had typed a number. He explained that the words in parentheses were the extra words he had managed to recover from the original using his equipment. The numbers were the amounts of seconds unaccounted for.

"On the parts that are audible, he speaks an average of three words per second," Travis continued. "So where the gaps are just a second or two, that means we're only missing a few words. In the longer gaps, obviously, we're missing far more."

"So, here, where you wrote a seven," I asked, pointing to the biggest number, "that means we're missing about twenty-one words?"

"Yeah."

"That's a lot."

"I know. That's why it's so frustrating. I worked on this most of the night, and as you can see, I was able to recover the last third nicely. But there's still lots of gaps in the rest, especially at the beginning. Like I said, there's nothing anyone could do to get those missing sections back because they never made it onto the recording in the first place."

I asked Travis to play the message, and I braced myself for the sound of my father's agonized voice to fill the vehicle. Sure enough, suddenly he was talking, and so I read along. I noticed that where Sam had written "bins" and "bins totter" Travis had put "Ben's" and "Ben's daughter," which made more sense. He had also made notations of other sounds, such as the cutting of the boat engine and the noise of that boat scraping on the bottom of the bayou. The most important part of what Travis had done, though, was to recover the last few sentences in their entirety.

Once the message ended, we sat quietly together in the car. Up the street, music played from a boom box where two little boys were tap-dancing their hearts out.

My poor dad. I knew he had suffered before he lost consciousness, but I hadn't fully grasped the extent of that suffering until I heard his voice on this message. I couldn't help but focus on the urgency and despair, so I told Travis to play it again, and this time I tried to listen more fully to the words themselves. As I did, two sentences jumped out at me near the end.

I always told you we had an insurance policy, our special recipe. I just didn't know it would end up getting me killed.

"There," I said. "Stop there. What does that mean, 'I always told you we had an insurance policy, our special recipe'? What is he talking about?"

"I don't know. Maybe you should ask your mother."

The "special recipe" could have been almost anything, the salt-crusted fish that Ledet's was famous for, something from one of my father's many published cookbooks, even the recipe for his pink secret salt. Travis was right. I needed to call my mother back. Though I really didn't feel like talking to her, I thought she might be of some help. When she answered the phone, I read that sentence to her and asked her if it had any special meaning.

"'I always told you we had an insurance policy'? 'Our special recipe'?" She sounded puzzled.

"Yes. If Daddy said that to you, what would you think he was talking about?"

"Hmm. I'm sorry, Chloe, I just don't know. I do remember him saying 'If anything ever happens to me, babe, that's your insurance policy,' but he wasn't talking about a real insurance policy."

"What was he talking about?"

"Some poetry he wrote, back before Ledet's ever opened. He had it framed and hung it in the entranceway. It's still there. It was just a poem and not a legal document. Whenever he called it an insurance policy, I just thought he meant symbolically, like it represented the restaurant itself."

"How about your 'special recipe'? Does that ring any bells?"

"Gosh, Chloe, that could be any one of a thousand different things. The man is a chef, you know."

"A poem framed and hanging in the entranceway," I said, trying to remember it. "Are you talking about the one that's matted with the photo of the ribbon cutting?"

"Yes, that's it."

I knew what she was talking about, where it hung, and what it looked like, but I hadn't bothered to read the verses in years. I also just assumed it was a memorial of the origins of Ledet's restaurant, a gesture of sentiment to remind my father of where it had all begun. Now that I thought about it, Ledet's had all begun with a loan from friends who accepted my father's treasure as collateral.

The treasure.

Quickly, I concluded the call with my mother, and as I hung up I had the sudden urge to throw my arms around Travis and give him a big hug. I didn't, of course, but I couldn't help but place one hand on his arm and give it a squeeze as I thanked him for his hard work with the tape.

"This may be my first big break," I said, a plan forming in my mind. I didn't tell him about the treasure, of course, but I did explain that there was something I needed from inside the restaurant, something that might go a long way in helping me figure everything out. Once I had that, we could take a quick look in Sam's apartment, and then I would be out of Travis' hair, in my own car, and heading to the hospital.

Five minutes later, I was hovering just outside the front door of Ledet's, an empty tote bag from Travis' truck in my hand, pretending to read the menu featured in my window.

Though I had every legal right to walk inside and take that poem from the wall, I didn't want to do it in a way that might attract attention. Primarily, I didn't want to tip anyone off who might be watching that this inane little poem that had been hanging on a wall of the restaurant for forty-two years was of any significance to the things that had been going on in the past few days.

On a more personal level, I was just so embarrassed at how I looked and what everyone in there must be thinking about me and my murder charge that I didn't want to show my face inside the restaurant unless I had to. My hope was that whoever was working the welcome station would be someone I didn't know and who wouldn't recognize me. As my ace in the hole, I was sending Travis in ahead of me, to distract attention while I nabbed the picture. As long as the hostess on duty had eyes, she would no doubt be quite distracted with the likes of the handsome and charming Travis Naquin, even if he was wearing jeans and a T-shirt and a backwards-facing baseball cap.

"Meet you back at the truck, *cher*," he said softly as he brushed past me, pushed open the door of the restaurant, and stepped inside. I slowly counted to twenty and then summoned my nerve and stepped inside as well.

"So you're telling me if I bring my family here for dinner, you can't make little Susie a peanut butter-and-jelly sandwich?" Travis was asking the woman at the front counter. "I know it sounds weird, but she's a weird child. All she eats, day after day, is peanut butter and jelly."

The hostess was not someone that I knew, thank goodness. While she explained to Travis that their chefs would be happy to try and put together whatever his family would like, within reason, she said she would have to check with the kitchen to get a definite answer on a PB&J.

"Super. Why don't you go check right now?" he asked, no doubt giving her a broad dimpled smile.

"Certainly," the woman said, pausing before she went to look over at me and ask if I had a reservation.

"No, I'm waiting for someone," I replied. "You go ahead and help him first. I'm in no hurry."

"Okay. I'll be right back."

As soon as she was gone, I stepped over to the frame and tried to lift it off of its hanger. Unfortunately, the wire wasn't simply on a hanger, it was bolted to the wall! As I struggled to work it loose, I gave Travis a look of panic, and he responded with a tilting of his head toward the dining room. Stepping into there, he just barely headed off the hostess at the pass, talking to her in the next room in order to buy me time to get the frame loose. Finally, as specks of plaster sprinkled to the floor, the bolt came loose from its mooring with a soft *thwunk* and the frame was finally in my hands.

Dropping it into the tote bag, I turned around and carried it out the front door. I knew that taking the poem wasn't stealing, but I still felt as though I had committed a major crime. My heart was in my throat all the way to Toulouse. I had hung onto the keys, and so once I reached the truck, I clicked the remote to unlock the door and quickly slipped inside, locking the door behind me. The tap dancers were gone, but there were plenty of other people milling around.

Travis would be back in just a minute or two, so in the time I had I pulled the tall, narrow frame from the bag and quickly skimmed the poem. Later, I would take the frame apart and look inside and see if perhaps my father's "insurance policy" had been an actual insurance policy, something tucked inside behind the poem and picture. I had a feeling, though, that the poem itself was the key. Even just skimming the first few verses, I thought it sounded like a mind game, a puzzle of some kind. The title of the poem was "Recipe for Success."

This had to be it, their own little insurance policy, their special recipe.

Above the poem was a photograph that had been taken back in 1967, a picture of my father with giant scissors in hand, cutting a big red ribbon just outside of the restaurant. He was in his late thirties, wearing a white chef's jacket, his hair long and pulled back into a ponytail. As that was the era of the hippie, lots of men had long hair, but I had a feeling his had been more an affectation of European style than a sign of the times in America. Not far behind him stood my mother, young and beautiful at just twenty-three. In the photo, she was wearing a leopard skin cape and huge dark sunglasses, looking like a blond Jackie Onassis or a French fashion model.

My phone rang, startling me, and I quickly grabbed it from where it sat, still charging, in the drink holder. The number on the screen looked familiar, and when I answered I realized it was Wade, my father's old friend who had visited me in jail.

"Hello?"

"Chloe? Wade Henkins."

"Hello! Thank you for calling me back."

From the corner of my eye, I could see Travis approaching, so I gave him a little wave to show that I was on the phone and would be just a minute.

"When we spoke earlier today," I said, "I had a feeling there was something you weren't telling me. Do you have more information for me, something that might help me out of the situation I'm in?"

He cleared his throat and asked if I was alone. Outside of the truck, Travis was killing time by fooling with the parking meter.

"Yes, I am."

"Okay. Listen, it's not much, but I think it's important."

"I'm listening."

"There was one other thing a little strange about yesterday. Down at

Paradise. It was after we finished working and I was about to leave to go get groceries."

"Yes?"

"He said something to me, Chloe, something I've been thinking about ever since. It was almost like he knew something terrible was going to happen."

I sat up straight, my chest tightening.

"What? What did he say?"

"After he handed me the keys to his car, he looked at me, real intense like, and said, 'Wade, if anything ever happens to me, would you give Chloe a message for me? Don't tell anyone else but her.' I didn't take it serious at the time. It was just one of those things a person might say if they was feeling sentimental or something."

"What was the message?"

"He said, 'Tell Chloe to follow the recipe.'"

SIXTEEN

Holding the phone against my ear, I closed my eyes, knowing that very recipe Wade was talking about was sitting on my lap.

"I don't know what your father meant when he said that, but it's been bugging me that he might have known he was in danger."

Outside the car, I noticed a trio of attractive young women coming up the sidewalk toward Travis. They were obviously tourists, wearing Mardi Gras beads, weaving a bit, and drinking from bright green plastic cups.

"I might have a few ideas," I replied. "It's kind of complicated."

"Well, listen, if I can be of help in any way…"

I watched as the girls caught sight of Travis and paused to talk to him. They were obviously drunk and ready to have a good time. That he smiled and chatted with them in return was a bit disconcerting, though I couldn't say why.

"You've already been more help than you know, Wade."

"Well, listen, you keep my number close at hand, okay? Let me be the first one you call if you get into any more trouble."

"Will do."

"I'm glad to help you out in any way I can. Your daddy and I go way back, you know, before you were born." Much to my dismay, he launched into a long drawn-out tale about how his father died when he was fifteen, and my father and Alphonse sort of took him under their wing after that.

"My family lived on a little houseboat just a few miles up from Paradise, and though I was a lot younger than them, I used to join up with their whole group to go out in the woods sometimes. They were like big brothers to me, especially your daddy. I was a young man angry at the world about losing my father. Julian had a temper too, you know, but he handled his better than I did mine. I tried to learn from that."

I didn't comment, but my head filled with a thousand tirades, echoes of my father's temper. If he handled it well, that was news to me. As far as I knew, he had never struck anyone physically, but he could whip a person to death verbally. I had seen grown men wither and fade under a Julian Ledet tongue lashing, sometimes for crimes so absurdly unimportant that I couldn't believe they had even been mentioned, much less yelled about.

"Anyhoo," Wade continued, "it was your daddy who helped me get out of the swamps altogether. We was so poor, you know, really hard up. After your pop opened his restaurant in New Orleans, he helped me find a room to rent near the Quarter and gave me a job at Ledet's." Wade chuckled. "I didn't have no skills and I couldn't do nothing right. But instead of firing me, your daddy helped me figure out what I really wanted to do with my life and then go for it. Even after I made it through police academy and was working the force, whenever money was tight I could always call up your dad for help and he'd throw odd jobs my way, give me a little extra work on the side. He's a real stand-up guy, that man. I'm sorry he's not doing so well now. If I can pay back just a little of his kindness by helping out his daughter, I'm more than happy to do so."

I thanked him again and finally managed to conclude the call. My mother had always thought of Wade Henkins as a crude and crass back-woodsman. He had a few rough edges, but his heart was obviously in the right place. I was just glad to know I had an insider on my side.

Glancing out at Travis, I could see that he was in no hurry to embark on our next errand. Though I was eager to get to Sam's apartment, I decided to take another minute or two and read the "Recipe for Success" all the way through.

It was getting dark outside, so I turned on the cab's dome light and began reading:

Recipe for Success
By Julian Ledet

There is a place of great repast,
Where promises and friendships last.
Where patrons dine on meals of kings,
And Quarter boys can live their dreams.

Yet not alone do I succeed,
But with your help in word and deed.
And so I give you at this time
Security inside a rhyme.

Here in the City Care Forgot
We'll make a gumbo in a pot.
So grab your spices from the shelf.
We start with Chef Ledet himself.

In gumbo, always make a roux,
4T oil heated through.
Then add 5T flour, white,
Stirred over heat till the color's right.

For the one who loves chou and chouchou,
I couldn't have done it without you,
I add to the roux your trinity,
First learned in your vicinity.

For the Bürgermeister, a man of means,
Who learned to fight in old Orleans,
I add some andouille sliced fine as can be
'Cause you Allemands love your boucherie.

For king of the Sunday breakdown raids,
Whose ancestors brought seeds in their braids,
Professor of juré extraordinaire,
I add fresh okra into the pot there.

Next comes the stock to fill up the pot,
Seasoned with mirepoix, heated till hot.
For my hoghead friend I shall not scrimp,
As I add to the gumbo a helping of shrimp.

And finally for he who has always been there,
Son of a traiture, kind and fair.
We grind up filé to add at the end,
Then the dish is finished and ready for friends.

For all who dare make this recipe,
There is one secret you'll not get from me:
The measure of how much each item to add.
Unless you know that, the recipe's bad.

Divided among those named in this poem,
I give each a quantity that's theirs alone.
Together they come to solve this rhyme,
The treasure they only together can find.

But if all else fails, I will tell you this:
North and West you may search for things gone amiss.
'Tween hill and dale and dock and dune,
It's out there, under the Cajun moon.

I was dumbfounded.

It suddenly struck me that in all our conversation last night, Kevin had never once said where the statuettes were now, just that they had long ago been put away for safekeeping. Through all these years of fruitless research and angry infighting, where had the two men safely stashed the statuettes? I had a feeling this poem was the key, a sort of treasure map—or a treasure puzzle, really—one that led to the millions of dollars' worth of gold my father and Alphonse Naquin had been fighting over for decades.

Outside, Travis was pointing toward something up the street and still talking to the girls. If this was the kind of person he was, I was glad he and I would part ways soon. He had been a huge help with the reporters at the courthouse, and his work with the taped message had gotten me this far, but once we finished going through Sam's apartment to see if we could figure out where he might be, I was going to thank Travis for his help and gladly retrieve my own vehicle from the parking garage up the street. I needed to get to the hospital as soon as possible, anyway.

Tucking the poem back into the tote bag, I hid it under the seat and hoped it would be safe there for just a little while. Fortunately, the girls were walking away by the time I got out of the car.

"Bye, sugar!" one of them called back to Travis, giggling. "Thanks for your help!"

He smiled and waved, but as soon as they were out of earshot he turned to me and said, "I don't know what these young girls are thinking, going around like that, half dressed and completely hammered. That's what *Grandmere* Minette calls 'trouble waiting to happen.'"

"You didn't seem to mind when trouble came calling," I said sharply, turning to head up the street toward the entrance to Sam's apartment. As he fell into step with me, I added, "You weren't exactly turning them away."

"They were looking for Pat O'Brian's, and I was trying to explain where it was. But they were so drunk, I had to repeat myself about five times. *Mais non,* I can't stand drunks, not the ones who think they're so charming and funny when they're really just sloppy and irritating."

We continued up Toulouse toward the archway that would lead to the alley that ran behind Ledet's and Sam's apartment.

"I thought Cajuns were big drinkers," I said. "Do you mean to tell me you don't toss back a few out there in the swamps when you and your buddies are fishing?"

Travis was silent for a long moment as we walked in step down the dark sidewalk. It took a moment for me to realize that he had stopped walking and was standing still behind me. I paused, turning toward him.

"What is it?"

"And there she is, the Chloe Ledet I remember," he said, slowly shaking his head from side to side. "I thought maybe you had changed, but now I see you haven't, not at all."

"Excuse me?" I asked, stepping toward him.

"You're still the snobby, judgmental, rigid little *bon á rien* you always were. Cajuns are all drunks? *Mais non!*"

"*Bon á rein?*" I asked. If the man was going to call me names, at least I wanted to know what those names were.

"'Good for nothing,'" he translated. "Nothing but judging others with broad stereotypes that do not apply."

"Okay, I'm sorry, you're right. That was a stereotype. But don't pretend to know who I am just from one careless remark."

"One careless remark? *Pooyie!* You have got to be kidding."

It was my turn to be silent for a moment.

"Do you have a problem with me?" I asked finally, lowering my voice and taking a step back.

"Same problem I always had, *cher*. For a girl who's supposed to know all about good manners, you seem to forget the most important rule of all."

"And what's that?" I asked stiffly, thinking that he was treading on dangerous ground here. No one impugned the knowledge and etiquette of Chloe Ledet. I wrote the book on good manners. I was the queen of rules.

"You can know all the etiquette in the world, *cher*, but if you use it to make a person feel small, then I hate to tell you, that's not good manners. Not at all. That's just ugly."

With that, he started walking again. I stood and watched him go and then ran to catch up with him, grabbing the hem of his shirt to get his attention.

"Is that what you think I do? Make other people feel small? I've got news for you, Travis. I make my living teaching people to respect other cultures, other ways of life. I teach entire seminars based on the principle of respect!"

"Yeah, I've heard about those seminars," he replied, stopping again. "Seems to me like you can say all you want about other cultures in other countries, but when it comes to the cultures right here in your own back-yard, Chloe, you haven't got a clue."

We simply stared at one another there on the street. There was too much going on in my life right now to be having this argument, an argument

I didn't even understand. Suddenly, I had the feeling his anger wasn't coming just from today but from something in the past, maybe from our long-ago date, the one I couldn't quite remember.

"Did something happen when we were teenagers, Travis? Did I do something wrong?"

He surprised me by laughing.

"You talking about our one big date? The one that went down in flames, so to speak?"

"I don't remember much about it. What did I do? Obviously, I hurt you in some way."

He grunted, shaking his head from side to side.

"Hurt me? *Cher*, you *eviscerated* me. Took me five years of admiring you from afar before I finally got the nerve to ask you out. I thought you were the nicest, most beautiful, most intelligent girl I had ever known. You were coming home from your fancy boarding school for the summer, and I had a job running deliveries for a seafood supplier, so I knew I'd be in town a lot. It was my last summer before college, and I had this vision that you and I would fall in love and share that whole summer together. I asked you out as soon as you got home. Tol' you I wanted to take you to dinner and a show."

"I remember that much. We ate at the Camellia Grill and went to the movies."

"Yeah, well, guess I should've made it Antoine's and the Saengar Theatre, because nothing less would have been good enough for you. My *grandmere* raised me right. I had sense enough to hold doors open for you and know what fork to use with my salad. But you found fault in everything, Chloe, every single little thing I did. I started out that night feeling so sure and confident of myself, but by the end of the evening you had me questioning everything I ever knew about myself and my family and where I had come from and where I was going. It was just one night, but I cannot begin to describe the impact it had on me. Long-term impact. After that, I made some stupid decisions, trying to be somebody I wasn't, trying to 'better' myself. Trying to get things so right that no one else would ever look at me and decide I wasn't good enough again. Problem was, I nearly sold my soul in the process. Thank the good Lord I finally came to my senses and made my way back home to Louisiana where I belonged."

I was stunned by Travis' speech, stunned that a night I could hardly recall had etched itself into his memory like engraving on steel. If what he said was true, if I had indeed spent the evening looking down my nose at him and making him feel small, then I was very sorry about that, and I told him so now.

"I was not a happy person back then, Travis. Whatever went on between us, I can guarantee you the only one on that date I hated was myself, not you. If I was acting like a snob and clinging to a bunch of silly rules, its only because that's all I had to hang on to. Who was I if I wasn't the well-bred product of the Windsor School for Girls, the rich daughter of the great Julian Ledet himself, the Ice Queen who didn't need anyone else in her life because she could do just fine on her own? I'm terribly sorry that I hurt you, but it was only because I was lashing out from the stuff that was going on in my own life."

Travis took off his hat and ran a hand through his hair. After tonight, I might not ever see him again, but I wanted this to end well. I felt bad about what I had done all those years ago, and I hoped he believed me.

"All right," he said finally. "Apology accepted."

"Thank you."

"Who knows, Chloe. Maybe sometime when your daddy's better and this whole mess is behind us, perhaps I can educate you a little bit about Cajun culture. My people spent a lot of years being forced to hide who they were. In my grandparents' day, they weren't even allowed to utter a single word of French in school—not even out in the schoolyard during recess—or they'd be beaten by the teacher. We had already been perse-cuted in the past, when our ancestors were kicked out of Nova Scotia and forced into the Grande Dérangement. That's how so many Acadians came to live in Louisiana in the first place, because it was one of the few places in the world that didn't turn them away. We're proud of our heritage, proud it has endured for all these years and is finally thriving again. If you let me, I could introduce you to a whole world, one you would quickly come to see was a fine and beautiful thing, not one to be scorned and dismissed."

"I hear what you're saying, Travis. And I think you're right. I've been so focused on foreign cultures that I've managed to dismiss one of the ones that was here under my nose."

Travis showed just a hint of a smile, one dimple appearing on his cheek.

"And a very pretty nose at that," he said softly. "*Aiyee*, no wonder I was so crazy 'bout you back then."

I was taken aback at his sudden about-face.

"You're flirting with me? Two minutes ago you tell me I eviscerated you and now you're flirting with me?"

He laughed.

"That's a Cajun for you, *cher*. Lesson one. We lay it all out there, work through it, then make up and move on."

"Given the world I grew up in, that's about the most foreign way of dealing with differences I've ever heard," I said. I didn't add that it actually sounded kind of refreshing, openly airing your issues instead of going on raging tirades, like my father, or silently swallowing them down where they could eat at you from the inside, like my mother. "For now, can we focus on the task at hand? We're here to look for Sam, remember?"

"*Si tu veux*," he replied with a wink, and then we were walking again. I didn't speak Cajun French, but I knew regular French enough to understand many of his expressions. *Si tu veux* was simply a way of saying, *If you want* or *As you wish*.

Soon we reached the archway that led to the courtyard and the alley that ran behind Ledet's. We stepped inside and went down the walkway and then up the stairs that brought us to Sam's kitchen door. There didn't seem to be any lights on inside, but Travis knocked loudly anyway. When Sam didn't come to the door after a second knock and another brief wait, I pulled out my key ring, flipped around to the old key, and slid it into the lock. For a moment I was afraid that perhaps Sam had changed locks in the last few years, but with one quick turn and a single click, the knob freely twisted in my hand.

It was dark inside, so I moved forward and ran my hand along the wall to find the switch. When my fingers finally found it, I flipped it upward, knowing that the kitchen light was a fluorescent fixture that always took a few moments to come on. As it flickered to full power, Travis stepped inside behind me and shut the door. Something smelled bad in there, and I told him that we should probably take out the trash for Sam when we were ready to go.

With a soft buzz overhead, the light sprung fully to life, and as it did Travis and I both froze in our steps. Though I gasped, I did not scream. In fact, I don't think I could have screamed. I couldn't even breathe. In the middle of the kitchen sat a single, hard wooden chair. On that chair was Sam.

There was no question that he was dead.

Worse than the fact that was he dead, though, was what he had obviously gone through before death. Someone evil had done this, someone who had been willing to beat him first. His poor body was bloody and battered, his hands and feet bound to the chair with duct tape.

"*Le travaille de diablo,*" Travis whispered. The work of a devil.

He was right about that.

SEVENTEEN

FRANCE, 1719
JACQUES

Nothing had been simple about getting to Les Halles, not from the moment Jacques started trying to find a ride in Charenton at one thirty to the moment he finally caught sight of St. Eustache Church, which was near Les Halles, at two twenty-five. In the past fifty-five minutes, despite a desperate need for expediency, Jacques had been held up first by one thing and then another. Unable to catch a ride with anyone heading to Paris, he finally had to hire a fiacre for the trip. The journey was harrowing to say the least, with several near-collisions and one sharp turn that Jacques thought would flip the carriage completely. They became mired in a bottleneck at the Paris city gates, and after being stuck for five minutes, Jacques finally told the driver he would pay now and go on foot from there. To Jacques' astonishment, the man charged him thirty-five sous anyway, almost double what the fare should have been.

Had everyone gone mad?

Jacques had run as fast as he could through the busy streets of Paris after that, weaving among carts and people and horses and structures, even taking a detour down an alley when the street he needed was blocked by a flock of sheep. As church bells pealed in the distance, he hopped over fences and skirted along narrow walkways and banged his head on more than one low-hanging flowerpot. He kept going, edging his way through the throngs of people and vendors and animals. When he reached Les Halles, it seemed that all of France was crowded into the public meeting area, a collection of fortune seekers all straining to hear the words that were being spoken from a podium on the dais, words that would tell them whether or not they qualified for a golden statuette. Studying that dais now from a distance, Jacques could see that it held four men, all of whom he recognized, one of whom was Freneau.

Jacques knew one thing. He had to get to M. Freneau whatever it took, even if it meant walking right up to the podium and handing him Papa's letter there.

Jacques tried to work his way through the crowd, but progress was nearly impossible. The closer he got, the more tightly people were packed in together. He pressed onward anyway, angering several. When he finally bumped into one fellow so hard that it knocked him over, the man jumped back up, grabbed Jacques by the collar, and threatened to punch him in the face if he didn't find a spot and stay in it. Given that the fellow was nearly twice his size, Jacques thought it best to do as he said. There was a stone wall not far off, so Jacques offered to go over there. Once he was sitting atop that wall, at least he could see and hear what was happening on the stage—and maybe catch M. Freneau's eye.

John Law was addressing the crowd, talking about his Compagnie des Indes and how it was creating opportunities for more and more Europeans to join the colonies in the New World. It didn't sound as though Jacques had missed much yet. As Law described a wondrous land filled with milk and honey, gold and diamonds, Indian kings and princesses, seafood-rich bays and vast lands of opportunity, the crowds began to respond—and not in a good way. They had heard it all before, the government's near-constant plea for God-fearing, hardworking citizens to move to the Louisiana Territory and settle the French colony there. Problem was, no one wanted to go. Not only was the voyage arduous—and oftentimes deadly—but word had been coming back to France that the Louisiana Territory was nothing but a swampy wasteland, a mosquito-infested pit of muck and mire.

"Enough about the New World. Tell us about the gold!" one man shouted, causing others around him to cheer.

M. Law, a wiry fellow with a patrician nose and a long powdered wig, peered in the direction of the catcall and raised his hand.

"Very well, my good fellow," Law cried. "The gold it is."

To cheers, Law walked toward the far side of the dais, and as he went Jacques saw for the first time that the trunk was there—sitting right *there*— up on the stage! Jacques said a quick prayer that whatever was about to happen would not be irrevocable, that the mistake made this morning in retrieving the wrong trunk could still be fixed without causing all sorts of very public problems.

As if in answer to that prayer, Law continued past the trunk, coming instead to a stop in front of a table that had been set up nearby. It was covered in a cloth, and as the crowd watched with great interest, Law bent down and pulled out from under the cloth three items, one by one, and set them on the table. First was a shiny gold platter, then a heavy gold candlestick, and finally a delicate gold medallion.

At the sight of all of that finery, the crowd began to murmur among themselves.

"Ladies and Gentlemen, let us be frank," Law said, crossing back to the center of the stage as the murmurs died down. "It is my understanding that rumors have been flying around town for several weeks, rumors that the royal goldsmiths have been carefully crafting two hundred fleur-de-lis statuettes, each one fashioned from solid gold. As you know, the fleur-de-lis is the very symbol of France and her monarchy, and as such is not a symbol to be taken lightly. Here to address this issue of these rumors is the royal goldsmith himself. I have invited him here today so that he may confirm or deny said rumors, for the record. Monsier?"

The crowd clapped politely as the king's goldsmith stepped forward, holding a polished wooden box and looking every bit as regal as the honor his high office bestowed.

"As the royal goldsmith," he said in a voice much softer than Law's but every bit as solemn, "I am here to state, unequivocally, that my department was recently commissioned to create a number of identical, solid gold fleur-de-lis statuettes, each based on my original design, at the request of John Law."

"And where did you obtain the gold to create these statuettes?" Law asked him.

"The gold was obtained as new from the Louisiana Territory and extracted from its ore, by amalgamation, under my direct supervision."

"And the quality of the gold derived from this ore? Was it sufficient?"

"Yes, sir. The product given to us for this job, once assayed, ended up being as fine as the finest gold from the Spanish territories in the New World."

That earned another murmur from the crowd. Now that the top goldsmith in the entire country had just publicly confirmed that gold was being mined in the Louisiana Territory, M. Law's claims to that very fact were given sudden validity. In an attempt to induce Parisians to become colonists, Law had already been circulating brochures and posters to that effect. Papa was skeptical, but M. Law's literature claimed that when walking down a wooded path in the New World, one could simply bend over and scoop up fistfuls of gold and diamonds from the ground.

"And this project concluded satisfactorily?" Law asked.

"Indeed it did, monsieur."

"So, just to reiterate, you can confirm the rumors that two hundred gold statuettes were recently created right here in Paris?"

"No, sir. I cannot."

Jacques sat forward, listening intently to what might come next.

"Why is that?" Law asked, looking out at the crowd with such exaggerated confusion that Jacques realized this exchange was preplanned.

"Because we did not make two hundred, sir. We made two hundred... and one."

With that, the royal goldsmith lifted up the box that he had been holding in his hands and presented it to M. Law. Law took it from him in delight, tilted it at an angle for all to see, and slowly opened the lid.

There, nestled among rich blue protective fabric, lay a single fleur-de-lis statuette, an exact duplicate of the ones Jacques and Papa had been making for the past month.

The crowd went insane. Though the statuette was small and decoratively austere, this was the item they had all been waiting for, the one that had brought them here today.

"How do we win it?"

"Who gets it?"

"Am I qualified?"

Voices called out from the crowd, but Law refused to continue until order had been restored. At last, as the din dropped back down, he held up one hand and spoke.

"Monsieur, on behalf of the good citizens of Paris, I thank you for your honesty here today, your fine design, and your impeccable workmanship."

As the man bowed to M. Law and then to the audience, everyone clapped. Jacques was still incredibly confused as to what was about to unfold next, but at least now he knew whose molds he and Papa had been using to make the statuettes. They had been created by none other than the royal goldsmith himself, who was just now crossing to the back of the stage to sit in one of a row of chairs waiting there.

Law took the statuette from its box and held it high over his head, to the delight of the crowd.

"Would you like one of these little things too?" he teased.

The people went crazy, whistling and cheering and stomping their feet.

"You can have one," Law continued. "In fact, *two hundred* of you can *each* have one—though, if you don't mind, I plan to keep this extra one myself, as a commemorative of this grand and glorious day."

Everyone laughed and cheered.

"So how do *you* get one?" Law asked, looking around at the people who paid rapt attention as they waited for the man to answer his own question. "My dear friends, listen carefully, and I will tell you exactly how."

EIGHTEEN

Sometimes in life there are moments so profoundly shocking or disturbing or frightening—moments where life and death intersect in the most earth-shattering ways—that once those moments happen, nothing can ever be the same.

For me, seeing Sam was one of those moments.

Had you asked me, prior to then, to rate my mental health on a scale, I would have given myself a good score, despite my dysfunctional childhood. But after seeing what had been done to Sam, after knowing that what had been done to him might have somehow been caused by me or my family, I don't know that I didn't slip all the way off that scale for a while. If I had been alone when I found him, I would have run to him. As it was, Travis had to physically restrain me, though at the time I didn't understand why. I don't think I ever made a sound. I remembered wanting to vomit but not even daring to do that. I just stood there with Travis' arms wrapped tightly around me from behind, holding me in place as I tried to step closer, to crawl toward something, anything, that would turn back the clock and stop this from happening.

I remembered the sound of Travis' voice, his lips speaking softly at my ear, but I couldn't recall what he said. Maybe my soul briefly left me. All I know was that I wasn't even there in that room anymore. I was floating, sailing away, existing in some alternate reality, one where people you loved did not meet with violent ends.

On the floor near Sam's feet was a small triangle of blue gingham with a wisp of fluffy white fibers attached. I couldn't tear my eyes from that sight, because somewhere in my mind I knew what that gingham belonged to, knew that it was wrong, somehow, to be there, torn and on the floor. Just like the image of Sam was wrong, broken and in that chair.

I remember walking out of the apartment and wondering why Travis was wiping down the wall and the light switch. Once he pulled the door shut, again he used the tail of his T-shirt to wipe off the doorknob. I couldn't understand why.

I remember walking down the steps and out of the courtyard with his arm around me, firmly holding me up at the waist. His hold was strong and warm and I lost myself in it. Somehow foot stepped ahead of foot, over and over, until eventually we were inside the truck.

I closed my eyes to the assault of headlights and car sounds and jazz music blaring from somewhere nearby. Leaning against the cold vinyl of the door, I went to sleep, an odd thing for a normal person to do, considering the situation. But I wasn't normal anymore. I had had my moment, the one that changed everything, irrevocably forever.

I don't know how long I slept.

When I awoke, it was to realize that I was being carried. At first I thought I was floating magically through the air, but then I realized that an arm was around my back and another under my knees and that the side of my face was pressed against the broad, muscular expanse of a man's chest. Somewhere in the deep recesses of my brain, I wondered if I was being kidnapped, if I was going to be tortured now. I was still wondering that as I fell asleep again.

The next time I awoke, there were voices nearby, and I had a feeling they were talking about me. I tried to tell them I was awake, but before I could even do that, I had fallen asleep again.

The next time I woke up, it was morning. I didn't know where I was, but I didn't have the energy to try to figure it out. Echoes of a different morning, one that had come before, bounced around in my brain: ringing phone, pounding door, dead man on the couch. This time, at least no phone rang. No one came and carted me off to jail. No one seemed to be here at all.

I dozed for a while, waking now and then, and each time I did I felt a little more back to earth, a little more me again. At one point I wondered if I had had a nervous breakdown. Then I wondered if that term was even used anymore. Whatever it was, I knew that I had stood at the edge of an abyss—and, for a while at least, I had fallen in. Years ago, a girl from school maintained in debate that there was a bit of madness in all of us. I didn't believe her then.

I believed her now.

My final awakening was markedly different than the ones that had come before. This time, when I came to consciousness, I simply knew certain things again. I knew that Travis and I had gone into Sam's apartment and found him dead. I didn't know where I was now, but I knew who I was, and that was more important anyway.

Sitting up in the bed, I looked around, wondering how many more times I would have to awaken in strange places with no real knowledge of where I was and how I had come there. The room I was in was small and rustic. The only furniture was the single bed I had been sleeping on and a small wooden bedside table holding a lamp, a cup of water, and a Bible. The sheets were crisp and white, and with a jolt I realized I wasn't in my clothes anymore. I was in a light cotton nightgown, with buttons down the front and sleeves gathered at the wrists. Someone had changed my clothes.

I swung my legs over the side of the bed and carefully attempted to stand. The room had one window and I walked to it now, my feet cold against the polished wood floor. At the window, I first peered through the sheer white curtains to see what looked like woods and trees outside. There didn't seem to be any people out there, so I reached up and pulled aside the sheers for a better view.

From what I could tell, I was in a cabin in the woods, though it wasn't completely isolated because I could make out other rooflines among the trees. In the distance was the telltale sparkle of a body of water.

Needing to use the restroom, I opened one of the doors, only to find myself looking into an empty closet. Closing that one, I crossed the room to the other door and swung it open. That led to a second room, one that was furnished as simply as the first, with a table and chair under the front window and the second, more cushioned chair in the corner next to another small table with only a lamp and a Bible. Besides a door that obviously led to the outside, there was one other door which I hoped was the bathroom and not another closet.

I was about to open it and look when the door swung open and a woman stepped out, causing us both to jump. Before I could react any further, her face lit up in a smile.

"You're awake," she said in a drawl so soft and melodic it was almost like a song. "How are you feeling, honey?"

She looked to be in her forties, with sparkling green eyes and graying hair pulled into a soft braid on the back of her head.

"Okay, I think."

"Do you know what day this is?"

"It should be Wednesday," I said, clearing my scratchy throat. "Is it?"

"Yes. You've been here since last night."

"Where am I?"

"I'll let Travis explain that. Let me go get him."

Travis. So at least I hadn't been kidnapped.

"Can you point me to a restroom?"

The woman gestured to the door she had just come out of, saying she had been putting a change of clothes, a towel, and some toiletries in there for me.

"Why don't you shower and dress, and I'll get you some breakfast and find Travis. He's been very worried about you. He'll want to know you're all right."

I hesitated, afraid to ask the question that was burning to come out. Finally, I knew I had no choice.

"This isn't...this isn't a mental hospital, is it?"

The woman smiled, a melodic chuckle escaping her lips.

"No, dear. It's a retreat center. Though sometimes in the summer when the junior campers come, I'm tempted to seek out a mental hospital for myself."

With great relief I thanked her and went into the bathroom as she headed out the front door.

The shower helped bring me further to life. Standing under the faucet, I let the hot water pound my back and shoulders, working off some of the tension, though washing away none of the grief. When I was finished, I pulled on a pair of jeans that were about the size of the woman I had just met and had to be belted at the waist. Given that they were about six inches too short, I simply rolled up the cuffs and turned them into capris. The shirt was a simple cotton button-down in a blue-and-green plaid. Black flip-flops that fit my feet well enough completed the outfit. Using the handful of toiletries there, I was able to brush my teeth, comb out my hair, and dab a little Vaseline on my lips. There was no other makeup, nor were there any hair products or tools, so I simply stepped back to get a look at myself in the mirror, knowing this was the best it was going to get.

Studying my image, I was grateful for my naturally rosy lips and dark eyelashes that helped pull off my lack of makeup. Although I always wore my long hair straightened and sleek, already it was starting to dry into soft waves. Oh, well. In a way, it was a relief having no choice but to forgo my usual morning routine and just be who I was.

After emerging from the bathroom, I opened the door and stepped outside. It was a beautiful day, with birds chirping and somewhere in the distance church bells ringing. Counting the dings, I discovered it was 11:00 a.m. I thought I could hear voices, so I walked around the side of the little cabin to find Travis and another man sitting at a table in the shade. Both of them stood when they saw me, a Southern gesture of good manners that I always appreciated. The man sat back down, but Travis came over to me and surprised me by giving me a big hug and asking me if I was okay.

"You could probably answer that better than I could. I don't remember much, just the parts I wish I didn't remember."

Travis nodded and solemnly led me to the table, introducing me to the man as a friend and inviting me to sit. A covered plate was waiting there, and when I removed the lid it was to see scrambled eggs, bacon, and a fruit cup. I wasn't very hungry, but I didn't want to be rude, so I took a bite of the bacon, picked at the eggs, and focused on the mixed fruit. As I sat there eating, I could tell both men were sort of sizing me up, trying to figure out if I was stable enough now for normal, intelligent conversation. Finally, I put down my fork, looked from one to the other, and told them I wasn't nuts, I wasn't out of my head, and I wasn't made of glass so they needn't be afraid I might break.

Both men laughed and visibly relaxed. I wasn't sure how much to say in front of the man, but he didn't seem to be going anywhere and there was a lot I wanted to know. I decided to follow Travis' lead, and right now they weren't talking about anything more important than a boat engine.

"You folks have a lot of talking to do, I'm sure," the man said finally, rising from the table. "Before I go, may I pray for you, Chloe?"

I looked up, a little startled. Though I didn't feel like praying, it seemed rude to refuse. I nodded, and I was surprised again when the man placed a hand on the top of my head before closing his eyes and speaking to God on my behalf.

He started his prayer by asking for healing and hope at this time of despair, as well as guidance, wisdom, and truth. He continued on from there, but my mind hung onto that one word: truth. *Yes, God, if You are listening, please help me find the truth.*

The man's hand stayed on my head through the whole prayer, and though it was a weird sensation, it felt good somehow, as if a deep warmth was running through his hand into me. Once he reached his "amen," he gave me a final pat and took his hand away, offering to return my plate to the kitchen. I thanked him, and after he was gone, I turned and looked at Travis, suddenly feeling very shy. We had been through a lot together since first seeing each other yesterday afternoon, yet in most ways we hardly knew each other at all.

"Ordinarily," I said, "I would make some stupid joke about now, something to help make light of the vulnerable and embarrassing position I find myself in. But not one witty comment springs to mind."

Before he replied, Travis reached out and placed a wide, warm hand on top of mine.

"Yeah, I know what you mean, *cher.* I tend to make jokes at times like these too. But who are we kidding? There aren't times like this. There's never been a time like this, not in my experience. I've never seen anything like that, and I only knew Sam as a friend. I didn't love him like you did. I didn't think of him as a second father."

"Travis—"

"No, just let me say this. Please don't be embarrassed, and please don't feel vulnerable. We may not know each other very well, Chloe, but our families go way back. Despite whatever rift has divided your father and my grandfather, I think they would both be glad to know that in this horrible time at least we have each other."

I appreciated Travis' sentiments, and I decided he was right about not being embarrassed. Maybe I had gone off the deep end, but I was suddenly grateful that he had been the one who was there when it happened. I told him so now. With a sweet smile, Travis squeezed my hand and then let go, and as he pulled his away, I found myself wishing he wouldn't. Meeting his eyes, I couldn't help thinking how handsome he looked. Gone was the baseball cap he'd been wearing last night, and his freshly shampooed hair looked far less shaggy without it. In fact, I decided, I really liked the length of his cut and thought it suited him well.

"So where are we, Travis, and what are doing here? Are we in hiding?"

He replied that we weren't here so much to hide as to regroup.

"By regroup, do you mean verify my sanity? I think I'm okay now."

"Good, because we have a lot to do."

I looked out at the water through the trees. I had thought it was a lake, but from this vantage point I realized it was a river. A lazy, beautiful, slow-moving river.

"Please tell me what happened. I don't remember much beyond walking into Sam's apartment and seeing him there."

According to Travis, my first instinct had been to run toward the body. To keep me from doing so, he had been forced to physically restrain me. There was no question that Sam was dead, he said, so there was nothing we could do to help. Travis explained that he had asked me several times if I thought we should call the police or simply leave and let someone else be the one to find the scene and call it in. Considering that I had already been framed for one murder, his inclination was that we should go.

"But I know you, Chloe. I know that you like to play by the rules. That's why I kept asking. When you wouldn't answer me, I realized that you were overcome with shock, so I had to make a decision for us. You were moaning a little, but otherwise you were pretty docile. With my arms around you, I was able to get you all the way back to the truck, but then once we got inside you really scared me by just laying your head down and going to sleep. Even when you were awake, it was like you weren't there. I wasn't sure what to do."

"So you brought us here, to a retreat center?"

"I knew it wasn't open for the season yet and would be pretty deserted. The owners are good people, old youth directors of mine. I jus' told them that a friend and I had run into a little trouble and needed a place to come where we could get some rest and figure out what to do next, but that they had to keep this to themselves. They said come on down. By the time we got here, they had made up one of the cabins for you and set up the sofa bed in the house for me. God bless 'em, they haven't asked me for any details about what's going on."

"I assume you weren't the one who changed me into a nightgown?"

His face colored, and I was surprised how easily my words had made him blush.

"No, *cher*, that was not I."

I took a deep breath, looking around at the beautiful terrain that surrounded me, the oak trees dripping with Spanish moss, the birds twittering in the trees, the water sparkling in the distance. Truly, I would have loved nothing more than to stay here and soak it in for days. But there was much to be done, many questions still to be answered.

"Has the...body...been discovered yet?"

"Not that I know of. I entered some media alerts on my phone, so if any relevant news stories come out—anything at all that contains words like Sam, Samuel, Underwood, Ledet's, or Chloe—I'll know about it. I've received a couple of texts, but they were all false alarms."

"How about my father? Is he still alive?"

"Yeah, but still in a coma. You weren't going to make it to the hospital last night, and I didn't want your mama to worry 'bout you, so I texted her on your phone, pretending I was you. Hope that's okay."

He pulled my cell phone from his shirt pocket and slid it across to me. Curious, I read through their exchange of text messages, which had begun last night but had continued on through the morning:

11:30 pm—*Hi, cell reception not good so am texting instead. Hope you get this message. Something came up and I won't get there tonight. Didn't want you to worry. Keep me posted. I'll be in touch.*

11:34 pm—*Something came up? Better be something important! Your father is still in a coma.*

8:02 am—*How's Dad this morning?*

8:15 am—*Doctor says vital signs stronger. Coma or not, might get out of ICU soon.*

8:17 am—*Thanks. Keep me posted.*

8:25 am—*Can't take another night on this couch. Need a shower. Soon as you get here am going to take a break, go home, and get cleaned up.*

8:30 am—*Might not get there soon. Don't wait on me.*

9:15 am—*Good news! Doctor said vitals stable. Will move to regular room in a few hours. Still in coma, though. Are you coming?*

9:17 am—*Not yet. If you leave hospital, make sure you take bodyguard with you and that Dad has one too.*

9:19 am—*One what?*

9:22 am—*Bodyguard. One for you, one for him.*

9:25 am—*Oh, good idea. Will hire second bodyguard. Where are you?*

9:31 am—*Hard to explain. Keep texting for now. Love you.*

9:45 am—*Get here soon as you can. Am so bored!!!*

The messages ended there.

"Gee, Travis, you're a better daughter than I am. I just hope she wasn't tipped off by the 'love you.'"

"You don't tell your mother you love her?"

"Not really. Please note she didn't respond in kind." I clicked out of the saved texts, glad to know at least that my father was now stable enough to be moved to a regular room, even if he was still unconscious. "Thanks for being so resourceful. That was a nice thing to do, considering the circumstances."

"I'm just glad we could charge your phone in my car. I noticed you had some voice mail too, but I didn't feel right going through that."

While Travis waited, I checked the messages, all three of which were from Jenny. The first two calls were about the lawyer, asking if he worked out, how the bail hearing had gone, etc. In the third call, she said that so far she had seen one small mention on the TV news about my father's hunting accident, but that otherwise there had been nothing about me or the fact that I had been arrested, at least not that she had seen, and there had been no calls from the media.

That was a relief. Hanging up, I decided I would get back to her later. Right now, I had some thinking to do. At this point, as badly as I wanted to go see my father, I thought it was more important to figure out who shot him, who drugged and killed Kevin, who drugged and framed me, and who tortured and killed Sam. Sadly, the list was growing longer with each passing day. Given that my dad was still in his coma, my visiting him wouldn't necessarily make any difference to him anyway, though it would have made me feel better.

"You sure you're okay, *cher*?"

I looked at Travis and saw the concern that wrinkled his brow.

"I don't think I'll ever really be okay again," I said honestly. "But I'll survive. And I will find out who's behind all of this if it's the very last thing I do."

"Correction, *cher*. We."

"We?"

"*We* will find out who's behind all of this. Together."

"No, Travis—"

"*Ain*, don't forget that I saw Sam's body too. I fled the scene of a crime, in the company of an accused murderer, no less. I'm also the one who worked on your father's phone message at the request of Sam, who is now dead. Given all that, I'd say I'm as mixed up in this as you are."

I wanted to object, to tell him that it was too dangerous, that Chloe Ledet didn't need anyone to fight her battles for her. But the truth was, I needed his help.

The truth was, I couldn't even bear the thought of trying to do this alone.

NINETEEN

FRANCE, 1719
JACQUES

From his perch on the stone wall, Jacques watched the figure of John Law on the stage, holding up the golden fleur-de-lis statuette and promising to tell the people how they could qualify to get one for themselves.

"But before I tell you," Law said, "I want to bring up one more expert, a master assayer from the Goldsmiths Division of the Merchants Guild. Not to question the testimony of the royal goldsmith, but simply to make sure that everyone here understands the purity and value of this fantastic object d'art, the assayer will now inspect this statuette and authenticate it for us. Monsieur?"

Ignoring the catcalls of those audience members who were running out of patience, the well-dressed assayer strode to the center of the stage. As he did, Jacques recognized him from his dealings with the guild, a man he and Papa secretly referred to as "Monsieur Pomp." Papa didn't like the man much, as he felt he was all show and no substance, a flatterer of kings who was always last to do the quiet, thankless jobs of the guild but first in line to hold up a corner of the royal robes during processionals.

Now Jacques watched as M. Pomp reached into his pocket with his right hand, and with a great flourish pulled out a touchstone. After holding the small black chunk of basalt up in the air for all to see, he stepped closer to M. Law and slowly rubbed the touchstone back and forth over the side of the statuette. Jacques knew that this action would cause a telltale, temporary metallic streak to appear, a sign of pure gold.

Sure enough, after pulling his hand away and taking a look, the assayer nodded and smiled.

"The mark of the touchstone indeed proves that this is gold," he announced to the crowd in his high-pitched, nasal voice as M. Law turned the statuette toward the people so that all could view it. They cheered loudly, though Jacques doubted that more than a few of them could even see the mark from where they stood. He couldn't, and he knew what he was looking for. As the cheer died down, the assayer nodded at M. Law and slid the touchstone into his pocket. "Nevertheless, I shall now attempt a second test to be absolutely sure, that of the application of nitric acid to the surface."

That earned another soft murmur from the crowd.

"If an item is not gold," he continued, obviously relishing the attention, "then one drop of nitric acid will turn it green, black, or brown, depending on the alloys used."

To demonstrate, he walked over to the table where the three gold items had been waiting, forgotten, ever since Law first pulled them out from under the table and put them there. Standing behind the table now, the assayer pulled a small brown bottle from his pocket.

He slowly removed the thin glass stopper from the top of the bottle and held it over the shiny golden platter. After a moment, a slight flick of his wrist allowed one tiny drop of nitric acid to fall onto the platter's surface. Once the drop hit its mark, he quickly tilted the platter upward, and immediately the rolling drip created a streak of green down the shiny surface. As the crowd gasped at this bit of magic, Jacques shook his head, marveling at the sheer theatricality of the presentation. He had watched assayers do this test hundreds of times, but always in the quiet of the mint or the workshop, never for the delight of a crowd.

"Now, if the product is gold but is of a quality between eight and thirteen carats, then a drop of the acid will create a slight tarnish or discoloration in the surface."

Taking a step sideways, M. Pomp inverted the candlestick, held up the brown bottle, and again pulled out the stopper to allow another small drop to fall on its surface. The acid hit its mark, and after a moment, he nodded and then held out the candlestick for all to see.

"The tarnish is faint, but it is there. By my practiced eye, I would say this candlestick is approximately ten to eleven carats. That's still gold, of course, but not of the highest standard."

He displayed the candlestick with its tarnished spot for a long moment, and then he put it down and moved to the medallion.

"If gold be pure," the assayer declared dramatically as his eyes scanned the eager crowd, "then a drop of nitric acid will cause no discoloration nor tarnish at all. This is the surest test for purity."

Correction, Jacques thought. *This is the surest test that you can do in front of a crowd, with visible results.* There were other, more accurate tests to be had, but they involved furnaces and crucibles and the like—all things that could not logically be employed here on the stage at Les Halles.

Slowly, the assayer pulled out the stopper, held it over the medallion, and allowed the acid to drip down on the bulging curve of the golden surface. As predicted, it had no effect whatsoever.

"As you can see, the metal of this medallion does not respond to the acid in any way. That's because this medallion is made of twenty-four carat gold."

People nodded and whispered to each other, as if to say, *Yes, I thought so. I thought it looked like twenty-four carat.* Soon they returned their attention to the stage where the assayer was rejoining M. Law and his statuette at the center.

"I will now conduct this same test on the fleur-de-lis statuette."

The crowd seem to hold its collective breath. They all watched and waited until one tiny drop of nitric acid fell from the glass tip onto the gold surface. The assayer, obviously more for dramatic effect than the actual necessity, paused for a long moment, and in that moment the people who watched him remained still and silent, the suspense nearly unbearable. Finally, the assayer nodded at John Law, who took a look himself and then held up the unblemished statuette for all to see.

"As predicted, the nitric acid has had no effect," M. Pomp announced to the crowd. "This test, along with confirmation of the touchstone, proves conclusively that these statuettes were created from gold of a quality greater than thirteen carats. I would stake my reputation on it as an assayer of His Royal Highness Louis XV, and his regent, the duc d'Orleans."

The crowd went wild. As they clapped and cheered the assayer moved to the back of the stage to sit by the others, and Jacques could only shake his head, wondering what all of this drama was leading them to.

He was soon to find out.

The crowd now held firmly in the palm of his hand, Law walked to the trunk and stood directly behind it. By that point, Jacques was so caught up in the spectacle of it all that he even forgot to feel nauseous.

"Ladies and Gentlemen," Law said solemnly once the crowd had quieted down, "as founder of La Banque General and director of the Compagne des Indes, I would like to make the following offer to the sons and daughters of France. Right now as we speak, at the port in La Rochelle awaits a new ship, an ocean-worthy vessel which has been christened *Beau Séjour*. Aside from crew, *Beau Séjour* has room for exactly two hundred passengers."

Murmurs began among those in the crowd, angry murmurs, as if they knew what the man was about to say next.

"I am here to tell you that the two hundred people who choose to take passage to the New World on that ship—"

Law was interrupted by angry calls from the crowd, but he raised his voice and continued.

"Whoever they are, those two hundred who choose to take passage and subsequently remain in the Louisiana Territory for exactly three years may at the end of those three years present themselves to my agent, Monsieur Pierre Freneau, who will be escorting the gold all the way to New Orleans and guarding it there. In three years, upon presenting themselves to M. Freneau, each of those two hundred people will be given their very own solid gold fleur-de-lis statuette. It will be theirs to keep, either to melt down and use as a financial reward, or saved intact as a priceless memorial of their homeland, a gift of the Compagne des Indes."

At that, the crowd was about to explode in fury, angered at this sudden turn for the worse, this cheap attempt, yet again, to lure them to sign up as colonists. Obviously expecting this reaction, however, M. Law thwarted it at that very moment by reaching down and dramatically flinging open the lid of the massive trunk.

There, sparkling brilliantly in the afternoon sunlight, were the two hundred statuettes, gleaming in all their glory. As if one person, the crowd's angry yells were suddenly swallowed up in gasps and silence.

Their anger was understandable, but the sight of that gleaming mountain of finely polished gold was utterly breathtaking. No wonder they didn't know how to react.

"As soon as we are finished here," John Law said as he reached down behind the trunk and lifted up a massive padlock, "I will close and lock this trunk and allow it to be escorted by M. Freneau and the palace guards and anyone else who wants to follow along all the way to La Rochelle. There, it will be loaded on the ship and put under guard. That guard will remain until the ship sails two days from now."

Law strode to the very front of the dais and gestured toward a man who was sitting directly in front of it, down on the ground level, at a small table that held a long sheet of paper, a bottle of ink, and a pen.

"Citizens of France," Law said earnestly to the crowd in a softer voice, both arms raised high for his final plea, "if you want to be among the lucky two hundred, all you need to do is line up here at this table and in your turn sign your name or place your mark on the ship's roster. A new world ripe with opportunity wants you. A crown eager for settlers salutes you. Best of all, a priceless gold treasure awaits you. Thank you for your attention, and may God bless you all. Good day."

With that, Law turned and strode to the back of the stage, signaling the end of the big event. As the other men on the stage stood to meet him and converse quietly among themselves, it seemed to Jacques that the crowd was stunned, unsure of what to do or how to react. There were a few smatterings of applause, but mostly people just looked at each other, talked among themselves, and considered the opportunity that had been placed before them.

In that moment, as the crowd stretched and shifted to get a better look at the gold and the first few braves souls presented themselves to the man at the table, Jacques finally understood what was going on, what had been going on since the day his father had first received his commission from the palace. Reaching into his pocket, Jacques fingered the letter Papa had written and sealed, the letter whose delivery had nearly killed Jacques in his race to get to this forum on time. Now that he knew what he knew, Jacques had a sick, dark feeling that he could not hide behind the anonymity of a letter after all.

He would have to explain what had happened in person.

TWENTY

Travis and I needed to map out a plan.

First, I realized, I was going to have to tell him about the treasure. As I launched into the tale, I could see that he was as dumbfounded as I had been when Kevin had explained it to me. Though half of that treasure belonged to Travis' grandfather, Travis had no idea that it existed. He said that his grandparents' house—the one the sale of the gold had paid for back in the fifties—had been nice but nothing special.

Travis explained that his grandparents had never been the type of people to care much about money anyway. They valued their faith, their family, their health, and their heritage. Money came far down the list.

What I hated to bring up but felt like I should was the possibility that his grandfather had met with some foul play just as my father and Kevin and Sam and I had. As far as we knew, Alphonse Naquin was still out of touch and unaccounted for, and though Travis said it was the old man's usual pattern to simply disappear on a fishing trip for a while, he agreed that there was a slight chance that someone had gotten to his grandfather in some way too.

"Well, then, you might also want to think about this," I added. "If my father told my mother she was in danger, isn't there a chance that your grandmother could be in danger too? Whoever wants the treasure may have started with the two men, but from my father's message it sounds like they might then move on to the wives."

Travis' eyebrows rose high on his face as he considered that possibility for the first time.

"I need to make a call," he said, standing up and pulling his iPhone from his pocket. "Don't worry, I won't say anything about the treasure or Sam or where we are now. I just need to get my *grandmere* somewhere safe."

He began pacing as soon as he finished dialing, and I thought I should give him some privacy. Standing and stretching my legs, I decided to stroll closer to the water. Oddly enough, the earth was hilly here, despite the fact that this part of Louisiana was mostly flat for miles around. Moving down the gentle slope toward the water, I marveled at the geological phenomenon that could have caused an anomaly like this, rolling hills amidst the flatlands. Whatever caused it, it made for a beautiful piece of land.

Despite all of our personal turmoil, it was so peaceful here. My mind kept going back to the prayer Travis' friend had said on my behalf. Though I had been a part of corporate prayer numerous times, I think that was the first time in my life anyone had ever prayed specifically for me, with me. It had felt good, for some reason, and infinitely calming to my soul. Maybe, I decided, the man's intervention on my behalf had now cleared the way for me to go to God myself sometimes. Maybe now I wouldn't be that rude person just calling for a favor, but instead a friend of a friend, someone who had a right to show up and ask for something every now and then.

Then again, I realized, maybe that was the whole problem, that I was thinking about prayer specifically as a way to get something from God. I had heard enough sermons over the years to know that that wasn't all prayer was for. It was also for worship, confession, and intercession...things like that. Maybe instead of starting with "God, help me," I should try something less self-oriented.

Unfortunately, that would have to wait. Travis was calling my name, obviously finished with his phone calls. When I got back to him, he said everything had been taken care of. I had a feeling that with such a large family, there were plenty of big, strong Cajun relatives to take in *Grandmere* Minette and keep her safe, even if they didn't know why Travis wanted them to do so.

"So what's our next move?" he asked, returning his attention to the task at hand.

"I think we should take a closer look at my father's 'special recipe,' since that's what he told me to follow."

Travis retrieved the poem from under the seat of his truck, and we started by taking the frame apart. There was nothing inside that frame except the mat, the photo, and the poem itself. The "insurance policy" my dad had always told my mother to depend on was the poem and/or the photo themselves and not an actual document of some kind. We put the empty frame back in the truck, and just to play it safe, Travis ran and got the key to the office and we let ourselves in to make some photocopies. I put one copy in an envelope I addressed to myself, and another addressed to him. We also each kept a copy ourselves to use as a reference.

As for the original poem and photo, we decided to hide them in plain sight for now, creating a folder that looked like a camper's medical records and simply tucking it into one of the file cabinets of the retreat center's office. According to Travis, those files were never purged, hardly ever touched, and no one would notice. As a private joke, Travis suggested we name our fictitious camper Antoine Saenger, a lighthearted reference to the argument he and I had had last night. Thus labeled, we slipped the file marked "Saenger, Antoine" into the drawer between "Sabatino, Maria" and "Saia, Clovis."

After locking up behind us, Travis returned the key to his friends while I made my way back to our comfy little table beside the cabin and studied my copy of the poem. My father had sent the message that I was to "follow the recipe." Given that the recipe obviously led to the treasure, I thought I was safe to assume that that's what was at the center of all of this tragedy. Someone else wanted the treasure and was doing whatever they could to get to it. I explained all of that to Travis when he joined me there.

"If that's the case," he said, taking the seat across from me, "then why do you think you were framed for murder?"

"Because for some reason they must think I'll stop them, or I'll get to it first, or I'll somehow keep them from getting it themselves. They wanted me out of the way. The problem is, I never heard of the treasure before Monday, and I don't have a clue where it is."

"None at all?"

Feeling antsy, I stood and began pacing as we talked.

"Okay," I said, "my best guess—and this is just a hunch—is that it's hidden somewhere down in Paradise. After all, that's where it was found in the first place."

Looking at the poem, Travis began shaking his head.

"*Mais non, cher,* look at this last verse. It says, 'North and West you may search for things gone amiss.'"

"And?"

Travis put down the poem and looked at me.

"If New Orleans or even Ledet's is his starting point, Paradise isn't north and west. It's *south* and west."

"Okay, so maybe he means the northwest corner of Paradise. Or north and west of the dock there. Or north and west of some sort of other landmark."

"Maybe," Travis said doubtfully, still studying the poem.

"In any event, what I'm trying to say is, there are only a handful of people who even know that the treasure exists: my father, your grandfather, their old buddy Conrad Zahn, their old lawyer Ruben Peralta, Sam Underwood, and one other investor, though I don't know who that was. Kevin never said. Anyway, when Ruben died and Kevin took over his father's practice, he found out about all of this. Until Kevin filled me in on Monday night, no one else knew, period. Of course, now I've told you."

"So not counting you and me, that makes seven people total who have known about the treasure," Travis said, holding up seven fingers and then counting them off as he continued, "but of those seven, Ruben passed away a while back, Kevin and Sam were murdered this week, your father was shot and is in a coma, and my grandfather is unaccounted for and may or may not have met with foul play."

"Which leaves us with two people still standing who know about the treasure: Conrad Zahn and the other investor."

"Whoever he was."

"Right. Those are the two people we need to see, Travis," I said, placing my hands down on the table and leaning forward. "This secret has been kept for fifty-eight years. If something slipped out now, it had to have slipped from one of the men in this inner circle. They might be able to shed some light on things."

"Of course, it could be that one of these two guys is the killer himself. Maybe this violence is going to continue until there's only one left, and all he'll have to do is grab the treasure and walk away with it."

"*If* he can find it, that is. Remember, no one knows where it is except for my dad and your grandfather. From what I can tell of this poem, each man has some sort of clue, but it takes all of the clues, put together, to get to that treasure." I pointed to the second-to-last verse. "It says it right here: 'Divided among those named in this poem, I give each a quantity that's theirs alone. Together they come to solve this rhyme, the treasure they only together can find.'"

"Like a treasure map."

"Right. The thing is, I'm far less interested in finding the treasure than I am in finding the person or people who are after that treasure—the ones who keep leaving bodies in their wake. Still, I have a feeling that we should look for both at the same time."

"Both?"

"The killer *and* the treasure. The sooner we can find that treasure and take it public, the sooner we foil the killer and remove the danger. Our mission is to find the killer or at the very least find the treasure. Either way, if that's really what this whole thing is all about, once we do that the killing will stop."

Thus, with the big picture in mind, Travis and I went through the poem, line by line. Decoding the first verse was simple:

> *There is a place of great repast,*
> *Where promises and friendships last.*
> *Where patrons dine on meals of kings,*
> *And Quarter boys can live their dreams.*

The "place of great repast" in the first line was Ledet's restaurant. The

"Quarter boys" in the last line were my father and Sam, who had grown up next door to each other in the French Quarter. Both of them had found jobs in the restaurant industry at a very young age and continued to stay with it in one capacity or other. For many years, my dad dreamed of owning his own restaurant, and he always promised Sam that once he did, Sam would be his manager and right-hand man.

Given what we knew, the meaning of the next verse was also quite clear:

> Yet not alone do I succeed,
> But with your help in word and deed.
> And so I give you at this time,
> Security inside a rhyme.

Clearly, these were references to the financial deal that Ruben Peralta had arranged between my father and the investors. We decided "Security inside a rhyme" was just another way of saying, "I'm using the treasure that this poem leads to as collateral for your loans."

Thus, the next verse also made sense:

> Here in the City Care Forgot
> We'll make a gumbo in a pot.
> So grab your spices from the shelf.
> We start with Chef Ledet himself

To keep the whereabouts of the treasure's location a secret, the poem had been written in the pretense of a recipe for gumbo when what it really was, was a recipe for finding the treasure. As for the first line, New Orleans was often called the City That Care Forgot.

I didn't quite get why my father had included the next verse:

> In gumbo, always make a roux,
> 4T oil heated through.
> Then add 5T of flour, white,
> Stirred over heat till the color's right.

I expressed my confusion on this one to Travis.

"That *is* how you start a gumbo," Travis said. "Maybe he had to put this part in there just to make the poem seem realistic, like it really was just a recipe for gumbo."

"Okay," I said, skimming the rest, "so then why is this the only ingredient for which he gives a precise measurement? Four tablespoons oil, five tablespoons flour. Those numbers must be important somehow."

"Maybe."

"What do you think he means by 'till the color's right'?"

"The color is the most important part of a roux, *cher*. Don't you know how to cook gumbo?"

I shrugged, not explaining about my one disastrous experience at gumbo when I was sixteen years old. My father had taken a rare day off from work and we were both at home, so in yet another desperate attempt to get his attention, I had had the brilliant idea of asking him to teach me how to cook.

Much to my delight, he was pleased with my request at first, eagerly gathering the ingredients from the kitchen cabinets and describing for me the origins of gumbo and the infinite number of variations that people had managed to create over the years. His version started with a roux and ended with filé, he said, though many folks believed you didn't need filé if you had a roux.

He prattled on and on, and though I didn't care much about the specifics, I remember beaming in the glow of my father's undivided attention. With him watching over my shoulder, I stood at the stove and stirred the flour into the oil exactly as he directed.

"The trick is to keep stirring and stirring and watching and watching as it changes colors," he said.

Sure enough, the longer I stood there and stirred, the mixture began to change from a light brown he called "béchamel sauce" to a darker one he deemed "sauce piquant." As it slowly grew even darker, I thought the mixture might burn, but he assured me that as long as I kept stirring we could push it to the very limits, to that precise dark brown moment that waited between "not quite enough" and "disaster."

Unfortunately, the phone rang as we were coming into the home stretch. He answered it, motioning for me to keep stirring. My arm was getting tired, though, so when he ducked around the corner to talk, I took a moment to shake out my arm and switch the spoon to my other hand. That one didn't work as well for stirring, though, so I switched back, accidentally dropping the spoon in the process.

Mortified, I wiped up the globby mess from the front of the stove and the floor as quickly as I could, knowing that that sort of clutziness in Ledet's could get a person fired. Hiding the dirty paper towels in the trash and the spoon in the sink, I ran to get a new, clean spoon from the drawer. I made it back to the stove, spoon in hand, just before my father hung up the phone and returned to the room.

I thought I had gotten away with it, but the moment he came around the corner, he screamed. Apparently, in the few seconds it had taken me to clean up my mess, my lack of stirring had caused the roux to burn.

My father went into a rage so extreme that one would have thought I had burned the house down. He took over then, pushing me away from the smoking pan as he banged and clanged and continued to yell. By the time his tirade had run his course, I was still there in a corner of the kitchen, determined to make things right.

"Can we still make gumbo, Daddy?" I asked softly, trying not to cry.

At that, he turned to me and gave me his most withering glare.

"You burned the roux, Chloe. There's no going any further when you burn a roux."

All these years later, I could still feel the sting of that moment, of standing there alone after he left, our happy time together having gone up in smoke.

"I know how gumbo is made," I said now to Travis. "I just wonder if there's some significance to the mention of color here."

Unsure, we moved on to the next stanza:

> *For the one who loves chou and chouchou,*
> *I couldn't have done it without you,*
> *I add to the roux your trinity,*
> *First learned in your vicinity.*

That one made no sense to me whatsoever, but Travis laughed, saying this one was about his grandfather. Apparently, Alphonse Naquin's favorite song was an old Cajun tune called "Chou and Chouchou."

"'I love my chou and my chouchou too. Give me both and be gone wit' you,'" Travis sang in a surprisingly good voice.

"What does it mean?" I asked, smiling.

"*Chou* is 'cabbage' and *chouchou* is 'darling.' It's just a silly song, meaning 'All I need is some good food and the woman I love and I'll be happy.'"

"Does it mention religion? Down here, he refers to the trinity."

Travis shook his head, explaining that the "trinity" is what a lot of people in Louisiana call the three basic ingredients to almost every dish: onion, bell peppers, and celery. Obviously, those were the ingredients that my father had attributed to Alphonse, though he gave no specific amounts in the poem of how much to add.

Given all that, the last line, "learned in your vicinity," made sense. Much of what my father knew about Cajun cooking he had first learned from Alphonse and his family down in Paradise.

The next verse stumped Travis but was clear to me:

> For the Bürgermeister, a man of means,
> Who learned to fight in old Orleans,
> I add some andouille sliced fine as can be
> 'Cause you Allemands love your boucherie.

In Germany, a *Bürgermeister* was a form of public office, much like a mayor, I explained to Travis. Given that Conrad Zahn was of German heritage and was a politician, I felt sure this verse was describing him. I didn't know who or what he might have had to fight about, but again in the last line he is referred to as an "*Allemand*," or a German.

"Here's his ingredient," Travis added, pointing to the word *andouille*, which was a sausage made from lean pork and garlic. That was reinforced in the next line, because a *boucherie* was a sort of community pig butchering, one that resulted in various pork products, including pork sausage.

I paused, looking up at Travis.

"Pig butchering," I said, feeling something rise up in my stomach. "A person who likes to butcher pigs might have no problem torturing someone and then killing them. Like someone did to Sam."

Travis met my solemn gaze with his own.

"I hear you, *cher*. If we go talk to Conrad, we had better watch our step."

TWENTY-ONE

I didn't know how much more I could take. In the last forty-eight hours my father had been shot, I had been arrested for Kevin's murder, and Travis and I had discovered Sam's brutal death. I closed my eyes, and then I opened them when I felt Travis' warm hand covering mine again and giving it a comforting squeeze. I wasn't alone, and I knew the only way out of this situation was to go forward. Taking a deep breath, I smiled at him and then we moved on to the next stanza.

> *For king of the Sunday breakdown raids,*
> *Whose ancestors brought seeds in their braids,*
> *Professor of juré extraordinaire,*
> *I add fresh okra into the pot there.*

I had a feeling this one was for Sam, because I knew that "Sunday breakdown" was an old restaurant expression. When I was little, sometimes he would play restaurant with me, and he'd always order things like a "coal yard," which was a cup of black coffee, and a "flat car," which was a pork chop. If I remembered correctly, a "Sunday breakdown" was simply fried chicken and grits.

As for the okra, I knew that this vegetable had first been brought to America by enslaved Africans. I hadn't heard of seeds being smuggled in braids, but it was possible.

I didn't know what juré was, but Travis said that it was a form of music, one that had also come out of Louisiana's African American culture. Unlike zydeco or Cajun music, juré had no instruments. Instead, it involved clapping and singing, and the words formed a sort of testimony or truth, hence the name *juré*, which translated as "truth."

"Give me an example," I said.

Travis told me to clap with him, and then he began to sing in time. The words were Cajun French, but even though I didn't understand what he was saying, I loved the sound of it. A memory began to stir in my mind, and I could see myself with Eugenie and Sam in their apartment, clapping along to an old recording they had put on their phonograph.

Tears suddenly welled in my eyes at the memory, and I was overwhelmed at the thought that I would never sit and listen to music with my dear friend Sam again. I blinked hard and took in a deep breath. I would mourn later. Right now I had to concentrate on this task. Travis stopped singing, and somehow I managed to hold it together as we moved on to the next verse.

This one left us both clueless:

> *Next comes the stock to fill up the pot,*
> *Seasoned with mirepoix, heated till hot.*
> *For my hoghead friend I shall not scrimp,*
> *As I add to the gumbo a helping of shrimp.*

We knew mirepoix was the bundle of spices used to season stocks. Other than that, we had no idea to whom this verse referred. Neither one of us had ever heard the term "hoghead" except for hog's head cheese. We decided to move on.

Next came this one:

> *And finally for he who has always been there,*
> *Son of a traiteur, kind and fair.*
> *We grind up filé to add at the end,*
> *Then the dish is finished and ready for friends.*

I was thinking of a traitor, but Travis said that *traiteur* was the word for a folk healer, a practitioner of holistic medicine. That didn't ring a bell for either one of us. I couldn't imagine how we were going to be able to narrow this one down. The phrase "he who has always been there" led me to think that it had to be of my father's very oldest friends. But as far as I knew, his oldest friends were Alphonse, Sam, Ruben, and Conrad. Beyond the four of them, I was stumped.

We moved quickly through the rest of the poem. The next two verses were the ones that explained how the puzzle worked:

> For all who dare make this recipe,
> There is one secret you'll not get from me:
> The measure of how much each item to add.
> Unless you know that, the recipe's bad.

> Divided among those named in this poem,
> I give each a quantity that's theirs alone.
> Together they come to solve this rhyme,
> The treasure they only together can find.

Obviously, the men each got an amount of their ingredient to be added, and somehow when those ingredients were all combined, they pointed to the treasure.

It wasn't until we were on the very last verse that a lightbulb went on over my head.

> But if all else fails, I will tell you this:
> North and West you may search for things gone amiss.
> 'Tween hill and dale and dock and dune,
> It's out there, under the Cajun moon.

As I read through it, yet again, something about the words North and West finally clicked for me.

"North and West," I cried. "Of course!"

"What?" he asked, looking down at the page in front of him.

"North of the equator. West of the prime meridian."

"Points on a map?" he asked as the lightbulb began to turn on for him too.

"Latitude and longitude," I replied, grinning. "What do you want to bet that the amount of ingredients each person was given somehow combines to give us a set of coordinates?"

We stared at each other across the table, both of us smiling from ear to ear. In the midst of an enormous amount of suffering, grief, and anxiety, it was nice to enjoy a single moment of absolute victory.

In the distance, bells pealed to announce that another hour had passed, and it wasn't until then that I realized how long we had been sitting there working through the puzzle. There was much to do, and not a lot of time to do it in. Travis and I had to get moving. Though I still desperately wanted to be with my father, I didn't dare show up at the hospital until Sam's body was found and I learned whether or not I was a suspect. In the meantime, I was doing exactly what my father most wanted me to do: I was following the recipe.

After several discreet phone calls, Travis had been able to ascertain the whereabouts of Conrad Zahn. Though he had an apartment in the city and a home in Slidell, according to his wife he was out at their camp on Bayou Calas, where he had been for almost a week. Once we knew that, Travis got a map and showed me where we were and where we needed to go.

Currently, we were about sixty miles southwest of New Orleans, just below Houma. Bayou Calas was another thirty miles west of us, near Lake Palourde. The large property the Naquins called Paradise, where my father had been shot, was another fifteen miles beyond that, also heading west, in a swampy region above the town of Patterson.

"I have friends and relatives all along in here," Travis said, running his finger across the map between Lake Palourde and Paradise. "*Ma tante* lives here, near Duck Lake, and I've got a little camp myself across the bayou from her, right about here."

On the map, the whole region was marked as swamp and looked uninhabited, but I knew that was deceiving. Plenty of people lived in the swamps of the Atchafalaya Basin, mostly on houseboats, with no roads or towns showing up on a map.

While Travis mapped out the logistics of our trip, I went inside and made sandwiches in the kitchen. It seemed rude to eat and run—or in this case, run and eat—but the kind couple that offered us their hospitality did not seem offended. Outside, Travis and I both thanked his friends profusely for their help.

"Let's go, *cher*," Travis said to me, moving toward the truck.

He unlocked the driver's side and reached in to grab his shotgun, the GPS unit, and my purse. Then he shut the door, handed my purse to me, and began moving down the lawn, toward the water.

"Where are you going?"

"*A la bateau.*"

Running to catch up, I asked him why we were taking a boat when we had a perfectly good truck.

He glanced at me and kept walking.

"Because Sam's body has been found. Came through on my phone a few minutes ago."

"Am I now officially a fugitive?" I asked, the knot in my stomach twisting. On one hand, I was deeply relieved Sam had been found, because I couldn't stand the thought of his body just sitting there, undiscovered. On the other hand, I had known the clock would begin ticking on me the moment someone found him.

"It says you're being 'sought for questioning.' Doesn't sound like there's an APB out yet."

"Sought for questioning. Yeah, I know what that means. It means back to jail."

"Probably. Anyway, given that I was caught on film outside the courthouse yesterday helping you escape from those reporters, there's a good chance the police have connected the dots between us and are on the lookout for a black truck with my plate numbers. I figure we can move around more easily by boat without being caught."

We reached the dock, where a ski boat sat bobbing in the water.

"'Course," Travis added, "if we go traipsing all over the swamps asking questions, somebody's bound to turn us into the police sooner or later."

"I know, but we have to talk to the men on this list."

"I agree, so we'll just have to take our chances and do the best we can."

I took off my borrowed flip-flops, tossed them into the boat, and then climbed in after them. Boating hadn't been a big part of my life growing up, but a few years before I had dated a man who kept a sailboat on Lake Michigan, and if I had tried to board his vessel in a pair of sandals with black soles, he would have had my head. In fact, it was his stupid boat that had finally led me to break up with him. While out on the lake one day, he went on a rampage because I didn't coil the rigging lines neatly enough, and I thought he was sounding just a little too much like my father.

Somehow, Travis didn't seem the type to stress over the small stuff, though he certainly seemed to know his way around a boat. This vessel we were borrowing was about fifteen feet long, with seating for six and an inboard/outboard motor. Together, we unzipped and unlatched things until the boat was opened up and ready go. Reaching into the storage up under the bow, Travis pulled out a big, floppy hat and some sunscreen, both of which he handed to me.

He started up the engine while I took in the rest of the rope, and soon we were off. The wind made it too noisy for conversation, but the ride was beautiful, the lush banks overflowing with weeping willows and giant oaks on both sides. I put sunscreen on my face and arms and then gave it to Travis for him to do the same. Settling back in my seat and eating one of the sandwiches, I could only hope that between the floppy hat and my sunglasses I was fairly incognito. Glancing down at my outfit, I couldn't help but smile. If I showed up at my office in Chicago in this getup, surely no one would recognize me.

As we ventured up the winding waterways, we passed all sorts of homes and camps, ranging from the most elegant of mansions to the most humble of shacks—sometimes right next door to each other. There were even elevated mobile homes out here, propped high above the earth by steel beams and accessed via exterior stairs or ladders.

Everywhere we went, people were outside, enjoying the sun and the water and the beautiful spring day. Even though I had grown up in Louisiana, I'd never had much opportunity to get out on the waterways like this, and I found the experience exhilarating. We passed through other regions where there were no homes or camps at all, and those were even more enjoyable. In my mind, I felt like an early explorer, coming to this land and discovering its beauty for the first time.

An hour and a half later, we turned north and passed through a more populated strip that Travis said was the town of Amelia. Beyond that, we skirted along Lake Palourde and then made our way into the swamps just east of there, where Conrad kept his camp. Puttering along more slowly, I saw that there were no real houses here at all, only camps and houseboats. Some were closed up tight, but others were overflowing with people, and everyone always waved as we passed by. I had never understood why boating was such a friendly event, but just the simple act of waving from a boat and being waved to in return had always made me feel that I belonged to a little club, one whose members shared a love of the water and a knowledge of its etiquette.

I wasn't sure how we would know when we had reached the right camp, given that there weren't any house numbers on them. Soon, however, I realized that it didn't matter. As we neared a tidy little blue structure up on the left, I spotted Conrad himself, sitting on the end of his little pier, fishing.

Conrad gave us a smile and a friendly wave as we drew near, obviously thinking we would continue past. He seemed a little surprised when instead Travis gunned the engine in reverse and we eased up to his dock. It wasn't until I removed the hat and sunglasses that understanding crossed Conrad's features.

"Chloe Ledet? This is certainly a surprise!"

Despite the fact that Conrad had to be in his late seventies, his movements were sprightly and energetic. He hopped up from his chair and tucked his fishing pole into a holder so he could help us with the rope.

His greeting was friendly enough, but I found myself studying his features, trying to decide if I could detect a glimmer of anger or fear or any other emotion he might not want us to see. Then I remembered that this man was a former politician, and I realized that no matter what he was feeling, he'd probably spent years perfecting the ability to keep it from showing on his face.

After polite chitchat, I told Conrad we had come here to ask him some questions. Glancing up and down the waterway at the few camps that dotted the shoreline nearby, he suggested we move inside. While I did want to speak beyond the hearing of nosy neighbors, I was also quite comforted that they were there. If Conrad was the killer and he decided to make a move on either one of us, the sound of our yells would carry to at least four camps that I could see.

Conrad's place was small but not typical by any means. Instead of a haphazard mix of geegaws and garage-sale furniture, his decor was well coordinated, its tasteful colors and textures suggesting an interior decorator's touch. In the cozy living room, the wall over the couch was filled with dozens of framed photos and plaques, so artfully hung that the effect was striking. The room was stuffy, but once Conrad opened some windows, warm afternoon breezes swept in.

Conrad invited us to sit while he went to the kitchen to make tea. Remembering my adventure at Ledet's the other night, once he was gone I gestured to Travis, telling him through hand motions not to swallow. Once Conrad came back and put ice-cold beverages in our hands, however, that was easier said than done. I was thirsty, and several times I almost took a sip without thinking. Mostly, I just held the sweating glass in my hand as we talked, occasionally tilting it against closed lips and feigning a sip.

"So what can I do for you, Chloe dear?" Conrad asked as he sat on an easy chair across from us. "As nice as it is to see you, I know you two didn't come all this way just to sit and drink sweet tea with an old man."

Given that he'd been here at this camp for almost a week, I wasn't sure how much Conrad knew about what had been going on—unless, of course, he had been the one behind it all and had just used this camp as a home base and alibi. Paradise was just fifteen miles away, a distance that he could cover by motorboat in less than an hour.

I introduced the subject of my father, and from what I could tell from Conrad's responses, he was aware of the shooting and also of Kevin's death and my run-in with the law. He didn't say anything about Sam, however, so we didn't, either.

Instead, I focused on the conversation I had had with Kevin the night he died. Though Conrad was surprised to learn that Travis and I now knew about the treasure, he actually seemed pleased to talk about it. I realized that in a way it must have been a relief to be able to discuss openly something that he had been forbidden to mention for many years.

When he was finished telling us about his own experience regarding the treasure—how he had almost hoped Ledet's wouldn't turn a profit so quickly, just so he would end up owning a part of that treasure himself—I asked him specifically about the poem.

"Your father was so proud of that," Conrad said, a bemused expression on his face. "I think the whole idea struck his fancy because our little group was about as multicultural as Louisiana gets. That's why he used gumbo as the overriding theme, because it comes from such a mix of cultures: okra from Africa, sausage from the Germans, filé from the Native Americans, and so on."

"Native Americans?" Travis asked, glancing at me. "In the poem, that would be the 'traiture.'"

"Yeah," Conrad replied, explaining that when the French settlers first came here, the Choctaws had taught them to crush sassafras leaves to make filé, which is the perfect thickener for gumbo.

"So who's the Native American in the poem?" Travis asked Conrad, who seemed surprised by the question.

"I'm sorry, kids," he said, looking to each of us in turn, "but you know I can't tell you that. In fact, I've already told you far too much."

TWENTY-TWO

Conrad would soon find out we weren't taking no for an answer.

I pulled a copy of the poem from my pocket and gave it to him. I wasn't sure if I should tell him we were on the hunt for the killer or the treasure, so instead I simply said that my father had told me to follow the recipe if anything ever happened to him and that's what I was doing.

"I think we've figured out who most of these people are. We also know that each one was given an ingredient, and that the amount of those ingredients actually correlate to a point of latitude and longitude."

Conrad seemed impressed that we had figured it all out, but from the corner of my eye, I noticed Travis watching the man intently as he spoke, obviously still very suspicious.

"So what is it that you want from me?" Conrad asked.

"Decode this for us. Tell us what we haven't been able to figure out on our own."

Conrad continued to seem disconcerted by our request. Handing the poem back to me, he said that he was flattered that we had come to him for help, but he wasn't comfortable discussing this matter without getting an okay directly from Julian first.

"Julian is in a coma," Travis replied. "Someone shot him, probably because of the treasure. Chloe and I are just trying to figure out what's really going on, who's committing all these crimes, and where that treasure is."

"The way I hear it, Chloe is the one behind Kevin's killing, and quite possibly Sam's as well," he said, eyes narrowing in suspicion.

At our look of surprise, Conrad nodded and said that yes he had just heard the news that Sam's body had been found in his apartment, and that the scene of the crime had not been pretty.

"Conrad, you've known me since I was born. You've known my father since you were both kids. Can you honestly look me in the eye and tell me you think I could murder someone? Do you really think I could've hurt Sam in any way whatsoever?"

Conrad and I locked eyes for a long moment, each studying the other for signs of rage or madness or whatever quality murderers must possess to do what they do. I didn't think I could see that in him, and I could only hope he realized it wasn't in me, either.

Rising and stepping forward, Conrad reached over my head, and for a moment I was afraid he was grabbing some kind of weapon. Instead, he pulled down a plaque and handed it to me. It was small and rectangular, a brass plate mounted on a walnut backing, and engraved *16" Andouille*.

"I have to confess something, but you can never tell your father."

I nodded, and he continued.

"Julian was so dramatic about this whole thing, you know, so Hardy Boys about the buried treasure and the intricate puzzle rhyme and all that. When he gave us each a sealed envelope with our individual ingredient inside, he was so solemn you would've thought he was handing over nuclear codes."

I smiled, as I could easily picture that side of my father, the side that took himself far too seriously.

"Anyway, later, as a private joke, some of us took our precious ingredient and rather than hide it away in our safety deposit boxes as we had been instructed, we decided we would each find a way to discreetly post it on a wall. After all, Julian hung his right there in Ledet's, so we figured we should be able to put ours up too. I got mine engraved. I figured with so many plaques on the wall, who would notice? Ruben actually framed and hung a photograph of his kids on the beach, and if you looked closely enough at the photo, you could see that he had written in the sand at their feet the number twenty-nine and placed next to that a shrimp. Twenty-nine shrimp, get it?"

"So Ruben is the hoghead in the poem," Travis said.

"What is a hoghead, exactly?" I added.

"That's slang for a mud engineer on an oil rig. Ruben's first job out of law school was for a firm that represented the oil companies. He spent so much time learning about the science of drilling for oil that we teased him that he was becoming a hoghead. The nickname just stuck. 'Course, years later, once he and I had our own practice, all that knowledge came in handy. He represented some of the plaintiffs in the Lake Piegneur disaster."

"Wow," Travis said.

I wasn't sure what the Lake Piegneur disaster was, but it didn't sound relevant to our quest. I just wanted to keep things moving. I gave the plaque back to Conrad. He chuckled softly as he looked at it.

"It seems silly and childish now, but Julian can be such a difficult person that sometimes we just needed to strike back, even if he wasn't aware of our private rebellion."

Travis and I looked at each other.

"Do you think that might be what this rash of crime is all about?" Travis asked. "Someone who's had enough and is trying to strike back at Julian in a big way?"

Conrad considered the question for a long moment.

"No, I don't think so. As tough as Julian is, and as frustrating as he can be at times, he's very loved. His friends are loyal to a fault. It's hard to explain, but people are just drawn to him. He's funny and fun and the life of the party, of course, but it's way more than that. There's something so dynamic about how he moves through life, noisy and stubborn and energetic, and bringing all of his friends along with him. He's very loved, actually. Except for his rift with your grandfather, Travis, I can't think of a single person in Julian's circle of friends who would wish him harm."

As I listened to Conrad's description of my father, I realized that it answered a long-standing question for me. Deep in my heart, I had always wondered why he was so popular, why anyone would choose to befriend

Julian Ledet. Given his legendary temper tantrums, I couldn't fathom why so many people voluntarily subjected themselves to that, over and over. Hearing Conrad speak of my dad with such fondness, I felt I could finally understand.

"So, again, the verse about filé that represents a Native American. Who is it?"

Surrendering to our persistence, Conrad told us that that was Ben Runner, an old friend of Alphonse's who just happened to be a Chitimacha Indian. As soon as we heard that, Travis and I both looked at each other, as the words "Ben" and "Ben's daughter" had been part of the phone message my father had left after he was shot.

"Ask a Chitimacha when his forefathers first settled in this region, and he will tell you that they have always been here. Isn't that what the poem says, 'For he who has always been there'? That's Ben." Conrad went on to say that Ben was a quiet man but nice, and very intelligent. He had grown up poor, but as a young man his dream had been to go to college.

"When they had those four little statues melted down so your father could get to Europe, Chloe, and your grandfather could build a house, Travis, the two men decided to share the wealth and give their friend Ben a small scholarship as well. They had me 'anonymously' present him with a thousand dollars, but of course he eventually figured out where it had come from. Ten years later, when it came time to return the favor, Ben was a successful pharmacist back in Charenton and eager to help his friend and benefactor Julian get Ledet's off the ground."

"Does he still live there now, in Charenton?" Travis asked.

"Far as I know."

"Do you know what his number was, the amount of filé for the recipe?" I asked.

Conrad shook his head.

"Sorry, I don't, and he wasn't in on the whole private joke thing, so it wouldn't be posted on his wall anywhere."

"How about the others? Do you know their numbers?" I asked, glancing at the window and wondering how much daylight we had left. If Conrad could save us some steps, that would be incredible.

"Well, your dad's is right there in the poem. Four and five, though I guess you're supposed to put that together and make it forty-five."

Travis and I glanced at each other, feeling dumb that we hadn't figured that one out ourselves.

"I don't know Alphonse's number, and he wasn't in on our private joke. That was just Ruben and Sam and me."

"Sam?" I asked, setting my full glass down on a coaster. "I practically lived in that apartment. I don't remember anything hanging on the wall that had to do with okra."

"I can't remember his number, but it was in the kitchen, on a pot holder or a towel or something like that. He had had it embroidered. He said Eugenie thought it was an odd thing, but the color was nice so she let him keep it where he had put it, hanging from a hook near the stove."

"The pot holder!" In a flash, my mind went to Tuesday night, and suddenly I was standing in that kitchen again, looking at my dead friend, Sam, with Travis' arms wrapped tightly around me. On the floor near Sam's feet had been a blue piece of gingham with a tuft of white cotton batting still attached.

I told the two men I needed some air, and without waiting for their reply I stood and raced through the door and to the end of the dock, trying to catch my breath there.

Conrad and Travis seemed to sense that I needed a moment to myself because they didn't rush out after me. I was glad. There, beside the silent, gently flowing water, I practiced my deep breathing until my pulse rate finally returned to normal.

Eighteen. Sam's blue gingham pot holder had been embroidered with the words "18 stalks okra." I could still see it, as vividly as if I were a teenager again, working in the kitchen with Eugenie, using the pot holder to pull a tray of cookies from the oven. It had made no sense to me then, but it sure did now.

When we saw Sam on Tuesday night, that pot holder had obviously been torn up and disposed of somehow, though one telltale piece had remained. More than anything, I now knew for certain that the killer was also on the trail of the treasure. Sam must have tried to hide the pot holder from whoever had gone to his apartment and demanded to know his share of the recipe.

When Travis and Conrad finally came outside, I explained all of that to Conrad and told him to be careful, that he might be in danger too. He didn't seem too disturbed by that possibility, which led me back around to wondering if he was involved or knew who the killer was.

As if reading my mind, Conrad suddenly blurted out that he believed that I hadn't killed Kevin Peralta after all.

"You didn't seem so sure earlier. What changed your mind?"

He smiled.

"Your tea in there. I've never seen two people take so many sips of tea and yet consume not a single drop from the glass. My guess is you were afraid I was going to drug you. If you think I'm the killer, then that tells me you're *not* the killer."

We all laughed, but I didn't say the next thought that popped into my mind, which was why would he even have noticed something like that unless he was watching us drink and waiting for the drug to kick in?

With my mind swirling with questions and answers and all we had learned here, Travis and I said our goodbyes and climbed into the boat. I wasn't sure where we would go from here, but I had a feeling our next stop would be Charenton, to visit Ben Runner, the Chitimacha Indian.

"You know, Chloe, I always felt so sorry for you when you were small," Conrad said as he helped us with the ropes. "Between your father's ego and your mother's reinvention of herself, you didn't have much of a life. I have to say you turned out amazingly well, given the circumstances."

I was surprised by his words but also oddly vindicated.

"I had a pretty rough childhood myself," Conrad continued. "If your father hadn't rescued me from the bullies in the Quarter, I don't know what would've happened to me."

I thought of Conrad's verse in the poem, the line that said he "learned to fight back in old Orleans" and asked him what it meant.

"I was a rich little nerd from the Garden District, but my parents were having some issues, so when I was about eight years old I went to live with my grandmother in the French Quarter. I did not fit in there, and it didn't help that I went by the name of Connie back then, fodder for being called a girl. I was tormented until the day Julian and Sam saw what was going on and stood up for me. The two of them sort of ruled the block, you know, so after that, I was left alone. I was so grateful that I kept hanging around them, and eventually we became good friends."

Travis turned on the engine, but it was making an odd sound, so he turned it back off again.

"Sorry, this'll just take a second," he said, moving to the back of the boat to fiddle with the motor. "It's been doing this for a while."

As we waited for Travis to make the necessary adjustments, I looked up at Conrad as his earlier words popped back to mind.

"So, what did you mean when you referred to my mother's 'reinvention of herself'? Reinvented how?"

An almost sheepish expression came over his face.

"You know," Conrad said, reaching for the fishing pole he had set down earlier. "Her days on Bourbon Street and all of that?"

Dumbfounded, I simply nodded and said, "Uh-huh?"

"I saw the toll it took on you, Chloe, the way she went overboard always making sure you did everything so perfectly and followed all the rules. But really, I've never seen such a transformation in anyone as I did when that woman came back from finishing school. Your father was right to send her there once they were married, given the lifestyle to which they both aspired."

"Finishing school," I echoed. I knew she had gone to a finishing school at some point in her life, but I had always thought it was when she was a teenager.

"Yes, so she could step in as hostess when the restaurant opened."

"Oh, right."

"It was amazing. We were all floored when she came back. I mean, gone was the crass, bleached blonde exotic dancer who went by the stage name of Fifi LaFlame, and in her place was this other woman, the elegant, classy Lola Ledet. Your dad knew all along that Lola had it in her. She just needed a little polishing around the edges."

TWENTY-THREE

FRANCE, 1719
JACQUES

No question, this was one message Jacques would have to deliver in person. After all he had seen and heard today, he knew Papa's little violation of confidentiality was the least of the issues to be dealt with, one of no real consequence. Greater by far was the swindle perpetrated by M. Law, a man who had just made a very public promise to two hundred citizens of France, a promise he had no intention of fulfilling. As if in one brilliant flash, Jacques understood everything now, how this whole event was *supposed* to have gone today.

If M. Freneau had brought back the trunk he was supposed to have brought, the statuettes up on the stage would have been the gilded ones. Law's ploy was to promise solid gold fleur-de-lis to the crowd but in reality give them only gilded fleur-de-lis instead. Thus duped, the people would have seen the trunk carted off to the ship and loaded in the cargo hold in full view, and everyone involved would have thought that the promised treasure was real. Given that this deception would not be discovered for three years, Law must have thought he would deal with the repercussions later, when the offended parties were too far away and too poor to have any legal recourse.

If that were the case, why bother with having the real ones made at all? If the real ones were never meant to see the light of day upon this stage or be carried off to the New World, what was their point?

Jacques began working his way through the murmuring, shifting crowd as he thought about that. *Why had Law bothered with making the real set at all?* Jacques could think of several reasons.

To start rumors and get people talking, which would help draw a crowd.

To trick the royal goldsmith himself into testifying to their validity. After all, he made them. Of course he thought they were valid.

To trick the assayer into performing public tests on the one and only statuette on that stage today that really was solid gold. Once the assayer's test proved it, the audience extrapolated, as Law wanted them to, that the proof applied to *all* of the statuettes, not just that one. What the audience—and indeed the experts—had failed to consider was that the statuette Law had tested was the one that had been presented to him by the royal goldsmith, not one of the statuettes from the trunk.

To use all of the above to make people to want the gold so badly they'd be willing to go across an ocean for it.

Jacques thought of Law's comment, when he'd said to the crowd, *If you don't mind, I plan to keep this extra one myself, as a commemorative of this grand and glorious day.* What a liar! The only reason Law had kept that one for himself was because he knew it was real—and that the others were all fakes.

As far as Law knew, the other real ones were currently secreted away in a distant, isolated location where a goldsmith who had been paid to keep his mouth shut was quickly melting them down into bars. Had things not gone wrong and Papa been able to do as he had been told, by morning there would have been no evidence left in France of this grand deception. The gilded statuettes would have been on their way to the New World, the real statuettes would have been transformed into bars and likely moved into Law's private vault, and no one except Papa, M. Law, and M. Freneau would have known the truth.

Unbelievable.

As it was, now the swindler himself had ended up being the one swindled.

Jacques was tempted to leave well enough alone and let the real gold sail with these two hundred trusting people to the New World as they had been promised. But if he did that, then what would happen two days from now when M. Freneau came back out to pick up the gold bars and learned what had happened? Papa might be held responsible for returning gold he didn't have.

By the time Jacques reached the stage, the trunk had already been locked up and was being loaded onto a cart bound for La Rochelle with great fanfare. M. Freneau was supervising the loading, but Law and the other two men from the presentation were merely standing nearby, watching the proceedings and chatting softly among themselves. Law's eyes darted frequently to the sign-up table, where the line was slowly growing longer and longer.

Jacques chose to go to M. Freneau first. After all, there was still a chance that this morning's mistake hadn't been a mistake at all. The only way Jacques could know for sure was to speak to Freneau himself.

"Monsieur, a word with you, if you please," Jacques said to him as politely as he could.

Freneau turned and looked him over, from his sweating brow and windblown hair to the mud on his shoes.

"Sign-ups are over there, boy, not with me," Freneau said, gesturing toward the table and dismissing him.

"I have to talk to you about the statuettes. I am Jacques Soliel, Henri Soliel's son."

"Sorry, don't know the man."

"That's funny, because you were with him just this morning, about ten miles past Charenton. Remember? He loaded the trunk with gilded statuettes while you tried to get yourself a hot breakfast and only came away with a biscuit."

Freneau's head snapped up, eyes wide with shock. He managed to recover quickly, but at least Jacques knew he had his attention now.

"That was a private arrangement between him and me," he hissed, moving in close to Jacques so no one else would overhear their conversation. "What do you want?"

"I came to deliver a letter from my father," Jacques said, pulling it from his pocket and handing it to Freneau.

He tore it open and quickly read it, Jacques studying his features as he did. The surprise and fear on his face told Jacques what he needed to know, that the mistake was genuine and not yet another part of this complicated ruse.

"What does he mean I took the wrong cart? I took the cart he rolled out to me!"

"Yes, but I was the one who loaded the trunk for him, and he didn't realize that I had moved the carts around a bit while loading. It was my mistake for moving the carts, his mistake for not double-checking them, and your mistake for hitching your horse to it without verifying that you had the right load."

Glancing around, Freneau crumbled the letter and shoved it deep into his pocket, his face flushing a brilliant red.

"So what you're telling me is that the real statuettes are here in this trunk, about to be loaded on the boat bound for the New World?"

"Yes, sir."

A dozen competing thoughts seemed to flash across the man's features as he considered the ramifications of what had happened.

"Please, we must discuss this further in private. Can you wait for me to finish here and then we can talk on the way to La Rochelle? You can ride in my carriage. There will still be time to rectify the situation, I assure you. I just have to think through the best way to do this."

Jacques glanced at M. Law, who was at that moment working the crowd, apparently trying to talk more people into signing up. The other two men, the royal goldsmith and the assayer, were just leaving the stage in the opposite direction, likely to head back to their apartments at the Louvre. Were Jacques to call their attention to what had happened here today, they would be angered, yes, and likely mortified and humiliated as well. They had served as pawns in a very clever scheme, after all. But they were good men, honorable and true. They wouldn't allow M. Law to go unpunished, nor would they keep silent merely to protect their own interests. Jacques couldn't be so sure about M. Freneau, as he simply didn't know him well. If he allowed Freneau to "straighten out this mess" in private, then Jacques would become a party to this swindle as well. His poor father, who hadn't a dishonest bone in his body, would have had a hand in deceiving two hundred people.

"I must speak to the royal goldsmith," Jacques said, quickly making his decision. Before Freneau could stop him, he was off and running, around the stage and through the crowds all the way past Les Halles, where he finally caught up with the royal goldsmith and the assayer.

"Sirs! Please! I must speak with you! It is urgent!"

The men paused, but before Jacques could say another word, the assayer had waved over a pair of royal guards who were advancing on him.

"Please! Listen! It is about the gold statuettes! There's been a tremendous deception!"

At that, the royal goldsmith's face turned a vivid red, and he began striding away even more quickly. The guards had Jacques tightly in their grip, but no matter how hard he struggled, he couldn't get free.

"Get this riffraff off the streets," the assayer said to the guards before trotting ahead to catch up with the other man.

"Please! I am a goldsmith! You must listen to me! You know my father, sir! Henri Soliel!"

At the sound of his father's name, the two men stopped.

Still red faced, the royal goldsmith marched back to him and told him to be quiet, that if he had something to say about the statuettes, they would discuss them in private.

"If you are Soliel's son, then I will hear what you have to say," he hissed. "But not here. Guards, bring this man to the Chambre de Jaune."

Much to his relief, the guards released their hold on Jacques as the other two men strode away. He didn't know where they were taking him, but he was happy to get an audience with the royal goldsmith. They had all been pawns of Law and Freneau. Once Jacques explained everything, the royal goldsmith would know what to do.

As it turned out, the Chambre de Jaune was a room at the Louvre, a comfortable sitting room decorated primarily in various shades of yellow. After a stop outside for Jacques to clean the dirt from his shoes, the guard allowed him in and told him to wait. Then the guard left and Jacques was alone.

The room was quite opulent, and ordinarily he would have enjoyed spending time in such a luxurious setting. But today he had no use for material pleasures. He needed to get back to his father, who was slowly dying outside of town.

Jacques didn't know how much time had passed, but it was at least an hour before the royal goldsmith finally showed up. The man was much calmer now, and when he came into the room he took a seat on the yellow silk sofa and actually apologized for the delay.

"I don't know what you have to say to me, young man, but I hope it was worth the display you put on out there for the crowd. I only hope your father was not there to see it, because he would have been mortified at your behavior."

"Sir, my father is on his deathbed right now, hidden away at an old blacksmith's shop about two hours east of town." Jacques went on to explain everything, starting with the secret commission that had come to his father and all that had happened since, ending with his conclusions about M. Law's intentions and the swindle he had perpetrated. As Jacques talked, the man across from him seemed to grow more and more upset. When Jacques' story was done, he was relieved to see that the man was giving him the benefit of the doubt.

"These are very serious accusations, young Soliel," he said. "If you are not telling me the truth, I am afraid there will be consequences. You will have been guilty of slandering the names and reputations of M. Law and M. Freneau."

Jacques sat up straight and looked the man directly in the eye.

"All you need do to see that I am telling the truth is come with me to the workshop where my father now lies dying and see the second set of statuettes for yourself. Once you have, you will understand. We are both victims in this situation."

"Very well. For your father's sake, a man I have long known and respected, I will do as you ask. Please wait here while I make the necessary arrangements."

The necessary arrangements ended up taking at least another hour. When someone finally came for Jacques and led him to the stables, there was practically a caravan waiting there for him. The best that Jacques could tell, that caravan included three carriages, two guards, and five officials from the guild, including the royal goldsmith himself. Jacques was told to sit up front with the driver of the first carriage to direct them where to go.

As they finally headed out, moving ever so slowly through the busy streets of Paris, all Jacques could do was pray that his papa would still be alive when they finally arrived.

TWENTY-FOUR

Travis started up the boat at that moment, and I was glad because I could not have come up with a reply to save my life. My mother had been an exotic dancer? Lola Ledet, the most beautiful, elegant woman I had ever known, had gone by the stage name Fifi LaFlame? Conrad might as well have told me that the moon was made of cheese and babies came out of cabbage patches.

At least Travis was busy guiding the boat back down the channel, so we didn't have to converse. Moving past the same camps on the way out that we'd seen on the way in, I could barely bring myself to focus long enough to return their friendly waves.

"It's getting late," Travis said to me finally, "but I say we keep going all the way to Charenton."

"How far away is it?"

"'Bout forty miles west of here. I can cut across Lake Palourde and Flat Lake to get us to the Atchafalaya River, and then we'll be able to take that most of the way."

"Go for it. I don't think we have much choice at this point."

Using my phone, I went online and searched for an address.

Sure enough, a Ben Runner was listed in Charenton. I gave that address to Travis, and he plugged it into the GPS unit. After a few minutes, he made a sharp turn that brought us from the narrow channel into the wide expanse of Lake Palourde. He pushed down the throttle all the way, and soon we were soaring across the greenish brown water as fast as the boat would take us.

We only had a few hours of daylight left, but at least Travis seemed to know where he was going. All I could do was sit there in the boat, look out at the beautiful scenery, and try to calm the desperate swirling of my mind. I had been through so much already, but at this point it felt as though the shocks and surprises were never going to end. My mother's secret past surely had nothing to do with what was going on now, so I would have to find some way to put it out of my mind and focus on things at hand.

That was going to be easier said than done, though. Now that I had this knowledge about my mother, I tried to fit it into the puzzle that my life had been. I always thought I was drawn to rules on my own, that maybe I had taken after my mother in that regard a bit, but that primarily it was just a part of who I was, a refuge from the chaos and neglect I suffered at home. After what Conrad had told me, I realized it was more complicated than that. Who I was hinged in part on who my parents were, so if they weren't who I thought they were, who was I?

No wonder I had a headache!

The engine began to sputter, and I looked at Travis, but he just gave me a shrug and kept going. Eventually, we managed to make it across the lake, under a highway bridge, and into the next lake. Going slower there, the engine began sputtering again, and this time Travis told me that we should probably switch to a different boat if we could. He called a cousin with a camp not too far from where we were and made the necessary arrangements. Soon, we had worked our way up a narrow bayou to that camp. This time, the dock was on my side, so I stood and leaned out of the boat to grab a rusty pole mounted there and guide us into place. Travis cut the engine and quickly began to close things up. With my help, we had the boat zipped and sealed and tied up within minutes.

Climbing from the boat, I realized this wasn't really a camp at all, just a plot of land with a covered boat garage on it. Both of the open bays were full, and I wondered which of the two big boats we were changing to. Both of them were very nice but also quite big, and I couldn't imagine the amount of effort it was going to take to get one of them into the water.

I needn't have worried, because as it turned out we were taking neither. Instead, Travis led us to another one I hadn't noticed, a small aluminum fishing boat that was propped up on cinderblocks near a tangle of bushes.

"Might be a good idea to be in a different boat now anyway," Travis told me as he reached down and grabbed a large limb from the ground. "If Conrad tipped off the police that we're out riding in a Sea Ray Bowrider, then that's what the cops will be looking for, not this little aluminum fishing boat."

Travis approached that boat now and, much to my surprise, began whacking the ground all around it with the big stick.

"What are you doing?"

"Jus' scaring off any snakes that might be hiding here, *cher*. In Louisiana, you don't ever go near tangled brush like this without giving it a few good whacks first."

"Oh, great."

Between the two of us, we managed to get the boat into the water, but I was stunned to see how very low it rode compared to the nice boat we'd just gotten out of. These waterways were filled with snakes and alligators, I felt sure, though I hadn't yet seen any today. Given that, our little boat was far too close to the water for my comfort.

"Come on, *cher*. Time's a passin'."

Reluctantly, I climbed aboard and soon we were on our way again. This time, Travis had to sit in the back, steering the outboard motor via the handle that was attached to it. I sat across a wide metal slat closer to the front, taking care to keep my hands and fingers fully inside the boat lest they be snatched off by a roving reptile.

This ride was much bumpier as well, and as I was knocked and jolted along the waterway, I could only hope we didn't have much farther to go. At one point, Travis veered into a side channel, and though I hoped that meant we were almost there, instead he soon slowed down and told me that since we were so close to Paradise he thought I might want to detour past it.

"Past Paradise? Where is it?"

"This is it. Starts right here. Nobody lives here year-round anymore, of course, but my grandparents still own the land."

Travis gestured to our left, toward a vast expanse of shoreline that was mostly overgrown with thick trees and brush, punctuated by a small, rickety dock. I knew it went on for a while, because I could remember my one and only visit there when I was a young teenager. The place had been impressively huge to me then, a mix of cleared and developed land and undisturbed forest. From what I could recall, the Naquins' house sat somewhere in the middle and was surrounded with a rolling, shaded lawn, a fenced-in garden, and a network of woodsy paths and trails.

I remembered being skeptical of their claim that just by taking a ten-minute walk on the property, one could pick an entire fruit salad. To prove it, Travis' grandmother had taken me to do exactly that, starting with strawberries in the lush garden the Naquins had planted there, then moving to the various fruit trees in the yard and then finally venturing up a wooded path to get the wild berries.

That had been fun, but otherwise my trip to Paradise had been a major disappointment. Though I had begged my father to bring me along with him for once, he had ended up sticking me at the house with the women while he headed off with the guys and their shotguns into the woods. Between the noisy family that never stopped jabbering with each other in a language I didn't understand, the mosquitoes that left massive welts on my arms and legs, and the humidity that frizzed my blond hair into steel wool, I was mostly just miserable. Making things much worse, of course, was that I had wanted to go there so I could have some time with my dad, but as it turned out I barely saw him from the moment we arrived until it was time to load up and leave. In the end, I didn't understand the attraction the place held for him, not at all. And I sure didn't see how it had earned its name. Paradise, indeed.

"That leads up to the house," Travis said, pointing to the dock and the walkway beyond. "It's just used as a cabin now. Nobody lives there anymore."

"Is that the dock where my father was shot?"

"I don't know. We already passed one dock, back there, and there's another one around on the river side. Had to be one of those three, but I don't know which one."

As we puttered past, I studied the dock and nearby terrain for signs of blood or even police tape but didn't see anything. I did catch a glimpse of the lawn and the old white picket fence that delineated the garden. From what I could see, the fence was in disrepair, the slats faded to brown, the lawn and garden both overgrown with weeds. Remembering what a busy, well-tended place it had once been, looking at it now felt kind of sad.

Continuing along the banks of Paradise, I noticed that the property was hilly, in the same way that that retreat center had been hilly. I asked Travis how that happened, how hills could suddenly be a part of terrain that was elsewhere completely flat.

"Salt."

"Excuse me?"

"Wherever there's an underground salt dome, you can get hills like this. Haven't you ever been out to Avery Island, the place where they make Tabasco sauce? That whole island is one giant salt dome." He went on to explain that coastal Louisiana was full of underground salt, and that in many cases a single salt dome might extend two or three miles out—and up to eight or nine miles down, whether it was obvious at the surface or not. "I think Avery is supposed to have something like a hundred and fifty billion tons of salt. It's really amazing when you think about it."

As he talked about the geology of salt and how it had been left by evaporated ocean waters thousands of years ago and then pushed underground by the shifting of alluvial sediment, all I could think of was my father and his famous Secret Salt.

"Is there a salt mine here at Paradise, Travis?"

"There used to be, back in the early nineteen hundreds, I think. It's all sealed up now, but there are still a couple of good ponds here, where the salt from inside the earth leaches out into the water to create brine. That's where I learned to track animals, because they're always coming there, licking the salt where it crusts around the sides."

I studied the wooded shore, several puzzle pieces suddenly clicking together in my brain. My whole life, my father had been coming down to Paradise on a regular basis to hunt and fish. Sometimes he'd be gone for a week or two, yet he almost never came home with much more to show for his adventures than a few fish and maybe a rabbit or a duck. On one occasion my father had returned from just such a trip bearing his meager bounty and our new maid had actually laughed, saying that her husband could go off hunting for a single afternoon and come back with ten times that much.

The maid was summarily fired, of course, but later I got up the nerve to ask my father why he never brought back venison or buckets of catfish or ice chests filled with crawfish like the maid had described. He had brushed me off, saying that for some men—especially men who slaved over a hot stove day after day at work—the expression "hunting and fishing" often meant mostly "relaxing and resting." Later, my mother had scolded me for even asking him, saying that my father couldn't help it if he was a bad shot with a rifle and a rotten fisherman, and that I wasn't to embarrass him like that ever again.

Now, looking out at Paradise, I finally understood what had really been going on. The expression "hunting and fishing" had been a euphemism, all right, not for "relaxing and resting" but for "mining salt." My father had been coming here for years, going down into the old mine, and coming out with a bounty of pink salt. The south Louisiana company that packaged and shipped Chef Julian's Secret Salt was likely not just a packaging and fulfillment plant but also a salt cleaning and processing facility. No wonder he kept coming here after the Naquins moved away, and even after he and Alphonse had had a parting of the ways. My father had to keep coming here if he wanted to continue to acquire the central ingredient in Chef Julian's Secret Salt.

That also explained exactly why my father wanted to buy Paradise from Alphonse Naquin. According to Kevin Peralta, my father called him on Monday morning, before he was shot, sounding very excited and saying he was willing to lose the battle over the treasure with Alphonse Naquin as long as Naquin would finally sell him Paradise in return. I just knew that the excitement in my father's voice had come from something salt related, perhaps the discovery of a whole new rich vein of especially pink salt. Regardless of what my father had found here, it was important enough that he was willing to do whatever it took to buy this land and its mine, even if that required him to capitulate in a battle of wills, something Julian Ledet would otherwise never have done. Knowing my father as I did, I realized that for him the real treasure of Paradise wasn't made of gold and shaped like a fleur-de-lis at all. It was pink and crusty and came from a hole in the ground!

As we reached the upper boundary of Paradise, Travis turned left into the narrow channel that would bring us to the river on the other side. Our little boat chugging along slowly, I told Travis my theory, but he didn't seem convinced.

"Louisiana salt isn't good enough for food, *cher*. It's mined for rock salt. You know, like for deicing bridges and roads?"

"I live in Chicago, Travis. I'm familiar with rock salt and icy roads."

"Well, then, chances are you've been driving safely up there thanks to rock salt that came to you from down here. We've got a couple of big salt mining operations in the state."

"Okay, so Louisiana has its share of salt mines," I said, "and what they get from those mines is used as rock salt. That still doesn't mean edible salt couldn't be here too, at least in a limited quantity."

"I suppose," Travis replied, but he didn't sound convinced.

We reached the end of the channel and turned left onto the river, passing back down the other side of Paradise. More than anything I wanted to go ashore, take a look at the old mine, and see if I could find the pink vein my father had been secretly exploiting for years. But considering that he had been shot here just three days before and the person who shot him hadn't yet been apprehended, it simply wouldn't be safe. Instead, I contented myself with looking out at the wooded, hilly terrain from our motorboat and listening as Travis described how this land had been passed down through his family for many generations. Sooner or later, once it was safe, we would come back, and I would get my chance to explore.

"What's that?" I asked, pointing toward a crumbling structure on the bank nearly hidden by weeds and brush.

"That's the old mine office," Travis said. "Nothing left of it now but ruins."

There was a dock at the water's edge and I studied it closely, but again I didn't see signs of blood or previous policy activity. Passing further down the property, I could see what looked like the white tip of a rooftop in and among the trees.

"Is that more of the mine?" I asked.

"No, that's an old houseboat that washed up in Hurricane Betsy." We continued puttering past, and as we did I realized he was right. What I was seeing wasn't a roofline at all, but the crumpled, rotting bow of a big boat that had long ago been pushed from the river onto the land and set straight up on one end, like a toy boat cast aside from a bathtub.

"And that's about it," Travis said now. "The property line ends down there just ahead of us. See that big cypress tree? That marks the boundary. Everything beyond that belongs to somebody else, a timber company, I think. Looks like they're building something." I looked where he pointed to see some heavy equipment in and among the trees, a big crane and some bulldozers.

Travis sped up the motor again and we were off. I was glad he had taken the detour to show me Paradise, as it helped orient me to the place even without setting foot onshore. It also led to my revelations about the salt, something I felt deep in my bones wasn't just a theory but fact. I wasn't sure where we would be going once we left Ben's house, but if following the recipe reached a dead end, maybe we could follow the trail of the salt instead.

TWENTY-FIVE

FRANCE, 1719
JACQUES

 Papa was gone.

Not just Papa. Everything was gone.

The trunk, the cart, the worktable, the cot, the food, the supplies, the clothes. Everything. Gone.

Jacques ran to the back door and looked out, but there was nothing and no one to be seen. He returned to the gathering of men in the main room, nearly hysterical, demanding they speak with the farmer and his wife next door.

Two of the men stepped out to do just that, and while they were gone Jacques continued to probe every corner, every nook and cranny for some evidence of what had been here only hours before. The furnace had been doused with water, so there wasn't even any proof of hot ash at the bottom.

Finally, the men who had gone to question the farmer returned.

"They say they don't know what we are talking about. They said this old blacksmith shop has been empty for two years at least, and no one has come or gone on this road all day."

"They're lying!" Jacques cried. "They were paid to say that! The woman has been bringing my father two meals a day for over a month!"

It didn't matter what Jacques said; no one believed him. For the return trip, Jacques was no longer perched up front. He was forced into the back carriage and held there under guard. Before they even reached Paris, the caravan came to a stop and he was told to get out.

There, on the dusty road he had already traveled twice today, he stood face-to-face with the royal goldsmith, who had climbed out of the middle carriage. The man looked at him with a mix of pity and sadness.

"I don't know what has motivated you to perpetrate such lies today," he said, "but I can only hope your father might be able to shed some light on this. In the meantime, we have decided that it will be necessary to keep you under watch. There is great concern about your mental health, not to mention the damage that can be done by someone who is obviously so impassioned in their lies. Once I have a chance to speak with your father, I will make a final decision as to how we will proceed in this matter."

With that, Jacques was taken away, his wrists bound in chains, his body led into the Charenton institution that loomed so darkly in front of him, the home for the insane.

TWENTY-SIX

We finally reached our next destination about a half hour later. The sun was sitting lower in the sky by that point, and I hoped we wouldn't be there too long. I didn't relish the thought of having to set out again in this tiny boat in the dark.

Travis studied the GPS screen as we puttered along past a broad curve. About half a mile past that curve, he turned left into a break in the trees, heading up a narrow channel that was probably too shallow for our previous boat anyway. We passed a small dock on the left and then a few minutes later spotted another.

"That should be it," Travis said looking from his GPS screen to the dock ahead. "According to this thing anyway. See how God provides? We couldn't have come here in the Sea Ray."

We tied up the boat to the rickety dock and headed up a narrow walkway. The bushes were so overgrown near the water that we couldn't see the house until we were practically on top of it. It was a standard ranch home, single story and made of red brick with white trim. We knocked on the door, and as we waited for someone to answer it, I looked around, deciding that the whole place looked like it needed some TLC. Besides the overgrown shrubbery, there were rotted boards and peeling paint and even a tangle of wires where the carport light used to be.

We could hear noises from inside, so we knew someone was home.

We knocked again, and finally a woman appeared at the door. She looked to be in her late fifties, and though she was attractive with dark eyes and wide, smooth cheeks, the overall impression she gave was that of exhaustion. Suddenly, I felt very bad for this breach of etiquette in not calling ahead. Given the situation we hadn't dared, but it still seemed awfully rude.

"I'm sorry, I didn't hear a car in the drive. Did you come by boat?" the woman asked, looking nervous.

"Yes, sorry about that. Hope we didn't scare you."

"No problem," she replied, tucking a loose strand of hair behind her ear. "How can I help you?"

"We're here to see Ben Runner. Does he live here?"

"Yes, but who are you?"

I was hesitant to say my name or explain my connection, so I was glad when Travis replied with his own, adding that he was Alfonse Naquin's grandson. That seemed to be enough for her because she opened the door, probably assuming I was Travis' wife.

"Follow me," she said, and we did just that as she led us through the living room and toward a hallway off the other side.

"I'm Ben's daughter," she said as she walked, and I was glad she was ahead of us and did not see the look Travis and I gave each other.

"Heidi ho!" someone called from the other side of the living room. Startled, I glanced that way to see an old woman waving at us from a chair. I wondered if that was Ben's wife. I waved to her in return but couldn't stay to chat because Ben's daughter was moving too quickly.

The hallway she led us down was dim and smelled kind of like a hospital or a nursing home. There was more noise in a room off to our right, and as we passed the open door I looked inside to see two beds, an elderly person in each of them. Ben's daughter stopped in front of the last door on the left, gave it a knock, and swung it all the way open.

"Sometimes I think he knows what we're saying, but of course he can't really reply," she told us.

Travis and I both stepped inside to see an extremely old man sitting in a chair beside the window. He was surrounded by medical equipment, and again that antiseptic institutional smell assaulted my nostrils. Ben's daughter obviously provided some sort of in-home elder care.

"Daddy? Here are some people to see you. 'Member Mr. Alphonse Naquin? This is his grandson."

The man didn't move or make a sound but simply continued to stare out the window.

"Come on in, it's okay," the woman urged us. "He's real quiet, but he always enjoys having visitors."

Travis and I moved farther into the room even as we heard the old woman calling from the living room.

"Y'all excuse me," Ben's daughter said. "I was just about to give her her dinner when you knocked. My name is Josie, by the way. Holler if you need me."

With that, she left us alone with her father.

Though Travis sat directly across from the man and spoke to him, there seemed to be no recognition or response. As he did that, I wandered around the room, looking at the many cards and photos that had been taped to the wall. Obviously, the man had a full life, filled with people who loved him.

There was a sign hanging near the photos, one that was obviously written in another language, more than likely Chitimacha. It said *Caqaad kaskec nama qaxt xahyte.* I made a mental note to ask Josie what it meant. If we were lucky, it was Ben's measurement of filé for the recipe.

Travis paused in his talking to Ben to whisper that I should poke around a little more thoroughly. I felt creepy doing it, but it didn't seem as though Ben would notice or care. Tiptoeing to the doorway, I listened for Josie, and when I heard her talking in the living room, I summoned my nerve and began rifling through the drawers.

By about the fifth drawer, running my hand under a stack of boxer shorts and T-shirts, I couldn't help but think how very low I had sunk. Sliding it softly shut, I told Travis that was enough, there wasn't anything here that would point us to the treasure or the killer.

Bidding the old man goodbye, we went back up the hallway and emerged into the living room to see Ben's daughter sitting there across from the old woman who had greeted us earlier. Josie was holding a bowl of what looked like creamed corn and urging her to take a bite.

"Heidi ho!" the woman cried again eagerly.

"Heidi ho!" Travis replied, crossing to sit on the couch and give the old woman's hand a squeeze. "Got yourself some macque choux there, huh *cher*? That smells good." The old woman didn't reply, though she stared at Travis with sparkling eyes.

Though it seemed rude to simply insinuate ourselves into the room this way, we didn't really have much choice. After a moment's hesitation I joined Travis on the couch. Josie apologized for the mess, saying she didn't have enough time to get to everything. I wanted to reply that the place didn't seem too messy to me, just in need of repairs. Instead, I simply asked her about her father's condition. She said he'd had a stroke a few years ago and had been like that ever since.

"I noticed an interesting sign in his room. I'm guessing it's in Chitimacha?"

"'*Caqaad kaskec nama qaxt xahyte*'? Yes, it means 'Welcome to the village by the bend in the river.'" She went on to explain that the Chitimacha language had actually become extinct back in the forties, once "Miz Delphine," the last living speaker of it, had died. Lately, however, the language was being revived, thanks to a grant that was allowing the tribe to access old recordings of the language and create for the first time a written version of it. The children were learning it in school, and all of the tribe members were encouraged to use it whenever possible. She had bought the plaque for her father, hoping it might stir some memories of the language he had heard spoken in his own childhood, even if he never had seen it written out.

In reply, I brought up the subject of my father, who was also incapacitated at the moment. I told her I was the daughter of her father's old friend Julian Ledet and asked if she had heard about his accident. She replied that she hadn't, saying that with caring for four elderly patients around the clock, she barely had time to breathe, much less watch the news. I didn't know if she was telling the truth or not, but I acted as if I believed her.

As she spooned more corn mush into the old woman's mouth, I

explained that my father had been shot on Monday, and that after he was shot he had left a phone message for my mother at their house, one that referred to "Ben" and "Ben's daughter."

"Referred to us in what way?"

"Well, that's the thing. He was calling from up in the swamps, and the message is pretty garbled. He's in a coma now, and so we're trying to figure out what he said and what that has to do with him getting shot."

"Boom boom!" the old woman cried gleefully.

"Okay, honey," Josie said to the old woman, shaking her head as she scooped another spoonful from the bowl. "She's been saying that all week. Between heidi ho and boom boom I'm about to lose my mind."

"Boom boom!"

"Are you related to all of these people?" Travis asked.

Josie replied that her only relative here was Ben, but that she took in the others so that she could afford to stay home and care for him.

"Your father is a very lucky man," Travis said, giving her an encouraging smile. "Your hands must really be full."

"That's an understatement." We got an idea how full as she began to describe her days, an endless series of diapers and meals, medications and baths, living in a house with four other people, not one of whom understood a word she said. Still, she continued, she loved her father very much and was willing to make whatever sacrifices were necessary to keep him at home and be there with him. "I didn't mean to go on and on like that. Y'all caught me on a bad day. A bad week, actually. My relief worker usually comes in twice a week for a couple hours, but she quit recently, so now I'm stuck without any help at all."

"Doesn't the tribe offer support in a situation like this?" Travis asked.

"He's already in their elder care program. They do so much, bringing meals and performing health screenings and things like that. I just can't ask for more—especially because the other three who live here aren't even tribe members. They're just local folks who needed help and couldn't afford a nursing home."

Travis and I looked at each other, and the thought that kept going through my mind was that this woman couldn't have had anything to do with my father's shooting. Still, there had to be some reason my father referred to her in his message.

When she finished feeding the old woman, Josie wiped her face clean, patted her arm, and told her to sit tight as she was just going to see to the others, and once everyone had their dinner, she would get her bath.

"Bath! Heidi ho!"

Josie invited us to follow her into the next room down the hall, and I was touched to see that Travis offered to feed the man who was lying in the bed there so that Josie could focus on his wife.

"Sure, thanks. He manages pretty well, don't you, Colonel? Just sit him up and help him with the spoon to get him started."

As each of them tended to their patients, I suddenly felt like a third wheel. Travis tended to the old man so tenderly, I had to wonder if he had experienced caring for the elderly before.

I sat on the edge of the bed and asked Josie some more questions, still trying to figure out if she might be able to think of anything that could help us. About the only thing that was accomplished in the next fifteen minutes, however, was the feeding of the two old folks. Otherwise, our conversation was mostly fruitless, revealing only that Julian Ledet had come by only once or twice in the past few years, both times when he was in the area and wanted to stop in to see Ben and bring him a little treat.

"He brought my father a tray of his favorite sweets each time," Josie said, "ones he made himself. I guess it never dawned on him that my dad no longer has the teeth now to eat anything with nuts and caramel." Other than that, she said the two men had no real interaction. When asked, she said she didn't know anything about a quantity of filé, and that she'd never heard or seen something like that among her father's papers.

Eventually, I had to admit this visit was a dead end. I was ready to get out of there, but Travis was still helping the man with his spoon and didn't seem to be picking up my signals. We could hear the old woman in the front room calling out more booms and heidi hos.

"She sounds like a parrot in there," Travis said to Josie, smiling.

"The heidi ho's I can take," she replied, "it's this new boom boom stuff that's driving me crazy."

"When did that start?" Travis asked, and again I tried to catch his eye to tell him we needed to go.

"I don't know. Monday afternoon, I guess."

Travis looked to me and then back to Josie.

"Do you know what started it?"

Josie said she assumed it was something the old woman had heard on TV. I stepped forward, my mind racing.

"She's been hollering out 'boom boom' since Monday? What time Monday?"

Josie looked at me, obviously startled by my sudden interest.

"I'm not sure. Why?"

"Because my father was shot on Monday," I replied. "Monday at noon."

"Around here?"

I asked Travis where we were in relation to Paradise and he said that it was due east. Looking from Josie to me, he explained in more detail, saying that Paradise was about ten miles away as the crow flies, maybe fifteen minutes by car, but at least twenty or maybe even twenty-five minutes by water. Because there had been blood on the property, we had assumed that was where my father was when he got shot. But now I had to wonder if maybe the shooting had been in a different location, and that the blood had somehow gotten to Paradise later.

"Josie, did you hear anything unusual around here on Monday? Any kind of loud noise, something that would make her start saying 'boom'?"

Josie sat back, thinking, but as I waited for her reply, I observed a strange look coming across her features, a sort of comprehension combined with fear. I hoped for a moment we were on to something. Then she simply shook her head and avoided our eyes and told us that she had been around there all day every day for almost two weeks and in that entire time she had not heard a sound.

Clearly, she was lying.

Josie got rid of us almost immediately after that, and I found myself wishing suddenly that Travis and I had some sort of high-tech equipment, the kind they used in detective shows on TV. There was no doubt in my mind that once we were gone she was going to be contacting someone who was somehow related to all the questions we'd been asking her.

Lacking anything more sophisticated than a pair of ears, I did the next best thing. When Travis and I reached the dock, I told him that I was going to sneak back up to the house and try to listen in at a window because I had a funny feeling she might call somebody and have an important conversation. Travis wouldn't hear of it. He agreed that her behavior had turned very suspicious there at the end, but he said that if we really had scared her in some way, it would be a mistake to stick around now.

"What do you mean? This might be the big break we need."

"Yeah, and sometimes to catch a gator, you gotta stick a pole in its nest. That doesn't mean you stand around with your ear hanging out, waiting for him to bite it off!"

"Come on, Travis! We're wasting time."

"Fine," he said, pulling off his hat, smoothing back his hair, and putting the hat on again. "But if we're going to listen in, it's going to be me at the window, not you."

With that, he was off and running, ducking into the bushes and carefully making his way back toward the house. Half of me was offended at the chauvinistic basis for his behavior. The other half was flattered.

The first half won, of course, and soon I was in the bushes myself, trying to get up to the house from the other side. The windows were open, and I could hear conversation coming from inside. I crept behind a big wisteria bush that was right under the window, not realizing until I was in the thick of it that a sticker bush was hidden there as well. Trying not to cry out at the sharp pinpricks of the bush against my leg, I stepped the rest of the way over it and crouched there, straining to listen. From what I could tell, it didn't sound like an urgent phone call. Instead it was Josie, speaking in a singsong voice to the old woman in the front room.

"Honey, did you hear a big boom?"

"Boom boom!"

"Listen to me, sweetie, you can have your bath now, but you have to stop saying boom. Can you do that, can you not say those words anymore? No boom boom." Both women were silent for a moment, and then Josie spoke again. "Do you understand? No more boom boom. That's our little secret, okay?"

"No boom."

"That's right. No boom. You want your bath now?"

"Bath! Bath!"

The scrape of the chair followed by footsteps told me that Josie had left the room. More than anything, I knew we needed to call the police and get them out here right away.

Otherwise, I was afraid that this bath might be the old woman's last.

TWENTY-SEVEN

Despite the sticker bush behind me, I needed to disentangle myself from the wisteria as quickly as possible without being heard or observed. Looking around, I figured out my plan of escape. Inching forward behind the brush, I made it past the window and stood to step over an old black garden hose. At least I thought it was a garden hose. As I was about to move across it, however, suddenly it reared its ugly head, and I realized that it was a snake.

A long, dark, nasty-looking snake.

I froze. Just as the snake darted in for the kill, with a swish and a ping suddenly that snake was in two parts, both of them wriggling for a long moment before slowly growing still. My heart pounding furiously, I backed away, trying to catch my breath, and looked up to see Travis crouched nearby, a rusty old hoe in his hand.

He had saved my life, cutting that snake into two with the hoe.

We made it back to the boat in silence, though once we were there, I could see how furious he was. As for me, the adrenaline was kicking in, and I had to sit down in the boat fast, before my knees started buckling. Without a word, Travis started up the boat and drove us away from there, going a few minutes downriver until he finally turned up into an empty cove and cut the engine so we could talk.

"I know you're mad," I said before he had the chance to say anything, "but it's *her*, Travis. I heard her. She was telling the old lady not to say 'boom' any more that it was their little secret."

"Do you know what kind of snake that was?" he replied loudly. "It was a water moccasin, *cher*. One bite, and you would have been dead!"

"I know, but—"

"I don't think you do know, Chloe. Didn't I just teach you that you never, ever go up into any kind of brush in Louisiana without tapping a stick in it first to scare away snakes?"

"You did, but—"

"Snake like that, he was just minding his own business until you came along and scared him. He was responding the only way he knew how, by striking out. You should be dead now. If I hadn't gone around to that side of the house looking for a better place to listen from, you *would* be dead now."

I realized Travis was so angry at me that he couldn't hear the more important part of what was going on here. I apologized for stupidly putting myself in danger, and when he had calmed down a bit I added that in the end it had been a good thing that I did. I told him that not only was I afraid Ben's daughter was the one who shot my father, but that I had a feeling she might do something to the old woman too, just to keep her quiet.

"Did you see the way she took care of them in there?" Travis asked me, shaking his head. "She's not capable of murder."

"I heard what I heard, Travis. She was talking to the old woman, telling her she couldn't have a bath unless she stopped saying 'boom.'"

"That doesn't prove anything."

"You didn't hear her tone of voice. She was threatening her."

"Fine, then. Maybe she did shoot your father, but I guarantee you she wouldn't harm any of those old folks in there."

Regardless of what Travis said, I knew the old woman might be in danger. We needed to call the police and have them come right out. We just had to do it in the right way, so they wouldn't end up arresting me instead of her.

Travis came up with a plan that would buy us a little time. He called his grandmother and asked her if she knew Ben Runner' daughter, Josie.

"Good, good," he said, giving me a thumbs-up. "Then I need you to do me a favor. Can you call her house and just act like you're looking for me? Start chatting. I need you to keep her on the phone for a while...Uh-huh...I'll explain later...Okay...just talk with her on the phone ten or fifteen minutes, okay? Thanks, *Grandmere*." Travis hung up the phone and to me said, "Asking my *grandmere* to chat on the phone for ten minutes, that's like asking a marathon runner to jog around the block." Sliding the phone in his pocket, Travis laid out his intentions, saying that Josie wouldn't do anything stupid as long as there was someone else on the other end of the telephone line. In the meantime he and I could remain hidden here in this private location, call the police, and tell them what we had seen and heard. That way, whether they ended up arresting her or not, at least they wouldn't find us. I agreed that that sounded like the most prudent course of action.

Still, I was afraid the police wouldn't believe me, given that it was just my word against hers—and I was an accused murderer while she was an upstanding citizen who lovingly tended to a house filled with the elderly. I decided I might be better off calling my friend on the inside, Wade Henkins. He could relay the information to the local police, and the fact that he was a cop himself, albeit one who worked in New Orleans and not down here, would give it much more weight.

"You said for me to call you if I needed help. I need help," I told him once he answered my call.

Wade listened as I explained to him what I had seen and heard, and how Josie was clearly lying. I repeated the words that she had said to the old woman, and Wade agreed that it was very suspicious indeed. "Even if she's not the one who pulled the trigger, it sounds like she obviously knows more than she was letting on."

Wade seemed to understand my desire to avoid the police for the time being. He said that he would call them for me and then get back to me.

"Are you somewhere safe in the meantime?" he asked. "You don't need to tell me where you are. I just want to know that you're okay."

"I'm okay for now, but I'll feel better once the police have a chance to talk to Josie Runner and see for themselves what I'm talking about."

After we hung up, Travis asked me if I was sure that Wade himself could be trusted. He was the last person to see my father before he was shot, after all, Travis reminded me. And as a cop, he also carried a gun. In reply, I told Travis that I was just so grateful to the man for helping to move up my bail hearing that I hadn't given his guilt or innocence much thought after that.

"I guess we'll know for sure soon," I added, "depending on whether or not the police go to Josie's. If they do, then Wade's likely on the up-and-up. If they don't, then that means he's probably getting in his car in New Orleans right now, heading down here himself to come after us."

We waited there in tense silence until Travis' phone rang about ten minutes later. He answered and had a brief conversation, finally disconnecting the call and returning the phone to his pocket.

"Well, *c'est ca.* That was Minette, wanting to know why, in the middle of a conversation with her friend Josie, the police came knocking on the woman's door."

I couldn't help but smile, glad to know that I wasn't wrong about Wade.

"It would be bad manners for me to say I told you so, so I won't say it. That I told you so."

"Sorry, but you can't blame a Naquin for not trusting a Henkins. Our families have been feuding for years."

"Feuding? You mean like the Hatfields and the McCoys?"

"Not exactly. Wade's father and his father before him were not nice men. But I guess Wade himself is fine."

While Travis started our engine again, I thought about Wade's story of how his father died and my father and Alphonse stepped into his life, kind of like big brothers. Between that and the anonymous gift of the college scholarship to Ben, at least this whole experience had given me a different picture of my dad. He could still be a jerk, but at least I knew now he could also be a pretty nice guy sometimes too.

"So where do we go next?" I asked.

"I think we need to lay low until we find out what happens at Josie's. In fact, we should probably put a little more distance between ourselves and her place, just in case the cops decide to come after us once she tells them that we got there by boat."

"Good idea."

Travis started up the engine and I put on my floppy hat again, even though the sun had already set and the darkness was fast approaching. Before we took off, he unhooked a big flashlight from under the seat, handed it to me, and told me to be ready to shine it out in front of us like a headlight once we needed it.

Driving back down the river away from Josie's, I thought about how badly I wanted to clear my name, to learn that the charges against me had been dropped. Beyond that, I wanted to know the details, the who and why and how of what had really gone on down here the day my father was shot and after that as well.

As long as I was letting myself think of the things I wanted, I wanted to get out of this ridiculous getup and into some decent clothes, and I wanted to get back to New Orleans and go to the hospital. My mother and I had a lot of things to discuss, and I was not looking forward to that, but it would be worth putting up with her just to be able to finally see my father. I couldn't believe that I had landed in New Orleans on Monday night, and here it was Wednesday evening and I still hadn't seen him. After all I had been through in just two short days, I couldn't believe that there was a good chance that all of this was finally coming to an end.

From behind me, I heard Travis whistle, and I turned to see what he wanted.

"*Regardez!*" he said, smiling and pointing toward the shoreline.

I looked in the direction he indicated, to see a flock of huge white birds taking to the sky. As I watched them soar and dip in the encroaching darkness, I couldn't help thinking about the one downside of this whole thing coming to an end: That would also mean an end of my time with Travis.

It had been a very long time since I had met someone I genuinely liked as much as I liked Travis Naquin. Though he could come across as a *goo goo ga ga* or whatever he had called it, in truth he seemed very intelligent, quite talented, and most of all kindhearted. It struck me that he didn't talk very much about himself, and in a way that was refreshing. Having grown up with an egomaniac for a father, I think I just expected all men to act as if the earth revolved around them. Though Julian Ledet was an extreme case, it seemed to me that most of the men in my life were self-absorbed. Now, after spending so much time in the company of the unpretentious, unassuming Travis, I found myself wondering what it would be like to date him.

With a sad smile, I thought of the lost opportunity from the summer we were both eighteen. Had I not been such a prim and proper snob on our date, Travis' dream for that summer might very well have come true. We could have fallen in love and had one last fling before both heading off to college. Then again, I had a feeling that Travis Naquin was not the "fling" type. He was more the love-you-forever kind of guy, the type of man you bring home to Mama. The one you marry. I couldn't imagine how different my life would have been if things had gone differently so long ago.

We were still speeding along the darkening waterway when I noticed that this engine was beginning to make funny noises too. I turned around to look at Travis, wondering if someone had tampered with our engine while we were inside at Josie's.

"This seems to be my day for engine trouble!" he called to me over the faltering roar of the motor.

At least we had put some distance between ourselves and Josie's by that point. As I flicked on the powerful lamp and shone it ahead of us, Travis turned into a side channel, one that seemed to have no houseboats or camps on it, and then he turned again into an equally deserted one and finally cut the engine.

The bayou was wide here, but I kept my eye on the direction we were drifting, as I had no desire to float into the overgrown tangle of flora and fauna that hung from the shore on both sides. One snake encounter per day was more than enough for me.

"Did somebody sabotage us?" I asked fearfully, my voice sounding loud in the sudden quiet.

Travis was silent for a moment as he carefully tinkered with the hot motor. Then he replied that he didn't think so. This looked to be a timing problem. He asked me to turn around and shine the light where he was working, so I did just that.

"Should we call someone for help?"

"Not yet. I should be able to fix it."

"How far are we from all of those friends and relatives you were talking about, the ones who have places up in the swamps?"

"About another five miles or so, too far to paddle in this kind of boat. Speaking of paddles, *cher*, you might want to grab one and use it right about now."

I turned around to see that we had practically drifted directly under the very place I hadn't wanted to go. Putting down the flashlight and frantically grabbing a paddle from the floor of the boat, I used it to push off from a fat tree trunk and float us out toward the middle again.

Once there, I again picked up the light and shone it toward the engine. Travis certainly seemed to know what he was doing, and as he worked I allowed myself to watch the certain, strong movements of his hands.

All around us, though it was nearly dark now, the swamp sounds were coming to life. Between the crickets and the frogs and a dozen other noises I couldn't identify, it almost felt as though we were listening to a mood tape, one from the rain forest or something. Creepiest of all were the near-constant plopping sounds that came at us from all sides. I wasn't sure what sorts of things were causing the water to plop, but I hoped it was flying fish or frogs or something benign like that—and not snakes or alligators or other, more ominous creatures.

"Chloe! *Allons done.*"

"What is it? We're still out in the middle."

He gestured toward the light, and with a start, I realized that I had let the beam wander to the wrong angle. As I corrected myself, I noticed something sparkling on the water about ten feet away

"Hold on a second," I said lifting the flashlight to train the beam out toward the shoreline. I could see two pairs of lights reflecting back at me, though I wasn't sure what they were so I asked Travis.

"*Cocodrie.* Now can you shine the light this way, please?"

"*Cocodrie*..." I said, thinking, and then I gasped. "Alligators?"

"Of course, *cher*. We're in Louisiana. What did you expect?"

With a shudder, I wondered if they were just sitting there watching us and waiting for our boat to sink so they could swoop in for a yummy dinner. I had seen enough *National Geographic* specials to know that alligators could move pretty fast and jump quite high—when they wanted to. Fortunately, they rarely wanted to.

"Hey, at least it's just April," Travis added softly. "Wait till it gets warmer and they all start coming out. When that happens, you can shine your light across the bayou and literally see hundreds of glowing eyes looking back at you. It's really something."

He was just chatting, unaware of the terrifying effect his words had on me.

"And you really did catch your first gator when you were only seven?" I asked, trying to distract myself.

"*Oui*, thanks to *Grandmere* Minette. She wanted to make stew but we were all out of chickens, so we went for a walk in the woods instead, saying we would cook up the first thing we found. I guess we were both a little surprised when the first thing we found was an alligator, caught up in one of our traps. By the time my *grandpere* got home that night, there was alligator stew on the table and a new pair of boots waiting for him by the door."

I couldn't help but laugh.

"Aren't you exaggerating just a little?"

"Well, now, there's always that chance. Exaggerating is one of those things comes pretty natural to Cajuns, so sometimes it's kind of hard to know."

As Travis worked, he told me about more of the creatures of the swamps, the nutria and frogs and snakes and fish—not to mention things like wild boars and bobcats and even bears. Of course, that only served to scare me more, especially when a bat swooped down at the water right beside the boat, causing me to yelp.

"You know," Travis said suddenly, turning his attention from the motor to me, "if you're scared you can move a little closer."

I did as he suggested, carefully sliding from the front slat to the middle one. Turning around, my knees just fit against the side of Travis' leg. He was right. Being there next to him made me feel a lot safer. He went back to work on the engine, and as he did, I realized that sitting so close to him made my heart pound in a different way altogether. Judging by the way he kept looking back at me, I had a feeling Travis was feeling the heat between us too. Finally, he closed something on the top of the motor, turned to me again, put a hand on my arm, and asked if I was okay.

"I think so."

"Well, good. Because it just struck me that I might have to keep you *very* close, purely in the name of safety."

The tone of his voice and the way he was suddenly looking at me let me know that safety wasn't really what he was talking about at all.

"Oh?" I asked softly. "So if some big, nasty creature showed up right about now, we'd have to get even closer?"

He didn't answer my question at first but instead just looked deeply into my eyes. From the tilt of his chin, I could tell he wanted to kiss me. I leaned slightly forward and tilted my head the other way, suddenly wishing he would do just that.

"Hey, *cher*? I don't want to move in to anything you're not prepared for," Travis said softly, the heat of his lips very near mine.

"I think I've been preparing for this my whole life," I whispered.

"No, I mean we're drifting again," Travis said, suddenly pulling back. "Grab the paddle, *cher*, or we're going to end up under the trees."

I spun around, mortified to see that the heavy, ominous branches were now only inches away. This time, Travis and I both grabbed a paddle, and worked our way furiously back out in the middle. As we did, I felt like biting my tongue, taking back that last, idiotic comment I had made in the heat of the moment. *I've been preparing for this my whole life?* Had I really just said that?

"What are we going to do, Travis? We obviously can't stay out here all night, paddling like a pair of propellers every time we near the bank."

"No need to," he replied, sliding his paddle back onto the floor of our little boat. "I fixed the motor. Did I forget to tell you?"

With a wink and a grin, he reached back and pulled the cord, causing the engine to spring to life.

TWENTY-EIGHT

FRANCE, 1719
JACQUES

Something was going on, something that stirred and frenzied the patients like animals in the forest before a fire. Jacques could sense it as soon as he awoke. Up and down the halls, everyone seemed to be working themselves into a fevered pitch. The patient noises had frightened him at first, but over the last month he had grown to identify most of them, the screamers and the criers and the moaners and the babblers. Though Jacques was clearly sane, he had been placed in the building reserved for lunatics. According to a conversation he'd overheard between the two Brothers who performed the bloodletting each week, Jacques was better off in here anyway, as the other buildings housed criminals and the severely ill. Eventually, Jacques had learned to sleep through the noise. Not this morning, though. This morning it sounded as though every single one of the men on this floor was at his most vocal.

Jacques, on the other hand, was one of the silent ones. It wasn't that he didn't have anything to say, it was that there simply wasn't anyone worth talking to. The people here didn't listen, and the Brothers and maids and servants didn't believe him. The only choice he had was to keep his mouth shut and bide his time and wait for his case to be handled in its turn. He could only hope that he hadn't been forgotten. Jacques knew that it wasn't uncommon for a man to be locked away in Charenton for many years without even so much as a trial. Jacques didn't get much communication from the outside, but he knew two things: Papa was surely dead by now, and Angelique had been lost to him forever.

Given that, Jacques had come to the point where he didn't really care how things turned out. He wanted to be free, yes, and he wanted to clear his name. But as neither event seemed likely to happen soon, if ever, he spent most of his time simply trying to survive, one sane man in the midst of madness.

"Key man! Key man!" one of the screamers yelled from the doorway. That guy seemed to get worked up every time anyone opened or closed the massive iron doors at each end of the long hall. This time, however, it sounded as though he wasn't the only one yelling about it. Soon the phrase "key man" was being called out, up and down, in both directions.

Again, Jacques had an odd sense that something big was going on. He got up from his narrow cot and went to the doorway, which was packed with people. Pushing his way through, he finally got a glimpse of what the fuss was all about: The iron door at one end of the hall was propped open, something Jacques hadn't seen happen since he had arrived.

"What's going on?" he asked those around him, but of course he received no intelligible replies.

Pushing his way through the crowded hall, he tried to find someone sporting the telltale white garb of the servants, but he couldn't find any.

When Jacques reached the open doorway, he realized that though all of the patients were clustering there, none of them were venturing past, even though there was nothing to stop them. They simply hovered at the edge of freedom and peered beyond, trying to catch a glimpse of whatever might be on the other side.

Jacques didn't want to cause trouble or make waves, but the whole thing was ridiculous. Had the door come loose on its own? Had someone simply unlocked it and left it open? Jacques didn't know what was going on, but he kept thinking of Peter in the Bible, Peter who had been locked in a prison and then miraculously set free. Miracle or not, Jacques decided to explore.

Emerging from the crowd, he stepped through the open doorway and ventured several feet into the large area at the top of the stairs. As he did, the patients went nuts, their already frenzied sounds and motions exploding with renewed vigor. The rooms on his floor had windows but they were all set high, far too high to see out of. Here, however, Jacques saw that there was a normal window, one that looked down on the grassy knoll outside.

Moving to that window now, Jacques would have been happy simply to drink up the sight of the trees, the autumn colors, the sunshine. But there was more to see out there, much more. Something indeed was going on. The lawn was covered with people.

Pressing his face to the glass, Jacques tried to understand what was happening. There was order in the chaos, though he couldn't quite figure out the purpose of it all. From the looks of things, men and women were being paired together, tied at the wrists, and moved into some sort of line. Already, about twenty couples had been hooked together that way, with more in the making.

"Here's one," a Brother suddenly called from the stairs.

He was just coming up and had caught Jacques looking out of the window.

"I didn't do anything. The door was already open," Jacques said, backing up, afraid that he might be penalized for his infraction.

"I know, son. I'm the one who opened it."

The man stood there at the doorway, cupped his hands around his mouth, and began calling out instructions at the top of his voice to the frenzied crowd inside. Jacques hovered nearby, trying to understand how this could be happening.

"Attention, everyone! Today you have the opportunity to change your life. Another ship is leaving for the Isle d'Orleans, and it needs passengers willing to go there and help settle the new colony. Anyone who is of sound mind and willing to go to the New World will be released to do so. You must be unmarried and healthy. If you choose to accept this offer, please proceed in an orderly fashion down the stairs. You will be directed where to go once you get there. If you choose not to accept this offer, please remain..."

Jacques didn't even wait for the man to finish.

As fast as he could, he ran down the stairs and then eagerly continued on outside, to the place he was directed. There were plenty of servants out here, keeping everyone in line, making sure no one could run off. Blinking in the sun, Jacques got behind a short fellow in the same muslin pajamas they all wore, a man who kept giggling and rubbing his fingers together. What a joke, that the offer required one to be of sound mind. Who were they kidding?

Still, Jacques couldn't believe this was happening. Could it really be possible? Had he just been given his ticket out?

As much as he loved Paris, life there had been ruined for him the day everything went wrong. He had heard terrible things about the Isle d'Orleans, but surely living in a colony in the midst of a swamp could be no worse than trying to survive in an insane asylum. Better yet, if Jacques had his freedom, he would be in a position to right the wrongs that had been done to him. Even from half a world away, he had a better chance of clearing his name from over there than he did from inside here.

The ship carrying the statuettes had set sail for the New World more than a month ago. Jacques had no idea whether or not John Law and his minions had been able to switch them out for the gilded ones before sailing, but either way he planned to follow the statuettes wherever the pursuit led him.

The line was moving forward, and soon it was Jacques' turn at the front. He didn't know why, but a woman was grabbed from a different line and tied to him at the wrist.

She wasn't wearing the muslin pajamas of the asylum but instead the gray smock of the adjoining prison. They didn't speak at first, but after an hour of being bound together in line, Jacques finally asked her name.

"Lily," she said in a low, flat voice.

"I'm Jacques."

Lily didn't seem very healthy, and several times Jacques thought she might pass out in the heat of the warm autumn sun.

With his help, though, she managed to stay erect, and eventually they were herded onto a flat-bottomed rowboat with about fifteen other bound couples. From the talk on board, this boat would take them down the Seine all the way to La Havre, where they would then board the ship that was to bring them to the New World.

Jacques drank in the views like a man rescued from the desert. As they sailed past the vivid oranges and yellows and browns of autumn, he couldn't help but think that in the New World he wouldn't mind it even if he had to sleep out in the open air. Anything was better than the feral, fetid existence he'd been living in the asylum.

As they neared Paris, he spotted two other, similar passenger boats waiting there and tied up to the dock. They tied his boat up as well, though Jacques wasn't sure why as there were soldiers there with guns pointed at them, making sure no one got up to leave. They all sat there mostly in quiet until a fourth ship joined them from behind. Once it had been secured, a priest came out to the landing, opened his Bible and began speaking in Latin.

At first Jacques figured that the priest was blessing their journey. After a while, though, something about the words gave him pause. He had heard them before.

They were the words of matrimony.

This was a mass wedding! Stunned, Jacques tried to decide what to do, but there didn't seem to be any way to stop it. Several others tried and were nearly shot for their efforts. It seemed that this one small fact had been left out of the announcement earlier. When the Brother had said you must be single, it was because in order to go to the New World you had to marry first.

At least the woman tied to Jacques wasn't like some of the others, insane or toothless or ridden with lice. But then when the ceremony was over and he turned to look at her, he saw it: the brand of the fleur-de-lis on her shoulder.

The mark of a prostitute.

The irony was not lost on Jacques. After all that the two hundred fleur-de-lis had cost him, now he was heading across the sea with a fleur-de-lis of his very own. Too bad it was one he didn't want.

It wasn't until the boats were untied and continuing on their journey that he allowed himself to take in the vast skyline of the city where he had always lived, the city he loved. As they passed under bridge after bridge, Jacques looked up at the faces of the people who were lining the rails. Word had obviously spread about the seabound newlyweds, and everywhere along the way folks were staring down at them in curiosity.

As the boat approached the Pont Royal, Jacques turned his face downward, fearing that if the royal goldsmith saw him he might have him pulled from the journey and returned to the asylum. Once past the bridge, Jacques dared to steal a glance toward the Tuileries, the place where he and Angelique had first met.

What he saw there on the riverbank would haunt his dreams forever.

Standing alone, a dark cape draped around her petite shoulders, was Angelique herself. Their eyes met, and even from that distance he could see the hurt and the loss and surprise there. She really had loved him, but in the end it made no difference. Jacques realized that their love was never meant to be, that what had been doomed from the start was never going to happen.

Still, that knowledge didn't stop Jacques from loving her with all of his heart, a heart that was now breaking in two. As they floated past, Jacques turned so that he could keep watching her as she stood there alone on the banks of the Seine looking back at him. He stayed that way for a very long time, until Angelique was nothing more than a single dot on the horizon, and then she disappeared.

TWENTY-NINE

Half an hour later, we reached what Travis called Duck Lake. We still hadn't heard back from Wade about Josie and the police, so Travis suggested that we make landfall. He said we could wait things out at his cabin, which was a short way up a nearby bayou, but that we'd have to be very quiet getting there, lest one of his friends or relatives hear us out on the water and spread the news on the local grapevine, news which might eventually leak out to the police.

If Wade eventually called with good news, telling us that Josie had confessed or the killer had been found or the charges against me had been dropped or anything along those lines, then all we would need to do next would be to get across the bayou to Travis' aunt's house, which offered a choice of several vehicles we could borrow and access to a road. If Wade called with bad news, well, at least we would be safe and dry in the meantime and in a far better position to regroup and plan our next course of action.

When he finally turned in toward a dock, I was pleased to see that his place was much nicer than I had expected. From what I could tell in the moonlight, it was more like a cute little house than a camp, set back from the water with a covered picnic area along one side.

We got out of the boat and tied it there, but instead of heading up toward the house, Travis simply looked around for another big stick on the ground, picked it up, and began whacking at some bushes near an upside down canoe.

"You've got to be kidding me," I said.

"What's wrong?"

"Where are we?"

"This is my cousin T-Ray's house. He's out of town for a while, so I know he won't mind if we borrow his canoe."

"But why?"

"I tol' you, *cher*. Noise. We got to go up the bayou to get to my camp, and we can't risk running a motor."

Travis Naquin was simply pushing me too far. An aluminum fishing boat was bad enough, but now he expected me to climb aboard a canoe and paddle the rest of the way? Incredible!

"You honestly expect me to go out in that little thing in the middle of the night, in the dark, in the swamp?"

Travis seemed genuinely perplexed at my objections. As he flipped the canoe over and pushed it toward the water, he asked me what on earth was wrong with it, that this was a birchbark canoe, worth far more than the old motorboat we had just gotten out of.

"This is a gorgeous piece of equipment."

"Travis, I don't care if it wins a beauty contest. I am not getting in that boat."

Ignoring my objections, he simply climbed into the back and settled himself there.

"Okay, *cher*, then you can just stay here and take your chances with the snake that's hanging in the tree over your head."

With a squeal I raised my purse over my head as protection and got into the canoe. Once I was safely settled inside, purse tucked under the wooden slat, I looked back toward the tree. Sure enough, a snake was clearly visible there on a branch directly above where I'd been standing, its red, black, and white bands practically glowing in the moonlight.

"Don't worry, *cher*. It's just a milksnake. Even if it bit you, it wouldn't kill you."

I was fuming after that, astounded that he could be so insensitive about this on the very day I had almost been bitten by a poisonous snake. At first I wasn't sure if Travis didn't notice the intensity of my emotion or simply didn't care, because he handed me a paddle and told me to pick a side and a rhythm and he would follow. I did as he said, silently working out my anger with the paddle against the water. After we were well underway, Travis surprised me by suddenly apologizing for what had happened back there, saying that we had to keep moving and that meant doing whatever it took to get me into the canoe. Before I could even reply, he told me that we shouldn't talk from there on out.

Taking a few deep breaths, I acknowledged his apology with a nod and forced myself to calm down. The snake hadn't been poisonous and it hadn't bitten me. That's all that mattered—that and the fact that I was currently paddling through waters that held far more dangerous creatures. At least Travis had had the decency to apologize, which was something I encouraged often in my etiquette lessons but that many people found almost impossible to do.

With the sharp bow of the canoe smoothly moving through the water, I focused on my paddling rhythm and how good it felt to work the muscles in my arms and shoulders. At least the moon was nearly full, so we didn't have to use the flashlight. The night noises were in force here too, but I had almost grown accustomed to them by now. It helped that as my eyes adjusted to the light, I could spot a jumping fish now and then, which was one reason for the incessant plops. I didn't see any alligators, though they were probably lining our journey on both sides of the bayou.

As we paddled along, I decided that I might survive. I was still scared, but the bayou was smooth as glass here, and the canoe felt more stable than I had expected, so at least I wasn't afraid that we might end up capsizing into the black void below. At one point, I spotted another snake, this one zigzagging down the waterway. It was long and black, but as it was swimming away from us, not toward us, I wasn't going to let myself panic.

Mostly, I tried to focus on all we had learned and all we still needed to know. My mind kept going back to the treasure, the very thing that had started all of this, not to mention my new knowledge that an old salt mine existed underneath Paradise. The two had to be connected somehow.

Either my father had first found the treasure down inside the mine or he had hidden it there later—or maybe even both. Treasure or not, I wondered who also knew about the source of the secret salt. Surely Alphonse Naquin was aware of it, but perhaps no one else was.

In any event, I could only hope that Travis had a Louisiana map at his place. We still lacked two of the numbers we needed in order to find the treasure, but at least we had four: my father's, which was 45; Conrad's, which was 16; Sam's, which was 18; and Ruben's, which was 29. Using the coordinates of Paradise as our starting point, my hope was that we could juggle around the numbers and narrow down the range well enough to pinpoint the general location of the treasure.

On the other hand, if the numbers we had so far in no way matched any of the coordinates of Paradise, then we'd know that we were on the wrong track and Paradise hadn't been the site of the treasure's hiding place after all.

We rounded a wide curve of the bayou, and I could hear a stereo playing not too far up ahead. I turned and looked at Travis, but he merely held a finger to his lips. The closer we got, I realized that the music was live, not recorded, and that it was coming from a large, well-lit camp up on the right. It looked as though the dock and structures there were decorated with hundreds of tiny white lights, and they reflected on the water's surface like stars. Given how far out that light projected over the water, I couldn't imagine how we were ever going to make it past that house without being spotted. I needn't have worried. Before we reached the light, Travis tapped me on the shoulder and pointed off to the left, to a dock that was hidden in the shadows.

Aiming our craft toward that dock, we paddled silently until we pulled alongside and Travis leaned forward, whispering in my ear.

"I haven't been here in a while, so you had better stay in the canoe while I clear the way."

By "clear the way," I thought he meant he wanted to straighten up inside, as in throw the dirty clothes in the hamper or something. Instead, he got up on the dock still holding his oar and softly tapped it against the boards, making his way toward the porch. That's when I realized that when he said he would clear the way he was talking about snakes. The tapping went on so long I was afraid the people across the bayou might hear, but their music was playing so loudly that I realized it wasn't likely. When Travis finally gave me the all clear, I gingerly climbed from the canoe onto the dock and then we both hauled the craft up onto the grassy bank, got our things out of it, and turned it upside down.

Once inside, Travis propped his gun beside the door and then pulled back the curtains to let in the moonlight. Unfortunately, it wasn't enough for us to be able to see, so he fumbled around in a closet and ended up hanging towels and blankets over each window, even though they all had shades on them already. He went outside to do a sight test and I flipped on the overhead light for the count of three and then back off again. When he came back in, he fixed the corner of one window and then put the light back on for good, saying that except for that one corner, you couldn't tell from outside that the light was on inside.

"And we can talk in here?" I whispered.

"As long as we keep it soft," he replied.

Now that the place was illuminated, I looked around to see that it was a simple cabin consisting of one large room that functioned as a bedroom, living room, and kitchenette all in one. To one side was a bathroom and to the other was an exterior door that likely led to some sort of yard. I had been curious to see Travis in his element, but this place didn't tell me much about him. With its tan walls and light brown couch and bedspread, it seemed sort of bland and boring—words that I would never have used to describe Travis himself.

About the only decorative touches in the whole place were old record albums that had been framed and hung on the walls. Looking at them more closely, I realized that they were all Louisiana related, mostly jazz interspersed with Cajun and zydeco.

"*Lache Pas La Patate?*" I asked, reading one of the album titles.

"Yeah, it's an old Cajun saying: 'Don't drop the potato.'"

"What's it mean?"

Travis went to a cabinet in the kitchen area and began rooting through the cans, obviously hoping to find something we could eat for dinner.

"I've heard it used two ways. Sometimes it just means 'don't give up' or 'hang in there.' Most of the time, it's more specific than that and means 'don't let go of what's truly important, particularly your Cajun heritage.'"

I came over to the counter and sat on the bar stool there, watching as Travis pulled out several types of soup, chili, and beef stew.

"I can't imagine what that would be like, to belong to something that way."

"What do you mean, *cher*? You're French Creole, aren't you? That's something to belong to."

"Not these days. In the beginning, of course, early Creoles formed a very tight-knit people group, from what I understand. But that's back when 'Creole' meant one thing, someone who was born in the New World to parents who were from the Old." I added that over the years the term had slowly shifted and changed so much that nowadays most people weren't even sure what Creole meant anymore. "Some people think it's just a style of cooking. Others think that's what you call someone of mixed race, or anyone in Louisiana with a French surname. Take your pick. How can I belong to something that nobody even knows what it is?"

Smiling, Travis admitted that I had a good point.

"Listen," he added, "I could go outside and run lines or do some frogging or something and catch us a nice dinner, but I just don't dare, considering how busy things are across the water. Somebody might spot me. Right now, I think the best I can offer is this enticing array of canned goods."

"At least it's food," I said, realizing that I was hungry. "My vote's for the beef stew."

"Beef stew it is," he replied, returning the other cans to the cabinet.

"Anyway, from what I can see, being Cajun is really significant—it's an identity, a community, a way of life, a style of music, a form of cooking, a language..." My voice trailed off as I couldn't think of how to say what I wanted to say. How could I explain that I had spent my entire life on the outside looking in, in almost every circumstance? Whether at school, work, or play, I had never found a place where I belonged. Even in my own nuclear family I was the third wheel, the one left out in the cold while my parents enjoyed living in their little nation of two. "I'm just envious, I guess. It must feel good to be a part of such a thriving people group, even one that has suffered persecution as the Cajuns have. The whole Cajun experience defines you. It lets you be who you are within a safety net of absolute acceptance."

Travis was quiet as he opened the stew, dumped it onto two paper plates, and heated the first one in the microwave.

"Chloe, do you know what people called you behind your back when we were teenagers?" he asked suddenly.

The microwave beeped.

"Ice Queen?" I replied, stiffening.

"Yeah. I wasn't sure if you knew."

Pulling out the plate, he added a fork and a paper towel for a napkin then slid both across the counter to me. I looked down at the stew, my appetite suddenly waning, wondering why he had brought that up.

"Even back then," he explained, "I knew it wasn't true. The guys all said that you were snobby and aloof, but that's not the Chloe I could see. The Chloe I saw made herself an outsider on purpose, not because she was a snob, but because she didn't know how to be an insider. Just now, to hear you talking about Cajuns like that, I have to wonder if that's what the problem was, the whole safety net thing. Have you never had in your whole life the feeling that you belonged somewhere and that you were totally loved and accepted?"

I was dumbfounded, not just that he had had the nerve to say that to me, but that he had been so incredibly perceptive. I'm not sure why I was surprised. He was, after all, the first one to fully believe my innocence after I was released from jail. Obviously perceptiveness was his special gift.

"Eugenie and Sam. They gave me lots of love. But even as a very little girl I can remember standing at the sink with Eugenie, washing dishes together, and wishing my arms were dark brown like hers instead of pale and freckled like mine. Of course, I was just a kid. I didn't understand the issues they faced, had never heard of civil rights, and didn't know what prejudice was. All I knew was that I wanted so much to be their daughter.

I guess, even then, I didn't really belong. One look at my blue eyes and blond hair made that obvious. An outsider yet again."

A beep announced that the microwave was finished, and Travis pulled out his plate of stew. He set it on the counter and then surprised me by reaching out and taking both of my hands in his. I thought he was going to say something important to me, but instead he simply bowed his head and asked a blessing for our food. After his "amen," he gave my hands a squeeze and let go.

"Ah, well, at least you always have the love of your heavenly Father," he said before taking a bite of his stew. "He *is* love, after all."

"Yep, as long as I follow all the rules."

"What do you mean?"

I swallowed my bite of the stew and dabbed at my mouth with the paper towel.

"Religion. It's filled with rules. Do this, don't do that. Don't get me wrong, that's one of the things I've always liked about the Bible, that it lays things out very clearly. I guess you could say it was the original guide to etiquette."

Travis looked at me, his mouth agape.

"What?" I asked.

"The Bible might have rules for living a more godly life, *cher*, but not for being loved. God's love doesn't hinge on anything. It just *is*."

Leaving his stew to get cold on the table, Travis moved to a small desk, opened a drawer, and pulled out a Bible. For the next ten minutes, he went through it, reading me verses about the nature of God's love, ones that he said showed how it was unilateral and undeserved and unearned and unfailing and unending. As he read and talked, I began to think that he was right: God's love wasn't earned, as I had assumed, it just *was*. Here I'd been afraid to pray for fear of seeming like an ingrate, when in fact Travis said God didn't care what I came to Him about as long as I came to Him!

"This is what real love looks like, *cher*. It's about grace, not rules. Yes, there is judgment, and that judgment is fierce and eternal. But even that comes out of God's love. He sent his Son so that whoever believes can come. You don't have to be on the outside looking in on that one. There's your safety net, *cher*. There's your acceptance. If you're a believer like you say you are, then you're *in*."

In any other situation, I might have felt that I was being preached at or talked down to, but Travis was just so genuinely enthusiastic that it didn't come across that way. In fact, as he continued to share with me from the Bible and from his heart what the character of God really looked like, a new understanding began to dawn on me. Many of the things Travis told me I had heard before, but somehow the way he explained them made sense in a whole new way.

"If you want to know for sure what it feels like to be a part of something bigger than yourself, listen to this from Ephesians," Travis said finally. "'There is one body and one Spirit—just as you were called to one hope when you were called—one Lord, one faith, one baptism; one God and Father of all, who is over all and through all and in all.' If that's not His way of telling you that you belong, *cher*, then I don't know what is." With that, he closed the Bible and gave me a triumphant smile.

"Thanks, Travis. You've given me a lot to think about and a whole new way to look at my faith."

"Well, I'm sorry to go all preachy on you," he replied, "but all of sudden God just laid this stuff on my heart. He *loves* you, Chloe. He always has and He always will. No matter what you do. You can't earn it. It's just there."

I looked at this man who was standing in front of me, Bible clutched in his hands, earnestness written all over his handsome face. What I had done to deserve such passionate concern for my heart or soul I had no idea. I just knew that of all the people in the world who could have been pulled into this situation with me, I was infinitely grateful it had been Travis Naquin.

THIRTY

After we finished our stew and had cleaned up the kitchenette area, I asked Travis if he had a map of Louisiana. He felt sure that he did, so as he poked around in drawers and cabinets looking for it, I tried to remember the basics of latitude and longitude I'd long ago learned in school. From what I could recall, measures of latitude were those parallel, horizontal lines on a globe that were identified in degrees. Within those lines, even more precise lines could be indicated by the use of "minutes" and "seconds." All three numbers written together as degrees, minutes, and seconds were considered to be "coordinates." The coordinates of zero degrees, zero minutes, and zero seconds—expressed as 0° 0' 0"—fell right at the equator. All of the latitudes that came above that were considered "North."

Similarly, measures of longitude were those lines that ran around the globe vertically. Also measured in degrees, minutes, and seconds, the coordinates of 0° 0' 0" longitude passed through the prime meridian, which was in Greenwich, England. Left of there, all the way to the international date line, longitudes were considered "West." That was why the line in the poem, *North and West you may search for things gone amiss*, made so much sense, especially given that he had capitalized the words "North" and "West." By combining a pair of coordinates to find where a specific line of latitude intersected with a specific line of longitude, one could actually pinpoint an exact spot on the globe. No doubt, if we could find the coordinates we were looking for, the treasure would be waiting for us there.

"Found it!" Travis said triumphantly, pulling an old map from the back of a drawer.

He spread it out on the kitchen counter, and together we played with the numbers we had recovered thus far, which were 16, 18, 29, and 45. We weren't sure how those numbers should be arranged into coordinates, so I asked Travis for a pen and paper where I wrote down letters substituted for numbers: X° X' X" N/Y° Y' Y" W. Under that, I started listing the various possibilities of how the four numbers we had might slot in, starting with 16° 18' 29" N/45° Y' Y" W. But given the possible variations of four numbers plugged into six places, I decided that would take too long.

Instead, we worked backward, starting with the map of Louisiana. By doing that, we were easily able to conclude where one of the numbers in our equation fell, simply because 29° N passed right through Louisiana. Better yet, 29° 45' N cut directly across Paradise! Thus far, then, our coordinates could be expressed as 29° 45' X" N and Y° Y' Y" W.

Unfortunately, the 16 and the 18—the numbers from Conrad and Sam—weren't nearly so easy to pinpoint. Looking at the map, we realized that either latitude, 29° 45' 16" or 29° 45' 18", could be correct. To make things even more complicated, the 16 and 18 could have been a part of the longitude instead. A reading of 91° 16' 18", for example, crossed Paradise, though 91° 18' 16" fell west of there.

Combining the readings that did land squarely on Paradise gave us several possibilities, but without all six numbers to work with, the readings still weren't specific enough to pinpoint the treasure. Given that each degree of latitude was about seventy miles apart, it was obvious that even one mistake could take us far off course. Using the four numbers we had and looking at the map, we both thought it was safe to assume that one of the missing numbers was 91, making the known parts of our formula now 29° 45' X" N/91° Y' Y" W. But even if our guess was correct, it wouldn't do us any good unless we managed to discover the final, missing number and then figure out where that and the other two we already had should go. I thought of the line from the poem, *The treasure they only together can find.*

My father hadn't been kidding about that.

Truly, Paradise offered the perfect hiding place for a treasure, because without exact coordinates, a general search-and-dig approach would have been impossible. Given its inaccessibility and the variations in its terrain, Paradise could confound a treasure hunter for years. Between the swamp, forest, marsh, high ground, low ground, and more, there would be no way to search every square inch. In fact, even if heavy equipment could be brought in, the wrong move might end up sinking the treasure into the swamp and losing it forever.

Finally, in frustration, Travis and I gave up for now. At least we could be more sure about my hunch that the treasure was hidden at Paradise, but given the size of that property, finding it without all six coordinates would be like trying to find a needle in a haystack—regardless of whether it was hidden above ground or in the salt mine below.

Watching Travis fold up the map, I realized that I needed some air. The cabin had grown incredibly stuffy. I said as much, and he suggested we turn off the lights and go out to the screen porch, which would be much cooler. As long as we spoke in whispers, he said, we should be okay. Stepping outside, I was glad to find that it was, indeed, much cooler there. The party across the water was in full swing, and as we sat in folding chairs side by side, I asked Travis what they were celebrating.

"Nothin', I don't think," he replied. "They're just visiting, having some fun."

"What about all those lights and the live music?"

"*Mon oncle* put those lights up a few years ago when my cousin NoNar got married, and *ma tante* liked them so much, she just kept them up. I think they're nice, don't you?"

"I do," I whispered, not even bothering to ask what kind of a name "NoNar" was. "What about the music?"

Travis shrugged, saying that they were playing zydeco, which likely meant that his cousin JT had come over and brought along his *frottoir*. That led Travis to give me an explanation of the difference between Cajun music and zydeco. According to him, Cajun usually featured an accordion, a fiddle, and a guitar and sounded kind of like country. Zydeco, on the other hand, had a frottoir, or a rubboard, rather than a fiddle and was closer in feel to jazz or rhythm and blues or even hip-hop. As the zydeco music bounced happily toward our ears over the water, I couldn't quite hear the similarity, but I enjoyed the way Travis spoke so animatedly about his area of expertise anyway.

Curious about his work, I urged him to tell me more. Settling further into our seats, leaning closer together so we could speak in whispers, Travis opened up to me, answering my questions and describing the recording studio where he spent most of his time working primarily with Louisiana-based musical groups. It was fun to hear the enthusiasm in his hushed voice, and I found myself wishing I could visit the studio with him sometime and watch him at work behind the mixing board. Given his own musical talent, his even temper, and his uncanny perceptive abilities, I had a feeling he was very good at what he did. And though he wasn't name-dropping, I could also tell that he had worked with many of Louisiana's finest musicians. He was such an unassuming guy, it was easy to underestimate him.

As we talked, I held my cell phone in my hand, the ringer off, waiting for it to vibrate silently from Wade's call.

"Oh look, Tee Noon's got his glow-in-the-dark Frisbee out," Travis whispered. I looked where he was pointing to see what looked like a UFO sailing through the night on the other side of the bayou. With the moon shining so brightly, it was easy to see the bodies running after the glowing disk; laughing, tumbling forms in the dark on the distant shore.

After a while, simply sitting there side by side and listening to the night noises all around us and the music in the distance, Travis reached out and took my hand in his. He intertwined his fingers with mine, and I found myself warmed and pleased by the gesture. There was something incredibly romantic about being in the dark, all alone, with this man who had done nothing for the last twenty-four hours but repeatedly rescue me. While I was certainly not a helpless female, I was utterly out of my element here, up to my eyeballs in trouble and questions, and his presence had been more helpful than he would ever know.

Still, I found myself wanting to know even more about him, about the responsibilities that were being ignored at home while he was on the run with me, about his love life. Given that he was now holding my hand, I didn't think he had a girlfriend, but I wondered how it was that such an eligible guy was still single at thirty-two. I wanted to ask, and I was trying to figure out how to word my question, when Travis announced that he was thirsty. He suggested that we go inside to find something to drink and to call Wade, just to remind the man that we were still waiting to hear from him about what was happening with Josie Runner and the Charenton police.

Quietly, we got up and returned to the darkened living room, Travis softly closing the door as I dialed Wade's number. The call went to Wade's voice mail, so I left a message. As I hung up, I saw that Travis had gone into the kitchenette area and was rooting through the fridge. He came up with a juice box and a bottle of ice tea and held them both up triumphantly as he offered me first choice. I chose the juice and then changed my mind and asked for the tea instead. The next thing I knew we were both holding onto both drinks, engaged in a teasing game of tug-of-war, and standing very close.

In the dark quiet of the kitchen, I could hear the pounding of my heart, could see the intensity of Travis' gaze. There was chemistry here, no doubt, in a way I hadn't had with anyone else for a very long time—if ever. Not wanting to move apart, I waited there in front of him, wishing more than anything that he would kiss me.

"I hope it doesn't sound tacky of me to say that I've been enjoying our time together an awful lot," Travis said to me softly.

"Why is that tacky?"

"Because of your father and the situation and all."

"Oh," I whispered, ashamed that for a moment I had forgotten everything else that existed outside this moment. "I know what you mean, though. Don't worry about it, Travis. I couldn't have made it without you."

He stepped even closer, and I released my hold on the drinks. Setting them on the counter, he turned toward me again and took both of my hands in his.

"Glad I could be around to help," he whispered. "To protect you."

"Protect me?" I teased softly.

"Uh-huh."

"And just what would that look like, exactly?"

"Well, first, I guess, I would've made sure that nothing got hold of your pretty fingers, like this."

Slowly, Travis raised my fingers to his lips and kissed the tip of each one in turn.

As he did, the memory of what had happened to me in Central Lockup filled my mind, the policewoman rolling my fingers across the pad to scan my fingerprints. As Travis moved down one hand, fingertip by fingertip, and then on to the next, I allowed myself to go with the moment, deciding that each kiss was a countermeasure, a point of healing, a replacing of a bad memory with an incredibly good one.

"After that," Travis said, his voice growing lower and softer, "I guess I'd have to make sure nothing bad happened 'round here."

Travis slid his hands from my wrists up to my shoulders and then onto my back, his fingers tracing circles around my shoulder blades. As he did, it was all I could do not to reach up and pull him even closer. But his movements were so lazy and yet so intentional that the greater pleasure was simply to stand still and see where he might go to "protect" me next.

Shivering, I leaned forward, tilting my head to one side.

"Aw, yeah, then there's your neck, *cher*, your long, beautiful neck. Gotta protect that."

Responding to my body language, Travis moved aside my hair and then used a finger to pull open the collar of my shirt. Lowering his head, he kissed the skin of my exposed shoulder. Gently, slowly, he worked his way up the side of my neck all the way to my earlobe, his breath warm against my skin as he lingered there.

"What else?" I whispered, trembling all the way to my toes.

Travis pulled back just far enough to look me in the eyes. And then tenderly, ever so gently, he reached up one hand and brushed the hair from my face.

"Well, then, I guess I'd have to make sure nothing, absolutely nothing bad happened to your mouth."

"And how would you do that?"

"Probably something like this."

With that, Travis Naquin kissed me.

He didn't just kiss me, he practically inhaled me. As he opened his mouth onto mine and wrapped me in his strong arms, I wanted to meld into him, to be so close that we could never be apart again. Travis Naquin was kissing me, and no kiss in my life had ever felt so right.

After the kiss was over, he pulled me even more tightly into his embrace, one hand stroking the back of my hair. I could have stayed that way forever. In a sense, I wondered if this was the one embrace I was always supposed to have found. It just felt that right, that sure.

We stayed there in the kitchen, clinging to each other, for a very long time, all of our problems and worries a million miles away. Then I initiated another kiss myself, passion welling up inside of me as I was lost in the moment and the darkness. Finally, Travis ended that one and surprised me by pulling completely away.

"Sorry, *cher*. We had better cool it. This is all just a little too..."

He smiled sheepishly as he shook his head.

"Too what?" I asked stiffly, trying to figure out why I had suddenly been rejected.

"Too tempting. Too amazing. One more kiss like that, and we're liable to find ourselves in a heap of trouble. I'm thinking we had better head back out to the porch and cool off a little."

With that, he gave me a wink and a smile, grabbed both drinks from the counter, and led the way outside. After a beat, I followed, stunned at what had just transpired. Though maybe I should have felt rejected or at the very least embarrassed, the truth was, more than anything else, I felt *treasured*.

Sitting out on the porch in the darkness with this sweet and sexy and fascinating man, the irony of the whole situation struck me. In searching for treasure, I had finally felt, for the first time in my life, absolutely and utterly treasured. Without question, I knew that what Travis had shown me here tonight was worth far more than gold. Not only had I begun to gain a new understanding of God, but I had witnessed a man, a good man, placing my value over his desires.

For me, that was a real first.

Later, as we quietly held hands out on the porch and sipped our drinks, my head resting lightly on Travis' shoulder, my cell phone suddenly sprang to life, lighting up and vibrating. Jumping up to run inside where I could answer it, I accidentally knocked over my chair, which landed with a loud, metallic crash against the wooden floor.

"Go on, go on. It's okay," Travis hissed, urging me toward the door.

I stepped inside, pulled the door shut behind me, and answered the phone.

"Hello?"

"Chloe?"

"Wade? Hey. Thanks for calling! What's the word?"

"Well, I've got good news for you, as long as you can keep it on the QT for now."

"What is it?" I asked, my pulse racing.

"Charenton police have brought charges against Josie Runner. Among other things, they've got her as an accessory to the attempted murder of your father."

There in the dark, stuffy cabin, I made my way to the kitchen counter so I could sit on one of the stools before my knees buckled.

"Accessory? That means others are involved?"

"Yeah. That's why you can't say anything yet. They haven't rounded up the three guys who were working with her."

Across the room, the door opened and Travis slipped inside.

"What do we know so far?" I said into the phone, watching as Travis fixed the towel covering the window on the door and then turned on the light.

Wade explained that apparently Josie had admitted finding something interesting among her father's papers, a map that showed where my father had hidden some sort of valuables. Josie had shared that news with a boy-friend, who promptly rounded up a pair of buddies and decided to go after those valuables for themselves.

"Did she know that her boyfriend and his buddies were doing that?"

"Says she didn't, but so far the cops aren't believing her. Things don't quite add up, ya know?"

"Any connection yet to Kevin's and Sam's murders and what happened to me?" I asked.

"Not yet," Wade replied, "but hopefully by morning. The sherriff wants you to meet him out at Paradise tomorrow, to show you some things and get some more information about your father. I told them you wouldn't come until the murder charges against you had been dropped. Hope that's okay."

I closed my eyes and told him yes, of course that was okay. I could only pray that that would happen soon, very soon. Though I was trying not to dwell on it, the fact was that I was an accused murderer out on bail. No matter how hopeful things appeared at the moment, the rest of my life still hung very much in the balance.

"With any luck, Josie Runner will spill everything tonight and you'll be totally in the clear by morning," Wade continued. "She's pretty moti-vated, you know, because the old folks that were in her care have been taken away by social services. If she wants to get her dad back, trust me, she'll talk."

"She seemed so sweet at first. I really hoped she wasn't culpable in all this, at least not intentionally."

"Yeah, but as you said yourself, she was threatening an old lady, trying to shut her up. That tells me that even if she didn't know beforehand, she sure figured it out after the fact—and she didn't report it. One way or another, she's an accessory."

"As long as the police eventually get to the bottom of things, I'll be happy."

"Me too. Listen, wherever you are tonight, Chloe, make sure you're safe—and that you stay put. I know you want to see your father, but you have to lay low for now, at least until these guys are rounded up."

"Do you think I'm in danger?" I asked, looking at Travis, who was standing nearby and listening, concern wrinkling his brow.

"There's no way to know that for sure, but I wouldn't do anything careless if I were you."

Suddenly, I felt exposed, as if coming here to the swamp cabin of Travis Naquin was about the dumbest thing I could ever have done. Surely, if anyone was after me, they could easily have learned about Travis' involvement in the situation—and drawn the most logical conclusion, that if we weren't at his home or his studio then we were likely at his cabin.

I thanked Wade for his help and made him promise to call me if anything changed. After we hung up, I explained the situation to Travis. Though I didn't relish getting back in the canoe in the dark, it was still a better alternative than waiting here like sitting ducks even as the bad guys might be heading in for the kill.

"We have to go somewhere else, Travis. Somewhere no one would think of or expect."

He seemed to understand my request, and soon he was tossing out ideas, saying that our most logical choice was simply to break into a friend or relative's cabin or camp and wait things out there. From the way he talked, it sounded as though he knew where more than one key was hidden—he just needed to figure out which cabin to choose, based on proximity and safety and the untraceability of the connection.

We gathered a few supplies, including some clothes and towels and food, and then we turned off the light, slipped out the front door, and began to make our way to the canoe.

We didn't get very far.

After only a few steps, the distinct click-click of a cocking gun could be heard immediately behind us. Obviously, someone had already been there, waiting and watching from the front porch until we came out.

"Stop right there," a man said in a low, guttural voice.

Freezing in place, we did as he said.

I could only hope that Travis wouldn't do anything stupid. In his desire to protect me, I feared most of all that he just might end up getting himself shot.

THIRTY-ONE

LOUISIANA, 1721
JACQUES

"Look out, Jacques!"

Jacques turned just in time to see a sack of rice flying toward him, and he reached out his arms to catch it. Ten more bags followed in succession, coming in a rhythm that allowed each man to toss it down the line to the person behind him. Having five men in a row made short work of unloading the supply ship. After the rice came salt, which had been sent from Europe in tins and would be one of their most popular items, despite the hefty price tag.

Everyone enjoyed it when the supply ships came through, even the men like Jacques who had to work out in the noonday sun to do the unloading. Soon the shelves in the mercantile would be stocked again, settlers from miles around would to come into town to replenish their supplies, and the mailbag's contents would be carefully distributed by Jacques himself, who could read and write and thus doubled as postmaster.

As he unloaded the supplies now, Jacques wondered if there would be anything in the mailbag for him. He hoped so, but then again he always hoped so. Jacques had been writing home regularly for two years now, maintaining his innocence, outlining events as they had taken place, and trying to find news, any news, of his father. Though there was no doubt that Papa had died soon after Jacques last saw him, his body had still never turned up. Jacques could only assume that Papa was dead when the men came to hide the evidence in the converted blacksmith shop out there in the country. If so, they would have quietly disposed of the body, just as they had disposed of everything else.

Once the unloading was finished, Jacques took a break with the other men in the shade to cool off and drink some water. He knew that the store would be bustling with activity, so finally he put on his apron and went inside to work, helping the customers who seemed almost giddy with the range of choices the new ship provided for them.

Except for the fact that almost everyone here spoke German instead of French, it wasn't a bad job, and the German couple who owned the store seemed to appreciate his hard work and his rapport with customers despite the language barrier. Using skills well honed in his father's shop, Jacques found it easy to convince folks to part with their money for the right objects at the right price. The only problem was that the supply ships from Europe were still few and far between. Most of the time he had willing buyers but nothing to sell them. At least here upriver, folks seemed to face the challenge of shortages with determination and ingenuity—which was far more than anyone could say of the people in New Orleans.

From the moment Jacques' ship had arrived at that town's dismal shore, he understood why everyone called New Orleans the "wet death." Jacques could not imagine a more ridiculous location for a town, much less one that was supposed to become the capital of such a vast territory. Almost everyone who came there said the same thing, that this swampy, infested land between the lake and the river was uninhabitable. Even the Indians considered the region to be useless.

The site had been chosen specifically because it offered the shortest distance between the two bodies of water and thus would allow for easier portage. In Jacques' opinion, that might have been reason enough to establish an outpost there, but he couldn't fathom why anyone would choose to build an entire town in such a damp, mosquito-infested, flood-prone pit of muck. Had Lily lived to see it, she would have been as appalled as he was.

In their own way, the people of New Orleans were even more problematic than the bloodsucking mosquitoes that feasted on them. It seemed to Jacques that the colony was being populated with all the wrong people. There was the upper class, the moneyed French who had come expecting to live in the manner to which they had always been accustomed back home. Those folks had had a rude awakening, but circumstance alone was not enough to transform the lily white hands of aristocrats into the red, worn hands of one accustomed to work. The ladies of New Orleans, in particular, wanted to be waited on hand and foot, but there was no one to wait on them. They wanted to dine on rich foods as they had back home, but there was no one to cook for them. They wanted to dress in finery and strut around in their bonnets and lace for all to see, but there were no dressmakers, and scarce little fabrics and trims. Even if there had been, there was no strutting to be done in a town that was basically wall-to-wall mud anyway.

At the other end of the spectrum, New Orleans had more than its share of the lower classes. Numerous prisoners, the homeless, the insane, and the poor had all been rounded up and summarily shipped here from France. Some had been forced into weddings, as Jacques had, but the more desperate John Law had grown to populate his floundering colony, the more outlandish his schemes had become, according to the news that was brought from home. At one point, the French government was allowing anyone to be seized in the streets of Paris, and unless they could prove they had had gainful employment in the past four days, they were forced on board ship and carted off to the New World.

Like the upper class, most of these lowlifes had no desire to work. They were used to getting by, whether from prostituting or outright thievery. Here in New Orleans, there weren't enough pockets to pick or values to steal. Thus, the city was quite a miserable place, populated by the two ends of the spectrum and devoid of almost anyone from the mechanical classes, the blacksmiths, the shopkeepers, civil servants, and others who kept a community going.

Jacques hadn't stuck things out there for very long. The city was surrounded by natural resources, abundant with fruits and vegetables, its waterways teeming with seafood, but the people were practically starving. Gathering indigenous food and learning how to prepare it was far too much trouble for them. They would rather import their goods from France, even if the prices were obscene. Jacques, on the other hand, was no stranger to hard work. He enjoyed going out into the countryside, hunting and fishing and learning from the Indians how to harvest and prepare the strange products that were so unfamiliar, such as sweet potatoes and catfish.

When Jacques heard about a settlement of German farmers fifteen miles upriver, hardworking folks who intended to cultivate the land and become the very breadbasket of Louisiana, he had left New Orleans without looking back. Here in the German settlement, he had found work in the store and had made a friend or two. These people had been recruited and sent here by John Law as well, and though the man hadn't offered them golden statuettes, he had widely distributed a pamphlet throughout Germany, one filled with all sorts of falsehoods and undeliverable promises.

Thus, Law was a frequent topic of angry conversation around here too. Jacques couldn't understand German well enough to catch everything that was said, but the man was despised everywhere. Today his name had been popping up a lot, and everyone's glee was so evident Jacques had to assume that he had finally been paid back for all of his dastardly deeds.

The last ship that had come through told of the crumbling French economy, the great rise and fall that was already being called the "Mississippi Bubble." With the backing of the regent, John Law had almost single-handedly converted the currency of France from gold to paper and then driven the value of that paper high, far higher than their stores of actual gold could back up. Just as Papa had predicted, with all of the speculating and inflation and sudden mass wealth, there had been a run on the bank, and the economy had begun to topple. Angry fingers were pointing to John Law, of course, but Jacques could have told them all along that the man was nothing but a swindler and a cheat.

Law had destroyed many lives. Here in the New World not a day passed that Jacques didn't miss his father or think of Angelique, though at least the sharp pain of the early days had faded into something a little more manageable, a little more dull. Poor Lily, his "wife," really had been sick that day they met and were joined in marriage. On the ship, she had been one of the first to die, and a quick burial at sea had left Jacques feeling sad and relieved at the same time.

Death was by far the most prominent passenger on board that ship. Of the 210 who embarked that day at La Havre, only 40 had still been alive by the time they reached Biloxi, where they disembarked for the final transport to New Orleans. Jacques didn't know why he had been one of the lucky ones to survive, but after watching so much death in so short a period in such prolonged quarters, he learned not to make friends too deeply or take for granted each day that continued to bring him new breath.

Now, as the surge of activity in the store lessened somewhat, Jacques turned his attention to the distribution of the mail. There was a big bag this time, and it took him a while to sort everything. As he did, he ran across not one but two letters addressed to him. Surprised, he tucked them into the pocket of his apron to save until he had time for another break.

Finally, in the glow of late afternoon, Jacques took that break. Sitting against the trunk of a tall tree out behind the store, he opened the first letter with trembling hands.

THIRTY-TWO

Travis and I stood frozen in place, our arms filled with supplies, our backs to the man with the gun.

"I want you to put everything down on the ground real slowlike, 'specially that shotgun, and then raise your hands up in the air," the man instructed.

I did as he said, but Travis surprised me by barking out a sudden laugh.

"Wait a minute," he cried. "Is that Tee Noon?"

More noise followed to our right and left, and then suddenly I realized that we were surrounded on three sides by men bearing guns. The extra two had been hiding on each side of the cabin, in the shadows.

"Travis? *C'est toi?*"

Suddenly the guns were lowered, and all four men began laughing and talking at once. It took me a minute, but from what I could tell, these were three of Travis' cousins, and they had come over here to stop what they thought were intruders robbing his cabin. Apparently, from across the bayou they had heard the crashing of my chair and then seen a strip of light behind one of the windows. Coming over to investigate, they had arrived and slipped into place for an ambush just as we were heading out the door.

As the laughter and the explanations subsided, the guys seemed to take notice of me, and they began eyeing me curiously, obviously waiting for an introduction. Travis moved next to me protectively, and then smiled and winked at me, saying I was a new singer he had been working with at the studio.

"We just came out here to get some of my Boozoo and a little Chenier," he added.

"You ain't got Boozoo up at your house, *cher*?" one of them asked, a twinkle in his eye, as the others laughed.

"*Non*, not 'Paper in My Shoe,'" Travis replied easily.

That earned another laugh, as all three cousins asked if he had never heard of iTunes. I wasn't quite sure what they were talking about, but I had a feeling that "Boozoo" and "Chenier" were either singers or songs. The cousins weren't buying Travis' explanation that we had come here to get some of his music, especially given that he could simply have downloaded it onto his computer from the Internet. Obviously, they seemed to think that he had used the music as an excuse and had brought me out here to the cabin for a little hanky-panky instead. As long as they didn't know the truth, that I was Chloe Ledet, accused murderer and probable target of Josie Runner's unnamed accomplices, I didn't care what assumptions they made. Travis, on the other hand, seemed offended on my behalf.

"My friend here is a lady," he said, his jaw firm. "I'd appreciate it if you'd treat her as such."

The others swallowed their laughter at that point, and one of them even took off his hat and said it was nice to meet me, a gesture I appreciated.

"Well, now that you're here, why don't y'all come over and make some music wit' us?" one of the cousins said. "We gots *sac-a-lait* and *breme*, and Tante B just brought out a *gateau de sirop*."

"Oncle Dennis even said he'd make us up some *oreilles de cochon* if we want," another one added.

My mind was racing to translate, but all I could make out was "syrup cake" and "pig's ears." Good grief. I left it to Travis to figure out a way to decline, but he surprised me by accepting their invitation instead.

Soon we were in our canoe and the cousins in theirs, paddling together across the black waterway. I didn't know what Travis had in mind, but I shot him a few stern glares when the others weren't looking. Giving me a slight nod, he seemed to be saying that he had things under control.

At the house, the three cousins returned to their game of glow-in-the-dark Frisbee on the lawn as the back door swung open and a woman in her fifties appeared there.

"Travis!" she cried gleefully, sweeping him into a hug and calling to her husband to come say hello, that their way-too-busy nephew had stopped by for a visit.

The uncle appeared and warmly greeted us both, and when the aunt finished hugging Travis she hugged me as well. There in the glow of hundreds of white twinkle lights, Travis introduced me as his "singer friend."

The aunt and uncle were both very sweet, and as they welcomed us inside, I could hear even more voices coming from further within. Their house was bigger than it looked, rambling along in a haphazard style that had likely come from addition after addition being built on over the years. Following the aunt and uncle, we ended up in a large, screened-in room, where several kids, a teenager, and an older man were clustered around a board game. They gave us a hearty greeting and then returned to what they were doing. Nearby sat several abandoned instruments, and at the other end of the room sat a table overflowing with half-empty platters of food.

Even though I was still full from our can of stew, they insisted we eat something, and soon Travis and I were both seated at the table with plates of food she had made up from the platters and then reheated in the microwave. Travis dug in, but I was afraid to try anything, lest I find myself munching on a pig's ear.

"You are too skinny, *cher*. You gotta eat," the aunt urged me, taking a seat next to me and practically feeding me herself.

"It all looks so delicious," I replied. "What is everything?"

She named the foods, pointing to each one in turn, as Travis translated. Apparently, *sac-a-lait* was a type of fish and *breme* was simply the Cajun word for eggplant, which in this case had been battered and fried and looked delicious.

"Did I hear something about *oreilles de cochon*?" Travis asked. Pig's ear. Great.

"Yah, yah, I make de *oreilles de cochon* for everybody," his uncle replied eagerly, jumping up from the table and stepping out of the screen door into the darkness beyond. As he did, I could only pray he hadn't gone back to a pig pen to do some quick butchering.

Seeing the concerned expression on my face, Travis' aunt explained that in Cajun households, the men could cook as well as the women, but they preferred to do their cooking outside, on the grill or the barbecue pit.

"I guess dat's more macho," she laughed. "He got his deep fryer out there tonight. Y'all 'scuse me while I brings him some paper towels and the sugar."

She got up and went to the kitchen, leaving me free to whisper to Travis across the table.

"Whatever you do, do *not* make me eat a pig's ear," I hissed.

He just laughed and wiped his mouth with a paper napkin.

"I'm thinking we can hang around just a little bit, then maybe I can borrow my uncle's car and we'll hit the road, find somewhere safer by car."

"That's not a bad idea, considering that the last anyone heard we were in a boat. I just don't want your family endangered by us being here," I whispered, looking toward the happy group at the other end of the room.

"You kiddin'? There's more firepower in this place than you could imagine—and every person here knows how to use it too."

"What's that about firepower?" his aunt asked, bustling through the room with a roll of paper towels and a box of confectioners' sugar.

"I was just saying how you used to make Sunday dinner," Travis replied, giving me another wink.

"Not that old story," his aunt laughed, shaking her head as she moved out the back door.

"How did she make Sunday dinner?" I asked Travis, curious.

"The chickens ran loose in the yard, and when she wanted to cook one up, she'd just go upstairs, open the window, pick out a good one, and shoot it. She had such good aim, she'd always get it right in the neck."

I thought maybe he was exaggerating, but then we were joined by the teenage girl who had been at the other end of the room, playing the game. She nodded adamantly in agreement, saying that Tante B was such a good shot with a rifle that the local gun club had to change their rules.

"She kept winning in the competition every year, and the men were getting mad because they were being shown up by a woman."

"Of course, that was a long time ago," Travis added. "Things aren't quite that bad anymore."

The screen door opened and the woman in question stepped inside. She was so small and unassuming, I had a hard time picturing her with a rifle in her hand, picking off chickens in the yard.

"Yes, indeed, it's a different world. It's nice that women have more opportunities and things nowadays, but I kind of miss some of the old-fashioned ways too."

"That's why a real man does both," Travis said. "I fully respect women as equals, but don't ask me not to open doors for them or stand up when they come in a room, because that's going to happen regardless."

"That's a good boy," his aunt cooed, pausing to pat her nephew on the shoulder. "Your *grandmere* done raised you right."

As an expert in etiquette, I didn't comment, but I couldn't help thinking that Travis' chivalry might fly here in the South, but if he insisted on holding doors and pulling out chairs in certain parts of this country, his actions might be misconstrued as condescending or even disrespectful.

I thought of the fight Travis and I had had about what had happened when we were teens, the argument where he claimed I'd had no respect for Cajun culture and that I had overlooked a people group that was essentially right under my nose. Sitting here with this group, I realized that I wanted to know more about Cajun rules of behavior, those unwritten rights and wrongs that could convey respect or disdain without saying a word.

"So if you had to describe Cajun culture to an outsider," I said to the aunt, "what would you say is unique about it? Besides the obvious, I mean."

"The obvious?"

"Language, food, music. Other than that, what's different about Cajuns than the rest of the world?"

She stared at me blankly, obviously not understanding my question.

"My friend here is an expert on good manners," Travis explained on my behalf. "I think she just wants to know what proper behavior looks like inside a Cajun home."

"Proper behavior? We're civil to each other," his aunt said, still confused.

"I know what you're asking," the teenager added, "like how it's rude to put your fingers in your mouth in China?"

"It is? Even if you have a hangnail?" the old man called from the other end of the room.

"That's right, *Grandpere*," the teen answered back to him.

"Yes, exactly like that," I said, smiling encouragingly at the teen. "Are there any rules like that for Cajuns, ones that are unique to this culture?"

"Well, goodness, if I couldn't put my fingers near my mouth, I couldn't eat crawfish," the aunt said, shaking her head.

"What do you think, Travis?"

He had a bemused expression on his face, and while he looked as though he would rather observe the conversation than take part in it, he nodded, saying that for one thing, Cajuns never left anybody out, no matter their age. Whatever they did, wherever they went, the whole family was almost always welcome to tag along, from the very youngest to the very oldest.

That led the aunt to explain why a Cajun dance was called a *fais do do*. Literally, the term meant "go to sleep," because that's what the women would say to their babies on Saturday nights at the dances, waiting for their kids to drift off so they could keep on dancing.

"They brought their babies into bars?" I asked.

"Not bars, *cher,* dance halls. They was clean, family places, not sleazy joints."

Travis and his teenage cousin began brainstorming about other Cajun rules of etiquette. In the end, they actually thought of quite a few, from hospitality to the use of "practical charities," to the food-centric way that they socialized and entertained.

"What's the rudest thing I could say or do to a Cajun?" I asked. My question seemed to stump them, as they looked at each other and shrugged.

"I guess that would be if you turned down a good meal," the aunt said finally.

"Acting like you're better than us," the teen added.

"Failing to see that the best thing that could ever happen to you might be right in front of your eyes," Travis said slyly.

I was startled by his words, but he simply grinned. Across the room the old man made catcalls, the teenager burst out laughing, and the aunt simply beamed and patted us both on the arms. Before anyone could say another word, the screen door swung open and Travis' uncle burst in bearing a platter of deep-fried pigs' ears smothered in confectioners' sugar.

Soon, everyone was gathered around the table, grabbing at the disgusting treats and eating them rapturously. Even the three cousins showed up at that point, the delicious smell apparently strong enough to have enticed them in from their game of Frisbee.

"I've got to say," Travis declared, "now that I think about it, the rudest thing you could do to a Cajun is to not eat one of their pig's ears."

Up to that point, there had been such a commotion around the table that I'd been able to avoid partaking of that particular delicacy. Now, thanks to Travis and his big mouth, all eyes were on me, waiting to see what I would do. Though I didn't appreciate being put in this position, Travis had underestimated me. In my travels to various countries, etiquette had required me to eat more than my share of unusual or even repulsive foods. When faced with a choice of personal revulsion and proper etiquette, for me etiquette always won.

Meeting his gaze with fire in my own, I reached out toward the platter, grabbed the smallest pig's ear that remained, and popped it into my mouth. At least it tasted nothing like I had expected. Instead of a pork rind sort of flavor, this treat was surprisingly delicious and almost reminded me of beignets.

"You know what a pig's ear is made of, *cher*?" Travis asked. Before I could answer, his uncle supplied the recipe, which was primarily a mixture of eggs and flour and sugar.

"Why is it called 'pig's ear'?" I asked, wondering if maybe the pastry was fried in pork fat.

"Because of the little twist you make when you drop it in the oil. See the way they puff up like that? Looks just like a pig's ear."

I kicked Travis under the table and promised with my expression that I would be getting even.

Soon, the three male cousins were back to playing zydeco music and the children and adults were dancing, the table pushed back against the wall to create more space in the screened room. I think I danced with everyone there, and though I obviously didn't know the steps to their well-practiced Cajun moves, they were generous with their good humor and their instruction.

At one point I found myself in Travis' arms.

"This is nice," he said softly, leading me in a Cajun waltz. "It's just right, you know?"

"I know," I replied, thinking I had never felt quite so comfortable so quickly with any man in my life. As Travis' aunt beamed at us from the sidelines, I found myself being swept around the room by a handsome Cajun and loving every minute of it.

After a few minutes the music slowed, and when I felt his hand gently pressing the small of my back, I responded by moving closer so that we were cheek to cheek. Closing my eyes, I inhaled the musky scent of him, feeling the warm, sharp smell sink into my very being. It conjured up visions of pine and Spanish moss and old oaks and the slow, lazy bayou. It brought back thoughts of our time together earlier in his cabin, his mouth seeking mine in the dark.

He obviously was thinking about kissing me too. I could feel his warm breath against my neck, and where our skin touched it felt like fire. Yet somehow, when the music came to an end, we managed to pull apart without moving into a kiss in front of his entire family—though it wasn't easy for either one of us.

Travis looked into my eyes, smiled, and then turned to the others and said that we needed to go, but the family seemed determined to keep us there. They begged Travis for a song on the guitar first—and for me to sing along. Earlier, he had introduced me as a singer, and I could see the panic on his features now as he took the guitar that was being offered to him and tried to think of a way of getting me out of having to join in. I wasn't good enough for a recording contract, but Travis would have been surprised to learn that I actually could sing fairly well. I had been a frequent soloist throughout my years of boarding school, and in college I had even had a good part in a musical. Of course, I wasn't going to spell that out for him now. Instead, I let him squirm for a bit before agreeing to sing, as long as he would lead and I could harmonize. Though I didn't know any Cajun or zydeco songs, we tossed some ideas back and forth and finally agreed on an old hymn we both knew well.

Once we began, the surprise on his face secretly filled me with glee. There, sitting on the screened porch in a modest house in the Louisiana swamps, my Cajun hero artfully strummed his guitar and sang in a voice that was rich and true. When he reached the refrain, I joined in a third down, artfully blending my voice with his. Around us, his family simply took in the music, smiling and tapping their feet and one even closing his eyes in prayer. The moment was perfect, and I truly didn't want it to end. There was no escaping the fact that I was falling for Travis Naquin, and falling hard. Singing with him now, enjoying the surprise that reflected back to me in his eyes, I knew this relationship might turn into something that could change my life forever.

Our song ended to an enthusiastic round of applause, and I could only hope that my singing had been good enough not to blow my cover.

"You're just full of surprises, aren't you?" Travis whispered as he leaned across me to hand the guitar back to his cousin.

"Untold depths," I replied with a wink. "Trust me, Travis. You've barely scratched the surface."

Rising, we told the family we simply had to go. They tried to talk us into spending the night, insisting that it was silly to take off when there was a perfectly good guest room right there for me, not to mention a sofa bed in the living room for Travis.

"Besides," the aunt added, "Minette and them are going to be here any minute."

I glanced at Travis, who looked sharply at his aunt.

"Minette? I thought she was staying over at Ophé's house."

"She is, but I thought she'd want to see you and maybe meet your new friend, so I called her while I was heating up y'all's dinner." She glanced at her watch. "They should be here real soon."

I wasn't sure why Travis was so upset, but it probably had to do with wanting to keep his grandmother safely away from any danger that might be looming around here. Besides that, there was also the little matter of me and my false identity. I hadn't seen Minette Naquin in years, but there was a good chance she might recognize me once she saw me and my telltale icy blue eyes. We had been so careful to keep me incognito that it would be a shame to blow my cover now.

Travis seemed torn, so when no one else was listening I put a hand on his arm and softly told him that we should probably hang around until Minette arrived, at which point he could give a more stern warning to the cousin who was supposed to be keeping her safe. We could all leave at the same time, and as long as we headed in opposite directions, any bad guys who might happen to be out there would surely follow after us and not her.

"It's more complicated than that," Travis said curtly.

Five minutes later, when we heard a car crunching in the gravel driveway and voices echoing in from outside, I would learn just how complicated it actually was.

THIRTY-THREE

LOUISIANA, 1721
JACQUES

Jacques' heart pounded as he read the letter he had been waiting for for two long years. It had been written by the royal goldsmith himself, and the very first sentence contained an apology. According to the letter, on December 10 of last year, the French economy collapsed and John Law was forced to flee Paris. In his wake, an inventory of his home and offices had been conducted, and much to everyone's surprise, a trunk filled with two hundred brass fleur-de-lis statuettes covered in gold leaf had been found hidden away in an office basement.

Faced with such irrefutable evidence, a former servant of Law's confessed to having been a party to the very deception that had fooled all of them that day. According to the servant, as soon as Law heard what was going on, he had sent several of his men out to the blacksmith's shop to retrieve the statuettes, destroy all evidence, and bribe the neighboring farmer and his wife. Though that part of the mission was a success, there had been no way for Law to change out the trunks unseen before the *Beau Séjour* left port. Though he had hoped to rectify the situation in a later exchange via transatlantic shipment, it was now, of course, too late for him to do so.

> As to your father's remains, the servant alleges that they
> found a sickly old man on a cot in the room that day. He

was feverish and out of his head, so they carried him as far as Charenton and left him at the hospital. Upon hearing this news, I sought to confirm the matter with the prior, who told me that a man suffering with a lung disorder had indeed shown up on the doorstep at Charenton that very day, and though the Brothers took him in and cared for him, the man never regained consciousness and died the next. He was buried in the cemetery, name unknown. Ironically, that cemetery lies not twenty feet behind the very building where you were being housed at the time.

I know this apology cannot erase the pain and shame of the last two years, but I hope it will be a start. As your father's shop in the Place Dauphin had already been closed down and its contents impounded, I asked the bookkeepers to provide an estimate of the value of the goods seized from within. Enclosed please find that amount, paid in full.

As you know, the passing of a master goldsmith leaves a vacancy for another, so that title has been awarded elsewhere and your father's name has been engraved on the plaque of former masters that hangs in the guild's central office. I hope in some small way this helps to make up for the pain and misery that M. Law's actions have caused you. Should you choose to have your father's bones reinterred elsewhere, please remit instructions, etc.

As a final form of restitution, I would invite you to attend the ceremony in New Orleans at the conclusion of the three-year waiting period and accept one of the gold statuettes on behalf of yourself and another on behalf of your late father. Of the two hundred people who signed up for that particular voyage, only forty-six survived, so I have convinced the court to allot these two extra before the remainder is returned to the royal vaults here in Paris. As you may know, M. Freneau passed away enroute to the New World, but his replacement will be in charge of distributing the statuettes and he has been advised of your situation in particular.

The letter ended with general good wishes and an open invitation, should Jacques ever return to France, to visit him at the guild and see the plaque with his father's name on it.

Overwhelmed with emotion, Jacques' hands began to tremble anew when he read the next letter, one which had come from Angelique. She said only that she had heard the news about the clearing of his name, and she wanted him to know that it came as no surprise to her, for she had always maintained his innocence. She went on to say that her father's entire fortune had been lost through speculation when the bubble burst.

> *Considering all that has happened, I took the liberty of asking my father to secure a few treasured items from those confiscated from your father's shop. I am sending them with this letter in the hopes they will reach you safe and sound. Thank you for writing to tell me of the circumstances of your marriage, and my condolences on the loss of your wife.*
>
> *Yours,*
> *Angelique*

Jacques folded the letter and placed it in the envelope, and then he brought it close to his nose and inhaled deeply, trying to capture the scent of his lost love. When he allowed himself to miss her, the pain was as sharp as any dagger slicing through gold leaf.

Back inside the store, Jacques turned his attention to the stack of parcels that were piled under the mail slots and had not yet been sorted. His was near the bottom, and when he opened it up what he saw brought tears to his eyes. The package contained three tools of his father's: his crucible, his tongs, and his muffle. Leave it to Angelique to think of this! Pulling the items from the box, holding their heft and weight in his hands, Jacques almost felt that Papa was with him now. The man would never know all that Jacques had gone through to clear his name, but considering how important his reputation was to him, Jacques could only hope that he had finally made his father proud.

"Soliel? Jacques Soliel?"

Jacques looked up to see the captain of the supply ship calling for him from the doorway.

"Yes?"

"I had one more delivery for you, but I was told to bring it to the Ursuline Convent up the river. It's waiting there."

The Ursuline Convent? Jacques couldn't imagine what it would be, but in his heart he could only hope that Angelique had taken it upon herself to send Papa's masterpiece, the golden communion plate, cup, tankard, patents, and candlesticks. It made sense, given that the package had been delivered to the convent instead of to the store.

Jacques' work was finished by six, so as soon as he was done, he tossed aside his apron and headed up the long, quiet road toward the convent. It was situated just slightly more than a mile away, and by the time he arrived, the sun had formed brilliant golden streaks in the sky. Before going in, Jacques stood out front and looked up at the cross mounted on the steeple, and he was filled with a sudden, deep sense that all along the way God had been watching out for him. Like Joseph, who had been betrayed by his brothers and sold into slavery, what others had intended for evil, God would use for good. If, indeed, Papa's full communion set was here, then Jacques only wanted to see it and touch it, and perhaps share with one of the Sisters its significance and a little bit of the history of the man who had so lovingly crafted it back in Paris long ago.

Jacques found what looked like the main building among a cluster of other buildings and knocked on the door. The woman who answered wore the dark garb of the sect and a simple silver cross hanging from a chain around her neck. Jacques explained to her that a package had come from Paris today and had been delivered here. She asked him to wait a moment while she tried to get more information. She left him standing outside the closed door, but after a few minutes she returned, and this time when she greeted him she was smiling warmly.

"Yes, indeed, this special package arrived just today. I must say, it's quite beautiful."

With that, she pulled open the door, revealing the masterpiece inside. There in the center of the room was not a communion plate or goblet or tankard or anything else constructed out of gold.

It was Angelique herself, who was more valuable by far.

THIRTY-FOUR

"Would you please tell Minette and Ophé to meet me out back?" Travis said to his uncle as soon as we heard the noisy group entering the house. Then, turning to me before he headed out the door, he added that I should wait there, that this shouldn't take long and then we would be on our way.

Soon, the cluster of visitors made their way through the house and into the screened room. Minette and a younger man were ushered straight out the back door to talk to Travis. That left three children, who rushed over to embrace their young cousins and immediately engage in a discussion about a board game. Behind them came a woman carrying a baby. She looked around the room and suddenly thrust the baby into the arms of the teen, saying that she would be right back. Giving me a polite smile, she made a mad dash up the hallway, obviously to the restroom.

I was impressed with the teenager and how naturally she handled the baby that had been forced upon her. Propping the child on her hip with one arm, she teased it with a pointed, wiggling finger, cooing as she brought it in close and pulled it away, again and again.

I could hear voices from out back, and though I wanted to know what Travis was saying to his grandmother and cousin, it was clearly between them. Feeling suddenly out of place, I forced myself to go over to the couch and sit among the kids and engage myself in the conversations they were having. From what I could tell, it sounded as though they were debating whether to play Risk or Monopoly. I didn't know many children, and I was always uncomfortable around them, so it felt especially odd when one of them suddenly turned to me and asked my opinion.

"Oh, we're not staying, so what I think doesn't matter. You guys play whatever you want."

"But which one would you choose if you were us?" asked one of the little boys who had just arrived. He was a cute one, about seven or eight, with curly brown hair and long, dark eyelashes.

Suddenly, all of the children were looking at me, waiting for my opinion. Squirming under their attention, I decided that since I didn't know how to talk to children, I would simply treat them as short adults.

"You have to be careful with Risk," I said. "Claiming territories and challenging others can lead to a lot of arguments. When I was in boarding school, so many of the kids fought over that game that it was banned. In larger groups, it just doesn't work."

"You're right," the boy said, clearly surprised and pleased by my insight. "Last time I was here and we played it, everybody got all mad over a bunch of nothin'."

"There's other games to choose from," the teenager said, suddenly rising and thrusting the baby into my arms. Once she had passed it off to me, she went over to a cabinet and began going through it, calling out the names of the various games inside.

I was mortified. Never having held a baby in my life, I had no idea what to do. At least it wasn't crying, but it just lay there, looking at me with wide eyes, as I tried to remember where all the danger zones were. I knew it had soft spots and a very fragile neck, and I was so afraid I might snap or break something that the best I could do was emulate the position the teenager had been holding it in before. Unfortunately, the baby didn't seem to like me very much and soon it was wiggling and swarming to get free.

"He doesn't like to lay back that far," the little boy said to me, reaching out to guide my hands into a more suitable position. Even at his young age, he obviously knew more about childcare than I did.

As the rest of the children clustered around the cabinet and debated the merits of the various games, the boy stayed there next to me on the couch, obviously sensing that I was too uncomfortable to be left alone. Grateful for his presence and the way he interacted with the baby, playing peekaboo and opening and closing his hands over his face, I attempted some more polite chatter.

"Is this your baby brother? He sure likes the way you play with him."

"Nope, he's my cousin. But we're together so much it's kind of like we're brothers."

And with that, this kid had expressed one of the deepest, saddest regrets of my life, that I had never had any extended family at all, that I had never met a single cousin on either side of my family tree. In my mind, I had always wondered if people actually had gatherings like this and relationships like this with people who shared their same bloodline. Given what I had learned about my mother, now I wondered if maybe that was why there was no extended family in our lives, because they had disowned her when she became an exotic dancer.

"What's your name?" I asked the boy.

"Everybody calls me TJ."

"TJ? What does that stand for?"

The boy once again guided my arm to raise up the squirming baby to the correct position.

"Travis Junior," he said.

Before I could react, the back door opened and in stepped Minette, Ophé, and Travis.

"Daddy!" the boy cried gleefully, jumping up and running across the room into Travis' arms.

Lucky for the child I was holding, its mother showed up at that moment and scooped him out of my lap—just in time to keep me from dropping him right on his soft-spotted little head. Stunned, I looked from her to the baby in her arms to the boy named TJ to Travis, who had picked up his son and was holding him tightly in a hug.

"How are you related to Travis?" was all I could manage to say to the woman who was now standing nearby and patting her baby's back.

"He's my brother, *cher*. Don't I know you? Haven't we met somewhere before?"

I couldn't even reply. All I could do was look across the room at the man I thought I had been falling in love with. He set his son down on the floor, and keeping a hand on the top of the boy's head, finally met my eyes with his own. Maybe his sister and I had met before, all those years ago at Paradise. As for Travis, I realized I didn't know him.

I didn't know him at all.

Had I not been deep in the swamps and in very real danger, at that moment I would simply have stood and walked out. I would have left this absurdly jovial family reunion behind and take taken care of my problems on my own. As it was, however, I could not make that choice. Even if I hadn't been in danger, I still couldn't have left, for there was no way I would have been able to find my way back to civilization from where we were by myself.

Travis obviously knew I was upset, and to his credit he didn't do anything stupid or placating. For a while, he didn't even look my way. Instead, he seemed to be waiting as everyone else in the room settled into their various activities. The kids finally chose a game and gathered around the coffee table to set it up. Travis' sister parked herself in an easy chair in the corner and began feeding her baby a bottle. The older folks, with Minette among them, went to the table and sat as the uncle went out the back door, ostensibly to make more pigs' ears. Cajun etiquette being what it was, I had been greeted in turn by both Travis' cousin and grandmother before they sat, but Minette didn't seem to recognize me. Fortunately, Travis' sister had also become distracted without my ever having to answer her question.

Everywhere there was chatter, some of it in French, some of it in English, all far outside the realm of what I felt like listening to at that moment. All I could do, in fact, was sit there on the couch among the children and their game as I wondered how many more times this week I would have to be shocked before I realized that no one, absolutely no one, was who they said they were or who they pretended to be. For all I knew, Travis Naquin was married. For all I knew, there were a couple of more kids back at home with their mother.

Travis seemed equally uncomfortable, and for a long moment he stood in the middle of the room, obviously unsure as to whether he should join me and the children at the game table or his grandmother and the other adults at the dinner table. Finally, he asked me if we could speak out front. Without a word, I rose and walked out of the room, retracing the steps that had led us through the house in the first place. Soon, we were outside on the lawn, and truly a big part of me didn't even care if we were putting ourselves in danger by being out in the open like that, by standing in the glow of the little white lights where we would be easy targets. Travis seemed to have other things on his mind as well. He looked as upset as I felt, his easy-going stance all but swallowed up by this new and very different, far more duplicitous and dishonest version of the same man.

At first, he didn't say a word, and though good manners made me inclined to break the heavy silence between us, I refused to give him the satisfaction. This was a mess he had created with his own omissions. It was up to him to initiate his explanation.

"I know you're mad," he said at last. "Trust me, Chloe, I almost told you about TJ a dozen times. But you have to understand how things are. On the rare occasion that I might interact with a young lady, I do not involve my son. He's been hurt enough, and I see no point in bringing women in and out of his life just because they are in and out of mine. What he doesn't know won't hurt him. I always figured that when the right one finally came along, that's when I would make him a part of my relationship."

"Well, aren't you just the noble hero, protecting this precious son? That all sounds well and good, Travis, except for one thing: I'm not angry that you didn't want TJ to know about me or to meet me. I get that. I'm angry that you didn't want me to know about TJ."

"I know, Chloe, I—"

"At what point, exactly, was it going to come up? When you were kissing me? How about this? Maybe you just should've waited until I was in love with you. You should've waited until I had imagined a whole world for us, one where we were starting fresh together, just you and me, and then that might have been the perfect moment to let me know that you were married, with children!"

Pacing there on the lawn, I had to remind myself that Travis and I had only been together for twenty-four hours. It seemed like so much more than that. It seemed, in fact, like a lifetime. I realized that I was more angry at myself than I was at him. How had I let myself fall so far, so fast? Was I that lonely? Or was it just that I was an easy mark, naive and optimistic and desperate to belong to something, anything, bigger than myself?

I wanted Travis to tell me that TJ's mother was completely out of the picture, that she had disappeared from their lives years ago. I wanted him to tell me there had never been anyone else, that he had never even considered the possibility of love or romance again until I had come back into his life, and that he had known from the moment he saw me outside the courthouse yesterday that both love and romance were inevitable. Here I was, so desperate to belong to his world. What I wanted him to tell me was there was room in that world, that there was no other woman who might rise up from the shadows and endanger the very thing I wanted so desperately for us to build together.

Before I could put any of that into words, in the distance a woman screamed. Shocked, I turned to look, though Travis didn't even flinch.

"Did you hear that?"

"Hear what?"

"That scream. A woman screamed!" We both stood frozen for a moment and then it happened again. "That! I know you heard it this time."

"That's not a woman screaming, *cher*. That's jus' a barred owl," Travis replied. There was another scream, and it was so real that I wasn't sure if I believed him or not. Suddenly, I had to wonder if not only had I been misled about the facts of Travis' life, but perhaps I had been misled about the nature of his character as well.

Obviously, I lacked any sense of discernment or judgment when it came to others. Maybe all of his Bible quoting and his sexual chivalry had been an act. In fact, maybe he couldn't be trusted at all, and here I thought he had been helping me when he had actually been pushing us toward his own ends. Could he have been behind the shooting, the deaths, my framing? It was awfully convenient that he had suddenly appeared on the scene at the courthouse in my most vulnerable moment. Standing there on the grass not far from the water, I stared at him now, adrenaline coursing through my veins. I'd had enough shocks in the last few days to last me a lifetime.

It was time I ended this relationship here and now. Inside that house was the safety of an entire family. If Travis really wasn't who I had been thinking he was all along, my smartest move at that moment would be to march inside, insinuate myself among the people he loved, and ask them to please get me out of there and drive me somewhere safe, like maybe the hospital where my father lay in a coma.

Before I could move, however, from off to one side I heard the familiar click-click of a shotgun cocking.

"What's that sound?" I whispered, though in my heart I already knew.

"I'd say that's the sound of trouble."

Suddenly, before we could even react, figures emerged from the shadows. Each of them was dressed all in black, with black ski masks over their heads. Before I could even get a breath to scream, a hand clamped firmly over my mouth. Struggling violently, I realized I was being dragged backward toward the water. Watching in horror, I saw more dark figures surround Travis and knock him into submission.

Dragged aboard some sort of boat, a gag was tied around my mouth and then ropes bound my wrists and ankles. Twisting around, I could see I was on an airboat, the kind that could sail through the swamps at high speeds and go almost anywhere. I had no idea where I was going to be taken, but as we backed away from the dock with just myself and two others aboard, I looked toward the lawn to find out what had become of Travis.

I didn't see him. I did, however, see the clump of dark figures moving into the shadows. Either they were carrying him away, or for some reason it had all been faked and he had gotten up and walked off on his own.

Fighting to break free, my efforts earned me a few quick kicks to my side. Curling defensively into a ball, I listened as the boat engine grew louder and then we were off.

Oh, how I longed for the canoe or even the rowboat that I had been in earlier! Compared to those low-lying, slow-moving vessels, this airboat was positively flying. The speed at which we soared through the night was horrifying. The only comfort I could give myself was that if we crashed and I was killed, at least my abductors would be killed as well.

Fifteen minutes later, a change in pitch told me that we were slowing down. The front of the airboat lowered toward the surface of the water, and though I strained to see where we were, it just looked like swamp and more swamp to me. It wasn't until we were at a dock and I was being lifted up and carried onto the shore that I thought I recognized my surroundings. I shouldn't have been surprised.

They had brought me to Paradise.

Whatever these people had in mind for me, they never said a word. As I continued to struggle against my bindings and the gag that cut into my mouth, I was carried in absolute silence up a long, shaded pathway. At one point, they untied my ankles, put me down, and let me walk, though firm hands held my arms at each side. Soon we reached the house, the one where the Naquins used to live year-round but now only used as a cabin.

When we got close, they stopped and one of them spoke to me for the first time.

"There's someone inside who wants to talk to you," the man's voice whispered. "I'm going to take off your gag and the rope. If you yell or try to get away, trust me, you won't like what happens next."

Something in his cold, hard voice reminded me of what had been done to Sam. I had no doubt these people were capable of torture. In fact, right now, for the sake of my own life, I was willing to play by their rules. I nodded and then stood very still as they undid the gag and the bindings on my wrists.

Once I was completely free, they gestured toward the door, and I stepped forward, hesitated for a moment, then twisted the knob and swung it open.

There, sitting in the light of a single lamp, was my mother.

THIRTY-FIVE

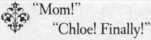"Mom!"

"Chloe! Finally!"

I stepped forward into the room, relieved when neither of my captors followed me inside. Instead, they seemed to have vanished into the night. I pulled the door closed behind me, locked it for good measure, and then turned back to face my mother. Even in the dim light, I could see that her eyes were red and swollen, as if she had been crying. I hesitated, not sure what I was seeing. Was she one of my captors or had she also been brought here against her will?

"What's going on?" I asked, moving toward her. "Are you being held captive here?"

"Held captive? Me? Good heavens, no."

I realized that though I had spoken on the phone with my mother, I hadn't actually seen her in person in about two years. She was as beautiful as ever, though for the first time it also struck me that she seemed older. Her forehead was smooth and unlined, as always, though looking at her now I realized it was likely Botox that was keeping it that way. I did notice the fine lines around her mouth and dark circles under her eyes. Still, given what she had been through in the last two days, with my father shot and her only child accused of murder, it was no wonder she didn't look her best.

She stood but did not approach me. Instead, we both just looked at each other, thirty-two years of disconnect and dysfunction and deceit thick in the air between us. There was so much I wanted to know and so much I wanted to say, but for the moment words failed me.

"What have you done?" I asked after some moments. I looked around the room and wondered how she could allow masked men to kidnap her own flesh and blood. The only thing I knew for sure was that my mother wasn't clever enough to have masterminded anything. If I had been some pawn in a complex scheme, then it had to be someone else's scheme, not hers. She was in cahoots with others, I had no doubt. Lola Ledet, or should I say Fifi LaFlame, was not even smart enough to play checkers, much less chess.

"What have *I* done? What have *you* done?" she cried, stepping toward me. In her eyes I could see a lot of different emotions: anger, fear, confusion. Clutched in her hands was a white linen handkerchief, now wrinkled and stained with mascara.

"I don't know what to say to you, Mother. You're not who I always thought you were."

"The same goes for you, Chloe. You're my own child, and I can't believe you're a murderer."

"A murderer? Me? Oh, that's right. You think I killed Kevin Peralta."

"You did worse than that!"

I hesitated, trying to understand her accusation.

"You don't honestly believe I'm the one who hurt Sam, do you? That I tortured and killed him?"

"I don't know, Chloe. I don't know you at all anymore."

"I didn't kill Sam and I didn't kill Kevin, and if you think I could have been capable of either one of those murders, then not only do you not know me now, you never knew me at all. Then again, I guess that's only fair, considering that I never really knew you, either."

"What do you mean?"

"Were you ever going to tell me about your secret past? Did you forget to bring up that one little fact about your former career, Mother? Or, excuse me, *Fifi*?" I threw her stage name out there like a dagger, expecting it to garner a big reaction. Instead, the only expression on her face was surprise and confusion. "Your days as a dancer? Fifi LaFlame? Bourbon Street? Does any of that ring a bell?"

I was practically yelling, but at this point I didn't care. My mother and I had been politely dancing around each other for years. It was time to let our hair down.

"What about it, Chloe? I don't understand your question."

"What about it? How could you have hidden something like that from me? How could you keep a secret of that magnitude for thirty-two years? I can understand not wanting me to know as a child, but what about when I was older? What about when I was off on my own? Did it never once cross your mind to tell me about your past? Or did you think you hid it so well that I would never ever find out?"

I studied her face, expecting to see shame. Instead, all that seemed to register there was yet more confusion.

"Chloe, I never hid any of that from you."

"Are you kidding me? I had to learn it from Conrad! He thought I knew."

"I don't see what this has to do with anything anyway."

Closing my eyes, I pinched the bridge of my nose and wondered how to get through to her.

"Mother, my whole life you have been this perfect person, this elegant, classy, rule-following Southern lady. Now I find out that that's not even who you are, that you remade yourself from something else entirely."

"Of course I did," she said, shaking her head. "When I married your father, I was just a stupid kid from rural Mississippi with no money, no brains, and a killer body. Exotic dancing was the only way I knew to make a buck. Julian and I made a perfect pair, you know. He was much older, of course, but he was still just a scrappy kid from the Quarter. We used to dream of a better life, an elegant restaurant that bore our name. Once it looked like that dream was going to be a reality, we decided that both the building and I needed makeovers. While Julian stayed home in New Orleans and renovated and designed and created and built Ledet's practically from the ground up, I went off to charm school, where they taught me to change my hair, my clothes, my makeup, my manners, my speech patterns, and everything else so that I would be good enough, classy enough, to serve as the hostess. By the time I got back, both the building and I were ready for our debut. I don't see what the big deal is. I never hid my past. I never kept it a secret. Over the years, sure, people forgot, and I wasn't going to remind them. But if you think there was some big secret conspiracy to keep it from you, you're wrong. I didn't know that you didn't know, honey. I guess it just never came up."

In a way, I realized, this was almost worse than if she had kept it secret. I didn't know about my mother's dark past simply because no one had ever bothered to tell me, and I hadn't been around her or their friends enough to hear it from anyone else. Unbelievable.

Crossing over to the couch, I sat and buried my head in my hands. At this point, I didn't know whom to trust or not trust. I didn't know where Travis was, if he could be trusted, or even if he was still alive. All I knew was that I had been captured and brought here against my will, only to come face-to-face with my very own mother.

"You're a monster, do you know that?"

"Because I danced for money?"

"No, Mother. Next subject. Try to keep up."

"Don't talk down to me that way, missy. Why am I a monster? The way I see it, Chloe, you're the one who needs to be behind bars."

Rage pulsed through my veins, and I stood and got right up in her face, her beautiful, elegant face, the face of a woman who was my own mother and yet a complete stranger.

"How can you not even know your own child?" I demanded.

She just shook her head, fresh tears springing into her eyes.

"How could you shoot your own father?" she replied.

I took a step back, feeling as if I had been punched in the lungs.

"What?"

"You shot your father!"

"What are you talking about? I didn't do that. I couldn't have. I was in Chicago at the time, if you recall. If you don't believe me, just look on the TV schedule. How could I have been appearing on live television up there at the same time I was supposedly down here?"

My mother shook her head, sobbing into her handkerchief.

"I don't know how you did it, Chloe. You know you're much smarter than I am. I'm sure you figured something out. I just don't understand what could bring a child to hold up a gun and pull the trigger on their own parent."

"I didn't shoot him!"

"Yes, you did!"

"Says who?"

"Says *him*, Chloe. Says your father. He's out of the coma. And he says you're the one who shot him."

THIRTY-SIX

LOUISIANA, 1722
JACQUES

"Here. Right here. Feel it?" Angelique said, smiling as she held Jacques' hand to her belly. He sensed the slightest rippling against his flattened palm. The kick of his baby felt like the kiss of an angel.

"I feel it," he said, grinning. He kept his hand there until the movement ceased. After that, he put his arm around her shoulders and pulled her close. With the other hand he clicked his tongue and tugged the reins to start the horses moving again. They responded by pulling the wagon back onto the roadway and continuing on down the bumpy, rutted road.

Jacques knew he had never done anything in his life to deserve this much happiness. One year ago, as the door of the convent had been swung open wide to reveal Angelique standing inside, he had done the only thing he could do: With a deep, guttural yell, he had moved into the room, wrapped her fiercely in his embrace, and openly wept, kissing her lips and face and promising her that he would love and care for her forever. Thanks to the startled nuns who then promptly sent for a priest from New Orleans, just a few hours later Jacques and Angelique were declared man and wife.

Jacques thought that would be the single happiest moment of his life. Now here they were a year later, and the child Angelique carried inside her womb was making itself known, giving its first real kicks.

Could his life get any better than this?

Jacques thought that perhaps all the trial and misery of that awful, uncertain time had created within him a heart more easily satisfied with life's blessings. All he knew was that he spent every waking hour of every single day feeling thankful and deeply blessed. To have the woman he loved, and to create new life within that woman, was more than any man deserved.

Now the two of them were on their way to New Orleans where they would finally claim the two gold fleur-de-lis statuettes that the royal goldsmith had promised to Jacques in his letter one year ago. Jacques already had a buyer arranged, a wealthy landowner who was going to pay him top value for the gold as long as Jacques melted it down first and used it to create a simple golden tray embellished with the man's family crest. Jacques could handle that job easily, especially given that he now owned a working furnace where he could use his father's smithing tools.

In fact, Jacques had his own shop in the German settlement, one he had purchased and outfitted using the money sent to him by the royal goldsmith. Through his previous work in the settlement as a store clerk, Jacques had seen the near-constant need among the local farmers for tools and implements. The shop he and Angelique built sold new tools whenever they could get the raw materials to make them and repaired existing ones when they couldn't. Knowing he could adapt his goldsmithing skills toward more general metalworking, Jacques was already becoming known for the fine axes, hoes, and other farm implements he crafted. He was pleased to realize that his lack of artistic ability made no difference here, for what did a farmer care if his plow was beautiful as long as it was sturdy and did the job? Free at last from the stifling guild system that had limited his occupation back in France, here Jacques was able to do as he pleased, and he found that creating and selling tools to the citizens of this vast territory pleased him very much.

Jacques and Angelique had been living over the shop, but once they cashed in their statuettes, they would have enough money to buy more land and build a home. That had been their plan, and so far everything had been working out perfectly.

"So many people!" Angelique cried, looking around them as they neared

New Orleans and began to come across other carriages and pedestrians. "It almost feels like Paris."

"Feels like Paris," Jacques replied, smiling. "Smells like a chamber pot."

Jacques had expected the mood in the city to be festive, considering today was the day that forty-six other people were about to get the statuette they had waited so long for. And though there were a lot of folks milling about, the mood seemed anything but light. In fact, almost every conversation they overheard was filled with griping and grumbling.

After securing the carriage with a livery service near the port, Jacques and Angelique made their way on foot to the Place d'Arms, a large central open square flanked on one side by the river and on the other side by low, wood slat fencing, a sure sign of construction to come. A crowd had already gathered there on the grass, and it seemed everyone was waiting for the agent of M. Law to appear and give out the treasure they had coming to them. Off to one side, Jacques could see a soldier standing guard over a trunk, the very same trunk from three years before. Just looking at it made Jacques ache with longing for his papa.

At precisely noon, a man entered the Place d'Arms and stepped up on a wooden box so that he could be seen and heard over the crowd. No doubt Freneau's replacement, the man announced that the three-year waiting period for the statuettes was over, and that those statuettes would be distributed today. His clerk had a list of the passengers who had sailed on the *Beau Séjour* and were eligible to claim the reward. He began reading through the list, and each person as their name was called came forward and accepted their prize. When the man finished reading off the ship's roster and called out Jacques' name, people began grumbling, reluctant to let Jacques make his way to the front to claim his prize.

"Why does he get one?" someone called out.

"Yeah, he wasn't on our ship," another added.

As Jacques finally made it through and was handed his statuettes, the man in charge told the crowd that Jacques was a special case, a man cheated by John Law and who was being awarded restitution by the French government.

"What are you doing with the rest of them?" someone yelled.

"Yeah, what happens to the ones that were supposed to go to all the people who died?"

The crowd was getting angry. One man yelled that he lost his wife and two children on that voyage and that he felt like he deserved their statuettes. He was probably telling the truth, but then ten more men shouted out, claiming that their wife and six children, eight children, twelve children had died, and they deserved their statuettes. The crowd worked themselves up in a frenzy, so much so that the man's answer could not be heard. Finally, he gestured to the soldier, who fired into the air. The resounding boom caught everyone's attention and soon they were again quiet.

"Ladies and Gentlemen, bear with me and I will attempt to explain the situation more fully. As you know, M. Law was not one hundred percent honest in his enticements to bring people to the New World. In all fairness, the populating of an entire territory is not an easy task."

An angry chorus of boos discouraged the man from justifying Law's actions again.

"In any event, you may recall M. Law saying that the gold for these statuettes had come from here, from the Louisiana territory. That, in fact, was a lie. The gold he used for the statuettes had been smuggled into France from Spain. The reason the royal goldsmith said that it was as fine as the finest gold from the Spanish territories in the New World is because the gold *was* from the Spanish territories of the New World. Law had procured the gold himself and lied to the royal goldsmith about its origins."

Jacques remembered the original propaganda that had been circulated by Law, posters and brochures that promised one could simply walk down the streets here and scoop up gold and diamonds by the handful. It had sounded ludicrous even then, but once Jacques had arrived in Louisiana he had seen for himself that it was not true. The only things one might scoop up by the handfuls here were mud, mosquitoes, and snakes.

"Given that France has strict sumptuary laws preventing the export of this type of gold," the man continued, "you will understand why the whole load is in violation of French law and should never have been sent here in the first place. The remaining statuettes, therefore, will be returned to

France, where they will go back into the royal treasury. It is only by the goodness of the regent's heart that he has agreed to honor the original promise made to you all by M. Law and allow me to distribute these here today."

The goodness of the regent's heart? As far as Jacques knew, he'd been as culpable in this as Law was! The regent was only serving until Louis XV was old enough to rule France for himself, and Jacques could only hope that would happen soon!

"How do we know these aren't fakes?" one man called out.

That seemed to rile up the crowd a bit, as they were all wondering the same thing.

"There has been some confusion about a second, duplicate set of statuettes. The truth is, a second set was made, but from my understanding there was a mix-up at the last minute, and the wrong ones were sent here by mistake."

"I knew it! They gave us the wrong ones!"

"Yes, but that is to your benefit," the man insisted, trying to explain that the wrong ones were solid gold and the right ones were gilded.

Things began to turn ugly very quickly after that. Jacques realized what was happening, and it was simply a confusion between the crowd and the agent as to what they each were saying.

No matter how hard the man tried to explain, the crowd simply didn't get it. When the agent confirmed, for the third time, that the statuettes he had just handed out were indeed the wrong ones, the ones that weren't supposed to come here, the entire gathering began to spiral out of control.

"It's a worthless piece of junk!" one man cried, and before anyone could stop him, he raised his arm behind his head and threw his statuette directly at the agent. It struck the man at the temple with a heavy thud, drawing blood and causing him to fall off of his platform.

After that, the crowd went crazy. Jacques tried to stop them, but to no avail. Soon both of the soldiers and the agent were down on the ground, and people were striking them relentlessly with their statuettes. It was as if the poor men were being stoned—all because of a simple miscommunication!

Jacques had to do something. Pushing his way to Angelique, he told her to leave the area and wait for him at the livery.

"Come with me," she said, clutching at his hand, her eyes wide with fear.

"Angelique, just go! I have to stop this! These two men are going to die for no reason!"

Reluctantly, he let go of her hand and watched her dart off toward the safety of a side street. Jacques again forced his way to the front of the crowd and tried to shout over all the noise, telling people to stop, please stop, but they didn't understand. He got the attention of several, but as he started to explain, saying that he was one of the goldsmiths who worked on the statuettes, it was as if all the rage and frenzy of the crowd shifted from the agent and soldier lying on the ground, likely dead now, to Jacques himself. Before he could stop them, Jacques felt a sharp blow to his cheek. The next thing he knew, what felt like a hundred more followed as he was pummeled. Curling into a ball against the earth, trying to protect his head with his arms, Jacques could only pray for mercy, begging God to spare him. At some point, he passed out.

Eventually, he awoke.

From the sound of things, the people were gone now. All was silent around him except for the soft weeping of a young woman, the tears of his beloved Angelique. Jacques tried to whisper her name, though all that came out was a low groan.

Still, that was enough to get her attention. Suddenly he could feel her hands clutching at the clothes on his chest, sobbing and begging him not to give up, not to go away. He opened his eyes, though even when he did it was as if everything was shrouded in a veil of hazy white. Slowly, he managed to form a few words, his voice just a hoarse whisper.

"I'm sorry, Angelique."

"This was not your fault, Jacques. You were only trying to help the poor men!"

"And I thank you for that, for trying to help," a deep voice rasped from nearby. "I fear I shall die regardless."

Jacques realized that it was the man who had first been stoned, M.

Freneau's representative who had not been able to make the crowd understand about the statuettes. Carefully turning his head to look, Jacques saw that the man was lying on the ground just a few feet away, blood trickling from his mouth, his eyes swollen shut. Between them and all around, though the scene was out of focus, Jacques could tell that the earth was littered with the statuettes, discarded by the angry crowd after their use for them was done.

"They have thrown the statuettes out as trash!" Jacques cried.

"Those fools," the man rasped. "They did not know...what they had in their very hands. And now we have suffered...for their foolishness."

"You suffer *now*, sir," Angelique cried angrily, "but Jacques and I have suffered for these infernal statuettes since their very creation! Oh, how I wish they had never been made at all!"

Sobbing, Angelique recounted their entire, sad tale from the beginning. Jacques wanted to reach up and comfort her, to stroke her hair or take her hand, but he found that he was unable to lift his arm.

"Girl, how many statuettes remain?" the man asked when she was finished with her story.

"If not all two hundred, then very nearly so," she replied, her voice sounding bitter. "They are everywhere."

"Then do as I say. Right now."

"Sir?"

"Gather the statuettes...all of them. Return them to the trunk that is on... the wagon there. Do it now...I beg of you."

Angelique objected, saying she must tend to her injured husband, but he was adamant in his request.

"Have you knowledge of anatomy or medicine?" he moaned.

"No, sir."

"Then you aren't doing him any good by...sitting there and crying. Gather the statuettes now. Please...give this dying man his last wish."

Reluctantly, she did as he asked. Jacques thought her energies would be far better spent trying to get both men to a doctor or, lacking that, a priest. But he was too tired and in too much pain to make his objections known. Instead, he lay there on the ground, going in and out of consciousness.

Every time he opened his eyes he spotted Angelique moving quickly between the statuettes she was picking up and the open trunk. She did not bother with the cloth wrappings but instead threw them into the wooden box with abandon, as fast as she possibly could.

"Done, sir, I have done as you asked," she gasped, collapsing on the ground next to Jacques, breathing heavily from the exertion. As she turned her attentions to her husband, he could feel her trembling hands gently wiping the sweat from his brow.

"Thank you. Now listen to me, girl. Listen carefully," the man persisted, a gurgling sound coming from his throat.

"What?" she asked, frustration clearly evident in her voice.

"These fools did not know what they had...when they had it. They have used the treasure as weapons and then discarded it." He gurgled again and coughed, and it sounded as if he was drowning in his own blood. "The government was...equally at fault in this, for allowing it to happen in the first place. The Mississippi Bubble was a shameful blot...on the noble face of France, and much harm has come to many because of it."

Though he could do nothing for the agent, Jacques was grieved at the sound of the man's labored breathing and hoped he would soon say what he was trying to say.

"I cannot ease the sufferings...of all the fools who held the gold in their hands and then gave it up...But I can do this...As an agent of the French crown, I bequeath the remaining statuettes, in total, to you, madam...and to your husband, should he live."

THIRTY-SEVEN

Clamping a hand over my mouth, eyes wide, I looked at my mother, knowing without question that I was going to vomit. She seemed to understand what was going on because she pointed toward a door and said, "That way!"

I made it down the hall and into the bathroom just in time. Retching into the toilet, the words that kept rolling around in my head were *He says you're the one who shot him*.

Was I destined to be betrayed by every single person in my life?

I could only hope that my father's bizarre accusation was merely a symptom of the trauma his body had been through. Surely, he was feeling confused. Perhaps he had even suffered brain damage. I knew a little bit about how blood loss affected the body. If he had lost two or three pints as they said, then there was a good chance the resulting lack of oxygen to his brain could have done some serious damage.

But of all the crazy things for him to come out with, how could he possibly say I was the one who did that to him? Either he was lying or I had an evil twin out there doing things I was being blamed for.

Of all the charges piling up against me, I wasn't worried that this one could stick. It was too easy to prove that there was no way I could have been in two places on the same day at the same time, especially given how far apart Louisiana and Illinois were. I wasn't worried about the legal ramifications of my father's claim. I just didn't understand how or why he could ever have said such a thing.

Sitting on the side of the bathtub, I remained as still as possible until I was finished being sick. I flushed the toilet and then moved to the sink, washing my hands and then rinsing my mouth over and over with water cupped in shaky hands.

I had to get out of here.

Despite the fact that I was in a swamp, despite the fact that there were no roads that led away from this isolated island called Paradise, my chances of surviving this night were surely far greater outside, on my own, than they were in this house with my mother, guarded by masked kidnappers.

Thanks to the boat ride Travis had given me earlier, at least I understood how Paradise was laid out. There were three docks here, and at the very least if I could get myself close enough to one of them without being seen, there might be some sort of watercraft that I could sneak onto and take off in. Out on the water, I might not know how to weave in and out as Travis had to make my way toward civilization, but having studied the map at his camp earlier looking for coordinates, at least I understood now how this general region was laid out. Paradise was north and west of Morgan City, so as long as I stayed on the main waterways and headed in a southeasterly direction, I should be able to get to civilization eventually.

But I was getting ahead of myself. Right now, it was more important that I get away from this house and the masked men who lingered outside. First, though I already knew it wouldn't go through, I pulled out my cell phone and tried to make a call. Sure enough, the phone could not get service. Slipping it back into my pocket, I continued making my plan for escape.

This bathroom had a window at the far end, one that looked like it would be just large enough for me to climb out of. Quickly, I turned off the light and then crept to the window, pulled back the curtain, and looked outside. I could see trees and vines and brush, but there were no people, not that I could tell.

Just as I was about to slide open the window and make my escape, there was a banging at the bathroom door.

"Chloe? It's Mom. Are you okay? Do you need anything?"

There wasn't a maternal, nurturing bone in my mother's body, but just listening to the sound of her voice I was reminded how she always at least pretended there was. When I was a child, we'd had an unspoken agreement about moments like these. She would offer to help and I would turn her down. That pretense allowed her to feel like a mother while sparing me the disappointment of how inadequate she really was those few times when I had called her bluff and accepted her "help."

"I'm all right," I called toward the doorway now. "But I threw up all over myself. Do you think it would be okay if I took a quick shower?"

"That's probably a good idea. I'll wait for you in the living room."

Case in point: A real mother would have offered to dig around for a change of clothes and a towel and whatever else I might need. Not Lola Ledet. She had already done her job by offering; it was up to me to handle things from there.

Making sure the door was locked, I turned on the shower and let it run as I moved quickly to the window, slid it open, and popped off the screen. The house was elevated, so even though the bathroom was on the first floor I still had a jump of about seven feet. Looking from side to side and seeing nothing but flora and fauna in the shadows, I hoisted myself onto the window sill and out the other side, making the leap and landing with a soft thud, my feet burning with tingles from the jolt.

I didn't know how long my mother would wait for me to finish my shower before she would get suspicious and try to figure out what was going on. I hoped that I would have a good ten minutes, maybe fifteen. That should be time enough to get to the closest dock, anyway, and if I had any luck at all there would be an unguarded boat there for me to steal.

Blinking as my eyes adjusted to the dark, I moved along the back of the house. I didn't have the luxury of banging a stick on the ground in the way Travis had taught me, so I could only hope that I would have no snake encounters there in the brush.

Peeking around the side, I saw no people or movement, so again I skirted quietly forward until I reached the front corner. Peeking again, I wasn't so lucky this time. Not five feet away stood one of my captors in black, a shotgun slung over his shoulder. His back was to me, so quickly I held my breath and retraced my steps, putting as much distance between him and me as possible.

If there were people in front of the house, my next best bet would have been to head in the opposite direction. Unfortunately, starting just a few yards behind the house, the woods were so dense and thick that there was no way I could have made my way through them. I would have to move sideways.

Given the general layout of Paradise, I knew that going in one direction would bring me to the river and the other would take me to the bayou. I felt sure that the airboat had come in on the bayou side, so that was my first choice. Of course, the chances were greater that people would be there too, people I really didn't want to run into.

There had to be a way to get to the water a little farther down, at a point where I could see the dock and gauge the situation without being seen. That would mean moving through brush and tangles and vines and trees, but at least the undergrowth was not as thick off to the sides as it was heading back.

Taking a deep breath, I sprinted from the shelter of the house to the nearest big tree in the direction of the bayou. From there, I picked out another tree and prepared to advance again, but as I did a twig snapped under me and my footsteps crunched loudly against debris that littered the forest floor. I froze, hoping no one had heard me. Moving more slowly, trying to be as quiet as humanly possible, I gave up trying to sprint and carefully crept instead. Eventually, I looked back and was pleased to see that I had put a good distance between myself and the house. So far, at least, it didn't appear as if anyone had spotted me or that my mother had even realized yet that I had snuck out. I kept going, the sounds of the swampy forest reverberating all around me. I was glad that I'd had all evening to get used to the sounds, because already they didn't scare me as much as they had before.

Beyond one particularly large tree, the ground grew wet and boggy. Afraid I might be sucked down into quicksand or something, I thought about grabbing a vine and swinging across the wet parts like Tarzan. That wasn't really an option, however, so I did the next best thing. Taking my chances with the snakes, I climbed up onto a low, fat branch of the massive oak and scooted myself along it like a bridge over water.

Where the branch tapered off at the far end, I hung down and tested the ground with my feet, and it felt firm enough. Lowering my weight onto the soil, I took another look behind me, but at that point I was so enveloped by the forest that I could no longer tell how far I had gone. All I knew was that I could no longer see the house.

Unless I had veered off at an angle, I should reach the water soon. Unfortunately, the closer I got to it, the softer the ground grew and the thicker the foliage. I was ready to give up, not sure whether I was more frightened of getting sucked into the muck or being eaten by an alligator. But then I heard the familiar plops and I realized I was nearly there. In front of me, I could even see the moon sparkling on the black water of the bayou. In order to see up the waterway and catch a glimpse of the dock, I briefly considered slipping into that water and swimming out, but that was just too dangerous and terrifying a prospect, so instead I stepped up on a large cypress knee, balanced myself, and then moved forward to another one. After doing that several times, I was finally able to look up the water-way and see the dock. I leaned forward, clinging to the trunk of the tree and squinting in the darkness as I tried to make out the scene there.

As I had hoped, the airboat was still sitting there, though now it had been joined by a second one. And as I had feared, people were there as well—several people—all of them dressed in black, though it looked as though their ski masks were off for the time being. I wished I had a pair of binoculars so I could get a better look at their faces. From where I was I couldn't ascertain much more than that they were Caucasian and they had what looked like brown hair. As that described almost everyone around these parts—or at least the Indians and the Cajuns—that knowledge didn't do me much good.

My heart sinking in frustration, I realized I would have to retrace my steps, pass behind the house yet again, and move in the opposite direction. I had less hopes of finding some means of escape on the other side of the island, but at this point it was the only real choice I had.

My movements were faster and more sure on the return. As I scooted myself back along the branch that served as my bridge, I was startled by my first real sign of wildlife: It was some sort of small, furry mammal, and at the sound of my movements it suddenly darted out from under the brush and scampered away into the dark.

Most terrifying was the moment that I had to pass behind the house. It had been at least ten minutes since I turned on the shower, so there was a good chance that my mother had already investigated and realized I had given her the slip. In a very real sense, though, I was cornered and had no choice. There was no way to get from where I was to where I needed to be without taking that chance.

Holding my breath, I moved quickly, dashing across the overgrown weeds, skirting the back of the house, and not even bothering to look before continuing on at the other side. There was an expanse of lawn there, and I ran across it as fast as I could in flip-flops. At least I heard no telltale sounds, no yells or gunshots that might tell me they knew that I was gone.

When I finally reached the cover of some trees, I was relieved to see that there were paths there. Choosing one that seemed to angle in the general direction of the river, I made fast work of it, jumping over fallen logs, splashing through puddles, and ducking under low-hanging vines. It was dark there under the thick canopy of trees that blocked the moonlight, but I did the best I could at staying on the trail and pressing onward as fast as possible.

More than once, I crashed headfirst through sticky spider webs, but I kept going, running my hands over my face and hair as I did. Trying not to think of the massive spiders that lived in the swamps, I increased my speed, though soon my legs were covered in mud, my arms in mosquito bites, and I swore I could feel a hundred crawling insects along my back, under my shirt.

I almost made it to the river.

I could see it there in the distance, the water sparkling at the river's edge. But then there was a log across the path and so I leapt over it. Had I not landed in mud on the other side, I would have kept going.

As it was, though, the angle that I hit the mud caused my foot to slide out from under me. The next thing I knew, I was smack on the ground, flat on my back, the wind knocked from my lungs.

It took what felt like a full minute before I could breathe again. Gasping for air, I sat up, and when that didn't help I flipped around onto my hands and knees. Getting the wind knocked out of me was a horrible sensation, and as I regained my breathing I had no choice but to remain there on the ground, heart pounding, and pray that I wouldn't be discovered before I could get moving again. After a few moments I steadied myself so that I could stand. Unfortunately, I didn't see the snake there, the one that was hidden in the shadow of the fallen log.

I didn't see it, that is, until its fangs were buried deep into the flesh on the back of my hand.

THIRTY-EIGHT

I'm not sure how I had the presence of mind not to scream. The moment I understood what was happening, I jumped up and flung my arm outward. With that, the snake let go, flying through the night air and landing with a thunk somewhere in the brush. Between my panic and the darkness, I realized I hadn't noticed its colors or markings. All I had seen were its beady eyes and its teeth, burying themselves into my hand, the hand that was now bleeding.

At that point, my entire snake education consisted of being able to recognize exactly two kinds: water moccasins, which were long, dark, and poisonous, and milk snakes, which had rings of red, white, and black and were nonpoisonous. I don't think this snake was either of those, though I wasn't sure what it had been.

I stood, waiting to see what would happen next. I didn't know anything about what I should do, and every bit of snake advice I had ever heard contradicted every other bit of snake advice I had ever heard. Suck out the venom, don't suck out the venom; make a tourniquet, don't make a tourniquet; hold the wound above my heart, hold it below my heart. Whatever my inclination was, I was afraid it might be wrong. Most of all, I could only hope that if indeed the snake had been poisonous that my death would come quickly and not as painfully as I feared.

I felt woozy, but I didn't know if that was the snake venom or my own hysteria. Steadying myself, I moved from the path on toward the water, thinking how ironic it would be if I made it to safety only to drop dead at the last moment because of a snakebite.

Whether my veins were coursing with venom or not, I still needed to staunch the bleeding. Trying not to think about infection—and knowing that if the snake really was poisonous then the venom would kill me long before infection ever had time to set in—I placed one filthy, muddy hand on top of the other and applied pressure to the wound.

I was closer to the river now, and again I tried to decide what to do. Plunge my wounded hand into the water or not plunge my wounded hand into the water? Doing so might wash away some of the germs and debris, but it could also introduce bacteria.

Was I delirious yet? Was I dying? I didn't know.

"My name is Chloe Ledet," I whispered out loud, just to see if my speech was slurred. It wasn't, which I took as a good sign.

Finally, as I stumbled from the wooded path onto the open riverbank, I realized I had come to the end of myself. The whole world was against me. No matter what I did right, it turned out wrong. Now even nature itself had reared its ugly head and taken a bite that would possibly end my life. For a moment, I almost felt like laughing. Stumbling toward the water, I knelt there on the riverbank, trying to decide how I should spend what might be my last few minutes on earth. I uttered a single, awkward prayer for help and hoped that God was listening.

The bleeding had stopped, for the most part, so I scrambled around for a stick, and there in the mud I gouged out block letters: CHLOE WAS INNOCENT. Looking down at my handiwork, I added OF ALL CHARGES and underlined the word ALL.

If I knew who was behind everything, I would have written their name there instead, as the killer or at least the mastermind of the killings. I knew my mother was involved, and I strongly suspected Travis was as well, but I still wasn't sure who was actually calling the shots, orchestrating my demise, and plunging me into what had probably turned out to be the final nightmare of my life.

I dropped the stick and thought about all Travis had said just a few hours earlier in his cabin as he read to me from the Bible. At the time, his words had been so inspiring and so instinctively needed that I had latched on to them with a kind of joy I hadn't experienced in years. Now that I knew he probably wasn't the man I thought he was, I decided that the God he had described wasn't the Being I thought He was either. Much like my own father, my heavenly Father had far better things to do than worry about someone like me. Vast and distant and uninvolved, He hadn't even sent me deliverance in my darkest hour.

I looked up at the sky, at a million twinkling stars, and thought about the power of something so mighty it could have created them in the first place. Travis had read a verse to me earlier, one that said God knew how many hairs were on my head. I knew now that was a lie. God didn't even know I had a snakebite. He didn't even know I needed Him.

Maybe He didn't even know that I existed.

I had nowhere else to turn. I was still waiting for the venom to set in, to do its job in stopping my heart or closing my airways or whatever it was that venom did. From where I sat, I couldn't see the dock that should have been somewhere along here on the river side of Paradise. Perhaps I should try to get to the dock after all, on the small chance that my death was not imminent.

Getting back to my feet, I dropped the stick I had written with and moved down the river bank some more, not caring whether I was about to stumble upon another snake or even an alligator. I decided that the sun would be up soon, so maybe even if there were no vessels at this dock, I could find a place nearby to hide and wait. Surely, come sunrise, there would be some activity on the river and perhaps I could wave down a passing boat.

It sounded like a plan, assuming I didn't drop dead from the snakebite first or get caught by my kidnappers.

As I got closer, I realized some sort of noise was coming from up ahead. Ducking behind a clump of trees, I moved toward the sound as silently as possible. Judging by the clinking and clanging, it sounded as though someone was working on an engine or a motor.

Moving closer, I could see something white bobbing in the water. A boat. It wasn't an airboat like the ones on the other side of Paradise. Again inching forward, I squinted and tried to make out the name of the boat that was painted on the side, *Miss Demeanor*, which didn't make a lot of sense unless it was owned by a cop—or a criminal.

I could only hope it was the former.

The old Chloe would have jumped out of hiding at that point, run toward the man who I could now see was hunched over the boat's engine, working away. I would have thrown myself at his mercy, trusting in the goodness and purity and devotion of an honored civil servant, confident that he would save me.

The new Chloe, however, understood that no one could be trusted. Sheriff or not, I still thought my best bet was to make sure he was alone and then attempt to ambush him and steal his boat.

Repositioning myself, it crossed my mind that for the very first time since this whole nightmare began, I was about to commit an actual crime. Assaulting a police officer had to be a serious offense. My only hope was that I wouldn't really have to hurt him so much as just knock him off the boat and into the water. Then I could make my escape and hope that an alligator or something didn't get him before he could climb back onto dry land.

At least he was in the right position to make my plan feasible. He was paying no attention to me, he was definitely alone, and I saw no telltale bulge under his clothing where a gun might be. Summoning my nerve, I grabbed a big, solid stick from the ground, emerged from the tree line, stepped onto the dock, and crept toward him. I could see that in the man's hand was a long wrench, and that concerned me, because I knew it could be used as a weapon and was likely to be more effective than my stick. I needed something even bigger. That's when I noticed the oar sitting on the side of the boat within easy reach.

Trying not to think about what I had become, I finally made my move.

Dropping the stick, I grabbed the oar and raised it over my shoulder like a baseball bat, ready to swing. At that moment, the man turned around, and I saw that it was none other than Wade Henkins. He seemed to recognize me instantly, despite the fact that I was covered in mud, bearing a weapon, and about to knock him overboard.

"Chloe!" he cried. "I been calling everywhere for you! Are you okay? What are you doing *here*?"

At this point, I trusted no one, not even this man who was my father's friend and who had been nothing but nice to me.

"I've been drugged, betrayed, kidnapped, and bitten by a snake. I guess you could say I'm not all that okay."

"Wait a minute. First things first. What kind of snake? When?"

"One with really sharp teeth, maybe fifteen minutes ago. I don't know if it was poisonous or not."

"Fifteen minutes ago," Wade repeated, the relief evident in his features. "Trust me, if it were poisonous, you would know by now."

So at least I wasn't going to die from the snakebite after all. That was good news, but I still had the little matter of my kidnappers and their guns, not to mention my mother. As politely as I could, I apologized to Wade for not trusting him and asked that he please get off of the boat.

"Wait a minute," he said. "Did you also say you were kidnapped?"

"Yep, I was gagged and tied up and brought here just a short while ago. I managed to escape, but they're going to be looking for me very soon. That's why I need to get out of here."

"But I can help you, Chloe. I am a cop, you know."

"I know, and you've been a big help to me these past few days. But I'm learning the hard way that I can't trust anyone."

Wade nodded, but he didn't move.

"I know how you feel, Chloe. Trust me, cops are probably the most cynical people of all. We've seen too much not to be. But I gotta tell ya, sometimes you reach a point where you have to *choose* to trust. Even if it's the wrong choice, it's still the one thing that keeps you human in the end."

Glancing at the dark wilderness behind me, I had to wonder if my mother had figured out yet that I was gone. Surely she had. I wasn't sure how much more time I had here before I would be overtaken by my captors once again.

"Thanks for the riverside philosophy, Wade. Maybe sometime when I don't have armed kidnappers breathing down my neck I'll think about it. Right now, I just want your boat. Climb off nice and easy and you don't have to get hurt."

I thought I could detect a small, brief smile at the corners of Wade's mouth. He thought I was a softie, that I wasn't up to this. Just a few days ago, I wouldn't have been. At this point, however, it was all about survival. I was ready to do whatever it took to get off this island and far away.

"You can have the boat, Chloe, but it won't do you no good," Wade said as he climbed onto the dock. "The motor's dead as a doorknob. Worse than that, the radio has been sabotaged. I got no way to communicate and no way to get out of here. I know you're feeling a little suspicious right now, but I think your smarter bet would be to trust me. Let me see if I can't fix the engine, and then I can get us both out of here."

Maybe it was the frank concern in his voice. Maybe it was the vague trace of light purple along the horizon that hinted at morning. Maybe it was simply that I had reached the end of my rope. Whatever it was, I decided to lower my weapon and surrender to the situation.

"If someone tampered with your radio, I'm guessing they messed with your motor too?"

"Sure looks that way. It's been running funny for the past half hour, and then it finally died about a half a mile away. Lucky for me that the current runs pretty strong through here, so all I had to do was watch for the dock and then use the paddle to get myself over to the side."

"Speaking of the paddle," I said, handing it over to him.

"Why don't we get back in the boat and I'll work on the motor and you can tell me what the heck is going on."

"What if the kidnappers find us?"

"I got a gun, Chloe. I'll keep us safe. You can be the lookout."

I didn't know Wade Henkins very well, but as he said earlier, sometimes we just had to make the choice to trust. Given that he was stuck here too, I thought I might as well fill him in a little, starting with the hardest news of all.

"If someone's been tampering with your engine, I have a good idea who it might be," I said as I climbed aboard and sat in a cold, vinyl seat, the one that would give me the best vantage point as the lookout. "You know Travis Naquin? I've been watching him fool with boat motors all night. I know for a fact he has the knowledge, but I'm just not sure why he would choose to use it this way."

"Probably just 'cause he's a Naquin."

Wade went back to work on the boat engine, shaking his head and telling me a tale about the Naquin family. According to him, this piece of land originally belonged to the Henkins family. In the bayou, there was something known as "trapper's justice," a law of the land that dictated who had the right to hunt and fish where. It wasn't just a matter of being a good neighbor, he explained. There were actual laws about usufruct and land ownership and hunting and fishing rights.

"In 1927, Louisiana had its biggest flood ever," Wade explained. "Back then, this piece of land here belonged to my grandparents. During the flood, the whole thing was underwater. Once the flooding was over, their home had been destroyed, their crops were ruined, and they had lost every single one of their possessions."

"That's awful. Did they have flood insurance?"

"In 1927, in a Louisiana swamp? A poor, backwoods trapper and farmer, are you kidding me?"

"You're right, dumb question. So what happened?"

Wade asked me to hand him the screwdriver, and as I did he spotted the wound on the back of my hand. Before he said another word, he stopped what he was doing, moved to the front of the boat, and pulled out a first aid kit attached to the side there. He handed it to me, telling me that even though the bite obviously was not poisonous, I was going to be in for a nasty infection if I didn't clean it up and dress the wound. I knew he was right, so as he turned his attentions back to the motor, I kept one eye on my lookout duties as I rifled through the first aid kit, pulled out what I needed, and sanitized and bandaged my hand.

Wade continued telling me the tale of his family and how they were forced to sell this ravaged piece of land to the Naquins after the flood. Sadly, because the Henkins had no money left at all, their only choice for housing had been to become squatters on an abandoned houseboat, one that was located just a quarter of a mile beyond the Paradise property line.

"Can you imagine what that was like for my grandpa? To have to live with his family inside that nasty hovel right up there, while the Naquin family took over the land here, building a home and putting in a garden and claiming it as their own?" He went on to describe how the Naquins had become selfish with the land, the Henkins had grown bitter and angry, and a grudge between the two families slowly grew into an out-and-out feud.

"I mean, I know they had bought the land free and clear, but in Louisiana, with trapper's justice and everything, my family just thought it was a given that they would have the right to hunt and fish here at Paradise forever, regardless of who owned the property."

I thought about Wade's story and how it had clarified the feud that Travis had referred to earlier.

"Anyhoo, Chloe, do you think you've calmed down enough now to explain to me exactly what's going on? I hate to push you if you don't feel ready to talk about it, but I want to know about this kidnapping thing. Were you exaggerating, or are you really escaping something that dangerous?"

Again, maybe it was the concern in his voice or maybe it was just that I needed to talk to someone, anyone, about all of my trauma. Whatever it was that caused the dam to break, I started at the beginning and soon found myself telling him everything—about the treasure, about my parents, about the clues and the coordinates and even the salt. He listened to the whole crazy story, though he seemed far less interested in hearing about the salt than about the coordinates that would lead to the treasure. The more we talked about it, the stronger the gleam in his eye grew, and it seemed as though there were things he wasn't saying. Suddenly, I had to wonder if perhaps the treasure had been put there not by a pirate or a confederate trying to protect his money during the war, but a Henkins. Maybe the reason Wade's face had lit up so was because he thought his family might have the more legitimate claim.

Frankly, at this point I didn't care who ended up with the treasure.

All I wanted was to be delivered safely from this island with the charges against me dropped. Given the lies my father was now telling about me, I wasn't even sure if I wanted to go and see him at the hospital. Mostly, I just wanted to head to Chicago, back to my condo in Old Town, back to my life before everything began to fall apart.

But life didn't have an undo function. Just because I wanted all of this to go away didn't mean that it would. I wasn't free to leave Louisiana, not as long as the murder charge against me stood.

"Okay, so tell me again about the coordinates," Wade said. "You got four out of the six numbers but you can't find the treasure without the other two?"

"Right."

"And the two you are missing belong to Alphonse Naquin and Ben Runner?"

"Yes. It's hard to explain, but Ruben and Conrad and Sam had actually played sort of a private joke and displayed their numbers in plain sight in their homes. It would be easier if everyone had done that, but according to Conrad neither Ben nor Alphonse were in on that particular joke."

"What do you mean they displayed them in plain sight?"

"Well, Conrad had a wall covered with photos and plaques, and on one of the plaques he had actually engraved his number. Rubin captured his in the photograph and framed it and put it on the mantle."

Suddenly, from the corner of my eye, I thought I spotted movement. I sat up, peering in that direction, but then I realized what I was seeing wasn't one of the kidnappers, it was a deer that had ventured from the woods to nibble at some grass along the waterline. The sun was coming up, and all around us the sky was a beautiful shade of purple-pink. Time was running out for us, though, and I knew that this might be the last sunrise I would ever be alive to see.

"Okay, so between the plaque and the photo and the pot holder, you were able to get those first three numbers," Wade persisted. "I thought you said you had four. How did you find out the fourth?"

"The fourth one was my father's. It was included in the recipe puzzle I told you about, the one that was hanging on the wall in the restaurant."

I looked at Wade, something shifting in my brain. "How did you know Sam's was on a pot holder? I didn't tell you that."

"Sure you did," he replied, his posture stiffening, a forced lightheartedness to his words. "When you was talking earlier." He went on to talk about the coordinates and trying them out in various combinations, but all I could think was how clearly it all came together. I knew what I said and what I hadn't said.

Wade. The one who had been there the morning my father got shot.

Wade. The one on who's boat my father had been found a short while later, bleeding and unconscious.

Wade. The one who had come to see me in jail and given me his number and told me the message that I was to "follow the recipe."

Wade. The only source of information we had about what was going on with Josie Runner and the Charenton police. For all I knew, everything had been a lie and she wasn't even in custody and there was no boyfriend and his buddies with a treasure map.

All along, I thought I had been framed for murder to get me out of the way. Now, with absolute clarity, I realized that it was the opposite. I had been framed for murder so that I would take on this treasure hunt. Unable to find the treasure himself, Wade had engineered everything so that I would do it for him. As Julian's daughter, he must have hoped that I would have insider knowledge and thus a better chance of finding the gold.

Once again, I had made the wrong choice and put my trust in the wrong person. I didn't know where Wade's gun was, but I had no doubt it was handy. Quickly, I considered my options, sorry that the oar had been put away at the front of the boat. I thought about jumping off the back, into the water, but for him that would be like shooting fish in a barrel.

At that moment, as my mind scrambled for what to do, a boat came chugging down the river. I spun around and waved frantically, trying to get them to stop and help. Instead, the boat continued by, the men on board returning my desperate waves with their own friendly response. Obviously, they just thought I was honoring boat etiquette with my mandatory, if overzealous, waves.

I would have to jump in and swim toward them. Surely then they would realize I needed their help. It looked like a boat of oil workers, heading off to a rig. Even from a distance I could see that they were big and strong and could easily turn things around.

"I wouldn't do that if I were you," Wade said from behind me as I was about to dive in. "Not unless you want to be Big Bertha's breakfast."

I glanced back at Wade, who was pointing toward the water. I looked where he indicated, to see an alligator floating nearby. It was at least twelve feet long, its yellow eyes hungrily taking in its surroundings.

The boat now passed, I again turned toward Wade, not surprised to see that he was holding a gun in his hand and it was pointed straight at me.

THIRTY-NINE

 With his free hand, Wade reached into his pocket and pulled out a small walkie-talkie. Pushing the button, he spoke into it.

"I got Chloe with me, on the boat. She figured things out, so I guess we have to move on to Plan B. Over."

"Copy that. Will meet you at the ponds with the others. Over."

Without another word, Wade forced me out of the boat and onto the dock. He moved in behind me, the gun's barrel pressing into my spine. I knew I would be crazy to try and make a run for it. Instead, I simply went where he told me, up the path past the old, crumbling remains of the salt mine. Switching between several paths to zigzag our way across the island, we eventually passed the upended houseboat as well, the one that had been washed ashore during a hurricane. Near the tip of its bow, I could almost make out the remnants of its name, two words that started with a *C* and an *M*, though they weren't quite readable because most of the other letters there had faded away.

Eventually we reached a clearing and came to a stop there. In the clearing were three strange, round ponds. The water in them was a vivid bluish-pink, and a crusty, pinkish-white foam encircled the edges like salt around a margarita glass.

Salt. Salt ponds. Of course.

On the far side of the three ponds was a fourth one, though something looked different about it. It had the crusty foam around the edges, but there was no water in it. Instead, at the center, was what looked like a foot-wide gash in the earth, almost as if the stopper had been pulled from a sink.

On this side of the ponds was a large hole in the ground with what looked like a rope ladder hanging down into it. That must be the old salt mine. Between that and these salt ponds, I realized that this really was it: My father's source for the pink salt that was sold around the world and had helped to make him famous.

I heard rustling off to our left, and then suddenly from another path emerged two of the men in black, their ski masks in place, my mother clutched between them. She looked terrified.

Before either of us could react at the sight of each other, there was more rustling from the woods across from us, and then there emerged four more men in black. Together, they were dragging a bloodied, beaten, and bound Travis Naquin. At the sight of him, tears filled my eyes. I couldn't begin to imagine what he had been through since our abduction hours ago. How could I have doubted him so fully, so quickly?

"You can lose the hoods, guys," Wade said, pressing the barrel into my back so I would move forward. "It don't matter if they see us at this point."

All around us, the masks came off. I didn't recognize any of them, though there was some common element to their features. My best guess was that they were brothers. Actually, looking more closely, I decided that they were Wade's brothers.

"Looks like the Henkins boys decided to take matters into their own hands against the Naquins," I said, testing my theory.

"That's right, Chloe. Sorry things had to end this way, but like I tol' you, this land was ours once. The Naquins, they *owe* us that treasure. We was here first."

My mother began crying, and between sobs she demanded to know what was going on. I wasn't completely sure myself, but from the exchange between her and Wade that followed, I realized that she had been lured here by him under false pretenses. Apparently he had told her that I had asked for her to meet me here at Paradise and had arranged for her transportation by airboat. She hadn't wanted to come, but Wade had said it was extremely urgent, a matter of life-and-death, and that I was ready to reveal who had shot Julian. Once she was here, however, Wade had called her on her cell phone and told her yet another lie, that Julian had suddenly come out of his coma and was fingering me as his shooter.

"Wait a minute!" I cried. "Mother, are you telling me you never actually heard Daddy say those words himself?"

Her face streaked with tears and mascara, my mother shook her head.

"No, but Wade told me that's what he said. I still don't know how you could have done that, Chloe, not to mention that once you got me all the way out here, you went and snuck out of the house! Do you know how much water you wasted by leaving the shower running? That was so rude, to me and to whoever pays the water bills."

I couldn't even dignify that with a response. But I did realize one thing, that my "escape" from the house had probably been engineered. By placing the masked men around the house and the dock on the bayou side, I had been left with no choice but to make my way to the river. There, Wade had already situated himself in the perfect spot. His goal, no doubt, was to get me to do exactly what I had done: feel secure enough to tell him all I had learned about the treasure. Every action I had taken had played right into his hands. No wonder he had been concerned about my snakebite. Had I dropped dead from poisonous venom, all of his hard work up to that point would have been for naught.

"You made me go through all of this just to find the treasure, but in the end you still don't have it," I said, shaking my head.

"At least we're closer now than we were before. I knew some of your father's friends were involved, but I never knew about the poem and the coordinates until all this started. In fact, I think I got Ben Runner's number yesterday, even though I didn't know what I had until I was talking to you back on the boat. When my brothers were there questioning Josie Runner, they took some boxes of papers and other personal stuff from under Ben's bed. I think I saw something in there about filé."

Before I could ask more of the questions that were swirling around my brain, Wade told the men who were holding on to Travis to get him "down in the hole." I watched in horror as they dragged Travis toward the ladder and threw him on the ground. While three of them held guns pointed at him, the fourth one untied the ropes that were binding his ankles and wrists.

"What happened here with my father on Monday?" I demanded.

As we both watched Wade's brothers handle Travis, Wade explained that he and his family had been taking turns coming out here to Paradise for months, searching for the treasure that they knew was buried some-where on this land. On Monday, Julian had shown up unexpectedly and caught Wade red handed, wandering around down in the old salt mine with a metal detector. My father realized what Wade was up to, and he had flown into a rage, angry that Wade's search for the treasure might end up jeopardizing his precious salt. Both men had come up out of the mine and continued their argument beside the ponds, and in the heat of the moment Wade had shot Julian.

"I wasn't no killer when all of this started," Wade told me now, as if that made things any better. "Even after I shot him, I tried to think of some way I could straighten things out and make it right. But your daddy tricked me. He said if I would get him to a hospital he would tell everybody we'd been out hunting and I had shot him by accident. To prove that I could believe him, he told me where the treasure was buried and offered to share some of it with me if I'd go dig it up. While I was digging over in the woods in the place he told me to, that skunk managed to crawl out of here to the closest dock on one good leg and steal my boat."

Over by the hole, Travis' bindings were finally off and the men were poking at him with their feet, trying to get him to get up and climb down that ladder into the mine. I wanted to help him somehow, but Wade's gun was still pressing firmly into my back.

"I had a feeling your daddy would head straight to the closest marina for help, so I ran up to the dock by the house here and took his boat since he had mine. I had to stop him before he could tell anybody what had happened. His boat—the one I was driving—was bigger and faster than my little fishing boat that he was on, so I was able to catch up with him and head him off before he could get there. After that, it was jus' a matter of playing a little cat and mouse out on the waterways. He did better than I thought he would, but I still stayed pretty close on his tail. Then he had the brilliant idea to head up the little channel to Ben Runner' house. I couldn't get up in there with the big boat I was in, so I took out my gun and shot at him as best I could from there. Even though I didn't get him, I had a feeling he would work his way farther up inside that swamp, maybe even get lost, and bleed to death before he could get back out. If he hadn't had a cell phone with him, that's exactly what woulda happened."

"You shot at him again near Ben Runner's house?" I asked, thinking of the old lady and her booms. "So Josie Runner wasn't involved after all?"

"Nah, but my brothers scared her good, showing up in uniform and demanding to know what she had seen and heard on Monday. Lucky for her, she did have one little secret, but she confessed right quick. Turns out she didn't see or hear a thing because on Monday at noon she had left the old folks there at the house all by themselves and had gone into town to do some grocery shopping. That's why she looked so guilty to you, not because she knew anything about the shooting but because she left those people there alone. Seeing as how she didn't know nothing, my brothers didn't have to kill her after all."

Poor Josie! I felt horrible, realizing that if she had indeed been a witness to Wade's pursuit of my father out there on the bayou behind her house, then she would be dead now—and it would be my fault because I was the one who called Wade and turned her in.

"You people are insane," I said, looking from one brother to another. No one bothered to reply, as they were all focused on Travis, who had finally managed to get up on his hands and knees. From there, he moved to the ladder and climbed on, though I could tell by the way he was favoring one arm that he wasn't just injured on the surface; he likely had some broken bones as well. Still, we watched as he managed to climb down, all alone, disappearing into the darkness inside. Not once did he look at me, not through any of it, and then it was too late.

"Her turn," Wade called to his brothers, gesturing toward my mother.

She shrieked and then tried to fight off the men as they dragged her toward the hole. Cursing Wade and his entire family, she called him just about every name in the book. He had a few choice words for her as well, and I could tell from their angry exchange that he knew all about her Bourbon Street past and that he found it pretty ridiculous that a girl who came from such humble origins had the nerve to look down her nose at him for the past thirty years just because he was from the bayou.

"So after you lost sight of my father," I said, trying to get Wade back on track with his tale, "what did you do?"

"The only thing I could do. Came back here and constructed an alibi. It helped a lot, being a cop. I knew what the police would need to see and hear to believe my story."

"So there never were any drunken fishermen? No blackberry bushes that needed clearing? No trip into town for groceries?"

"Nope."

"What happened then?"

He shrugged, watching as my mother struggled fiercely with his brothers at the ladder, swinging at them even as they laughed at her.

"I went to the hospital where they took your daddy. I knew I had to stay close to make sure he kept quiet if he regained consciousness. But with him in ICU and your mama calling around trying to hire a bodyguard, I knew I wouldn't be able to get near him. I stayed there a couple hours anyway, listening to her making plans with the lawyer and the restaurant and you, and then I came up with a different approach. Lucky for me your daddy stayed in a coma."

"But how did you engineer what happened at Ledet's? Who drugged us? Was it Graze? The waiter? Someone at the party?"

"No, that was all me. Don't forget, Chloe, that I'd done security gigs there for years. I knew how to get around the restaurant without being seen. I grabbed me some Georgia Home Boy from the station on the way, and then I slipped into Ledet's and went to the security room. The place was mostly empty, so it was easy just to sit there and watch things unfold on the cameras."

"Georgia Home Boy?"

"Sorry. GHB. Gamma hydra something. The date rape drug. I got it from a raid we did last weekend. Anyway, at that point, I just wanted to get a look at all that paperwork you and Kevin were going through, hoping it had information in it about the treasure. I figured once you and Kevin and Sam were out of it I'd sneak in there, grab the briefcase, and take off. I really didn't plan on killing anybody. But then stupid Kevin came back in the room and caught me fooling with the drinks, getting a good look at my face when he did. I made up a quick story about why I was there, but I knew I'd have to do something about him later."

My mother finally gave up the fight and gripped at the ladder to keep herself from falling down the hole. Then she climbed downward into the mine, cursing all the way.

"I didn't have time to put the GHB into every drink on the table, and I had to stop once Kevin came in. It still coulda worked out, though, excepting my plan got messed up even more when Sam grabbed the wrong drink first, one that didn't have any of the drug in it. Watching on the cameras, I knew what was happening. Soon as you passed out, I got to the room real quicklike and took over, before Sam could yell for help."

Pressing the gun into my back, Wade now urged me toward the ladder and the hole. He kept talking as we went, his tone almost proud of the elaborate scenario he had managed to construct and execute.

"I didn't know what to do about poor Sam, but at that point I kinda had no choice. I told him to turn off the light and shut the door and tell the staff you and Kevin were gone and he had cleaned up the room. He did exactly as I said, because I stayed there in the dark with my gun to your head and told him if he didn't do that and then wait for me outside the back door, I would kill you."

We reached the hole and I looked down into the darkness, the sounds of my mother's sobs echoing from within.

"I slipped out of the restaurant right after that," Wade continued as his brothers took over with me and began pushing me at the hole. "Went up to Sam's place. Tied him up. Tried to get him to tell me what he knew about the treasure. Again, I really didn't plan to kill him, but he made me so mad."

Wade sounded furious just talking about it, and I remembered what he had said to me the other day, that he had always had a problem with his temper.

"Go down on the ladder or we'll push you in anyway and you'll fall," one of his brothers said now as I struggled against them. With no choice, I reached out with shaky hands and grabbed hold of the rungs.

"But before I go down in there," I stalled, looking at Wade, "I have to hear the rest. What happened with Sam? Did he really die just to protect the treasure?"

"Nah. He died to protect you."

"Me? How?"

"I tol' him if he would tell me everything he knew about the treasure I wouldn't kill you when I got back downstairs to Ledet's. So that's when he finally let me know about the pot holder that was hanging by the stove. I tore it up, thinkin' there was a map or something hidden inside, but there wasn't. Sam said it was the number on the outside that I needed, that I had to use it to 'follow Julian's recipe.' The whole thing sounded so stupid I just knew he was lying. I worked him over a while, but his story never changed, so finally I gave up and finished him off."

Gripping the wooden ladder so tightly that I could feel the grains of the wood digging against my palms, I closed my eyes and tried not to picture Sam's final moments as Wade continued.

"Then I waited there until the party at Ledet's was over and everyone was gone. Thanks to your stubborn father and his lack of a good security system, it wasn't any big deal to use Sam's key to get back in. I went through all the papers right there, but never found nothing about the treasure. You were my last resort. Since I knew I had to kill Kevin anyway, because he'd seen me, I decided to get two for one: kill him and frame you, and then let you find the treasure for me. I just had to figure out how to make it all happen."

"The hotel setup was my idea," one of the brothers volunteered proudly.

"That's right," Wade said, acknowledging him with a nod. "A couple of us had to work together on that one, but we managed to pull it off. Even managed to slip a tracking device into your purse before we left you there. After that, all I had to do was show up at the jail the next day and convince you that I was your friend on the inside. Between watching the tracking device and getting your phone calls, I've been able to follow your every move since."

"Unbelievable," I whispered.

"Anyhoo," Wade added, looking up at the sky, which was finally a vivid morning blue, "it's just a shame that things had to end this way."

"Time to wrap it up, Wade," one of his brothers said, stepping toward me with his gun.

"Yep. You better get down there, Chloe, 'fore Bubba here has to do something drastic."

Taking one last look at the lot of them, I did as they said and lowered myself into the darkness. As I climbed down the long, long ladder, I saw that this was a central chamber, almost like an elevator shaft, and shooting out from it on each side were what looked like long, dark tunnels. Though the first few feet were made of packed dirt, there came a point where the strata changed to solid white, the hard, pockmarked surface of the salt dome. Continuing downward, the shaft widened considerably. I passed two levels of tunnels before finally reaching the third. Far above me, I heard the one named Bubba ask Wade if they should have confiscated our cell phones. Wade replied that it didn't matter since cell phones couldn't work from down inside the mine.

I didn't know what they planned to do next, but when finally my feet were on solid ground and I looked back up toward the opening, I wasn't really surprised to see them pull the ladder out. My guess was that they planned to abandon us down here, where we could die of natural causes, thus getting us out of the way and avoiding any appearance of murder.

Regardless of how we died, though, it was still murder, plain and simple.

Looking around the dark, salty chamber, I spotted my mother, crying and hovering against the wall. Beside her was Travis, lying on the ground, his eyes closed.

I ran to him, falling to my knees and laying my head on his chest, listening for a heartbeat. My own heart was pounding so loudly, though, that I couldn't hear. Then I pressed my fingers against his neck to feel for a pulse, and he opened his eyes.

"Did they hurt you, *cher*? Did they do anything to you?"

"No, I'm okay, really," I assured him.

"Then what's that?" he persisted, touching the bandage on my hand.

"Long story. I'll tell you about it later."

"I haven't stopped praying for you since we were kidnapped," he rasped. "I thank God He answered my prayers."

I wanted to say how wrong he was, that God hadn't helped or spared me in the least. But as I laid my head back down on Travis' chest and closed my eyes, I was overwhelmed with the thought that God had heard those prayers after all, and that He was the only reason we were both still alive.

Suddenly, something began to change in our surroundings, a subtle shifting of the dimness around us.

Looking upward, I could see the opening to the mine, the silhouette of something else began to cover it like an eclipse.

"What are you doing?" I shouted, but no one answered me.

"Looks like they're capping the mine," Travis muttered. "We'll never be able to get out now.

Soon, the opening was completely covered and everything went black.

FORTY

Plunged into a darker darkness than I had ever known, I realized I couldn't even see my own hand held up in front of me. Blinking, I tried, but my eyes simply couldn't adjust to the complete absence of light.

"Cell phones," I said suddenly, reaching into my pocket and flipping mine open. The light was dim, but amid the darkness it shone like a beacon. My mother and Travis quickly illuminated their phones as well.

"I doubt we'll get a signal, but at least we've got light," I said.

I held my breath as I dialed a number, but the call was quickly terminated with the words "Signal unavailable."

"Texting. Try texting," Travis said, explaining that right after Hurricane Katrina, even when they couldn't get a signal to make calls, sometimes texts slipped through.

"Who do we text?" my mother asked. "Should we try 911?"

Shaking my head, I replied that at least two of Wade's brothers were cops down here, dirty cops who might intercept a call for help if it came through the local dispatch.

"I've got cousins who live nearby and can be here in a flash—backed up by a dozen other strong, resourceful, well-armed Naquins," Travis said, reading off two numbers for us to type into our phones.

"Actually, we need the state police to come in too," I added, thinking that might best be accomplished through my lawyer. I read off the number

I had for him, and then together we worded the one message that would go out to all of the numbers, typed it into our individual phones, and saved it as a draft so we could keep trying without retyping if it didn't work the first time. We hit "Send," but after a moment the texts came back as undeliverable on all three phones.

"Okay. Mom, you keep trying while I take a look at Travis' injuries," I said, trying hard to keep a tone of desperation from my voice.

"All right."

"Tell me where you're hurting," I said to Travis, holding my phone so that the light shone on him. It was hard not to cry at the sight of his swollen face.

"I think they broke my arm and a couple of ribs," he replied, gingerly raising himself up to a sitting position. "And maybe my knee. Other than that, I'm probably okay."

"Would a sling on your arm help?"

"Why, do you happen to have one handy, *cher*?"

I looked at his face in the dim glow of the phone to see that he was smiling. That was a good sign, for sure.

"No, but I can make one for you. Mother, you're not wearing panty hose under those slacks by any chance, are you?"

"Are you kidding me?" she snapped. "We're about to die and you're worried about how I'm dressed?"

Rolling my eyes, I explained that I needed them so I could make a sling for Travis' broken arm.

"Oh. Well, no. I've got on knee-highs, but you can have those if you want."

She removed her shoes and then gave her stockings to me. I tied the ends of the stockings together, looped the makeshift sling around Travis' neck, and carefully arranged it under his arm.

"That already helps." Travis said, closing his eyes and leaning his head back against the wall. "Thanks, *cher*."

By the light of the phone, I took a moment to study Travis' features. If we really were going to end up dying down here, I wanted one of the last things I could see to be the face of this man who had done nothing but try and protect me. Finally, unable to help myself, I reached out and gently stroked the side of his cheek. He nuzzled into my hand, eyes still closed, and took a deep, sighing breath.

"I'm sorry, Travis, for everything," I whispered.

"Shhh," he replied. "You haven't done anything wrong."

"I lost faith in you. I stopped trusting you. For a little while, I even thought you were one of them."

"That's just 'cause I didn't tell you the whole truth about myself, *cher*. Don't blame yourself for jumping to the wrong conclusions. I'm the one who's sorry. And for what it's worth, I do owe you the courtesy of some pertinent facts."

"I just need one, Travis. Everything else I can learn later—if we get the chance to *have* a later, that is."

He opened his eyes and looked deeply into mine.

"Divorced, five years ago. Long story, but the bottom line is that she fell in love with the lead guitarist in a band we were recording and ended up divorcing me to marry him. She got life with a crossover star and I got custody of TJ. That's the bottom line, but I'll be happy to tell you more. As much as you want to know. Anything. Everything."

"Thank you, Travis. For now, that's enough."

I leaned forward and kissed his cheek as gently as I could, wondering if I was destined to have found love at what turned out to be the very end of my life. Placing my cheek against his for a long moment, I thought how ironic it was to be so happy and so sad all at the same time. Taking in the full extent of our situation, the sadness won, and I felt a sob bubbling up in my throat. I couldn't afford to waste time crying right now, though, so I pulled away and turned my attentions to other things.

My mother, on the other hand, was still at it, though at least her sobs had finally subsided to sniffles. As she continued to try and send out the text message over and over, she began to whine about the dire straights we now found ourselves in, saying that we were all going to die. I could tell that she wanted me to comfort her and pay attention to her and make her feel all better. I was sorry, but I had more important things to do. Lola Ledet would have to look beyond the end of her own nose for a change.

"I need to explore these tunnels," I said to Travis. "Maybe one of them will lead to a different exit."

"Trust me, they don't," Travis said. "My cousins and I used to play hide-and-seek down in here when we were kids. The only way out is up."

"Then let's figure out a way to go up. There must be plenty of debris down here. Maybe I could find some rope or some boards and maybe fashion a ladder."

"I know where there's a ladder in one of the tunnels, but it won't help," Travis said, explaining that the mine cap was likely made of cement and couldn't be removed from the inside without some heavy equipment doing the pushing.

Feeling antsy, I jumped up and used the light from my phone to explore our immediate surroundings. The chamber we were in was large, at least twenty feet across, with tunnels branching off in four directions. There were also the other tunnels on the two levels above ours. Surely somehow we could find a way out of here.

"What about our cell phones?" I asked, moving back toward Travis. "If I could get close enough to the surface, maybe I could text for help there."

"It's worth a try."

"So where's the ladder?"

He explained the route I would need to take through the tunnels to get to it. I could tell he wanted to go himself, but of course he was too injured for that.

"I'll be fine," I said, leaning forward and kissing him full on the mouth. "You stay here and pray. Mom, you come with me."

With that I headed down the tunnel Travis had indicated, my mother following closely behind. Feeling a new surge of confidence, I moved more quickly than I should have and soon bumped my head on the solid salt wall.

"Oh, honey," my mother cried, grabbing at my shirt from behind.

"I'm okay," I said, gingerly feeling my forehead for blood even as I pressed onward.

We soon reached the juncture Travis had described and took the tunnel on the right. About ten feet in, I slowed down, looking for the old wooden ladder that was supposed to be there but wasn't.

"I see it!" my mother said, holding out her phone for light and moving carefully toward the far wall.

The ladder was lying on the ground, its wooden rungs crusted over with white salt.

"Good catch, Mom," I said, moving to one end and lifting it. "With the salt, it was practically invisible."

Beaming from my compliment, she grabbed the other end, but it was hard to carry the ladder with both hands and shine our cell phones at the same time. Finally, we put the ladder on our shoulders, supporting it there with one hand while holding out our cells with the other. Turning the corner was a bit tricky, but we managed it. As we went, I couldn't help but think that this was one of the first times in my entire life that my mother and I had had to cooperate and work as a team in order to accomplish something. Despite the dismal situation we were in, at least that felt good.

When we finally reached the central tunnel again, it was to find Travis with his eyes closed and his lips murmuring in prayer.

"We got it," I said proudly.

"Amen," he said in response, opening his eyes.

Travis directed us from his place on the floor as my mother and I propped up the ladder against the wall directly below a tunnel opening. From what I could tell in the dim light, the ladder was tall enough to get me to the next level as long as the wooden rungs held up under my weight.

"Here goes nothing," I said, kicking off my flip-flops and glancing back at my two companions with what I hoped was an encouraging smile.

"Be careful," my mother urged.

"I love you," Travis added.

He loved me? We barely knew each other but he loved me?

Funny, but in fact I knew I loved him too.

"It's mutual, Cajun Boy," I said, flashing him a grin. "Now get back to praying while I try to get us out of here."

As I had feared, the ladder was partially worn through with rot. Still, though two rungs split under my feet, it held together enough for me to make my way to the top. My mother steadied it against the wall as I stretched upward, desperate to reach the next level of the mine. Finally, with a fierce surge of effort, I grabbed the lip of the tunnel and pulled myself up and in.

Victorious, I turned around and looked down at the other two who were there below me. "Well?" my mother asked. "Are you getting a signal?"

I pulled my phone from my pocket, flipped it open, and tried to send the text message. After a long moment, it responded with a beep. Service unavailable.

"Not here," I said, trying not to sound as devastated as I felt. There was no way to get any higher than this. "Let me go up the tunnel a bit and see if it's any better."

Summoning my nerve, I ventured into the darkness, checking the service bars on the screen of my phone as I went. Unfortunately, after a few minutes the phone beeped, and I looked to see that not only did I not have a signal, but the battery was low.

"Come on," I hissed, shaking the phone as if that would give it more juice. I tried again to send the message, but it simply wouldn't go through. As I continued onward, I thought about one of the Bible verses Travis had shared with me, the one that said He was one God who was over all and through all and in all. If that was true, then I knew that He was there with us now and we could turn our situation over to Him, for better or worse.

"I'm sorry I doubted before," I prayed suddenly, out loud. "Please, if You can, teach me the difference between the uncaring and distant God I usually think You are and the loving and ever-present God that the Bible— and Travis—says You are."

As I continued moving forward, I was filled with a sudden peace so overwhelming and pervasive that it could only have come through a divine blessing. My phone beeped again, and I thought of turning back, but something told me to keep going just a bit further. Pressing onward, I went around a corner and then, with a final beep, it died.

There in the darkness, I carefully turned around so I could exactly retrace my steps. I was scared, but I knew if I could just get back around that corner, I could call out to the others and use the sound of their voices to find my way.

The funny thing was, after a few steps I decided that the black blackness of before wasn't so black here. In fact, I realized, if I held my hand up in the air, I could actually make it out. Waiting for my eyes to adjust further, I decided that there was some light here, coming from somewhere, allowing me to see.

Please, God, let it be the sun!

Feeling my way along the walls, I slowly gravitated toward the light. I reached a point where the ground was littered with massive boulders, and I looked up to see that the ceiling of the tunnel had caved in there. Looking further upward, I realized that directly above where I stood was a crack high in the ceiling. With a gasp, I thought of what I had seen earlier, when I had been brought to the clearing by Wade Henkins.

When we had first arrived there, I had taken a good look at the ponds, and though three of them were filled with water, the fourth one had been empty with a small gash at its center. Thinking about that now, I had to wonder if somehow the bottom of that particular pond had actually broken through the ceiling of this tunnel. That would explain where the water had gone—it had simply drained down through the opening and into the mine below. That had to be it! Looking up, I decided that the crack in the ceiling was located right about where that pond probably was. Sunlight was pouring through the crack, illuminating the walls, which were not white, but pink. In fact, the boulders on the ground weren't even boulders at all but instead were giant, pink chunks of salt that had fallen loose from the ceiling. Surely, my father had discovered this new vein on Monday morning, and that had been the source of his excitement the first time he called Kevin Peralta and told him to make the offer on Paradise. From what I could see, there was enough salt here to fill a million bottles of Chef Julian's Secret Salt and then some. Given how proud he was of that salt, it was no wonder he wanted to own this place for himself.

I wanted to call down to Travis and my mother and tell them what I had found. First, though, I tried climbing up the salt boulders a short way, just to see if they would be stable enough to hold me. Torn between wanting to go further and wanting to let them know that for the first time we had real hope, I was ecstatic when I heard the sound of my mother's voice coming toward me and then I saw her approaching with her lighted phone.

"Chloe, you're okay!" she cried, coming to a stop at the bottom of the pile of salt boulders. "You were gone so long I couldn't stand it anymore."

"Look!" I cried triumphantly, pointing toward the ceiling. She looked up, and when she spotted the sunlight coming through the crack, her filthy, exhausted face burst into a beautiful smile.

"Mom, my phone died. Can you try sending the text with yours?"

As she did, I started to make my way back down the pile of rocks toward her, ignoring sharp edges digging into the skin of my feet. One of the rocks tilted when I put my weight on it. Scrambling to regain my balance, I knocked against one of the biggest chunks, dislodging it from near the top and causing it to roll down the back of the pile. It landed with a crash against the tunnel wall, busting through a surface I had thought was salt but sounded more like wood. As the dust settled, I peered into the cavern that the collision had exposed.

"It worked, Chloe! It sent the text out!"

Standing atop the pile of rocks in my bare feet, I was torn between wanting to explore the newly opened cavern and wanting to see what text messages my mother might get in return. Looking from her to the opening, I was about to make a decision when I thought I heard Travis calling to us from far away.

Scrambling down the rock pile, I told my mother to stay there and wait for any return messages while I went to answer Travis. Of course, I had only gone a few feet when I realized I had no way to illuminate my path. I could have borrowed my mother's phone, but we needed it to stay where it was in case texts came back to us.

Keeping one hand on the wall and inching one foot at a time out in front of me, I proceeded through the darkness. Except for a few scrapes and bumps, that worked well, though I was still afraid I might walk right past the end of the tunnel and fall to the main chamber one floor below.

Using the sound of Travis' voice, I was able to call back and forth to him until I was fairly close—at least close enough to make out his words without an echo. As I did and I understood what he was saying, my stomach lurched.

"Water, Chloe! Water is pouring in!"

Dropping to my knees, I crawled the rest of the way until I reached the overhang and could look down at him. There, by the light of his iPhone, I could see Travis struggling to make his way up the ladder despite his injured arm, ribs, and knee. Below him at least a foot of water swirled furiously around the chamber.

"How?" I cried. "Where's it coming from?"

"It's like Lake Piegneur all over again," Travis replied, looking up at me. "I should've known they were going to do something like this. They're trying to drown us."

Horrified at this new turn of events, I tried to reach down and help Travis up the ladder, but the distance was just too far. With only one good arm, even if he made it to the top, he would never be able to heft himself up on the ledge and I had no way to pull him.

But that was one bridge we didn't have to cross. When the rung he was perched on cracked under his weight, he fell back into the water, the cell phone in his pocket dimming and then going black.

Terror gripped at my heart at the return of complete darkness, but I had to remain calm for his sake.

"Travis! Can you hear me? Are you okay?"

"I'm here, but I've got terrible news."

"What?"

"It looks like I probably violated the warranty on my iPhone."

I couldn't help but laugh despite the circumstances. Leave it to him to make a joke at a time like this.

"My mother got a text out. Someone will come and rescue us soon."

"If we don't drown first," he replied, his voice echoing against the walls.

"Try climbing up again," I urged, wishing desperately that I could see. "Can you find the ladder?"

"I think it fell. Let me see."

I heard splashing sounds.

"Found it. No, wait. This is just part of it. Feels like it split clean in half."

My heart sank. Without a ladder, he couldn't come up—and I couldn't go down.

"This is not our lucky day," I said.

"With one arm, a bad knee, and some broken ribs, I think I was out of luck anyway."

Lying down on my stomach on the salt floor, I reached out into the darkness, wishing I could lift him up beside me.

"Maybe the water will float you up," I said. "By the time it reaches this level, you can swim right to me."

"Guess that's the only option we have left, *cher*."

As the water continued to rise, I asked Travis where it was coming from and what he had meant about Lake Piegneur. He gave the short version, explaining that about forty years ago an entire lake in south Louisiana had been lost down a salt mine. An oil company had been drilling in the wrong place by mistake when their drill bit punctured through the ceiling of a mine. Like pulling the stopper from a bathroom drain, the lake began to pour through the resulting hole, filling the empty caverns of the mine and forming a whirlpool in the lake that sucked down the drilling platform, eleven barges, and something like sixty-five acres of surrounding terrain.

"Is that what you think the Henkins did here? Punctured the mine?"

"They must have. I don't know how much time we have, but if help doesn't get here soon, Chloe, we're done for."

"Hang on, Travis. I know you can do this."

Unable to see anything, I had no way of knowing how quickly the water was coming in. I refused to think about drowning. Most of all, I just wanted Travis to be safe, to be next to me on this level, where we could make our way together through the darkness to my mother.

"How high is it now?" I asked, afraid to hear the answer.

"It's at my waist. You may be right. In the end I might just float up to you, if I can tread water that long."

All I could do was lie there and keep talking to the man I loved as the water rose around him. He continued to update me on its progress, and finally it was too deep for him to stand. Treading water with his injuries was harder than he had expected, and though I tried to keep him talking, I could tell by his voice that he wasn't going to last long.

"Listen, Chloe," he said in a voice filled with pain, "if I don't make it, tell TJ—"

"No!" I cried. "Tell him yourself. I'm coming in. Watch out."

Before he could reply, I scooted off the ledge, feet first, and passed through what felt like a mile of air before I hit the cold water. Plunging down into it, I forced myself not to panic lest I forget which way was up. Instead, I simply held my breath and let my body rise to the surface until it popped out and I could breathe again.

"Where are you?" I called as my teeth began to chatter, though whether from cold or fear I wasn't sure. Floating in complete blackness was a horrifying feeling—scarier, even, than jumping off the ledge had been.

"Right here," he replied from not too far away. "Chloe, you're crazy."

"About you, yeah," I said, paddling toward his voice until I felt his hand reaching for me. Moving closer, I slipped my arm around him to hold him up, and together we managed to propel ourselves to the wall. There wasn't much there to hold on to, but at least we could stabilize ourselves against something solid.

"Got any more boats handy?" I joked, thinking of the endless series of watercraft we had gone through yesterday. But then the image of that sideways boat outside filled my mind, the one that had long ago washed ashore in a hurricane. Trying to distract us both, I asked Travis to tell me more about it, if he had any idea what the *C* and *M* still visible amid the faded letters stood for.

"That boat belonged to my grandparents. I can't quite remember, but now that you say *C* and *M*, I'm thinking it might've been called the *Cajun Moon*."

Something bumped against my leg underwater. Trying not to imagine what might be floating in there with us, I kicked it away and focused on the man I was holding in my arms.

"The *Cajun Moon*? Travis, do you know what that means?"

"No, what?"

"My father's poem. That boat is the thing 'gone amiss.'"

"'Tween hill and dale and dock and dune, It's out there, under the Cajun moon,'" he replied slowly. "The treasure."

"The treasure. It must be buried under that boat, under the *Cajun Moon.*"

Chuckling, we managed to hug there in the water, relieved at least that we had followed the recipe to the end.

"Ah, *cher,*" Travis said, his breath warm and close. "Whether we make it or not, I want you to know—"

"Shhh," I whispered, holding a finger to his lips. "We are going to make it. I promise."

But, of course, I wasn't nearly as sure as I made my voice sound. If this really was the end, more than anything I wished I could see his face one last time, that I could look into his eyes. I wanted it so badly that my imagination even began playing tricks on me, for it was as if I really could see him.

I realized suddenly that I really *could* see him.

Whipping my head upward, I blinked at the sight of blue, blue sky. The cap was sliding away from the mine's opening.

"Depending on who that is," Travis whispered, "we're either saved or we're dead."

Peering upward, I watched as several faces appeared at the opening and voices called down to us. I held my breath until I knew for sure that these were friendly faces and not the Henkins. Sure enough, it sounded to me like the state police. With them was an old man, calling down to Travis.

"*Grandpere?*" Travis replied. "*C'est toi?*"

Could it possibly be Alphonse Naquin, the missing man himself?

"*Oui, c'est moi.* Looks like I got here jus' in the nick of time too. *Pouyee,* you two sure picked a strange place to go for a swim."

At least now I knew where Travis had come by his sense of humor.

Soon a rope was dropped down and a rescue worker began descending into the shaft. He tried to take me up first, but I insisted that Travis should go. Travis, however, would have none of that, despite his injuries. Finally, I compromised by letting the guy lift me first, but just to the level of the tunnel my mother was on. Once there, I borrowed a waterproof flashlight from the rescuer and promised I would be back right away.

"You and your mother should be able to get out at that end," the man replied. "You'll see what I mean when you get there."

Dripping wet, playing the light's beam on the white walls, I raced back up the tunnel toward my mother. I found her standing atop the pile of rocks, looking up to where more rescue workers where breaking through the ceiling at the crack.

"We did it, Mom!" I cried, mounting the pile of rocks to climb up and give her a hug. "We made it."

Despite my wet clothes, my mother surprised me by wrapping her arms around me and holding me tight. She stopped short of saying she loved me, but somehow I knew that she did. A voice called through the widening hole above us, telling us to hang on just a few more minutes and they would have us out of there. My mother released me from the hug and sat down on one of the huge pink rocks.

As we waited, I pointed my flashlight toward the small chamber that I had accidentally busted open earlier. From where I stood, I could see what looked like a very old wooden trunk, almost completely crusted over in salt, sitting inside. If my father's treasure was buried under the *Cajun Moon*, then what was this?

Holding my breath, I approached the trunk and forced open the lid. Nestled inside was row after row of fleur-de-lis statuettes. Even there in the semidarkness, their surfaces sparkled with gold.

FORTY-ONE

LOUISIANA, 1768

With a smack, the baby's first cry rang out loud and clear. Jacques could hear it through the window from where he sat out on the front porch in the rocking chair.

"It's a boy!" someone cried from inside. Like an echo, the words were repeated all over the house, upstairs and down, in voices both young and old.

A boy, Jacques thought, grinning. After four great-granddaughters, it was good to hear that someone had finally given him a great-grandson. Angelique had never cared whether the newborns were boys or girls, merely that they were healthy. Judging by the chatter coming from the window, the child and mother were doing just fine—and that was good news for all.

"Papa, did you hear? It's a boy," Simone said from the doorway. "Should I wake *Maman* and tell her?"

"No, dear, I'll do it. You take care of your new grandchild," he replied, reaching for his cane.

Gripping it tightly, Jacques rose carefully to a standing position. The old injuries ached even more today than usual, but somehow he didn't mind. In one way or another, this family was going to continue forward through the generations. His four daughters had all married good men and carried on the bloodline, if not the Soliel name, to children of their own. Now the grandchildren were having children, and life was rolling along as it should.

Moving slowly, Jacques ambled across the porch, down the front steps, and around the side of the house, choosing the well-worn path that led to the smaller home he and Angelique shared out back. She had been having a bad day and had taken to her bed soon after breakfast. Knowing their granddaughter was in labor, though, she had asked Jacques to keep vigil for both of them and to give her the news as soon as he had it.

Pushing open the door to their house, Jacques stepped inside, hobbled across the main room, and entered the bedroom. An oil lamp glowed on the table there, bathing the room in a warm light. Angelique was asleep, but she stirred when he came in, waving him over and giving him a tired smile.

Propping his cane against the wall, Jacques carefully slid onto the bed next to her, took her hand, and entwined her fingers with his. He asked how she was feeling.

"Not well, but that's not important now. What of the baby?"

"It's here, it's healthy, and it's a boy."

That seemed to wake her up a bit more. Shifting her weight so that her head tilted against his shoulder, she gave a long, contented sigh and thanked Jacques for being the bearer of such good news.

"How time flies, eh, my love?" she whispered. "It's been forty-nine years since our first child was born, but I remember it like it was yesterday."

"I've been thinking the same thing all day, Angelique. These children, they don't know how good they have it. How you did it, caring for me and the baby all at the same time, I'll never understand."

"You pulled through, Jacques. That's all that mattered to me. That's all that has ever mattered, that you lived, that you hung on even though you wanted to die." Her voice grew shaky with emotion as she continued. "I've been trying to do the same for you now, but I'm afraid I can't hang on much longer. I'm just so tired, you know?"

"Shhh, don't talk about that," Jacques said, holding her hand more

firmly in his. Truth be told, lately he had begun to think that it was a race
to the finish for both of them. While he couldn't bear the thought of losing
his precious wife, he, too, had been hanging on for her sake, just to spare
her the pain of losing him.

"We've been blessed with far more years on this earth than either of us
had the right to expect," he said gently. "Most folks never see sixty—or
even fifty, for that matter. Yet here we are, both still alive at seventy-one.
I'd say that's pretty amazing. We still have each other, we have our family,
we live in this beautiful place..."

"Coming here was the right decision," Angelique agreed, a comment
she had made often in recent months. Though it had been difficult to pull
up roots from the German settlement where they had raised their family,
the move down to this region had been the right choice in the long run.

The whole shift had begun several years ago when three of their
granddaughters had fallen in love with a trio of handsome young Acadian
refugees who had been temporarily stationed at their settlement. None of
the girls had ever found suitors among their mostly German neighbors,
but those three Acadians, cousins by the name of Naquin, were another
matter altogether. Handsome and hardworking—not to mention French-
speaking—there had been an instant attraction on both sides.

Soon, all three couples had married and moved down to the Atchafalaya Basin to live among other Acadian families there. The government
had been encouraging all Acadians to establish themselves along the buffer
zones and had even given them land, seed, guns, and tools in order to help
them do so. It had taken a while to carve out a new life from the wilderness, but with the Acadians' strong bonds of community—not to mention
a lot of help from local Indians—they had managed not just to survive
but thrive. When their new settlement was firmly established, they began
sending for others to come down and join them.

When an incredibly beautiful island was discovered in the midst of the
swamp, Jacques and Angelique's oldest daughter had come to them and
asked if they might consider purchasing the entire tract of land so that they
could all settle near each other there.

They had been such careful stewards of the gold over the years that it was not a decision they had made lightly. Their intention had always been to make the gold last as long as possible, passing it down through the generations.

Years ago, in the beginning, they hadn't touched the gold at all. Consumed with Jacques' recovery and Angelique's pregnancy, they had simply had the trunk stashed in a corner of the bedroom, where it sat, if not forgotten, at least ignored. They were both ambivalent about the statuettes, anyway, considering how much grief and pain they had caused them both.

Eventually, though, as the effects of Jacques' injuries had made it nearly impossible for him to work more than a few hours a day even after he was healed, he had broken down and melted one of the statuettes and turned it into an ingot. Selling it to a wealthy Indigo dealer had netted him even more money than he had expected. By his calculations, if he and Angelique continued to live frugally, they could survive for several years from the income of a single statuette. He had created a better hiding place for the gold then, and though he had never been truly happy with where it was kept, at least it had never been discovered inadvertently by anyone else. As time went on, he would melt down another statuette here and there to supplement the income from his part-time work in the tool shop. Many of his injuries were permanent, so the gold helped to compensate for his disabilities.

As each of their daughters reached maturity and married, Jacques and Angelique had enlightened them and their husbands about the treasure, its history, its value—and its true cost. To their credit, the children had never taken advantage of that knowledge. They knew the treasure would be theirs to administer eventually. Thus, when one of them came to their parents and asked for them to purchase the land, serious consideration was given to their request.

Angelique hadn't been sure she could bear to live out the rest of her life in a swamp, even if her home was on high ground, but then they went there for a visit, and she had fallen in love with the place at first sight, with the rolling hills and the massive, gracious oaks and the dark, lazy water, much as the others had done. That left only Jacques, who wanted to be absolutely sure before making any such commitment. He prayed about it and soon his prayers were answered in two ways.

First, he learned that the nearest settlement to the island had recently been christened "Charenton." Apparently, the rumor went, it was so far out of the way that people who chose to live there were obviously crazy and belonged in Charenton, referring, of course, to the institution back in France.

Though Jacques shuddered at the thought of the month he had spent in that institution, his revulsion was eventually overcome with gratitude that the Brothers there had taken in his dying papa, nursed him in his final days, and buried him in the cemetery. Somehow, living near a town called Charenton made Jacques feel connected with his father's final resting place.

The second reason that Jacques felt like the island would make a good home was because it offered a perfect hiding place for the remaining statuettes.

As they had toured the entire property with Simone and her husband, Jacques had noticed one very unique characteristic of the geology there: open pits dug into the ground that revealed what looked like white sheets of ice underneath. But it wasn't ice, they said, it was salt. The pits had been dug by the Indians, who liked to break off great chunks of it with picklike implements and use them in trade elsewhere.

When they reached one such pit, Jacques was surprised to see that the salt there wasn't white but pink. Simone said that the Indians weren't interested in the pink salt. As far as she knew, that particular mound had been dug up and then abandoned.

Studying the marks that had been made by the picks and the stability of the mineral, Jacques couldn't help but think that a hollowed-out chamber inside the salt might make a perfect place to hide the treasure—especially if he could use his metalworking skills to fashion some sort of waterproof seal. If the Indians didn't want the pink salt, his hiding place could go undetected for years.

As Jacques had been very impressed with the place as a whole, this final discovery made it too good to resist. In the end, he and Angelique had melted down some of the treasure and used it to purchase the land and supplies for the construction of several houses there, including their own. The other Acadians in the region had surprised them with a coups de main, a community effort that made short work of the house-building process, and soon they were all getting settled into their new homes. All that remained was to name the island that was now theirs. The whole family was always tossing around ideas, but so far nothing had seemed quite right.

Later, Jacques had supervised his sons-in-law in the secret excavation and construction of a sealed, hollow chamber in the pink salt, one to hide the trunk with the remaining treasure. It had gone even better than expected, though getting in and out of that chamber was more trouble than he had thought it would be. To solve that problem, they finally decided to take some of the statuettes out of the trunk, put them into a canvas bag, and place that bag in a separate, smaller, more accessible spot, also underground. That way, the bulk of the treasure remained deep in hiding, while they could still easily get to a portion of the treasure should they need it. They found a place about twenty feet away where the salt was also pink, though perhaps not as vividly so, and created just such a chamber.

Thus far, everything had gone according to plan. Jacques' biggest concern wasn't that someone might find the treasure but that there would come a day when someone might *not* find it, when for some reason word was not passed down to the next generation and knowledge of the treasure and its location somehow got lost. Jacques supposed he couldn't worry about that but instead would simply have to trust that each of his descendants would handle that responsibility on their own.

"We did okay, didn't we, Jacques?" Angelique said suddenly, startling Jacques from his thoughts and giving his hand a squeeze.

"What do you mean?"

"With the children. With our life. With the treasure."

Ignoring the pain in his shoulder, his hip, his back, Jacques moved fully onto his side and took his beloved into his arms. She went willingly, a perfect fit in that spot right under his chin where she had always belonged.

"*You* are my treasure, Angelique, and always have been."

She tilted her head up and kissed him sweetly on the lips.

"As you are mine, Jacques Soliel. I do love you so."

Moving even more tightly together, they both closed their eyes and rested.

Later, much later, Jacques awoke to the feel of a hand on his arm.

"Papa," a voice was saying softly beside him. He opened his eyes to see his daughter Simone and her husband, hovering there next to the bed.

"What's wrong? Is it the new baby?"

Clutching a handkerchief, Simone stifled a sob.

"No. It's...it's *Maman*. She has passed."

Jacques looked beside him in the bed to see the very still form of his beautiful wife. Reaching out a hand, he touched her face, and though the skin was still soft, he knew that her soul was gone.

"You two didn't come up to the house for dinner, so we got worried," Simone explained, crying harder. "As soon as we came in the room, I could see that we were too late."

"It's okay, though," Jacques said, smoothing the hair from Angelique's lifeless face. "She knew it was her time. She was ready."

"Let us help you up, Papa, and then we can tell the others. My sisters and I can prepare the body. You'll sleep up at the house."

Instead of rising, Jacques laid his head back on the pillow. Looking up at the ceiling, he was surprised to see that his vision suddenly began to fade just like it had so long ago, after the stoning, when everything went blurry and white.

"Can you give me a minute, sweetheart?" he said. "You don't have to leave the room, just don't make me get up right away."

"Of course, Papa," Simone whispered. "Take your time."

They stepped away from the bed, turning to give him privacy.

Lying there next to Angelique, Jacques closed his eyes and tried not to think about how he was going to survive without her, without this woman he loved more than life itself.

As he thought about that, an odd warmth began flowing through his limbs. Though it was strange, he almost thought he could hear the tinkling laughter of angels. That laughter grew until it turned into song and became the music of the heavenly hosts. Was it possible that he was dying too? Dare he dream that when he opened his eyes, it would be to behold paradise? How could that be, when he felt no pain at all?

"Paradise," he whispered with his final, physical breath, and then amazingly, he let go.

When at last he did open his eyes, it was, indeed, to view paradise: the glory and the golden, sparkling magnificence of holy splendor.

Best of all, waiting for him there was Angelique. Just as she had come to Louisiana to find him so very long ago, now he too had come to find her, to join with her in heaven.

Behind Angelique stood others, many who were waiting to see him as well. And at the very front of the line was Papa. He was there waiting, just as he had promised, smiling and welcoming Jacques home.

EPILOGUE

Because of the potential for rain, an outdoor wedding in Louisiana in April could be a risky thing to do. We decided to chance it anyway, and in the end it paid off: On a beautiful spring Saturday evening at five o'clock sharp, under a canopy of live oaks and Spanish moss, Travis Naquin and I vowed to love and honor and respect each other forever and the minister pronounced us husband and wife.

My groom thoroughly kissed his bride. After that, nearly bursting with joy, we joined hands with each other and with TJ and headed down the aisle, ready to begin our new life together.

We would be a blended family, but if I had learned anything in the past year of dating this man and getting to know his son, it was that finding our way through the ups and downs of that scenario was a journey worth taking. These days, whenever I looked at the two newest loves of my life, I couldn't fathom that I had ever thought I didn't want children. I already loved TJ as if he were my own, and our hope was to give him a baby brother or sister in another year or two.

Even the logistics of merging two such disparate lives hadn't been as complicated as either one of us had expected. Though Travis had offered to make the move to Chicago, we both knew Louisiana was the better choice for us. Not only would that help TJ remain closer to his extended family, who lived in Houston, it also allowed me to be near my parents, especially my father, who had aged greatly in the past year.

At least my business was easy to relocate, and much to my surprise, Jenny chose to follow as well. Tired of the snowy Chicago winters, she had been eager to move south and start a new chapter in her life. Already she was becoming an expert on all things Louisiana, and the fact that she had recently begun dating one of Travis' cousins was simply icing on the cake.

The past year had not gone nearly so well for my father. After the shooting, his coma had ended up lasting for ten days. When he finally came out of it, though he still looked like his old self, it was obvious to those who knew him well that he wasn't quite the same. He didn't laugh as hard or yell as loud or engage with life as he had before. Even after he was out of the hospital and back home, he moved slowly and carefully, as if he had aged ten years in those ten days. In a final, tragic irony, the saddest aftereffect of his whole experience wasn't the way in which it aged him. It was that somewhere through that physical trauma, he permanently lost the ability to smell and taste.

It had broken my heart to learn that, knowing that for him such a tragedy was akin to a master pianist losing his hands or an Olympic runner losing his feet. Though he could still cook for others as magnificently as he always had, Julian Ledet had now been denied the single greatest pleasure of his life. Making matters even worse was the fact that the Henkins had destroyed the salt mine at Paradise when they flooded it, thus putting an end to the source of Chef Julian's Secret Salt forever. Because the mine was relatively small, the impact on the surrounding terrain wasn't nearly as severe as it had been in the Lake Piegneur disaster, but the damage inside the mine itself was permanent. Once the flooding had ceased and the water pressure equalized, officials had capped off the openings with cement. At least they successfully removed the trunk I had found and its contents first, but the salt was a lost cause.

After that my father had sunk into a deep depression, one that had lasted for months. During that time, as sad as it was, at least some healing had taken place as well. He and Alphonse managed to patch up their differences and reestablish their friendship—an especially good thing considering that our families were now going to be joined together in marriage.

My father also took great pleasure in getting to know Travis better, and I was deeply heartened and touched to see how patient Travis was with him, how sweet. He spent a lot of time talking with my dad about the Lord and sharing with him from the Bible, and though my father hadn't exactly fallen to his knees in surrender and repentance, he was at least willing to listen. Travis and I both prayed that someday soon my dad might finally take that final step and come to accept the truth that would set him free.

My mother had also changed in the past year—or at least our relationship had changed. Though she would probably always be self-centered and shallow, the time we endured together down in the salt mine somehow managed to soften our hearts toward each other. We would never be the best of friends, but I felt that we had finally at least made our peace and found a way to start over again.

Travis was a big part of that. As he helped me understand what forgiveness really looked like through God's eyes, I realized I had been carrying around for many years the burdens of my own unforgiveness. Surrendering my anger and frustration and resentment at both of my parents had been a huge step for me. Once I did that, many of the elements of my spiritual walk fell into place more fully as well.

By moving back to Louisiana, I felt that my life had come full circle. In the months leading up to the wedding, I had managed to develop a whole new appreciation for my home state. Though I still didn't like snakes or alligators, I couldn't get enough of the beautiful scenery and the colorful culture and the extended Cajun family that seemed to welcome me in with open arms as if I had always belonged.

My snake bite had left a scar, two shiny circles on the back of my hand, and I considered them my badge of courage. As a private joke, Travis had given me the honorary Indian name of "Twin Fang."

The wedding of Twin Fang and Cajun Boy was held at City Park, but, of course, there was only one place the reception could be, and that was at Ledet's. My parents had gone all out for the event, even surprising me by closing the restaurant for the day.

Once the private party was fully under way, Travis and I had fun simply meandering from room to room, greeting our guests, listening to the strains of the Cajun and zydeco music wafting in from the courtyard, and dining on the Creole high cuisine my father had chosen to serve. Out of respect for Travis, my dad had tailored some of those courses to the Cajun palette. Had there been a restaurant reviewer there that night, no doubt the Michelin guide would not have had enough stars for the rating Ledet's would have received. My father had outdone himself that much.

Ironically, our wedding had fallen on the one-year anniversary of our discovery of the treasure, so in a way we were celebrating both. When we finally understood that the treasure had been divided into two parts, everything that had happened one year ago made much more sense. The portion my father had found in his youth had been discovered in a pink vein of the mine in a disintegrated canvas bag. At first, he and Alphonse Naquin had decided to leave it right there where he had found it, thinking it would be safe. Later, when they chose to tell the investors about the treasure, they moved it to a better location, one they felt sure no one would ever find unless they had the coordinates. Thanks to Hurricane Betsy's handiwork with the *Cajun Moon*, they had been able to create a hiding spot underneath the upturned boat, one that was accessible only to the two men who knew how to climb inside, get to it, and open it up.

The wooden trunk I had discovered in a different, pinker vein of the mine contained a treasure no one had ever known about before. Inside the trunk were one hundred more of the statuettes, the value of which was legally halved between me, as the finder, and the Naquins, as the landowner. Now that Travis and I were married, it didn't really matter as it was all in the family anyway.

Once news of the treasure came out, the truth of its origins finally surfaced as well. A French historian who read about it contacted us to explain, saying how the gold had originally been created as an enticement for settlers to the New World but was supposed to have been switched out for gold-plated statuettes instead. Having that information to go on had made the rest of the research easier. Eventually, we were able to uncover the story of two of Travis' ancestors named Jacques and Angelique Soliel. From what we were able to piece together, Jacques Soliel had been a gold-smith with ties to the treasure and at one point had nearly been killed by an angry New Orleans mob over its mix-up. The Soliels' Creole grand-children had married the Acadian Naquins and relocated the whole clan down to the Atchafalaya Basin. Obviously, they had brought the treasure with them, though we would probably never know why it was divided and hidden in two different parts of the mine. Legend had it that Jacques and Angelique were so deeply in love that they died in each other's arms. The last word Jacques uttered before death was "Paradise," so that's what his children named the island where they lived in his honor.

Knowing that whole story made a big difference in refuting Wade Henkins' territorial claims to the land. In fact, his family had bought Paradise from one branch of the Naquin family in 1925 and sold it back to another just a few years later. We weren't sure why knowledge of the treasure hadn't passed down through the generations, but with further research we hoped one day to find out.

At least we finally learned how Wade Henkins had come to know about the treasure in the first place. According to court testimony, it had simply been a matter of his having been in the right place at the right time. Working security at Ledet's on the night of Ruben Peralta's funeral, he had been fine-tuning the alarm system down in the wine cellar when he overheard a conversation between my father and Sam. They had thought they were having a private discussion about the need to tell Kevin Peralta all about the treasure now that he would be taking over his father's practice. Putting two and two together, Wade had begun snooping around after that, embarking on a greedy pursuit that would eventually end up in murder.

About six months after the treasure was made public and just before it was about to go up for auction at Christie's, we were contacted by a representative of the French government and told that the treasure rightfully belonged to them. Just as my father had always feared, by revealing the statuettes to the world, it looked as though we were going to lose them entirely.

But my father hadn't counted on my help in the matter. The day the representative showed up to claim the gold and bring it back to France, we all decided to meet for lunch at Ledet's and give the treasure a proper sendoff.

I'm not sure what tipped me off about the representative first, if it was the "okay" sign he flashed during conversation (which, to the French, meant "zero," not "okay") or the fact that he politely kept one hand on his lap during the entire meal (when the French politely keep both hands on the table). But at some point, because of his very American etiquette, I began to suspect that the man wasn't actually French at all. Discreetly, I managed to quiz him about French protocol, French manners, and even the order of the seven courses in a Parisian restaurant. He failed on all accounts, and so, as we were waiting for our desserts, I excused myself to go to the restroom and called up the police instead. The man was under arrest practically before the others at our table even understood what was going on. I was afraid he might be an extended relative of the Henkins, maybe one who hadn't participated in the original crime and wasn't serving time at Angola like the others. But as it turned out, this guy was just a petty criminal from Shreveport who had apparently planned to con the gold right out of our hands and then disappear.

Two weeks later we were all stunned when the fleur-de-lis statuettes sold at auction for $96 million dollars. Once we all had our money, it was fun deciding how to utilize it. I was especially touched when my father established a huge memorial scholarship fund in honor of his late best friend and right-hand man, Sam. Because he had been in the hospital and missed Sam's funeral, my dad had rented out Preservation Hall just last week, on the anniversary of Sam's death, and thrown a huge musical party in his honor instead. Travis and I had been there, and it was one of the first times I had ever interacted with my parents in a social setting and hadn't felt in any way excluded or overlooked. I still wasn't sure if that was because I was changing or they were, or both.

Following his example, I had established a scholarship fund of my own, one in honor of Ben Runner that would benefit Chitimacha tribe members who were interested in majoring in the fields of medicine or pharmacology. I also made a sizeable donation to the Tribe's already-outstanding senior care program and managed to convince Josie Runner to take advantage of all the services available to her there. With the help of her fellow tribe members, we even engineered a complete renovation of her house. Given the fact that I had nearly gotten her killed, I thought it was the least that I could do.

As for me, all charges had been dropped by the time we were rescued from the salt mine. Many inconsistencies had led Detective Walters to rethink his original impressions about the case, especially when blood samples taken from me and from Kevin Peralta had both tested positive for the date rape drug known as GHB. Wade Henkins, on the other hand, was convicted of numerous felonies and had recently begun serving concurrent life sentences at Angola State Prison. His brothers were at Angola as well.

In fact, many parts of what had gone so wrong one year before had actually turned out so right in the end. As the wedding reception drew to a close, my father gave a beautiful toast to the bride and groom, welcoming Travis into our family. Later, I found myself thinking about my father's choice of words. Had my parents and I ever been a family? Maybe not, but we were getting there.

As TJ happily stayed at home with his numerous aunts and uncles and cousins, Travis and I headed off for ten heavenly days in Hawaii on our honeymoon. Though the scenery was amazing and the nights breathtaking, the highlight of the whole trip for me actually came one afternoon when we were lounging around together in our rented condo. Travis decided that his new wife absolutely had to learn how to make a gumbo before the week was over. We rounded up the ingredients we needed and started with a roux, but soon Travis moved in close behind me so that he could perfect my stirring technique. That led to some kissing of my neck and a warm hand around my waist, and soon we both forgot all about the gumbo.

Ten minutes later we were so lost in each other that the smoke alarm had to go off before we realized what was happening. As it beep-beep-beeped from high up on the ceiling, Travis moved the smoking pan from the burner while I raced to open the windows and doors to fan the smoke outside. When the alarm finally stopped, I nervously turned to look at my husband's face.

"You're not mad that we burned the roux?" I asked, biting my lip.

"Why?" he replied, seeming genuinely perplexed. "It's just a roux."

At that moment, my eyes filled with tears. He didn't understand my reaction at all, and I had to assure him that they were happy tears, not sad.

"If you say so, *cher.*"

Standing there and looking at each other, I recognized yet another facet of the character of God. Somehow, He had a way of bringing into my life people who were helping me to heal and grow. Chief among them was my new husband.

As he wrapped his arms around me and we picked up where we had left off, I knew one thing for sure: I would love this man forever.

ABOUT THE AUTHOR

Under the Cajun Moon is Mindy's eleventh novel from Harvest House Publishers. Previous books include the bestselling Gothic thriller, *Whispers of the Bayou*, and Amish romantic suspense, *Shadows of Lancaster County*, as well as the Million Dollar Mysteries and the Smart Chick Mystery series, which includes *The Trouble with Tulip*, *Blind Dates Can Be Murder*, and *Elementary, My Dear Watkins*.

Mindy is also a playwright, a singer, and a former stand-up comedian. A popular speaker at churches, libraries, civic groups, and conferences, Mindy lives with her husband and two daughters near Valley Forge, Pennsylvania.

In any story, where facts are used to mold and shape fiction, sometimes it becomes hard for readers to tell the two apart, particularly when learning about a history or culture that isn't overly familiar. For more information and to find out which elements of this story are fictional and which are based on fact, visit Mindy's website at:

www.mindystarnsclark.com.

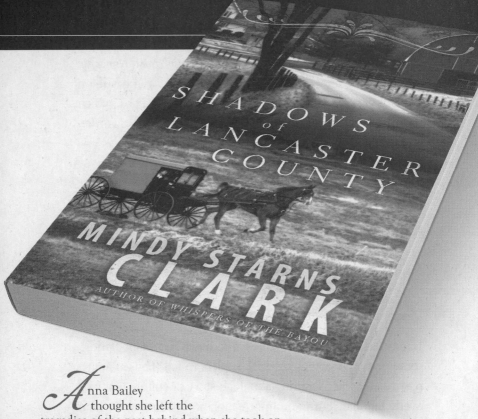

If you enjoyed *Under the Cajun Moon,*
you'll love *Shadows of Lancaster County.*
Here's a sample...

ONE

BOBBY

I'm dead. The powerful engine gunning behind him drowned out every other thought. He held on to the handlebars of the borrowed motorcycle, crouched low on the leather seat, and accelerated as far as he dared. When the dark car struck his rear tire the first time, he managed to hang on through the jolt, though just barely. Regaining control, he crouched even lower and gripped the handlebars more tightly, adrenaline surging in the piercing cold. In vain he searched the blackness ahead for an escape, for some point of diversion where the motorcycle could go but the car pursuing him could not. Caught on the wide curve of a hilly highway, there were no shoulders here, and no way to know what lay in the darkness off to the right beyond the metal guardrail. Worse, he knew he couldn't swerve back and forth on the blacktop to dodge the next hit, because moves like that on a motorcycle would end up flipping the bike and high-siding him whether the car rammed into him again or not.

A second jolt came just as the guardrail ended, a collision that nearly managed to unseat him. Barely hanging on, he regained his balance, scooted forward on the leather seat, and took a deep breath, conscious of the vehicle still roaring aggressively behind him in murderous pursuit. In a choice between certain death on the road and possible survival off of it, he steeled his nerves and made the decision to leave the pavement no matter what he might run into. Holding on tight, he shifted his weight and angled the handlebars to the right, veering into the unknown darkness. The action was punctuated by a series of bumps and jolts as his tires went from blacktop to gravel to crunchy brown grass.

Let it be a field, God. Let it be somebody's farm.

The headlamp of the borrowed motorcycle was strong, its beam slicing through the February night air to reveal the unfamiliar terrain he had driven himself into. Before he could discern what lay ahead, however, before he could even slow down or adjust his direction or see if the car had tried to follow, he spotted the looming gray mass in front of him—a solid, four-foot-high cement retaining wall. He knew this was the end.

The sudden stop flung him heavenward, propelling him in a broad arc across the night sky like the flare of a Roman candle. As he went, he thought mostly of the ground far below him, the frozen and unforgiving earth that was going to greet him by shattering his bones or snapping his neck upon landing. He prayed for the latter, less painful option.

Let it end quickly, God.

As his trajectory continued, his limbs instinctively flailing against the void, his mind went to one person: his younger sister, Anna. He hoped beyond hope that his message would get to her, that she would understand what he wanted her to do. For a guy who didn't even own a computer, he found it vaguely ironic that the last thought that raced through his mind just before certain death was of an email. But the message he had sent her was the only chance he had, the only hope that Lydia and Isaac might still be protected. That one email was the only way his desperate efforts might save his wife and son and the unborn child Lydia was carrying.

Let it end quickly, God, he prayed again just before impact. *And please, God, please guide Anna to the truth.*

TWO

ANNA

The nightmare started up again last night.

That was the first thought that struck me as I turned off the alarm. Somewhere in the early hours of the dawn I had gone there in my sleep for the first time in many months. Now as I sat up and swung my legs over the side of the bed, I couldn't understand why it was back, this nightmare that had plagued me off and on for the past eleven years.

Why now? Why last night?

Sometimes all it took was an external cue, like a house fire spotted from the freeway. An Amish character flashing across the television screen. A news report about a dead newborn baby. But I hadn't experienced any of those things lately. There was simply no reason for the nightmare to have returned like this, out of the blue.

Standing up, I traded my nightgown for shorts and a T-shirt and then padded into the bathroom. As I stood at the mirror and brushed my teeth, I tried not to relive it again now that I was awake, but I couldn't help it.

The dream was always beautiful at first: rolling fields that look like patchwork on an Amish quilt, cars sharing the road with horses and buggies, colorful laundry flapping in the wind. But then there was the farmhouse, the rambling old farmhouse. Without electricity or curtains, as I came closer the windows would turn into dark, empty eyes staring at me. My nightmare always ended the same: black to orange to hot white.

Sirens. Screams. The acrid stench of smoke, of terror, of unspeakable loss. When I woke up, guilt would consume me like flame.

Wishing I could spit out that guilt along with the toothpaste, I rinsed my mouth and then reached for my hairbrush, attacking my long, blond hair with vigor.

It happened a long, long time ago.

You paid your dues.

All has been forgiven.

Telling myself that over and over, I swept my hair into a ponytail, turned out the light, and headed downstairs. In the kitchen, judging by the mess on the counter and the fact that the door was ajar, I realized my housemate was already up and doing her exercises on the back porch. Kiki was always trying out some new fitness trend, the latest and greatest plan guaranteed to shed pounds and inches by the second. I had given up long ago trying to convince her that if she would just come jogging with me a few times a week, she would eventually achieve the results she so desperately sought. Still, I thought as I put away the juice carton and wiped off the counter, on days like today I was glad I could jog alone. I needed the quiet to clear my head and wash away the last remnants of my nightmare.

Once the kitchen was tidy, I grabbed a bottle of water from the fridge and opened the back door the rest of the way; a warm ocean breeze wafted in to greet me. I stepped out onto the uneven slats of the porch and let the door fall shut behind me as I inhaled the salty sea smell of morning. Gorgeous. As someone who had grown up in snowy Pennsylvania, I knew I'd never get used to the year-round warm weather and sunshine of Southern California.

"Howdy," Kiki said cheerfully. She was doing stretches on the far side of the porch, past the square of rotten boards near the door. "Wanna see my new Piloga move?"

"Piloga? What's that? Some cross between Pilates and Yoga?"

"No, it's named after the founder, Manny Piloga. He teaches the fifty-plus class down at the Y."

I smiled, glancing at my watch. It was early yet; I could spare a few minutes to encourage her efforts—not to mention that a quick chat might help distract me even further from my nightmare. As Kiki sat on the wooden floorboards, I reached for a folded aluminum chair that was propped against the wall and told her to be careful on the floor lest she get splinters in her bottom.

"Aw, I've got so much padding, I probably wouldn't even feel it if I did," Kiki laughed, adjusting the waistband on her pajamas and stretching her legs out in front of her.

"Hey, I saw that guy at the grocery store flirting with you yesterday," I reminded her as I sat in the chair. "He didn't seem to mind a little extra padding at all."

"That's 'cause he works in the deli department. He likes it when the scales weigh in heavy."

I rolled my eyes again, refusing to laugh at her joke, but she laughed loud enough for both of us.

"Okay, check out the ab work I've been doing," Kiki said as she leaned back, arms jutting forward parallel to the ground. Slowly, she raised her legs into the air and held them there. "I can stay like this for three minutes, just long enough for you to tell me about your date last night. A fancy dinner at Harborside, hmm? He must have had something in mind. Maybe a certain question he wanted to pop?"

"Good grief, Kik, it was just our third date."

"Sometimes true love can speed things along. I got engaged to my Roger during our first date—and we were happily married for twenty-five years before he passed, God rest his soul."

"Yeah, well, you were one of the lucky ones. Very impressive stance, by the way."

"Thanks. Manny says it strengthens the core."

I opened up my water bottle, took a sip, and looked at my housemate, who also happened to be my landlord, coworker, and best friend despite the twenty-one-year difference in our ages. As she maintained her bizarre position, I thought about yesterday evening, about my third and final outing with Hal, or as I had come to think of him, Hal-itosis.

"We decided not to see each other anymore."

She let out a long grunt, though I wasn't sure if it was from exertion or exasperation.

"'We' who? 'We' him or 'we' you? Or do I even have to ask?"

"Well, like you expected, he did take me to Harborside for a reason. He told me he wants to get more serious."

"Exclusive dating serious or engagement serious?"

"I have no idea, Kik. His exact words were 'I think it's time we should take this to the next level.' I didn't even want to know what the next level was. I suggested he would be happier with someone who enjoys day-old-coffee breath."

A loud laugh burst from Kiki's mouth. "You didn't say that!"

"No, I didn't. But I thought it. I just told him I didn't think it would be fair to him, because I wasn't interested in a long-term relationship."

"Yeah, right."

"I'm *not* interested in a long-term relationship...with him."

"Uh-huh." She was quiet for a long moment, but her silence was louder than words.

I looked her way to see that she was still holding her pose, though beads of sweat were now forming along her hairline.

"What?" I demanded. "What is it you're not saying?"

"I don't know, Anna, it's just that you're so picky about who you're willing to go out with, which is fine. Not every fellow who comes sniffing around a pretty girl is worth her time or attention. But how come the ones who make it through the first elimination never get to the next round?"

"What am I, a game show?"

"You know what I mean. How come every one of your relationships ends this way, with you breaking it off just when the guy wants to get more serious? How can you be so sure one of these fellows isn't The One?"

I shrugged, wondering how I could explain. I kept dating because I hoped someday to find the man who would make me forget all about Reed Thornton. He had been The One, as far as I was concerned, but I had lost him eleven years ago when the fire that burned in my nightmares had also extinguished my dreams with him. Even though I hadn't seen or spoken to Reed since, I still thought of him often, no matter how hard I tried not to. Somehow, I had yet to meet the man who could even begin to compare.

"I'm not waiting for the perfect guy. I just want a guy who's perfect for me. If I can't find that, I'd rather be alone."

With a loud groan, Kiki finally collapsed, breathing heavily as she lay sprawled on the floor. I glanced at my watch. I needed to get moving soon if I wanted to get in a full run before we needed to leave for work. Still, as Kiki recovered from her efforts, I could tell she had more to say.

"Go ahead, Kiki. Don't hold back now."

With a chuckle, she rolled on her side and propped up on one elbow.

"Fine. You're a very private person, Anna, and I know you have trouble letting people in. But if you want to find someone, stop giving up so soon. True love starts when you open yourself to chances."

Chances? It had been a long time since I'd allowed myself the luxury of chances. Once I broke with my past seven years ago and created my new self, my new identity, my whole life had become one big chance. Back then, finding Mr. Right was the least of my worries—especially because my heart was broken from all that had happened with Reed. As time went on and I finally escaped from my past and found peace in my new life here in California, the daily risk factor had greatly lessened. Maybe it was time to take a few chances in life.

"Thanks, Kiki, I'll think on it," I said as I stood and moved toward the steps in my bare feet. "Gotta run for now though, or we'll be late for work."

Careful to avoid more rotten boards, I made my way down one side of the steps to the sandy beach.

"Without shoes?" Kiki asked, moving into position for another exercise.

"Yep, and no sunscreen either," I said, grinning. "See? I can take chances."

I turned, my bare feet digging down into the sand, and took off. My movements were awkward until I reached the damp packed sand near the water. There it was easier to run, easier to find traction in the gritty ground. I tucked in my elbows and sprinted along the water's edge until I could feel my heartbeat pounding in my chest. I slowed to a jog and ran farther than

I had intended, which was not a wise choice given my bare feet. I would pay for this later, but for now it just felt good. It was calming. Sometimes I thought God used the sand and water and my quiet morning runs as a special gift for me, just to keep me sane.

At the jetty I turned around, picked up the pace, and headed home. As I jogged, I thought about Reed and how loving him had spoiled me for any other man. In the years since I last saw him, I had probably built him up in my mind to be far more special than he actually was. I decided it wouldn't hurt to remember that he wasn't perfect, that in fact he had at least one very serious flaw I knew about—and probably tons more I had never had the opportunity to discover. Maybe I really did need to take a chance or two. Maybe I should stop cutting off every single relationship the moment it began to get serious. Here I was waiting for someone to come along who instantly lit that spark inside of me the way Reed had, someone who made me feel as though the world ceased to exist beyond the intensity of his gaze. But maybe I wouldn't ever find that again. Maybe I should learn to settle for less—either that, or decide to stop looking and find contentment in being single the way Kiki had after her husband died.

As I neared her ramshackle beachfront house, I slowed my run to a walk, fingers to my wrist as I studied the second hand on my watch. Pulse rate was good, lungs open and clear, leg muscles burning nicely. Too bad the soles of my feet were throbbing.

I climbed up the side of the steps, grabbed the empty glass Kiki had left on the porch, and carried it through the open back door to the kitchen. I decided to stop thinking about my love life for now and focus on getting ready for work. I hoped Kiki had finished showering and I could take my turn right away. I wouldn't have time to blow-dry my hair, but at least I could put on some makeup in the car.

"Hey, Kik, you out of the shower yet?" I yelled.

"One more minute and then it's all yours," she called back, her voice echoing from the bathroom directly above the kitchen.

My stomach growling, I grabbed an energy bar from the pantry and another bottle of cold water from the fridge before leaving the kitchen. I had just unwrapped the bar and taken my first bite when the phone started ringing. I hesitated at the bottom of the stairs, listening as it went to the machine, knowing I didn't have much time to spare.

"We're not here, leave a message!" Kiki's recorded voice said cheerily from the box on the kitchen counter. That was followed by a beep and a long silence.

"Annalise?" a woman's voice finally uttered, sounding very far away. "Is this the number of Annalise Jensen?"

Annalise Jensen? I hadn't heard that name for years, not since I left Pennsylvania behind, moved west, and became Anna Bailey. Quickly, I dashed to the machine, heart pounding and praying that Kiki hadn't overheard.

"I hope this is the right number," the voice continued in a lilting accent. "I guess I leave a message and wait and see."

One glance at Caller ID confirmed that the woman was calling from Dreiheit, Pennsylvania. I didn't recognize the number, but I recognized the voice and its familiar Pennsylvania Dutch lilt. I steeled myself and answered, closing my eyes as the past came rushing toward me through three thousand miles of telephone line.

"Don't hang up," I said, turning off the machine. "It's me. I'm here."

"Annalise? Is Lydia. Lydia Jensen." My sister-in-law.

"Lydia? How did you get my number?"

I had given this number to my brother in confidence and told him to keep it somewhere private, never share it with anyone—not even his wife—and never use it himself except in an extreme emergency.

"Bobby gave it to me last night. He said to call you if anything went wrong. Otherwise I would never..."

I struggled to listen as Kiki started making clunking noises overhead. What was she doing up there, a tap dance?

"What was that last thing you said?" I asked.

"So sorry. You cannot hear me *gut*? I am calling from my sister's farm, out behind the milk house."

I held a hand over my other ear, closed my eyes, and tried to focus, picturing my sister-in-law standing in one of those Amish phone shanties that looked more like an outhouse than a telephone booth.

"It's okay. What is it, Lydia? What's wrong?"

She exhaled slowly, and as I waited for her to explain, I tried to calm my pounding heart and push away a feeling of impending doom.

"I am calling about Bobby. He...he is *verschwunden*. Missing. He has gone missing, Annalise. I am so frightened for him. I do not know what to do."

I cleared my throat, genuinely surprised to hear that my brother had abandoned his wife and child. He had always seemed so happily married, but maybe there was trouble in paradise.

"Um, it's Anna now, not Annalise," I corrected, leaning over to reset the tape on the answering machine, erasing the part of her message that had been recorded before I picked up. "Anyway, so he left you? Like, moved out?"

"No, no, nothing like that. Is complicated to explain."

"Go on," I said, stretching the cord as far as I could to get to the fridge. At least I could make lunches as we talked.

"Well, it started last night. Bobby was working late at the lab, and little Isaac and I had choir practice. When we got home from church, there was something wrong with the apartment. The lock on the door was broken, and it looked like someone had been inside, going through our things."

"What do you mean?" I asked, setting a pack of sliced ham and some condiments on the counter.

"Closets and drawers were half open. Items were emptied out of baskets. Our belongings were intact, but they were *ferroontzled*—uh, like messy, out of order. Like someone had been here looking for something."

"Were you robbed?" I asked, wondering what that had to do with Bobby's decision to leave. I grabbed a loaf of whole wheat from the bread box and began assembling our sandwiches.

"I did not think so. I could not find anything that was missing. Still, I was about to call the police when the phone rang. It was Bobby. Before I could even tell him about the apartment, he said for me to take Isaac and get out of there, that we were in danger. He said for us to go to my sister's farm and to wait there until he contacted us. When I told him about the broken lock and the *ferroontzled* apartment and everything, he was even more upset. I told him I was about to call the police, but he said, 'Don't call the police, Lydia. Just go right now. *Go.*'"

"Did you?"

"*Yah,* he was so insistent, we left right away. Bobby had already talked to my brother Caleb and told him to watch for us, and for him and my brother-in-law Nathaniel to protect us from harm once we arrived."

"Protect you from harm? Why?"

"I have no idea. I do not understand any of this. I was just glad that Caleb has a cell phone so that Bobby could call us back once we got there—"

"Wait," I interrupted. "You're telling me an Amish boy has a cell phone? Since when is that allowed?" I had only been gone from Pennsylvania for seven years, but I couldn't imagine that in that time the Amish community had gone from having no phones in homes to letting their kids run around with cell phones in their pockets.

Lydia hesitated and then explained.

"Caleb is nineteen, not such a boy anymore. He is on *rumspringa* right now, so the rules for him are bent a bit. He is not allowed to use the cell phone in the house, but in this case an exception was made so Bobby could call back."

Rumspringa, I knew only too well, was that time in every Amish teen's life when they were allowed extra freedom and more access to the outside world. The whole point was to let them see what was "out there," what they would be giving up—and what they would be gaining—if they chose to join the Amish church and commit to a lifetime of living by Amish rules. Bobby and Lydia's romance had begun during her *rumspringa,* and in the end she had chosen to forgo Amish baptism, leave the faith for a less restrictive denomination, and marry a man the Amish considered an outsider, an "Englisher." At least she had made her radical decision prior to baptism. Had she been baptized Amish first and then left the faith, she would have been punished through shunning. As it was, though no one in the Amish community had been happy about her decision, at least they were allowed to have contact with her and her husband and children and could remain somewhat involved in their lives.

"So did he?" I asked, trying to get back to the point. "Did Bobby call you again?"

"*Yah*, soon after we arrive at the farm, Bobby called on Caleb's phone to make sure we had arrived safely. I asked him what was going on, but he said it was a long story and that he would explain everything as soon as he got to us in just a few hours."

"And?"

"And those few hours came and went, but Bobby never showed up. Now it is almost ten fifteen in the morning and we still have not seen or heard from him since that phone call last night."

"So he's a few hours late—"

"Nine hours, Anna. Almost nine hours since he should have gotten here, twelve hours since his phone call!"

"Maybe he fell asleep at his desk. Maybe he was really tired and went to the wrong farm by mistake." I didn't add that it would be an easy error. All the Amish farms in Lancaster County had always looked the same to me.

"No, it is not like that. Something has happened to him. Something terrible. I know this."

Putting the sandwich fixings back into the fridge, I took a deep breath and held it for a moment. I felt bad for her, but I didn't know what she expected me to do. Though my brother and I emailed occasionally, I hadn't spoken to him in weeks—maybe a month, even. He and I had always shared a special bond, especially since the fire and its aftermath, but that didn't mean we stayed in constant touch.

"Lydia, I don't know what you want from me."

"I have no idea, Anna. I just know I need your help—and Bobby specifically said for me to call you if something went wrong."

"But how can I help from way out here? I don't have any way of knowing where he might be."

"This is what you do, *yah?* You find people who have gone missing?"

"Yes, I'm a skip tracer. But—"

"Your brother has gone missing. Please, Anna. Please, help me find him before it is too late."

THREE

Turning around, I leaned against the counter and looked through the kitchen window at the glistening sand and the blue-gray expanse of the Pacific Ocean beyond. I thought how very far I was—both literally and figuratively—from the gentle plains and rolling hills of Amish country back home.

"That is not all," Lydia added before I could form my response, and from the tone of her voice, I could tell the situation was about to get more complicated.

"Okay, then wait a second," I said, once again almost unable to hear thanks to the clunking noises Kiki was making upstairs. I couldn't fathom what she was doing, though from the bumps and scrapes, it sounded as though she was rearranging the furniture. If so, that was a good thing as it meant I'd still have a chance at carpooling. I asked Lydia to give me the number she had called from, explaining that I needed to switch our conversation over to my cell phone. We hung up, and immediately I retrieved my cell from the charger, turned it on, and called her back.

"Sorry about that. Go ahead with what you were telling me. There's more?"

"Yes. All night, I have been thinking about the apartment, about the mess that had been made, about our things. I worried that whoever had been there *did* take something." She hesitated, and as I waited for her to go on, I assembled our lunches into brown paper bags and set them near the door along with my purse, keys, and sunglasses. "Bobby has a metal box filled with all of our important papers: birth certificates, marriage license, things like that. Early this morning I started thinking about that box, that maybe they took our papers, our information. A woman at the bridal shop where I do alterations had identity theft once, and I worry that we might have that too. So when Caleb went over to the apartment a while ago to fix the lock, I asked him to bring back that box. I knew it had been gone through, because last night it was open on the floor in front of the cabinet."

"And?" I prodded, leaving the kitchen and moving through the living room toward the stairs.

"And Caleb brought me the box and everything was there, even our Social Security cards. Even the credit card we keep for emergencies. Only one thing was gone. I am so sorry, Anna."

I paused halfway up the stairs as her words sunk in. *Why was she sorry?*

"It was a sealed envelope. Inside was your new name, your address, your phone numbers. When Bobby put it in there years ago, he told me what it was but said I was never to open it unless something happened to him and I needed to contact you. That envelope...it is gone, Anna. Someone took your information. If he had not given me this number last night over the phone, I would have had no way to reach you."

"Lydia, hold on a minute," I managed to say.

"*Yah*, sure."

As she waited, silent, at the other end of the line, I walked slowly up the rest of the stairs, trying to understand the implications of what had happened—and what I could do about it now. I needed to think.

When I reached the top, I took a deep breath and knocked on Kiki's door, intending to tell her I was running late and she would have to go to work without me. Getting no response, I crossed the hall to my own room and reached for the knob. It twisted, but the door wouldn't swing open.

"I'm sorry, Lydia. Keep holding," I said into the receiver. Then I tucked the open phone in my shorts pocket so I could use both hands and a hip to work open the door that was always getting stuck. More than anything, I needed to sit in the privacy of my room, finish this call, clear my head, and *think*.

"Come on," I whispered, jiggling and pushing until the door finally broke free.

As it swung open, I stepped inside, startled when my foot caught on something—something big and warm and lying on the floor. Before I could stop myself, I was falling. My knees and hands hit the ground as the phone shot from my pocket and skittered across the room. I turned to see what had tripped me and gasped. It was Kiki, lying on the floor, her eyes closed, her face covered with blood.

Trying not to scream, I turned back around, and that's when I saw him, a man standing across the room dressed in black and wearing a ski mask. At his feet was my open cell phone.

Without a word, he reached down with a gloved hand and gave the phone a push so that it slid back across the room to me.

"Finish your conversation and hang up," he said softly, his voice menacing and unfamiliar. "Don't do anything stupid."

I swallowed hard, trying to find my voice. Slowly, I picked up the phone, weighing my options.

"Anna?" Lydia's voice was saying over the phone line. "Anna, are you still there? Please do not be too upset. I do not know why anyone would go to such desperate measures to find you after all these years. I just wanted you to know that someone might call you."

I tried to reply, but my voice was lost somewhere deep in my throat. I swallowed again, watching with wide eyes as the man pointed a gun straight at me.

"Anna? Are you there?" Lydia persisted. "I'm sorry, but I suppose it is possible that someone might even come looking for you."

I cleared my throat and took a deep breath.

"You may be right about that," I said finally into the receiver. "More than you know."

With the man's gun still pointed toward me, I somehow managed to conclude my call, promising the distraught and confused Lydia that I'd be in touch as soon as possible. As I disconnected, I wondered if I was cutting off the one chance I had to scream for help and be heard. Then again, how could she possibly help me from an Amish farm three thousand miles away?

"Who are you?" I asked as I put the phone in my pocket and tried not to sound as scared as I felt. "What have you done?"

Instinctively, I reached for Kiki's wrist and felt for a pulse, which was faint but still there. Turning my attention to her face, I pushed back her hair to find the source of the bleeding. I expected to see a bullet wound, but instead it looked more like a gash, the result of being hit in the head by something hard and sharp edged, probably the butt of his gun.

"Your friend didn't want to cooperate," the man said. "Maybe you can learn by her example."

He took a step closer, and as he did, I stood, anger and adrenaline pumping through my veins.

"What do you want?"

"I think you know what I want," he replied, his eyes boring into me through the holes in the ski mask. "I'm here for the rubies. The whole set."

"The *rubies*? What rubies?"

He took another step toward me, with something like excitement flashing in his eyes.

"The Beauharnais Rubies. I know you have them."

He might as well have asked me for the Hope Diamond or the Crown Jewels. I had no rubies in my possession—and no idea what he was even talking about.

"I don't know what you mean," I said earnestly, stepping backward and nearly tripping again over Kiki's body. "I drive a car that's held together by duct tape. I have less than a hundred dollars in my checking account. Do you really think I'd be living this way if I had something as valuable as rubies?"

"Who knows why anyone lives as they do?" he replied. "Get them. Now."

"This is crazy," I said, shaking my head. "You're crazy. You have the wrong person, the wrong house."

He spoke evenly, cocking his gun.

"Your name is Annalise Bailey Jensen, currently going by the name of Anna Bailey. You are the sister of Robert 'Bobby' Jensen, the daughter of Charles Jensen and a descendant of Peter and Jonas and Karl Jensen, among others. I'm in the right house, and you're the right person. Now hand them over." Whoever this guy was, he knew more about my family tree than I did. But what he was asking for was ridiculous. I had never owned any rubies—and doubted I ever would.

Looking around, I tried to decide what my chances would be if I made a run for it. He was tall and looked strong under the form-fitting black shirt—though the ski mask could become a bit of an impediment. Unfortunately, as he spoke his steps had closed much of the gap between us.

"I'll ask you one more time, and then I'll have to get serious," he said, coming to a stop in front of me and resting the gun barrel against my temple. "Where...are...the...rubies?"

Discover the Smart Chick Mysteries
by Mindy Starns Clark

The Trouble with Tulip

Josephine Tulip is most definitely a smart chick, a twenty-first-century female MacGyver who writes a helpful-hints column and solves mysteries in her spare time. Her best friend, Danny, is a talented photographer who longs to succeed in his career...perhaps a cover photo on *National Geographic*?

When Jo's neighbor is accused of murder, Jo realizes the police have the wrong suspect. As she and Danny analyze clues, follow up on leads, and fall in and out of trouble, she recovers from a broken heart, and he discovers that he has feelings for her. Will Danny have the courage to reveal them, or will he continue to hide them behind a facade of friendship?

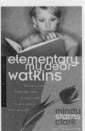

Blind Dates Can Be Murder

Blind dates give everyone the shivers...with or without a murder attached to them. Jo Tulip is a sassy single woman full of household hints and handy advice for every situation. Her first romantic outing in months is a blind date—okay, the Hall of Fame of Awful Blind Dates—but things go from bad to worse when the date drops dead and Jo finds herself smack in the middle of a murder investigation.

With the help of her best friend, Danny, and faith in God, Jo attempts to solve one exciting mystery while facing another: Why is love always so complicated?

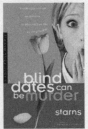

Elementary, My Dear Watkins

When someone tries to push Jo Tulip in front of a New York train, her ex-fiancé, Bradford, suffers an injury while saving her—and the unintentional sleuth is thrown onto the tracks of a very personal mystery.

Jo's boyfriend, Danny Watkins, is away in Paris, so she begins a solo investigation of her near-murder. What secret was Bradford about to share before he took the fall? And when Jo uncovers clues tied to Europe, can she and Danny work together in time to save her life?